Words We Never Speak

By

Scarlet Darkwood

DARK BOOKS PRESS

Words We Never Speak

Cover Design: Front Cover: Dale Reierson;
Back Cover: William Armstrong
Images: Depositphotos

CHAPTER 1

He stood there staring. The heavy silence amplified her discomfort. It had been so long ago. Why was he here now? What did he want? Black walls boxed in the darkness that nearly blocked her vision. Though she barely saw him, she knew he was inches away. The force of his presence pressed against her. Why didn't he say something? Part of her welcomed him. The other part dreaded him.

She really wanted to scream, tell him to go away. He must have read her mind. A rush of cold air blasted against her skin. Then, she felt it. Hot and stinging, something burned in the hollow of her throat. Wincing with pain, she clutched at the object. It was the tiny, gold heart. She knew it was golden without even seeing it. She'd touched it many times.

The metal had burned a raw place on her skin, and she rubbed her finger over the area. In her mind's eye, she saw the mark it made on her throat. Angry red, swelling and retracting, it chastised her. In a moment, she felt herself nearly suffocating. She struggled to breathe.

Kit awoke gasping, drenched in sweat. She glanced at the clock and groaned. God, she was tired. Curious, she crawled out of bed and looked in the mirror. There was no red spot in the hollow of her neck. Kit sat down on the bed, frustrated. This nighttime intrusiveness needed to stop. She'd either go mad or collapse from fatigue if this kept up.

Only one person could help her come up with a solution, one who understood circumstances like these. Kit knew she may be tired and on edge, but she wouldn't be beaten. The man in the dark room fooled her once. He wouldn't do it again. She stepped in the shower and got ready for work. Today, she would fix this problem once and for all.

* * *

A Cup Above the Roast hummed with patrons conversing in hushed tones. In one corner of the coffee shop, Kit sat stirring her latte, breathing in rich scents from the roaster. Songs from the radio competed with the whirring of the grinder behind a pastry counter filled with an eye-watering assortment of confections.

She wrinkled her nose and stared at her cup while her best friend and co-worker, Irene Westmont, sipped her espresso.

"You'll think I'm crazy if I tell you this." Kit looked up, considering whether or not to spill the beans on what had been eating away at her sanity. "You promise you won't laugh at me or think I've lost my mind?"

"Don't be silly. Why would I?" Irene furrowed her brow as she loaded up a fork for another bite of the crunch bar gleaming on her plate. "Coming from you, it won't be silly. So out with it."

"You're pretty spiritual, Irene. I mean, you believe in dreams, intuition, cosmic energy, and all that hocus-pocus stuff, don't you?"

"Not sure what you mean about the hocus-pocus stuff, but as far as the other, yeah. So, what of it?"

After taking a quick taste of her cake, Kit answered. "I keep having these strange dreams. They started several weeks ago, out of the blue. No particular reason why I should have them."

"Like what do you mean, strange?"

"I mean, strange. I keep having a dream about an old classmate I haven't seen since high school graduation six years ago."

Irene shrugged, tossing back her thick, charcoal waves of hair. Large sterling hoops swayed from her ears. "Okay, so what about it bugs you?"

"It keeps coming back, the vision of this guy. He shows up, and just stares at me. Nothing else going on. Just me and him. We're locked in a room with black walls. It's weird. We don't talk; we don't do anything." Kit washed down another bite of cake with a sip of coffee, and stared back at Irene. "What does it mean to have a person show up in dreams repeatedly?"

Drumming her fingernails against her cup, Irene remained silent, lost in thought. "Tell me more about this person. What feelings do you have during this dream? Are you happy to see him? Does he make you feel anxious? Do you feel nothing at all? Somehow I suspect this is no ordinary guy." She smiled across the table at her friend. "Is this the reason you're holding out on Dwight? You're still hankering after an old love?"

"Don't be ridiculous. I'm not holding out on Dwight. I'm just being careful, taking it nice and slow."

"From the blush on your face, I think you're lying to me, Kit Millinger."

Kit stabbed at her cake, loading up her fork again. She had connected instantly with Dwight Vandergard, the finance director, at the Windham Springs Historical Society. She'd accepted the position as conservation manager six months ago. With Irene as the collections manager, all three had been branded as 'The Three Musketeers.'

She loved her job, and she loved North Carolina for its mountains and historic folklore, but bringing personal old ghosts along for the ride hadn't figured into the equation. The last thing she wanted was interference between her budding romance with Dwight and the cozy life she'd created, which included living in an historic building only blocks from her job.

Irene doled out a playful kick from under the table. "Fess up. Tell me more about this person in your dream."

"His name was Austin, and we actually dated our junior and senior year of high school. After we graduated, he died."

Irene arched an eyebrow, eyes fixed on Kit. "How?"

Sinking back in her chair, Kit struggled with putting the memories together. "Apparently, he and a friend had been drinking during a day in the mountains and they had a car accident. Ran off the road and down a ravine. Killed them both."

"Ah, alcohol and winding mountain roads make deadly companions." Irene shook her head. "Was your friend driving?"

"No, his buddy was. And boy, did Austin's parents raise a stink with the other guy's family. Not happy times."

"Anything happen while you two dated?"

Kit's heart caught in her chest. Licking her lips, she glanced across at Irene. "No, we just went our separate ways."

"Just went your separate ways? Forgot about each other, just like that?"

"Pretty much," Kit said, shrugging her shoulders.

Irene sat still, not breaking eye contact.

"Come on, what did you expect?" Kit retorted, a scowl on her face. "That I went after him with a knife or made a diamond out of his heart?"

"That would have been a more interesting story."

"We were so busy near the end of school, and I'd been planning for college. Time just slipped away." Kit wrinkled her brow, tugging lightly at a hangnail.

"Okay." Irene finished off her dessert. "But here's what I'm thinking. You may be having this dream for a reason."

"A reason?" Kit eyeballed her friend. "What on earth do you mean by that?"

Leaning forward, Irene mumbled, "Look, when the dead come to us in a dream, they're usually trying to communicate in some way. They have some unfinished business, something they're trying to wrap up for themselves so they can move on."

"So how do I get rid of him?"

"The answer is simple. Talk to him."

Kit let out a laugh, but stopped short. Irene's somber face indicated she wasn't kidding. "Seriously?"

Irene folded her hands neatly on the table. "I don't ever recommend trying to contact the dead first, but this Austin dude has made the first move. It's okay to talk to him, get to the bottom of what's bugging him. You need to either meditate on him and connect spiritually, or we can use a spirit board I have. It'll give you a chance to ask questions and get a response from him. It works. I've used it lots of times."

"It's been six years, Irene, and he's dead. Honestly, what on earth could he want after all this time? Whatever it is, wouldn't he just forget about it?"

"Have you – whatever it is?" Irene's eyes bore straight into Kit's.

Shifting in her seat, she fluffed her hair, tucking a stray lock behind her ear. The knot forming in her stomach nudged at her conscience, the way it always did when she lied. She'd tried to forget about it; she almost thought she'd succeeded. Now, these dreams.

"I'll be honest with you. I have a sneaking suspicion there's more going on than what you're telling me. Personally, I think something happened between the two of you. Being a good friend, I won't pry, but you just think about what I'm saying here."

"You sure that'll make him go away?"

Irene winked. "Promise. Just think about it."

Kit lifted her gaze to the ceiling. "I should have known you'd suggest something this way out. But it's an interesting concept, I'll say that much."

"You asked for my opinion, so there it is."

"Yes, I did, and thanks." She smiled at Irene, patting her hand. "I appreciate it."

"Anytime. If you want to use my spirit board, let me know and we'll get together. I also have some good beginner tips for meditation, if you'd rather do that."

"Ugh, I'm not sure I'd be so great at that, but let me think on it some more. With any luck, it'll all just stop. You know what I mean?"

"Or, maybe it won't. Restless spirits want resolution, you know."

With a grimace, Kit shook her head. "Let's hope he never comes back. Maybe I'll get lucky."

As the ladies sat in silence, Kit's eyes wandered around the room, roving over a variety of unusual paintings on the old brick walls, accented by the occasional spattering of select coffee-related odds and ends. In the middle of the main wall stood an old studio upright piano, which had been converted into an art piece, with various musical instruments attached to the sides and peeking out from the raised top. A few customers remained, enjoying the ambience, reading books or lording over their computers, tapping furiously at their keyboards. Did they have secrets too? Did old boyfriends or girlfriends from high school romances haunt them in their dreams? Even the friendly atmosphere of a hip coffee shop didn't take her mind off Austin or rid her from the clenching in her gut.

Scooting her chair back, Kit grabbed her clutch bag. "I guess we better move on. I need to get back home."

"Me too." Irene stood up and slipped her purse strap over her shoulder. "Had a great time, and thanks for sharing this dream with me. Things happen for a reason, so it's all good." She smiled.

The ladies pushed their way through a heavy, squeaky wooden door, trading the smells of coffee and hot bistro sandwiches for the dull roar of cars on the street and the scents of trees and leaves. Fall approached, bringing with it crisp air and the promise of bonfires, spiced cider, and the spookiness that came with Halloween, an event that heralded the beginning of the holidays.

Kit watched Irene cross the street and disappear behind the old Stothwell Mansion, home to the historical society she had grown to love. The house stood fearless and somber in the shadow of the trees, shielded from the glow of the evening sun. A fine example of Greek Revival architecture, its solid white columns stood tall and strong, sending a message of fierce protectiveness – the same ferocity she used in guarding her emotions. The darkness shrouding the house reflected her mood, but, right now, her life should be anything but uneasy.

She considered the mansion that resembled a Greek temple, taking in the neat rows of windows and the front door. Another reason for coming to Windham Springs, North Carolina, a set of family ties luring her with an unseen force so strong it left her powerless to have done otherwise. In her mind and heart, she'd come home at last.

The mansion, a place she remembered from her youth, provided the elegant backdrop and stage on which she conducted her work. No, she didn't need anything spoiling her world, didn't need anyone or any restless being reminding her of the past, hell-bent on taking her down a path of bad memories. Austin just needed to go away, far away, wherever dead people go, and take his baggage with him.

Kit made her way back home, this time staying on the same side of the street, instead of crossing over to the opposite sidewalk like she usually did when she left the coffee shop. In the window of the building next door, a large 'For Lease' sign, complete with contact number, still hung in the large picture window. Out of curiosity, Kit peeked through the glass. The shop was one big room, with the walls covered in an icky mint green paint, which had now chipped off in several places. A cutout in the wall behind the counter hinted at a hallway leading to the back of the shop.

From the sight of dust and an occasional dead bug on the floor, this space had not been used in quite a while. Come to think of it, the space had not been rented since her arrival to Windham Springs, and she and Irene had never discussed who previously had owned the shop.

What a shame. This would be a wonderful spot for a new merchant, perhaps an artist, someone with talent and something creative and beautiful to sell. Though the Society didn't mind who took up space in the district, Kit remained partial to retail businesses only, believing another place to shop made the experience in this area even better. Stepping back from the window, she shook her head. *I wish someone would rent this space.*

She ambled down the sidewalk, nodding and smiling to the occasional passerby, sometimes stopping to peer through a shop window or admire a display of goods in a showcase. When she took in a deep breath, she caught the musty smell of the old buildings, an odor that would linger until the end of time, unless progress got them first.

That's what she liked about the square, the charming atmosphere, allowing a glimpse back to more nostalgic times. What had it been like to live in the Stothwell Mansion in the eighteen-hundreds? Life on the square surely moved at a different pace when there weren't so many choices. When life and commerce centered around this place, and urban sprawl had not spread its far-reaching fingers over the fabric of society like liquid that runs freely from a toppled glass.

When she reached Our Lady of Eternal Blessings Catholic Church, she crossed the street to her apartment, a one-bedroom studio above her landlord's law office.

Kit opened the glass door and locked it before climbing the steep set of black-painted wooden steps, losing herself in the dim light. Turning at the top landing, she opened a door to a large room with high ceilings, complete with wooden rafters. She'd decorated her space with simple antiques, down to an old vintage chime clock, a graduation gift from her aunt. Other than her bedroom and bathroom, the space consisted of one big room, with a small section serving as the kitchen.

In her bedroom, she stripped away her work clothes and slipped into a silk robe. Switching on a small, glass, satin-shade lamp on the dresser, she gazed long and hard into the mirror. The reflection of an older face stared back. Six years had taken away the rosy cheeks of the vivacious, young girl who had walked eagerly across the stage for her high school diploma, a bright future ahead.

Out of the corner of her eye she'd glimpsed Austin, his face somber as he watched her from the crowd, never attempting a wave or shouting kudos like the others had done when the assistant principal called her name into the microphone. She'd turned her eyes away, accepted the diploma with a gracious smile at the principal, and walked off the stage to her seat.

Over the years, all mementos and tokens of their dating days had been relegated to the garbage except for one item. The last time it dangled from her neck was before the end of senior year. Could she bear to see it again for real, the tiny, golden puff heart pendant he'd given her on prom night their junior year? The same golden heart that burned in her dreams? It still rested in a petite, art-nouveau metal jewelry box, where it had remained until lately, out of sight and out of mind.

She pulled open a small drawer, her stomach tightening as the antique gold-tone box came into view. The hinges let out a soft creak as the lid fell back, exposing the necklace resting on a puffy, pale blue chiffon fabric. Light glinted from the gold surface of the heart, the flashes infusing an almost magical quality to the piece. If she wore it, would a transformation occur, like the wave of a magic wand, taking her back in time so she could do things differently?

With trembling fingers, she picked up the necklace and fastened it around her neck, leaning her head right and left, studying the way the heart landed perfectly in the hollow of her throat.

It seemed like such a childish piece, one she probably should have given to a younger cousin or a child of a family friend, but no matter what, she could never part with it, would never get rid of it for someone else to wear. Some items became too sentimental, no matter the circumstances surrounding the giver.

Kit headed toward the kitchen and made a sandwich. After depositing her plate and a glass of water on the coffee table, she spent a moment staring at the bookshelves on both sides of the fireplace. Her gaze followed up the rows to the top right-hand corner where her high school yearbooks sat.

So, Austin wanted to communicate, did he? What would he say? The bigger question, what would she say? They'd been too young? She'd been foolish?

Meditate. That's what Irene had suggested. People did this, claiming they found peace, and answers to problems. She closed her eyes, took a deep breath, and let it out by degrees. Could she clear her head enough to concentrate, or did fear of what she might see hold her back? Through the darkness, images floated in front of her, jumpy, incoherent in their progression, void of reason.

Should she call out to him, ask him to come? Her eyes flew open. No, that wouldn't work. What if he did? What would it be like, seeing a ghost? Other people had their stories. No need to add to that crazy collection of fear fodder. But she could only hope Austin would grow bored with her, wherever he was.

Kit blinked a few times and focused on the yearbooks again, keeping her eyes fixated on the spines. Little by little they lulled her into an almost altered state, instilling a strong desire to leaf through the pages again. They held a certain power now, standing out in contrast among the other books on the shelf, an unusually bright glow around them. She dulled her mind to the present, concentrating on the books. Other than the ticking sounds from the old clock on the mantle above the fireplace, the room held a thick silence, a stillness pervading every inch.

Overcome at last by their spell, Kit pulled herself off the sofa, crossed the room, and reached up for the fourth book. The cover still looked as good as new, with the silver, foil-embossed year gleaming in the light. She plopped back down on the sofa and ate while leafing through the pages until she came to the section titled *Seniors*.

She scrolled through the lists with her index finger until Austin's name finally came up. There he was, smiling at her from the pages. Her heart leaped at the sight of his picture. The more she gazed at him, the more the flood of memories came pouring in: holding hands on their way to classes; her hanging around after school to watch him finish up an art project; attending school dances and holding each other close when the slow songs played.

Then there were the football games on Friday nights, where she and a group of friends gathered in the bleachers to cheer on the team. Austin was one of the best players that year, with rumors he'd been offered a scholarship to a well-known college. She didn't take the time to congratulate him or ask questions; they'd stopped seeing each before school ended.

She jumped at the sound of the phone. At the same moment, the clock sounded the nine o'clock hour. Scrambling to her feet, Kit tossed the book on the sofa and hurried toward the phone.

"Thought you might have gone to bed early." A rich masculine voice sailed over the line, flowing comfortably in her ear.

Kit smiled, relieved. "Hey, Dwight. No, I still have a while before I head off to bed. You okay?"

"Just thinking about you. Irene seemed hell-bent on getting you out of the office today. Is the coffee that good over there?"

"You're funny. Of course, the coffee's that good. I love that place."

"Any scuttlebutt I'd want to hear?" he chuckled.

Her heart paused a beat. Dwight definitely didn't need to hear about her dreams, especially when they involved an old flame. "Only idle gossip between two crazy girls. Nothing you'd be interested in."

"I'm sure anything you had to say would interest me, Kit. But you've seemed a bit preoccupied lately, like something's bothering you. I've been meaning to ask you about that."

"Oh?"

"I'm concerned. Is that what you and Irene were talking about? She's noticed it too."

Kit sank down on the sofa, pushing the book out of the way so she could stretch out and figure out an answer. "I'm still getting used to everything – new home, new town, new job, life without school. It's stressful learning something new, and then being manager on top of that."

"I understand. Don't burn out."

"Won't let myself get to that point." Time to change the subject away from her. "Did you stay over and work late? You've been doing that for the past week. Are numbers that fascinating?"

"It's a lot of work keeping up with Alexandra Stothwell's place. Always something going on."

"I love where we work and what we do, Dwight. Everything's like a dream come true for me." Alexandra Stothwell. The name rolled around in her head as she thought about her second cousin, the owner of the mansion and the one who'd helped her get the job. She'd insisted Kit come to Windham Springs for an interview. "Nothing like having you back here again. We used to have some good times, didn't we?" Kit remembered her smile, and how she'd squeezed her hand with excitement.

Dwight kept on speaking. "It's been better since you've come along," he sighed. Through the line, Kit heard him fumbling with something before he apparently found a comfortable position. "You want to get together this Saturday, grab a bite, maybe see a movie?"

"I'm game." Kit let her mind wander, imagining herself cuddled up next to him, his arms wrapped tightly around her. The real heat between the two of them was only three weeks old. Not one to rush anything in the romance department, she kept him just enough at arm's length to give her time to learn his personality, how he thought, his personal quirks and preferences. So far, so good.

"I say we go for some Italian food at Garabaldi's."

"Garabaldi's?" Her eyes widened in alarm. "Isn't that kind of pricey?"

"Not for you. I'll get the tab. Don't you worry about a thing."

"I couldn't let you do that. We'll at least go dutch."

"Never in a million years."

Just listening to him nearly intoxicated her. Fine dining, a movie, and maybe something after – if she dared. Intimacy after three weeks wouldn't seem too desperate, would it? Many girls didn't care how soon they became physical in a relationship, but she still used caution. No need for any problems from hasty decisions or a moment of weakness.

As she and Dwight chatted, a sharp heat centered on her throat, hot metal against her skin. She bolted upright from the sofa. A chill shot down her spine. Just like her dream, the heart was extraordinarily hot to the touch. The longer she wore the necklace, the hotter it got.

"Hold on, Dwight." Kit put the phone down long enough to unclasp the necklace and fling it on the table. "There, that's better. Sorry, had to get comfy."

For the next hour and a half, Kit and Dwight engaged in small talk. Throughout the conversation, her mind crept back to the necklace and how the heat of the gold heart stung her skin. Once, she ran to her room and peered into the mirror. No red mark like in her dreams. But even that left her with little comfort.

"I'll see you tomorrow." Dwight's voice had grown softer, a sign of fatigue.

"You too. Thanks for calling." Kit hated to end the conversation, but it was late now. She replaced the phone on the receiver.

Sitting back down on the sofa, Kit kept her eye on the necklace, nerves revving up the longer she stared at it. Did she dare touch it, put it back in the box in her dresser? Had it all just been a flight of fancy, transgression of the imagination? No. Let it sit there. Nobody would bother it anyway. Tomorrow she'd deal with it. The book, however, was safe enough to replace back on the shelf.

CHAPTER 2

A sound from the living room jolted Kit awake. She sat up in bed, straining her ears against the pounding of her heart. That thud sounded like something had fallen. Or was someone coming into her bedroom? Cringing, she gripped the covers.

Dear lord, was it that blasted yearbook again? Since her weekend date with Dwight, five days ago, this would be the second time the book had fallen. The first time it happened, she tried to ignore it as mere coincidence, that she'd replaced the book without pushing it all the way back. She'd gone about her business of working, shopping, hanging out with Irene and Dwight.

Kit listened a few seconds longer, praying hard that it was nothing more than the cracking sounds of her old apartment building, but the growing uneasiness suggested this wasn't so. Only one way to find out. Throwing off the covers, she sprang out of bed and headed toward the living room.

Glancing at the front door and the door leading out from her tiny kitchen, she saw nothing out of the ordinary. To her relief, the apartment was locked up tight, deadbolt in place just as she'd left it when she'd gone to bed. Kit still didn't rest too easy as it only confirmed her worst suspicions. With dread, she turned and viewed the living room, eyes widening with horror and dismay.

A book lay on the floor in front of her bookcase, where it had fallen, from a shelf wide enough to hold all the books without any of them toppling over the edge. Cautiously, she tiptoed over, groaning when she saw her senior high school yearbook. The pages lay open, exposing the neat row of faces and comical, fake smiles. But this was not a coincidence. Not this time. She had shoved the book back until it hit the back solidly. No way could it fall off. The most disturbing issue, it kept landing with certain pages open – pages showcasing pictures of Austin.

Grimacing, she stared down at the end of the fourth row of photos, a grim feeling creeping over her as Austin's eyes stared back, almost taunting. Like it or not, something strange was happening, and it seemed like she'd be tormented through cryptic dreams, hot pendants, and falling books until she paid attention and faced this issue head-on.

After talking with Dwight several nights ago, she'd managed to return the necklace to the jewelry box where she vowed she'd never open the lid again. Something had to give. Images of her old boyfriend kept disrupting her thoughts, slipping into her mind at work, during dinners with friends, especially when Dwight called or came around. When she wandered through boutiques, Austin's face popped up in her mind, just before an old song they'd danced to drifted through the store speakers.

"What do you want, damn it?" Kit stood in front of the bookcase, casting her eyes briefly to the ceiling as her shout broke the silence. She jerked up the book, shoving it back into the bookshelf. "Just go the hell away."

Though she'd tried to bury the memories of Austin forever, hiding them in the darkest recesses of her mind, he'd flatly refused to be cast into darkness, forgotten. Kit shook her head and headed to the bathroom to shower and get ready for work. Austin had done nothing more than dredge up sadness and haunt her psyche. For sure, he wanted her to pay attention to something. What could he possibly want?

She stepped into the old porcelain, claw-foot tub, pulling the white curtain around her. How she wished a hot shower would wash away bad mojo and life would get back to normal. Dressing quickly, without much thought to her wardrobe, she snatched up her purse and left her apartment, clambering down the long flight of stairs.

"Careful there, Kit. Don't want any broken necks around here." At the bottom of the stairs, Harold Crispin, the town's go-to attorney – and Kit's landlord – poked his head through the office door, giving her a questioning stare.

"Sorry, Mr. Crispin." She paused a moment to catch her breath when she reached the bottom. "I hope I didn't disturb you."

His lips curled up into a warm smile. "Oh, normally you don't bother me at all, but the herd of buffalo charging down the stairs actually made me curious enough to take a look."

Kit grinned. "Made you look!" She considered the gentleman a moment. "Mr. Crispin, I have a question."

"Okay." He blinked at her over his readers.

"Do you believe in ghosts?"

He raised an eyebrow. "Well, not really, though the square is loaded with stories. Tall tales, I call them." Crispin chuckled.

"I just wondered if this place is haunted."

"Haunted? My office, your apartment?" The gentleman glanced around, and then gazed back at Kit. "Not that I'm aware of. This building doesn't have anything special or historical attached to it. No murders, clandestine trysts where a lover got shot in the back for cheating, no hateful deals where something went dreadfully wrong." He grinned. "Why? Are you hearing things that go bump in the night?"

Forcing a grin, Kit replied, "I was just wondering, that's all. Just talking to some friends at the Society, and I realized I hadn't asked you that question about this place."

"Nope, nothing here. Not to worry." He glanced at his watch. "You better head on to work before you're late." He smiled one last time before retreating into his office and closing the door.

Squaring up her shoulders, she fluffed up her hair, rushing outside to the sidewalk. She picked up her pace and headed toward the mansion. This morning didn't hold the usual peace she felt during her walk to work, peeking into windows, sniffing the air, glad life had treated her well. When she reached the mansion, Kit headed toward her office, where she found Irene and Dwight sitting, waiting for her.

"What are you two doing in here? And what's with the long faces?"

Dwight and Irene exchanged glances.

"Sit down, Kit. We need to talk," said Dwight, waving a hand toward the chair behind her desk.

Kit sat down, pulse racing. The tone in Dwight's voice didn't sound promising at all. "What's up, guys? It looks pretty serious."

"Have you heard anything about this, by any chance?" Irene waved a paper before sliding it across to Kit.

She looked down at the paper and saw in large, bold print: "Stothwell Property to Become Future Site for New Condos." Confused, she jerked her head up at Irene and Dwight. "What?"

"Go on, read it." Irene's mouth flat-lined on her face, matching Dwight's grim expression. "We've read through it several times, and just can't believe it. I'm numb all over."

"Me too." Dwight shook his head, staring straight ahead.

Taking a deep breath, Kit skimmed over the article, eyes widening with every sentence. She reached the end. "Oh my god, this can't be true!" Stunned, she reviewed the article again, a little slower this time to make sure she hadn't misread anything. "I've never gotten any hint of something like this going down, not even once."

"Aren't you and Alexandra related? You mean you don't chat on a regular basis about things?" Irene frowned in Kit's direction. "This notice is also on the Internet. Now, everybody will know."

"I find it interesting that Alexandra didn't call you about this too." Dwight gave Kit a suspicious stare, tipping his head to the right as he studied her.

"Oddly enough, we don't talk that much. I spent some time here during the summer when I was much younger. For an older cousin, Alex was always so sweet, didn't try to keep away from me because she was older and didn't want kids hanging around."

"She let the Society use this house all these years, but if this place goes, you know what this means, don't you?" Irene arched an eyebrow.

"Yeah, unfortunately I do. We're going to lose the Historical Society. Or at the very least, we'll have to move somewhere else."

Dwight sucked in a deep breath. "The truth is, Kit, none of us want to move. We want to stay here. The ambience and antiquity of this place just makes this job even more enjoyable."

"You're crying already? What for? We haven't lost this house yet." Kit wrinkled her brow.

"I can't help it," Irene said. "I've been working here faithfully for the past three years. Others have been here longer than that. This house is home, right here, on this site!" Irene wiped her eyes and sniffled.

"Look, stop for a minute and take a deep breath. Here." Kit handed her friend a tissue from a box on her desk. "Let's think about this for a minute. I mean, we're a historical society, after all, so conservation and preservation is what we do. Maybe we can do something and try to stop this thing from happening. Tell you what, I'll give my cousin a call and see what she says. I don't know what's come up, but I'll get to the bottom of it."

Irene dabbed at her eyes and blew her nose. "I'm not sure about that, Kit. This house isn't on the National Register, you know. Didn't meet the state's criteria for inclusion. And Edmond Harsh Contractors wants the property. Harsh knows what he's doing, and he's probably putting the screws to Alexandra, pressuring her to sell. I've heard old Edmond Harsh lives up to his name, all right. He's a greedy, mean old bastard."

Dwight chimed in. "He believes in tearing down the old and making way for the new, especially when it puts bucks in his pocket."

"I'll have a chat with Alex. Let's not get ahead of ourselves." Kit bounced her gaze between her two co-workers, hoping they would find a way to share her optimism. She hoped her tone sounded optimistic, unlike the sense of dread spilling all over her. What on earth could be going on with her cousin?

"It's time to get back to work." Dwight stood up. "Kit, if you need any help from me, want me to join you and Alexandra, let me know. I'd really like to know how much money old Harsh is offering her. Sometimes an offer just may be too good to refuse."

"Let's hope she's not that greedy." Irene clapped a hand over her mouth. "I'm sorry, Kit. That was rude of me."

Kit waved her away. "No, it's okay. I can understand the feelings right now. The truth is, I don't know how greedy Alex is. I haven't really kept up with her through the years. We've just now kind of gotten re-acquainted. Know what I mean?"

Giving a slight shrug, Irene said, "True."

"Dwight, I'll try my hand at talking with Alex. If I run into anything complicated, I'll give you a yell. Thanks for the offer." She grinned, watching him nod and leave the office.

Irene moved from her chair and, with a light hop, landed on the edge of the desk, where she spent a few moments fluffing out her hair before tossing it all behind her shoulders. From her ears, the large, trademark, sterling hoop earrings glistened in the light. Her fingers fidgeted over her pale-yellow cotton blouse, while her pursed lips suggested a new preoccupation with a different matter.

"What do you want?" Kit grinned, fixing her gaze on Irene. "You've got something on your mind, and I don't think it's about this house or Alexandra."

"Have you given any more thought to what we talked about over coffee the other day?" She scrutinized Kit's appearance. "And you look a little ragged for some reason. That's not like you, either. Is something wrong?"

"Gee, thanks, Irene, you're a true pal. So, you're saying I look dumpy today? Is that it?" She smiled up at her friend before shaking her head.

"Well, your hair's limp, and you're not wearing any make-up. Your outfit's not too bad, except it doesn't represent your usual panache for style." She kept her eyes fixed on Kit. "And you simply look tired. Have you seen yourself in a mirror?"

"I'm fine, really. Probably staying up too late talking to Dwight. He's calling at night sometimes. A just-before-bed chat."

Irene let out a small huff. "I seriously doubt he'd keep you up that late when he has to come here early too. Besides, you should be skipping around with a smile on your face and a sparkle in your eye with a new love in your life, don't you think?"

"I'm joyful and liking where things are going, but the skipping thing? Nah, that's a little much." Kit reached over, delivering a small punch on her friend's shoulder. "You worry too much."

"I get a feeling you're not telling me something."

"Oh yeah, like what? If something big came up, I'd tell you." Kit lowered her gaze, pretending to fidget with items in her desk. If she told Irene what she'd experienced the past few days, she'd never hear the end of it. Irene would ride her hard.

"There's something eating at you. Part of me hoped you'd solve your problem, but I don't think so. It's getting worse, isn't it?" She tilted her head, giving Kit the 'I knew it' look. Irene leaned over the top of the desk toward Kit. "You can tell me. I can keep a secret." Sitting up, she mimicked the action of locking her mouth up with a key and tossing it away.

"God, Irene, you're too much!" Kit sank back in her chair, resting her feet on the desk. "You got me, though. There have been a couple of things."

"I knew it! You can't hide things from me." She propped up on one hand, ready for the story. "What's been going on that you've kept hush-hush about?"

For the next several minutes, Kit brought her friend up-to-date on everything that happened.

"Holy shit!" Irene frowned, shaking her head. "This is not good, I'm telling you. You have got to do something, or your old flame will never stop until he gets what he wants."

"I'm beginning to believe you." Kit gazed across the room. "I think I may just have to take you up on that spirit board offer. I'm honestly not much into that sort of practice, but at this point, I'm desperate. I'll do just about anything."

"We'll make plans. But when are you going to call Alexandra? You need to do that today if you can. Time's running out as we speak." Irene slid off the desk and headed toward the door. "Give her a call. Let me know what she says." She waved and left the room, closing the squeaky door behind her.

Good, now with her friends gone, she could spend the time alone thinking a little. Kit sank down in her chair and reviewed the article again. The Society had used the house and land as their headquarters for the last forty years, and now it seemed like Edmond Harsh wanted to strut and show off his fine rack of antlers.

She'd been fifteen years old when her cousin turned this house over to the Society. Engrossed in school and her personal life, Kit had put the old house and fun summers out of her mind a few years before that time.

Something was definitely up. Alexandra must be up against it for money, or she was tired of the place, Kit thought. But there had to be a way to stop this sale. Her mind raced. Before she called her cousin, she wanted to make sure she had her facts in order about the house.

For the next couple of hours, her eyes remained glued to the computer screen as she surfed the Internet for information on the Stothwell Mansion. Nothing much of value came up, except the website for the Society and the typical real estate address information. Hard as she searched, no articles showed up indicating the house had been part of an historical event or connected to anyone of historical importance. And there were no articles citing the mansion in special parties or charity events.

Of course, even if the house had been part of these events, too much time had passed for any of this information to show up on the Net. Worse, no blogs contained posts on the property.

She tried remembering whether her parents had mentioned any special events happening here when she was older. She shook her head. None. On North Carolina's website, she reviewed the state's criteria for inclusion on the National Register. With each bullet point, hope faded fast.

If Edmond Harsh bought this property, he'd be setting the stage for more demolition and construction of new sites adjoining the property. Windham Springs, unfortunately, stood a good chance of having its history whittled away, one knocked-down building at a time. But what nerve, jumping the gun and sharing news like this with the public before an actual deal went through!

Time to make a phone call to the only person who could give her answers. A twinge of apprehension nudged as she tapped out Alexandra's number on the keypad.

"Hello?" The perky sound of a woman's voice filled the line.

"Alex? It's me, Kit."

"Oh, Kit, how are you?" The cheerfulness faltered.

"I'm okay. Just wanted to call and chat for a minute."

"I hear you're settling in over there. You seem to like the job. That's good." The words came forced, filled with dread and nervousness as they slipped from Alexandra's lips.

"Love it. Sure wish you came around a little more. It'd be nice to see you every once in a while."

"I really couldn't offer very much. I'd just be in the way. You guys do such a great job with everything."

"You'd never be in the way. I mean, it's your house, after all. Don't you ever want to come by, check in, say hi?" Kit shifted in her chair. She sensed Alexandra's discomfort, the flatness settling into her speech, the silence creeping over the line. "Hey, Alex, I'll come clean and just ask. Could we talk about why you're wanting to sell the mansion? I don't want to pry, but surely you can understand how we all feel. We love it here." Closing her eyes, Kit braced herself, wishing she could shut out her cousin's sigh trickling into her ear.

"Yeah, I know Kit, but it's, well … yeah, it's a great house."

"Alex, are you okay?" The silence from Alexandra only spiked up the gloom. This was definitely not going to be a casual conversation.

"I'm okay." Alexandra forced a light laugh.

Kit knew one thing at this point. She did not want to talk on the phone. "Why don't we meet for coffee or let's go grab a bite and talk this out. You can't sell this house. It's been part of this community for decades, and I just got here.

"I know, I know. This isn't an easy decision for me, either." Silence. Kit furrowed her brow as she heard rattling in the background. "Sorry, hon. I'm just a little busy right now, but I want us to talk. I really do."

"You want to meet here on the square?"

"Why don't you come to my place? Come on over after work tonight, if it's not too short notice."

"Perfect, I'll swing by after work. Thanks so much, Alex."

Hanging up the phone, Kit breathed a sigh of relief. Spending time at her cousin's place would be a nice change of pace, especially since she lived on the outskirts of town in a charming old farmhouse. Some fresh air and a walk by the creek would do them both some good.

A knock at the door broke the silence. Kit sat straight up. "Come in."

The door creaked open, and Dwight poked his head his head through. "Are you busy?"

"No, not at all. Come on in." She propped her elbows on the desk, waiting.

He held out a soft, light pink rose resting in a tiny, quaint cut crystal bud vase filled with water. "Meant to give this to you earlier, but obviously, we all got side-tracked."

"Oh, Dwight, what's this for? How sweet." Smiling, she took the flower from him and buried her nose in the center of the fluffy petals. "Mmm, this smells so good." Narrowing her eyes, she glanced up at him, a big smile spread across her face. "You didn't pick this from one of the gardens outside, did you? How convenient."

"Very funny." Dwight chuckled and seated himself in one of the vacant chairs in front of Kit's desk. "I grew this myself, just for you."

"Really, now?" She laughed, plunging her nose into the soft petals again, breathing in the heavy scent. "You've created some nice gardens. I guess a huge back yard and some extra property behind it doesn't hurt."

"They're not as fancy as the ones around the mansion, but I'm pretty good with plants. I'm trying to decide what my next venture is – a Zen garden or a gazing pool. At least I could think about you when I'm in either one of them." His eyes gleamed, a dreamy grin tugging at the corner of his lips.

She laughed, gazing at Dwight, eyes roaming over his tall, lean frame. Maybe, if she put her skittishness aside, a romp through those gardens one night might end up with her running her fingers through his sandy blond hair. But what attracted her most was his scholarly look, complete with chestnut brown eyes shrouded by a pair of black-rimmed glasses. During college, she'd learned to appreciate the more studious men. They, too, held a passion for their interests, talking just as wildly as the most excited jock about a sports game.

"You've been so nice, Dwight. And thanks for calling me at night. Lately I've had a little trouble falling asleep."

"So, I bore you? Is that it?" He chuckled. "Not sure whether to take your comment as a compliment or an insult."

"You know what I mean." Kit fingered the tiny glass vase. "This is adorable. Where did you get it, if you don't mind my asking?"

Dwight considered her question. "It's actually from a collection of old cut glass my grandmother had when she was alive. Since we've visited a few antiques shops lately, I knew you'd appreciate the piece."

"I do, but are you sure you want me having something that belonged to your grandmother? I mean, don't you want to save that for someone ...?" She stopped, feeling the rush of heat to her cheeks.

"Meemaw would have loved for you to have it." He grinned. "I think she would have liked you a lot, Kit." His eyes moved from her face and over to the window behind the desk. She glimpsed the struggle brewing behind them. It had been harder for him to keep the slow pace of their relationship, but he'd hung on, having graduated from simple gifts and light flirting to sneaking up from behind and giving her small shoulder massages. At the touch of his hands, she wanted to melt, throw caution to the wind, and pay nature its dues.

At this point, she wasn't sure how much longer *she* could hold out. But being co-workers presented risks if things didn't work out. One had to be careful, she reasoned to herself.

"Next time we're in your gardens, are you going to play your guitar for me and serenade me under the moon?" Kit batted her eyelashes.

"Of course. No candlelight dinner, with fine, chef-prepared cuisine and all the trappings of a luxurious dinner, would be complete without a song."

"I totally agree. Can't wait."

Dwight stretched out, wrapped his arms behind his head, and stared at Kit for several moments before he spoke. "What are we going to do to save this house? I've been racking my brain since I left your office."

"Don't know. I'm meeting with Alex tonight. I'll let you know after she and I have a chat."

"You made the phone call. Good for you. That's what I like about you, Kit, you're a woman who gets things done."

"She didn't sound happy. Don't know what's up, but I'll get to the bottom of it and see what we can do."

"What was it like here, when you were a little girl, and this house was truly a home, with people who lived in these rooms where they ate, slept, bathed, and made love? Where there was happiness and sorrow, excitement and worry? Where life seemed kinder and ambled on with a much gentler pace than it does now?"

"Gosh, Dwight. You can wax poetic, can't you?"

"No, really. I want to know. Wasn't it hard for you to come back here and see all that gone, changed, filled with strangers, rooms converted to offices? The upstairs stripped of all the antique furniture you surely must have used when you visited? Don't you ever stop and try to re-imagine it in your mind all over again?"

Smiling, Kit rested her head back, remembering what it was like to be ten years old again. "This is an old house, Dwight, built in 1825. This place had that old house smell even when I was young. I've walked through that entrance hall in my jammies when I was little kid." Kit giggled. "The room where the administrative assistants sit now was a dining room. I ate many a meal in there. Upstairs in the first room on the left, the one we use for archives now, I slept in an ornate tester bed, feeling like a princess when I closed my eyes at night."

Kit stared intently at Dwight. "It was all so beautiful then. You're right, I hate to see all that gone, and I hate like hell to see this place knocked down just so progress can trample over what little history we have left."

"You have an even more vested interest in this old house than we do, then." Dwight nodded, face drawn up in thought. "It just seems that Alexandra is not quite on the same page as you are, willing to sell out to Harsh."

"You know all the finances around here. Why can't the Society just buy this place, give Alex her money, and conduct business as usual?"

"Um, Kit, I'm sure your cousin will be glad to tell you what Harsh is willing to shell out for the property. No doubt the amount would boggle our minds. Wish we had the funds to bid him up and throw him off, but we don't have anywhere near enough money to do that."

"Come on, Dwight. I'm still new here, but haven't you or Irene ever saved a piece of property in Windham Springs? A house, or an old building of some kind? If so, what did you do to save it?"

"Every property we've managed to save amounts to about two. To save each one, the Society held some kind of fancy shindig." A rueful smile filled his face. "We haven't had one of those since I've been here the past few years."

"Then you have a way." Kit snapped her fingers. "If you've done it once, you can do it again."

"Not for the kind of money we have to match now." He shook his head, adamant.

"Come on, Dwight, you seem like a fancy shindig sort of guy. Couldn't we just do one of those and see if we can cut some kind of a deal with her?"

"Kit, old man Harsh is in the bargain, and he won't give up easily. He'll fight off anyone like a screaming banshee if they cross his path. Personally, I think he'll make a deal Alexandra may find hard to refuse."

With a smile, she pointed at him. "Hey, we could throw a concert, and you be the star, Dwight. I know you can draw in a crowd if anybody can! With your voice, you can croon the socks off a snake."

He shrugged. "Sure, and I can bring in the clowns, poodles, and a dancing bear, how about that?" With a nod, he raised his hands to make the 'A-OK' sign with his fingers.

"You'd like all the attention. You know you would." Kit batted her eyelashes.

Dwight gave her a solemn look. "What I really like is *your* attention, Kit. I don't need all the other hoopla."

She stopped right there and said nothing else, fearful that any more teasing or wise-cracks would hurt his feelings. "Well, we need to come up with a plan. I say we don't go down without a fight."

"I'm with you, but go have your talk, and we'll regroup afterwards. We really don't know all the details right now. No matter what happens, I don't want to see you get hurt."

Kit grinned. "You'd come and bail a poor girl out if she got stuck, wouldn't you? I'm a tough cookie, but you never know." She shot him a quick wink.

He sat for a few seconds, staring at her in deep thought. Finally, he got up from the chair and strode to the door. "You can count on me for anything."

For the rest of the day, Kit worked on her projects, taking quick breaks to surf the Internet for more information about the house, about Alexandra, about anything that would help her find a way to save a big piece of her heritage. Alexandra may have owned the house, but Kit felt like this house was just as much hers.

Call her selfish. Call her sentimental. Call her a fool for probably over-stepping her bounds, but she'd fight for this house. She'd spent her youth here, done everything that Dwight alluded to, excluding the love-making. She grinned, wondering whether or not one day he'd spare a moment for a quickie upstairs behind one of the filing cabinets. She laughed. Where was a nice tester bed when a lady needed one? But tonight, the fate of this house remained locked in Alexandra's story. From the exchange on the phone, it didn't sound good.

CHAPTER 3

The sunny yellow VW Bug sped down the streets to Alexandra Stothwell's house, each stretch of road accelerating the anxiety in Kit as she gripped the steering wheel. A nostalgic drive through the old neighborhood behind the square didn't settle her nerves any better. She made her way to the main highway leading her out of the city and on toward rural life.

She thought it rather odd that her cousin had never chosen another house in the Victorian District, but instead settled down to country life just outside its boundaries. Still close, but far enough away from the call of olden times, where time stopped, trapped as if someone had placed the world in a glass globe, and only a brisk shake from a child's hand made the difference between calm and turbulence.

That's what Kit felt like right now – that Harsh thought nothing of picking up the ball, peering into it with greedy eyes, and shaking it with all his might, grinning as the water clouded with its make-believe storm. She slowed down at an intersection, turning left on the scenic route, and driving the last ten minutes to a pea gravel driveway up to the farmhouse.

The evening sun spread its brilliance, wrapping everything in golden hues, nearly blinding her. Thankful for the long row of shady oaks, she steered the car down the drive toward a soft, dusty, green brick structure topped with a hip roof, characteristic of Italianate farmhouses. Ornamental arch work bridged between four modest columns at the top, and the lower railings consisted of three-leafed clover styled cutouts in each slat.

From the inside, a large lace panel covered a wide pane of glass in the wooden front door. Kit scanned her vision upwards, studying the arched wooden moldings crowning each of the three windows on the upper level.

Shaking her head, she brought the car to a stop, marveling at how Alexandra's taste in homes followed her to the isolation and beauty of the country. Kit stepped out of the car, her vision gliding over the house, off to the right side, where she spied the creek, moving without a care into the forest. No wonder Alexandra liked it here. She truly had the best of both worlds.

The lace panel behind the glass moved slightly, and before she reached the door, Alexandra flung it wide open, a warm smile on her face.

"You made it. So good to see you." Alexandra's matronly arms held Kit in a brief, warm embrace as she planted a kiss on her cheek.

"I hope I haven't ruined your evening. I know this was so quick."

"Everything seems awfully quick these days. But no, you haven't bothered my evening at all."

Alexandra ushered her inside into a much more modest entrance hall than the one in the Stothwell mansion, closing the door to the afternoon sun as the last streaks of light died against the wooden floors and wall panels.

Within thirty minutes, Kit found herself sitting by the creek, cradling a plate with a sandwich and some chips on her legs and a tall glass of iced tea on the ground beside her. A small plate of cookies sat between her and her cousin.

"It just happened so fast. He called me one day, out of the blue, and said he wanted to buy the house." Alexandra's gaze bounced from Kit to her own plate as she spoke between bites of food.

"Alex, that house has been part of Windham Springs history for a long time. You grew up in that house. How can you just let it go like that, and why didn't you come talk to us about it?" Kit stopped short, taking note of her cousin's wide eyes. Embarrassed, she looked away, trying to regroup.

"Look, honey, I wasn't trying to be sneaky, but the money's too good to pass up, and ..." She turned her face toward the creek.

"And what?" Kit took a bite of her sandwich.

"He's been calling me on a weekly basis for the past month. The first time was one thing. Told him I'd think about it and get back to him. Same for the second time. After that, I just let the voice mail pick up when I'd see his number."

"He's that persistent?"

"Like a dog with a bone, shaking his head, determined he'll get it away from you. One time he even managed to catch me on my way to the car when I was out shopping. I nearly had a heart attack. He came running over to me, shouting my name, and pulled my car door open just as I was about to shut it."

"Wow, Alex, that's just crazy. So, what's made you give in all of a sudden? You've waited a month." Kit stared at the lady beside her. Time had tinged her complexion with age and rounded out her figure more. The vibrancy of younger years had faded away, and in its place, a more resigned demeanor.

"The truth is, I'd like the money. A trust will only go so far, and I don't want to use it up entirely and find myself in a predicament later down the road."

"Does our lease amount not help you in any way?"

Alexandra's expression turned more earnest. "Look at me, Kit; I don't have any skills. I'm getting older. I kept the lease amount affordable all these years because that's what mama did, and at the time, I was fine with it, didn't think about it a whole lot, either. Things have changed now. Not to be mean, but the Society can find an office or another old house to move into. It shouldn't be that hard. Nothing will affect the work you do." She turned a set of reluctant eyes on Kit.

"But condos? Really?" Kit stared in surprise at Alexandra. "I thought you loved preserving history, keeping the square intact."

"Honey, *you* like preserving history and keeping the square intact."

Kit put down her plate, dumbstruck. "Alex, doesn't that house mean anything to you at all?"

"Listen," Alexandra said, placing her hand easily on Kit's wrist, "I've owned it, lived there, experienced it as a home. Your family were invited guests."

"... You like preserving history ... you were invited guests ..." Kit blinked a few times, gazing down at the space between her and Alexandra, trying to take in what she'd just heard. Her cousin had dismissed her and the Society, a wave of the hand, not batting an eyelash.

"What I'm trying to tell you, dear, is that I don't have the same sentimental attachment to it that you apparently do. Ownership and experience can do that to a person. At some point, you're ready to let go. Don't take all this the wrong way. I love old homes and history too. May not sound like it right now, but look at this place. It's old. I love it." Alexandra leaned toward Kit. "With the money Harsh gives me, I can at least invest it, make more money. I'm just pooling my assets together and consolidating, that's all."

"I really don't know what to say, Alex." Kit stared out at the creek. Had she been so foolish to assume her cousin was a lot like her simply based on where she grew up? That owning a piece of history might have meant something? Of course, others found the historical aspect of living there worth it, fitting smoothly into their personal dogma, finances be damned. "What did he offer you?" Inwardly, she cringed at the question.

"Two hundred forty-five thousand dollars. That's what the property appraised for."

Without thinking, Kit blurted out, "What if you let the Society buy it from you? I mean, tell Harsh you're not selling, that you have another buyer in mind."

Alexandra shook her head. "Too late, hon, we've already signed a contract. Did it about three days ago." She glanced at Kit, a rueful look on her face.

Gazing down at her cell phone, Kit never wanted to call Dwight as badly as she did right now. He'd already warned her that the Society's finances couldn't handle an outright purchase.

Her adrenaline rush got the better of her. A memory that she loved, holding onto it for years, was slipping away from her each second the ink dried on the contract. "Alex, if the Society requested the Planning Commission to issue a stay of demolition until an appropriate buyer is found, one with the intent on keeping the house intact, would you consider selling your home to us?"

"Sweetie, are you crazy? You can't just up and make a decision like that. It has to go before the Board, which I'm on, in case you've forgotten." Alexandra shook her head.

"Resign, then." Kit's boldness took on a fierceness she'd not experienced until now. Never had she dreamed that she and Alexandra would have a conversation like this. Of course, what would a young child have to say to a woman old enough to be her mother? She choked back a wave of nausea. "I'm serious, Alex. If you're not into keeping the home of your youth, into preserving the square, you really shouldn't be on the board anymore. You've lost your fire."

Alexandra hung her head in sadness. "True, and I think you've found yours." She managed a wan smile, patting Kit on the back.

***

"The next planning commission meeting is when? Next Friday at one o'clock. Good." Kit clicked the calendar icon on her computer and input the information. "And this is open to the public so anyone can bring up an issue, right? Wonderful, thank you." Kit hung up the phone and rested back in her chair. "And just how am I going to scrounge up enough signatures to make a damn?" she said out loud.

"I don't know. Why do we need signatures?" Irene stood in the doorway to Kit's office.

Kit jumped. "I didn't hear you come in. And how long have you been eavesdropping?" She grinned at her friend.

"Long enough to catch bits and pieces of your phone conversation." Irene sat on the edge of the desk. "What's going on?"

Tapping a pen on the desk top, Kit grimaced at her friend. "I have less than a week to get signatures protesting Harsh's attempt to buy this mansion."

Irene frowned. "Why is that?"

"Because there's already a signed contract in place."

"You talked to her – Alexandra, that is?" Irene tapped a small piece of paper against her other hand. "That may explain why she's resigned from the board. Just got a memo in my box." She stared down at the paper.

"Yep. So, you and I will make the rounds to get signatures. You with me on this? We need them all by the end of next Thursday night."

The sound of a male voice came from the doorway. "If it's signatures you want, you can start with the protesters on the sidewalk out front."

"Protesters?" Irene and Kit spoke in unison, staring wide-eyed at Dwight, who rested easily against the door jam. "Word's gotten out."

"Then maybe I need to get the word out to you guys that I want the Society to have the option of buying the mansion." Kit's gaze slid from Irene to Dwight, ending with staring her new love in the eyes. "Sorry, Dwight, but I think we have a chance. Bring it up at the next board meeting with the trustees and let them know. You offer the subject first; I'll second it. We'll go from there."

"Is that an order?" He shot her a quizzical look.

"Take it any way you want, but I've decided we keep this house for us, because I can't purchase it myself. Besides, Dwight, you and I have the makings of a plan. If we think it through, we'll not only have a house, but something fun the community can look forward to each year."

"C'mon, Dwight, work your magic." Irene waved her hand like a fairy waving a wand. "Kit, my friend, I'm with you. We'll get those signatures. But I agree with Dwight, I'd start with the people outside."

Kit grabbed a yellow legal pad out of her desk, picked up a pen, and headed for the door. She'd create an electronic petition form for the front page of the Society's website later, before she went home. At this point, any attempts to get signatures would be a big help for her cause.

The number of people in front of the house surprised her, but the others who'd taken up various posts along the square touched her most. Some of the protesters paraded up and down the sidewalk, as cars drove by, honking horns in approval. She read the signs. 'Save the Stothwell Mansion.' 'Say Bye to Harsh.' 'No Condos.'

Kit's spirits lifted. They were already off to a great start. For the remainder of the day, she spent time gaining signatures from the protesters, followed by the merchants in the square and patrons in the shops. Stopping at *A Cup Above the Roast* just in time for the lunch crowd, she got signatures from people inside, then stood outside the door for an hour in the hope of catching customers as they entered.

At five o'clock she returned to the mansion, making a beeline to Dwight's office. Waving the legal pad, she marched inside. "I've got close to fifty-five signatures. That's not a lot, but it's a start at least."

Dwight glanced up from his desk, fingers pausing above a calculator. "That's all that matters. What's the plan for getting more? We'll need over five hundred to make a strong statement."

"Why don't you, me, and Irene work on hitting the neighborhoods this weekend? Maybe divide them up into sections and we each take one?"

"Sounds good to me. I'm coming with you to the planning commission meeting. I want to hear what that's all about."

"Oh, Dwight," Kit said, waving him away. "I think I can handle it. Shouldn't be that hard."

"You sure you don't want some of us from the Society to join you, at least for moral support?"

"Where I need your support is getting the bank loan." She winked at the man behind the desk, admiring the way his face glowed in the light. She liked the way he dressed, the way his long fingers gripped the pen he held. Maybe, just maybe she might be ready to take this relationship to the next step.

"Kit, are you listening to me?" Dwight snapped his fingers. "Think I lost you there." She turned her eyes up to his. "We'll have to put down twenty percent based on the final sales price."

"And that's going to be over forty thousand dollars at least." Kit arched an eyebrow while Dwight winced.

"I love this old house, but now that we're putting it into a different perspective, money-wise, does it still mean that much to you?"

"Of course, it does. I believe in the Society, the work we do." She gave him an intent look. "I believe in us."

He smiled, and she excused herself, heading back to her office.

CHAPTER 4

The brisk morning air hit her skin. Autumn was in full swing, and the cloudless sky above held a beautiful, glowing orb. After a quick shower, she emerged from her apartment wearing sweat pants and a sweatshirt. Behind her head, an old silver-tone barrette pinned the side locks of her hair in place while letting the rest blow freely in the wind. A new weekend had finally arrived with the promise of pleasant weather.

Talking with Alexandra and the small start to the petition filled Kit with a new energy and purpose, a more optimistic way to end the previous week. They still had far to go before the Committee would even begin to take their efforts seriously.

Tonight she, Dwight, and Irene would hit the neighborhoods, garnering every signature they could. Looking at a map of the Victorian District, she'd divided the area into thirds, Dwight taking the back, Irene the middle, and she would cover the front. Hanging out on the square during lunch hour each day next week ensured more signatures. At least if she were to attend the Commission meeting next Friday armed with the names of people who agreed with keeping the mansion, success would be more than sailing on a wing and a prayer. The Commission took petitions seriously, and she hoped they'd accept her proposal.

She wished Irene could have joined her in grabbing a fresh cup of coffee for a bit of a celebratory kick-off, but her friend didn't live close to the historical district. Dwight had some errands to run this morning, or he would have gladly joined her.

At least she had tonight to spend some fun time with her friends. Maybe they could talk about other things besides work.

Kit crossed the street and passed by Our Lady of Eternal Blessings, giving a sideways glance at the slate gray stone structure, its gothic roofline and spires ominous even in daylight. She'd liked the look of that church the moment she first laid eyes on it. Since her arrival, she had only attended mass five times.

Catholicism had never held her in its clutches with rigid rules and ideology, but certain ceremonies and practices captured her fascination. Perhaps she concurred with their intent, believed in the reasoning behind them, or maybe resorting to ritual offered a sense of power. On impulse, she stopped, gazing at the shadowy outline of the door tucked inside the portico.

Today the church called to her for a reason she didn't understand. The more she tried to pry her eyes away and keep moving on down the sidewalk, the stronger the pull. Did she need to go inside? Why? What would she do there? Kit moved toward the door. The brightness of the day dimmed as if it were an afterthought, the darkness inside the portico luring her in deeper.

The heavy wooden door squeaked on its hinges. Passing through the narthex, she moved down the aisle. Inside the church, the air stilled, cool against her face. The vaulted ceilings towering over her added a certain expanse to the building, building her sense of smallness to a more profound level. Large fluted columns lined both sides like soldiers guarding the space. The Tiffany stained glass windows, a rarity not found in many churches, depicted bright biblical scenes. Shaded panes illuminated the church in vibrant colors as if an artist had created a series of mandalas down the side of the building, each one unique and resting against a backdrop of grey. Along the far wall to the left of the main altar stood the rack of votive candles used for individual prayer requests.

Kit smiled. Of course, she'd light a candle. Not having done this in years, now was as good a time as ever. There were houses to save, contractors to stall, lovers to entice – and old ghosts to get rid of. She needed any saint or generous spirit that would help. When she reached the rack, she picked up the lighter, lit a candle, and began a prayer, making the words up as she said them silently in her head.

May a humble prayer reach the heavenly ear that listens as I solicit intervention from saints and angels. Please watch over and protect those things that bring joy to others. From evil, keep me from harm. From restless ones who are no longer with me, please offer resolution so they may find eternal peace.

She opened her eyes, focusing on the flame. There, she felt better already. With a sense of having completed a spiritual duty, she turned on her heel and headed out of the church.

As she walked by the shops, Kit resigned herself to a morning of enjoying her java alone. The chimes in the clock tower of the church rang out, signaling ten o'clock.

As if on cue, merchants turned on their 'Open' signs, neon orange lights blazing in windows. *What a great day for shopping.* Once she finished coffee, she would enjoy her time scouring the shops and treating herself to a few choice trinkets, if any caught her eye.

Would it be too forward or inappropriate to pick up something for Dwight? A vintage fountain pen or some oddity with a strange history behind it? Shopping with him was always fun, as he never seemed rushed, encouraging her to take her time, to look and feel. She peeped quickly into the window of *Madison's Jewelers*, admiring the 'sparklies,' as she liked to call them, glistening in the sun, iridescent flashes dancing from the surface of diamonds and other gemstones polished to a fine sheen.

Her eyes scanned the window until her gaze fell on a golden necklace in the back left-hand corner of the display. Her eyes widened in surprise. Or was it with dismay? A tiny puff heart dangled innocently from a delicate gold chain. Kit backed away from the window. Oh, shit! Why was she seeing this? Of course, *Madison's* was known for carrying vintage and antique merchandise, so why not this particular style of necklace like the one Austin gave her?

She loomed closer to the window again, hoping by some magical chance her eyes had been fooling her. The necklace glowed extra bright as if for her benefit. Creeped out by the vision, she moved on, definitely with no intention of browsing here today, maybe not ever.

As Kit continued toward the coffee shop, she did a double-take at the sight of the space next door, which had been vacant. Something struck her as out of the ordinary, but it took a few moments for her to digest what she saw; the 'For Lease' sign was gone! A new merchant had moved in.

Curious, she walked over and peeped through the large window, viewing a clean, polished floor. The right wall had already been painted a light pale yellow, and on the floor, several pieces of art work rested neatly in a row. Next to the left-hand wall stood a tall ladder, with a can of paint and a brush resting at the bottom. She strained her eyes, staring down the dim hallway in hopes of seeing someone inside.

She stepped back out to the edge of the sidewalk to read the store's sign and saw the words '*Celestial Temptation Gallery.*' No, this was not a dream. The space held a new owner and, from what she'd witnessed so far, one who admired art. At this point, Kit decided she may have to postpone her shopping excursion on the square for another day. After savoring a cup of coffee, she planned on returning here to welcome this new merchant.

Once she'd settled into her job at the Historical Society, she'd acted as the unofficial welcome wagon, making it a personal sworn duty to introduce herself to each business owner when they moved into a space on the square.

The door of the coffee shop swung open as a customer stepped outside. Distracted, Kit turned away from the new gallery and ran over to catch the door before it closed. Maybe the barista knew something about the new owner. When she reached the counter, she asked, "Do you know who's moved into the space next door?"

The barista, a pleasant-looking young lady, furrowed her brow. "Hmm, I hadn't really noticed. Has someone taken the space?"

"Yeah, I just looked in the window right before I came in here. And there's a sign up too."

The lady behind the counter shrugged. "I don't know anything about it. I just don't pay much attention to who comes and goes around here." Her lips spread into a wide smile. "But I'm glad someone has finally taken that space. It's about time."

"I agree. I hate to see empty spots around here. The more the merrier, I say." Kit's eyes roamed the glass case for a yummy pastry to chew on while sipping coffee.

"So, what'll it be for you this lovely, cheery morning?"

"You know what, let me try the *Red Velvet Fantasy*, and I'll have a medium *Hazelnut Creme* to go with it. No cream or sugar, either."

"Coming right up!" The lady smiled and busied herself getting the order together.

After paying the ticket, Kit carried her items to a vacant table, seating herself so she could watch customers come and go. While she ate, her thoughts turned back to the shop next door. A new merchant. Finally, after all this time. She couldn't keep this news until tonight. Unable to contain her excitement, she pulled out her cell phone and called Irene.

"Hello?"

"Hey, it's me, Kit."

"Kit? Hi, how's it going? You usually sleep in 'til noon on weekends."

"I know, I know, but listen, I've got something to tell you. Did you know someone has rented the space by the coffee shop? I know, because I'm here as we speak."

"Huh? Really?"

"Yes. I saw the space next door, and it looks like an artist has moved in. There's a sign outside, on the building."

"What's the name?"

Kit took a quick sip of coffee. "*Celestial Temptation Gallery*. Did you know about this?"

"Gosh, no. I sure didn't hear any rumors of anyone interested in the space, but I think it's great that it's rented."

"Yeah, me too."

"Are you going over there to check it out when you're done?"

"Are you kidding? You bet! I'm dying to find out who the owner is. I'll let you know tonight how it all goes. How about that?"

"Absolutely. I can't wait for tonight. I think we'll definitely get more signatures."

"Me too. See you later, Irene."

Kit pushed the 'End' button on her phone and took a bite of cake. As people filed in and out of the shop, she tried to see if anyone looked remotely like a painter, or at least someone dressed like they were in the throes of fixing up a new storefront. No luck. She gulped down the last bite of cake and swallowed down her coffee. After placing her dishes on the 'Dirty' shelf, she headed out the door.

For some strange reason, she became acutely aware of her appearance. A pang of self-consciousness hit her out of the blue as her gaze traveled down her dingy sweatpants to the worn sneakers that had seen better days. How silly! Who cared what she looked like today, and who would she impress, anyway? A merchant settling into a new shop wouldn't look the neatest, either. She reached up and fluffed her hair anyway, making sure her barrette hadn't slipped down or gotten crooked. With a deep breath, she walked over to the art gallery and pulled on the door, hoping the owner hadn't locked it.

Much to her surprise, the door was unlocked, and she stepped inside. The smell of fresh paint and polish filled the air, and a radio played some popular tunes in the background. Curious to see the artwork, she sauntered over, hoping to meet the owner soon. For the first few moments, the paintings didn't strike her as much out of the ordinary, though they were quite good. However, the more she focused on the canvases lining the wall, the more recognition started to seep in. The style and subject matter tugged at her memory. Had she seen these or something like them before? Somewhere?

She strolled back and forth, staring at each one, trying desperately to remember why these paintings held such a fascination for her. The radio played a new tune, and as the song continued, Kit's eyes widened. She and Austin had danced to this song. *Here we go again.* First the necklace, now a song. Would this ever end? Her prayer only went out about an hour ago, so maybe the angels and saints hadn't received it yet. Did prayer candles ever work? She couldn't remember. Her eyes fell back on the paintings, studying them in more detail. Without warning, a chill shot up her spine. She shivered and glanced up at the ceiling, expecting an open vent with cold air blowing from the air conditioner.

"Can I help you?" a man's voice rang out.

Startled, she whirled around, finding herself face-to-face with an attractive man, about her age, dressed in paint-spattered jeans and a T-shirt. A cropped head of hair rested neatly in place, and the deep blue of his eyes seemed to sear into her soul.

"I'm sorry, I didn't mean to scare you. Were you interested in a painting, or something?" The new smile on his face reminded her of the moment during a dreary day when the sun burst forth from the clouds, illuminating the world with brilliant sunlight.

Kit stood transfixed, unable to think straight.

"Are you okay?"

"Um, sorry." She shook her head, collected her thoughts, and forced a smile on her face, hoping she didn't look too much like a bumbling fool. "Hi, I'm Kit Millinger, and I'm the conservation manager for the Windham Springs Historical Society. I work in the mansion across the street." She paused, pointing in the direction of the house. "When I see someone new in the neighborhood, I always stop in and welcome them to the square. Looks like you've just moved in, so I thought I'd come over and say Hi."

He smiled and reached out and shook her hand. "Hi Kit, I'm Steven D'Astolo. I own the gallery."

When they touched, a surge of emotions welled up at once, a mix of joy, excitement, and confusion, topped off by a sharp pang of sorrow. She blinked a few times and took a deep breath, recovering from this unexpected assault on her senses. "Nice to meet you." Kit forced another smile on her face, hoping to still her excited nerves. What on earth was going on right now? Why did this stranger affect her like this? Even during the most stressful occasions, she could hold it together.

"So you get to work in that gorgeous old home." He leaned his head toward the shop window, in the direction of the old Stothwell Mansion.

"I do. I've only been there about six months."

"Do you like it so far?"

Her eyes brightened up. "Yes, I love it there. Love my job. Nothing like saving some beautiful buildings and homes around here." She refused to launch into a monologue right now about the mansion and what had transpired.

He kept his eyes on her, gazing from her face and traveling the length of her slender figure, and back to her face. "Maintaining old things must mean a lot to you, then. Are you a big history buff?"

"Yeah, always have been. I'm definitely into antiques and old homes. I love the craftsmanship and stories behind them. What about you?"

She blushed under his perusal of her. The intensity in his eyes, the way his lips twitched up in an easy grin, all triggered a memory, but what, exactly, she couldn't quite determine.

Steven hesitated a moment, running a few fingers through his hair as he thought about what to say. "I definitely appreciate people who try to save a piece of history. Someone took the time to create everything out there and, yes, it's nice when others care about it."

A few seconds of silence passed between them. Kit fidgeted, unsure whether to excuse herself and leave now, or find some other reason to stay a little longer. Personally, she wanted to stay longer! Something about this gentleman attracted her, a connection between them so strong it almost scared her.

"So were you interested in some of the art here? Or if you want, I can give you a brush, and you can help me finish up painting the walls. Either one is fine by me." He smiled again.

She laughed and shifted her weight to the other leg, praying she'd keep her balance and not fall in a heap at his feet. "Well, I was interested in the paintings. I'm so sorry for barging in, but I couldn't help myself, I guess."

He moved in a little closer to her. "I would never consider you coming into my shop as barging in. You're welcome here anytime." His voice softened to nearly a whisper, and a new spark lit up his eyes.

Kit's gaze fell to the floor, with a hot flush coloring her cheeks. "Thank you."

"Was there any particular piece you were interested in?" Steven walked toward the wall of paintings, with Kit following behind.

She stood there, eyes roaming back and forth. "How long have you been an artist?"

He turned his eyes toward the ceiling, thinking a moment. "You know, I've been drawing since I was old enough to hold a pencil or crayon in my hand and my brain could comprehend that I could sketch things I saw." He chuckled. "As much as I hate to admit it, I used to sit at the back of the class when I was a kid and draw all day long. I couldn't have cared less what the teacher was saying."

"I'd say you've had lots of practice, then." She'd managed to get her nerves under enough control to take a hard look at him. He stood about two inches taller than she did, with a strong, solid body from head to toe. Looking at him, she saw power, force, and energy. His personality seemed easy-going enough, and she liked his quick sense of humor.

"True, I've had all my life to practice." He stood still for a moment, surveying his work.

"Steven, when did you move in here?"

He straightened up a canvas that had slipped down to the floor. "Believe it or not, I started working on this place late last night. I figured if I could at least get a head start and do some basics, the quicker I could get this shop open and start selling my work."

Feeling more comfortable now, she wanted to ask more questions. "Where did you live before you came here to Windham Springs, and where do you stay now?"

Steven stared at her, hard and penetrating, before answering. "I come from the west coast. To save money, I just decided to live in the back. The hallway there leads to a pretty big area. I have all the bare basics I need." He pointed to the door behind the counter.

"Don't know about you, but I like living in a historical district." She waved a hand in the direction of her home. "I live in an apartment above Harold Crispin's law office, just down the street. Guess you haven't had a chance to see the area, yet?"

"No, I haven't. But I'm with you when it comes to living in an area like this. It's soothing to the soul, and I need a clear head to think so I can create the kind of art I want to." They both turned back toward the canvases.

"You know something? Your style seems so familiar to me, like I've seen it somewhere before." Kit turned her eyes to his.

"Really?" He pursed his lips, nodding his head lightly. "Well, some of the works are much older, and some are new. If you look at the older paintings, it's not anything like I currently do. I've changed my style over the years."

"Oh?"

He hooked his thumbs through the belt loops on his jeans and focused his attention back to Kit. "Of course. As we grow and mature and evolve, our style changes. I can see how different I am now from what I was before."

"That makes sense, though I guess I haven't thought about it much." She smiled back. "But you make a good point, and your work is beautiful." She leaned over and touched a smaller painting, depicting a pair of hands holding up the Earth. From the globe, rays of light emanated, creating a complete circle. Above the hands, a golden 'Infinity' symbol had been painted. "I think this one is awfully neat."

Rubbing his chin, Steven gazed at the painting. "That particular one is special to me, and it's one of my latest works."

"What does it mean?" Kit cocked her head, trying to figure out what it meant to her.

"It's actually supposed to represent 'The World,' which is one of the major arcana cards in Tarot."

"Huh?" She gave him a blank stare. "Tarot cards?"

"Yeah, I'm sure you've seen tarot cards before." Seeing her confusion, he thought for a moment before continuing his answer. "You see, the tarot cards represent all aspects of human nature and the different ways we interact with others, ourselves, and our environment. It reflects the journey we each take in our lives and all the nuances of change and growth. This particular painting signifies completion of a journey, success, victory. The symbol at the top here means our spirits endure forever."

Kit said nothing, but glanced at the painting and turned back to Steven.

He continued his mini lecture on the cards. "I painted my design a little differently than what you normally see for this particular card. Instead of a person dancing, I used hands because I believe we hold the power to create our own path and make our own choices."

"Wow!" She blinked a few times, trying hard to understand what he'd told her. "That's the most interesting story behind a painting I've ever heard –not that I obsess over why an artist paints what he does."

Steven laughed. "Don't worry if you don't understand right away. I'm just glad you like it. At least it made you pay attention, which is what I hope to do with my work."

Yes, and pay attention she did. During the past several weeks, it seemed like *something* wanted her to pay attention. They stood together, finding themselves in a new, awkward silence. Kit's shyness crept in again. She didn't know how long they'd been talking, but she knew if this man wanted to get his shop ready to open, she needed to get out and let him finish his work.

"Well, Steven, it was so nice to meet you, but I guess I'd better get going." She stepped back, taking a few steps toward the door. "I appreciate the tarot lesson too. Very interesting. I'll have to study up on that."

The light in his eyes dimmed. "I'm glad you stopped in, Kit. I enjoyed meeting you too." He followed her to the door, and touched her hand lightly with his fingers. "Hey, you know what, maybe you can show me around the area. I bet you're a terrific tour guide, working with the Historical Society and everything."

Her stomach clenched with excitement. She'd love nothing better than giving him the grand tour of Windham Springs, especially the historic district. His suggestion gave her the opportunity to see him again without trying to come up with some lame excuse. "I'd be glad to do that. Let me check my calendar, and I'll get back with you so we can set up a time."

"You know where I live." He touched the back of her shoulder as she stepped out the door, sending another round of shivers flitting through her body.

Once outside, Kit didn't look back. The inside of her belly fluttered like a ton of butterflies had been set loose. Wait until Irene heard about this! Her steps slowed. Irene – Dwight. She was meeting the two of them tonight, and most likely they'd be going out afterwards for dinner and some drinks. Her pulse sped up. With Steven, Dwight had all but disappeared from her thoughts. She frowned. This didn't bode well at all. Now all she felt was guilt muddled with confusion. The relationship with Dwight had been going so well, and now a strange, new man had come along and sent her mind into a tailspin.

Kit glanced around the square, hoping the sight of a certain shop would help persuade her to stay. No such luck. What started out as a promising, fun-filled day had done a U-turn. How could she enjoy herself while thoughts of Dwight and Steven tumbled around in her brain? Discouraged, Kit walked slowly back to her apartment. Back inside, she made a salad and spent her afternoon catching up on a novel instead. Her thoughts wandered back to Steven, his eyes, the way he looked at her, how being around him stirred up the strangest emotions.

Shaking off the imaginings, she forced her attention back to the words on the page, trying to get through the chapters. No need to make a fuss. Steven and she had just met, still strangers. Dwight had familiarity and a little more time to wrap himself around her heart. Yet Steven held an odd familiarity, too, and for some reason, that bothered her the most. When the clock on the mantle chimed four-thirty, she put the book down and grabbed up her legal pad and pen, ready to meet her friends on the square. There were signatures to collect and a fun-filled night ahead, if she could only put thoughts of Steven away for a while.

***

Wild Waldo hummed like a swarm of gnats, the usual Saturday night crowd packing the favorite bistro where the locals hung out. In one corner, a solo guitarist crooned out a soulful melody. Mugs of beer slid easily across the bar to eager patrons, and the bartender mixed drinks with assembly-line speed. Dwight, his arm around Kit, led the way to a vacant table, where an industrious server barely had time to wipe the top clean before the trio wiggled onto the stools.

"What'll it be for you fine people tonight?" She forced a smile, reaching for the pen behind her ear and whipping out an order book from her apron pocket.

"I'll have a *Wild Waldo Smash*," Irene said, after studying the drink list with a quick eye.

Dwight nodded at Kit, who ordered first. "Let me try the *Zombie*."

The server raised an eyebrow. "You know that's the strongest drink in the house? It'll knock you flat."

"Exactly what the doctor ordered." Kit's lips spread into an exaggerated grin as she watched Irene and Dwight raise their eyebrows at her choice. "And my buddy here will have the best merlot you have. It's my treat tonight, Dwight. I owe you after that fine dinner."

"You don't owe me anything, dear." Dwight pursed his lips. "You're worth every dime." Kit avoided his eyes as his hand ran smoothly down her back.

"I'll let you love birds figure out the bill. You'll have your drinks shortly." The server whirled on her heel and lost herself in the crowd.

"How many signatures did we get, guys?" Kit flicked her gaze between Dwight and Irene. After studying their sheets, the number totaled one hundred fifty. Kit sank against the back of her stool. "Rats! Still not enough. I'd hoped we'd have more than that." Her gaze moved between Dwight and Irene. "Dwight, you said we'd need way more than that."

"We'll try to get some more during next week, and add them." Irene patted Kit's hand. "Don't worry, we'll get the signatures we need. We may have to get more creative, maybe go outside Windham Springs."

"You've done such a good job on this, keeping your nose to the grindstone." Dwight leaned over, clutching Kit in his arm for a lingering hug and a quick kiss on the side of her cheek.

"I feel like I'm saving more than just a house," Kit said, pulling away and clearing her throat. "I'm preserving memories and keeping the place where we work the best."

After a round of drinks and dinner, Dwight excused himself a moment, heading toward the men's room. Kit barely picked at her sandwich, but guzzled down the *Zombie*. She rather enjoyed the tremendous buzz filling her head, making its way through the rest of her body.

"What the hell is going on with you? You've been acting strange all evening." Irene landed a scowl in Kit's direction. "Did you ever find out who rented the space next door to the coffee shop?"

CHAPTER 5

On a chilly Monday morning after meeting Steven, a dreamy-eyed Kit sat back in her office chair, drumming her fingers on the desk.

"So, what are you going to do now that you've met someone new?" Irene, perched on top if Kit's desk, delivered a playful smack on her friend's hand. "What about Dwight?"

"Ugh, that's what I've been thinking. I adore Dwight, but this guy who owns the art gallery ... There was something about him, Irene. I don't know how to describe it exactly."

"So, was he cute or what?" Irene tossed her hair back and smiled. "And does he have a girlfriend or wife? That's what you really want to know. You can't just be jumping to conclusions that he's available."

"He was really cute, with a gorgeous body, athletic and built like a brick wall. And you know what, I didn't ask him if he was married or had a girlfriend with him." Kit shifted in her seat to get more comfortable. "But he said he was living in the back of his shop. If that doesn't scream bachelor, I don't know what does. He also told me he came from out west. Didn't mention having any family here."

Irene narrowed her eyes and pursed her lips. "Where out west? He didn't tell you what town or state?" She nibbled on one of her nails, waiting for Kit's answer.

"You know what, he never did say exactly where, but I don't guess it matters. I mean, he's not a local guy or from a neighboring state or town."

"Sounds hedgy to me. Probably married!" Irene leaned back on one hand and crossed her legs. "So, tell me more. What was he like, personality-wise? What were his paintings like? Are they any good, or is it some newfangled crap, where we'll see him here today and gone tomorrow because nobody will buy his self-proclaimed masterpieces?"

"He was pleasant, funny at times, and his work is fantastic. Some of it is rather unusual."

"Unusual? In what way?"

"He had this one painting with some hands holding up the earth, and he gave me a speech on tarot cards, saying this particular piece was 'The World,' or something like that."

"I know which card that is." Irene nodded, rubbing her lower lip in thought.

"Of course, you do." She smiled at Irene. "You need some of his art. Don't you need a swanky painting or something to go in your house?"

Irene frowned and shook her finger at Kit. "No, ma'am, I don't need a painting right now. And let me tell you that arcane knowledge is very powerful. It was the first knowledge, and the ancients were spiritually connected. Unfortunately, we so-called modern folk have lost our way."

Kit smiled at her friend. "I guess vanity, lust, and greed do that over time, yeah?"

"You said it. When it comes to tarot cards, there's nothing magical about them, either. The cards just reflect what's going on inside of us, telling us where we are in any given moment of our lives at the time we consult them. They're actually esoteric in nature, if you really think about it."

"Great, you sound just like him. If I didn't have the hots for him myself, I'd offer to introduce you two."

"Sweet, but no deal. I'm madly in love with my darling Jim." Irene fluttered her eyelashes, fanning herself with one hand.

"Have the hots for whom?" Dwight leaned against the doorframe of the office, looking from one lady to the next.

Kit's face colored a bright red.

Irene blurted out, "Kit may have found her a new friend, and he's hot, hot, hot."

"Sh-h-h, Irene!" She shook her head in disapproval as Irene turned back, shoulders up in a questioning shrug.

"What else can we say?" she mouthed to Kit.

Like the skilled speed of a quick-change artist, Dwight's expression changed from one of idle curiosity to dismay, face pale and lips drawn in a grim line. For a few seconds, no one said a word, eyes averted elsewhere.

After a few seconds, Kit spoke up. "Someone rented the space next to the coffee shop, that's all. And you know me, I make it a point to introduce myself to new merchants."

"Hmm, I hadn't heard." Dwight's voice trickled over Kit's ears with a steely coldness she'd never heard from him before. "I see. So this hot man is also the new merchant about town. How nice."

Irene lifted up her wrist, viewed her watch, and slid off the desk. "I just remembered I have to make a phone call. Gotta go."

"How convenient," Kit murmured.

"I'll talk more to you later." Irene winked back at Kit and sidled past Dwight, patting him on the shoulder.

He walked on into the office and sat down. "So what wonderful, magical, mystical wares does this hot merchant of Venice have that will amaze and astonish us all?"

"Mr. Steven D'Astolo is our new merchant, and though he's not from around here, I hardly think he hails from Venice." Kit smirked back at Dwight, who engrossed himself studying his hands as if he'd discovered them for the first time.

"Did you get his signature on your trusty petition?" He shot Kit a withering look.

"Nope, as a matter of fact, I actually don't have his John Hancock." Her stomach tightened. How she was ever going to resolve this tangled issue, she didn't know. Every time her thoughts focused on Dwight, images of Steven's face pushed through, his eyes and smile crowding out anything else.

"Is that why you drank so much the other night? You sure guzzled 'em back." Dwight resumed studying his hands.

"You're Mr. Nice Guy today." Kit shot back, nearly reeling as his words shocked her, almost scary, as they fell from his lips.

"Sorry, that just slipped out. I usually see you in more control, that's all."

"Unlike you, right now." Several minutes of uncomfortable silence passed between them.

With reluctant eyes, she studied him in the chair, wondering if he'd be like a jealous lover, knocking someone off just as Mr. Crispin had mentioned the other day when they discussed some of the local history. Did Dwight even own a gun? He seemed like a perfectionist at everything else, so why couldn't he be a sharpshooter? She knew one thing – avoid hurt feelings at all cost.

"Thank you for getting my meal and drinks at Waldo's. I don't know if I ever thanked you." He pulled his gaze up to hers, his face expressionless, the tone in his voice sad.

"Oh, Dwight, you did thank me. And you don't always have to do that. I'm more than glad to treat you. It's nice that you appreciate things."

"Yes, I do." He stretched out his arms in a silent yawn. "I need to get back too. I came over to see what we wanted to do about earning money for this down payment we may have hanging over our heads."

"We definitely need to discuss that. The board meeting for the Society is Wednesday. If they give us the okay to be a buyer and the Commission grants a stay, we'll have all flags waving 'Go' for this project – that is, if we get the remaining signatures we need."

"The biggest project we'll have for many years." Dwight glanced up at her. His face softened somewhat, and his eyes regained a little of their old sparkle. "Talk to you later."

When he left, Kit came around from behind the desk and closed the door. After such an awkward situation minutes ago, she needed some time alone to catch her breath and get her head together. Seeing a glimpse of a smile at the end of their conversation brought on a sense of relief. Though Steven excited and intrigued her, new thoughts of having Dwight out of the picture didn't comfort her at all. She liked Dwight. He was a nice person, thoughtful, and she enjoyed his attentiveness. No, he wasn't the jock type, but he had an attractiveness about him that drew her to him. How odd one quick revelation had exposed strong emotions – for each of them.

Reclined back in her chair, feet propped on the desk, Kit reviewed her time with Steven, over and over, remembering each detail. The way his face lit up with a bright smile when he spoke to her, the way his eyes focused with great interest when a subject matter attracted his attention; all his mannerisms and gestures made her warm and tingly again.

She thought again of the yearbooks. Come to think of it, she didn't remember ever seeing Austin's art photographed. There weren't any hints of his work, not even in various sketches gracing the margins of title and ad pages.

Maybe elements in Steven's work reflected a style similar to Austin's –from what she remembered, anyway. The passing of time had faded all the memories to a point where reality blurred into what could now be simple imagination, a trick of the mind believing fiction as fact. However, many of Steven's paintings also displayed a fascination for the more cosmic aspects of existence, with much of the subject matter showing man in communion with the realms of the spirit, of God.

She didn't recall Austin having a great spiritual interest in things. But again, youth had not ripened into adulthood, a time when people came into their own. Steven seemed to possess an understanding of something greater, concepts she didn't grasp easily.

She swung her legs off the desk and continued working.

"I brought you something to eat. You've been holed up in here for hours." Dwight had knocked and let himself in, placing a cardboard carry tray in front of her, filled with a medium cup of coffee, a brie and turkey panini sandwich, and for dessert, her favorite: *Red Velvet Fantasy.* "I figured you might be starved by now."

"What do I owe you?" She pushed back the chair and reached for her purse in the bottom drawer of the desk.

"You don't owe me anything. It's always my pleasure to get you something from across the street." He flashed her a broad smile.

Sitting back in her chair, she stared at him from across the desk. His smile resembled Steven's, wide and full of warmth, radiating like the sun. "Thanks, Dwight." She closed her eyes and sniffed the steam from the coffee. "Nice! You got me a different flavor."

"It's a new blend they have over there, *Divine Angel.*"

Kit widened her eyes, pulled the cup out of the holder, and took a sip. "I like the cinnamon and chocolate taste of this one. It's spicy, sweet, and bold, all at the same time."

"Yeah, just like you, Kit." With a wink, he turned around and left the office, closing the door behind him.

She breathed a sigh of relief. Good, he was back to his old ways. Telling him about Steven clearly put him on the defensive, but not enough to keep him from backing down from his old pursuits.

Shaking her head, she smiled and unwrapped the panini, sinking her teeth into a world of goodness. She closed her eyes, savoring the textures of grainy pears, succulent turkey, and creamy brie as they all communed in her mouth in a perfect union of flavors. Nothing better than enjoying a good sandwich on an empty stomach. She swallowed the bite and chased it down with a sip of the new coffee.

Divine Angel. What an unusual name for a coffee blend. The words turned her thoughts to Steven again. He struck her as rather divine himself, with a strong body, soulful eyes, and lips so tempting, she wanted to dive right into him. On the other hand, didn't she think those same thoughts about Dwight, especially since their relationship had taken a step up? Who would taste more divine, him or Steven?

She stopped the new onslaught of lusty thoughts, embarrassed she'd even think of such things about someone she'd just met and, to top it all off, about two men at the same time. Nobody had incited feelings like these in a long time. Dwight had been inching closer to hitting the mark, and then came along Steven, sweeping her away in a flood of confused emotions. As much as the situation flattered her ego, she didn't want Dwight ending up with a broken heart, and she didn't want to blow Steven off as if he didn't matter. He did. Very much.

During her meeting with Steven, the emotional paradox of excitement, coupled with the underlying sense of loss, puzzled her. She finished off her meal, tossing the wrappings in the trash. For the remainder of the afternoon, she concentrated her energies on a new project she'd received the day before. The fight to keep old architecture intact and preserve history had, as of late, become more challenging at every turn. It seemed more people each day, like Edmond Harsh, saw no value in antiquity, choosing the mantra of 'out with the old and in with the new'.

Money seemed the biggest driving force, turning what had been proud, loving owners of their old property into people filled with desperation and greed. Sadly, enough, Alexandra had turned into one of them. If the Society became the new buyer, ousting Harsh out of the picture, what would happen if he didn't get his land?

The door opened with a creak, and the sound of a few light raps revealed Irene slipping her head into the office. "Hey, are you about to wrap it up for the day?"

"I am. Come on in. Let me make a few notes here, and I'll really be finished."

"Geez, you've boarded yourself up in here all day, haven't you? Did you even go out for lunch?"

Kit batted her eyelashes. "Dwight had my back, as usual. If it hadn't been for him, no lunch for me."

"He didn't!" Irene sat down and stretched out her legs. She shook her head as a grin broadened across her lips. "Thank goodness. I'm sorry I opened my big mouth. It just slipped out before I could stop myself."

"Don't worry, he survived. But all that doesn't get rid of the fact I want to see Steven again. I need to set up a time to show him the historical district. He's interested."

"You'll sort it all out, but boy, I don't envy you."

Both ladies turned their eyes in the direction of the shuffling noises in the doorway. Dwight strolled in, eyes steadfast on Kit. "Hey, I thought, if you'd like, I'd walk you home, maybe stop for a drink or something. Happy hour's about to start at *JJ's Grille*."

Her heart caught in her throat. *JJ's Grille* was another favorite hot spot on the square. Before Steven came along, she would never have dreamed of turning down time at *JJ's* with Dwight. "You know what, Dwight, I'd love to, but I think I've had my fill of alcohol for a while, don't you think?" As she grinned, his face colored.

Irene said nothing, but worked steadfast on pushing back the cuticles on her fingernails with the thumbnail of one hand. "I just want to go home and rest for the evening. Can I take a rain check on your offer, though?"

"Sure, dear." He hung his head in disappointment. "I hope you feel better. I'll call tonight and check in on you, see if you need anything."

"That would be great, Dwight. You're so sweet." She smiled up at him, cringing inside as she viewed a trickling in of the old sadness across his face.

Holding up his hand, he shook his head a little. "Sweet enough to let you have a rain check, this time." He grinned and left the office.

Irene and Kit waited until the sounds of his footsteps died against the wooden floors of the hall before either of them spoke.

Irene popped a hand over her mouth. "You're right, he's hanging in there. You must have a magic about you, Kit, juggling two men at the same time."

Kit stuck out her tongue. "You're so evil. You know all this makes me feel so guilty, don't you?"

Irene's expression sobered up. "Dwight's a tough guy. Don't know Steven, so I can't guide you in that arena."

"And I'm very sorry about that. I could use some advice, but we'll see what the future brings."

"I think Dwight handled it extremely well." Irene fiddled with a twisted earring until it landed back in place. "Any thoughts on when you're giving Steven the grand tour?"

"I don't know. I'll have to think about this one. I'm almost scared to go back in there."

"Don't be silly. I'm sure he's dying to see you as much as you are to see him. Why don't you ask him after you leave here?"

"No, I can't do that. I just saw him a couple of days ago."

"So what?" Irene stared at her, impatient. "I wouldn't keep tabs on how long I go before seeing a guy. That's so yesterday. No need for melodrama over this."

Kit grabbed her purse and came around to the front. "Tell you what, give me a few more days, and then I'll make the tour date with him. I promise."

Irene clicked her tongue. "Tick, tick, tick. Clock's a-tickin'."

"Quit worrying about a stupid clock. I promised you I'd take care of it." Both ladies turned out of the office and walked out the main door of the mansion. Kit turned to Irene. "Maybe *we* ought to go for a drink at the pub sometime. Coffee's good, but, as you see, a good stiff one now and then is nice."

"And let's face it, you need a stiff one, really bad." Irene enunciated 'stiff one' and jerked her head toward the mansion and back in the direction of Steven's gallery.

"I get it. Intimacy has its place." Kit grimaced.

"If you ask me, you have choices right now. Choose wisely. Take care, my friend." She patted Kit's back and left for her car. Kit turned right and started the walk back to her apartment. As she passed by the shops on the square, the urge to stop by *Celestial Temptation Gallery* became strong, and she questioned whether she'd be able to hold off seeing Steven much longer. Visions of him, his smile, his touch, had overtaken her thoughts since the day they'd said good-bye. What if he caught her staring at him? *So what? She'd simply wave and walk on. Or she'd step inside for a second, check in to see how's he's doing, and then leave.*

After kicking the idea back and forth, she decided to casually walk by and peep through the window. Maybe she'd catch a glimpse of him and be able to walk on unnoticed. The big deal for her was to not seem pushy. Guys she'd dated before didn't seem to care for over-eager women. Even as interested as Dwight was, she monitored her behavior.

She crossed the street, strolled over to his shop, and peeked through the window. Steven sat behind the counter, sketching in a large spiral book. Should she go in and just say hi, or move on? When he glanced up, her heart nearly stopped. He smiled, waving for her to come inside. Without another thought, she opened the door.

"Hi there, great to see you again!" The light in his eyes burned with excitement, and the sketch he'd been working on landed on the counter as an afterthought. Walking toward her, he gave her a quick hug. "You just get off from work?"

Kit struggled to calm her beating heart and took in a deep breath. "Yeah, finally. I was walking by on my way home and thought I'd check in on you, see how you were getting along."

"Doing great, settling in pretty well." He patted her on the shoulder. "I'm still holding you to that tour you offered. I'd love to hear more about this town."

"You know what, I haven't forgotten. Maybe this weekend we can do something."

"Sounds great. You want to swing by Saturday after I close?"

She blushed as he studied her face, a warm smile on his lips. In his eyes, she sensed a certain desperation, like one piecing together details long lost to memory.

Smiling and nodding, she said, "That'll be good for me too. Well, I don't want to keep you. It's hard to get back in the swing of something when your concentration gets interrupted." Without thinking, her hand smoothed up and down over his back, and she turned to leave.

"Bye, Kit. Feel free to come in any time. Looking forward to Saturday." He walked with her to the door. She felt his gaze burning hot and heavy on her back until she'd reached Our Lady of Eternal Blessings.

CHAPTER 6

Friday afternoon arrived. The room holding the Commission meeting was full. The chairs had been cleverly arranged in a circle, four rows deep. Two podiums fit with microphones broke the pattern of chairs up front. Kit sat in the fourth row so she could see everyone better. In her hand, she clutched the papers holding all the signatures she, Dwight, and Irene had collected. She glanced up at a light tap on her shoulder.

"Hey, honey. How are you?" Alexandra slipped into the vacant seat next to Kit, a guarded look on her face.

"What are you doing here?" Kit hugged her cousin, relieved that she didn't seem to hold any grudges. "I thought you'd be miffed after our conversation. I hadn't heard from you."

"Aw, Kit. We're family. I could never be mad at you." She leaned over and whispered, "You're my favorite cousin. I always admired your passion for life, the excitement you always had when we'd do the simplest things together." She smiled. "A bumblebee buzzing inside a rose fascinated you. You'd laugh, and those sweet blue eyes of yours would just flash with excitement. And when we spent Christmas holidays together, you were the first one to hop out of bed and fly down the hall to the tree. Your feet in those cute footed pajamas padding down the hall always made me laugh." Alexandra's smile faded. "The more I thought about it, the more I agreed that if I was ready to give up this house, then you and your crew deserve a shot at it."

Kit grasped her cousin's hand and squeezed it lightly. "You're right, Alex. The house means the world to me, and the Society loves working out of it. Thank you for seeing it my way."

"Are we ready to start this meeting?" Mr. Hale's voice boomed over the microphone, between the sounds of his fingers rapping over the top. Nods from several of the attendees gave him the affirmative answer he needed.

"All right, then, let's get started."

Kit barely listened to all the business agenda. Her thoughts were only on the mansion. On the first row to her right, she saw Mr. Crispin. His presence, along with Alexandra's, filled her with relief. Not only was he her landlord, but he was the Society's lawyer. At least he'd know all the details of this meeting.

"Hey, Ed's over there." Alexandra tapped Kit on the back, before discreetly pointing to a figure sitting also on the front row, directly across from Mr. Crispin. Kit's heart pounded. There he was, dressed in an impeccable, dark navy-blue suit, onyx-colored hair cut close to his head. The ceiling lights bounced off his watch, illuminating it in an exaggerated gold tone against the fabric of his clothing. From the look of his trim frame and expressionless face, he didn't immediately strike her as the most imposing man she'd ever seen.

"What's he doing here?" Kit murmured in her cousin's ear. "Do you think he suspects anything?"

"Don't know. From what I've heard, there's a lot of people unhappy with the notion of putting condos on the square." Alexandra stared in his direction, shaking her head.

"Has he called you? I mean, you haven't told him we've talked, have you?"

"I haven't talked about this to anyone. I've kept pretty close to home lately." Alexandra tipped her head, studying Edmond Harsh. "I think he wants to protect his interest, and he has other business reasons for attending planning meetings." She shrugged at Kit.

One by one, different people discussed agenda items, leaving Kit down to the last hour. She glanced at the clock, stomach tightening as the moment of putting a dent in Harsh's plans drew near. Alexandra would get her money no matter what. Whether or not Kit would get her house remained the big question.

Mr. Hale spoke into the microphone. "Anyone else need to bring up an issue before we end this session in the next hour?" Alexandra elbowed Kit in the ribs.

Kit raised her hand.

"Come on up here, Miss Millinger." Mr. Hale placed a thick hand on her shoulder when she approached, guiding her in front of the microphone.

"Thank you, Mr. Hale." Kit straightened up, looking out across the room. The sound of the door opening drew her attention away from the microphone. Dwight and Irene slipped in, speeding to two empty chairs on the back row. Irene threw up a few fingers in a quick wave of acknowledgment while Dwight smiled and nodded, encouraging Kit to continue. She blinked and nodded back, relieved at the support. They must have finished their meetings early and driven at breakneck speed to get here.

Gathering her thoughts, Kit spoke in the clearest, steadiest voice a body could muster, praying she wouldn't pass out from an attack of nerves. "On behalf of the Windham Springs Historical Society, I would like to bring up an issue of great urgency to those of us who conduct business in the Stothwell Mansion, located at 17 East Main Street at the end of the square in the historical district. It is our understanding that a sale agreement has been made between Alexandra Stothwell and Edmond Harsh.

It is Mr. Harsh's intent to destroy the property and build condominiums on the site. The Society is requesting a stay of demolition to allow an alternate buyer the opportunity to purchase the property with the intent on keeping said property intact." Kit didn't fail to see Mr. Harsh jerk himself upright in his seat as she made her announcement. She turned her head to Mr. Crispin, who winked at her and offered a light smile of reassurance. In the back row, Alexandra blinked and nodded, silently urging Kit on.

"I see," said Mr. Hale. "And why should we grant you a stay, Miss Millinger?"

Catching her breath, Kit gazed out at the audience again, glimpsing Mr. Harsh's face, brows furrowed in dismay. He craned his neck, searching the room until he apparently spied Alexandra, who sat with averted eyes, staring across the room at nothing in particular.

"First of all, I have family ties to that house, which I know is not a reason it shouldn't be sold, but the Society conducts business out of the mansion. People know us, the work we do, and using that house as our headquarters makes it easier for people to reach us. It's a beautiful house that has stood in the square since the town came into existence, and it would be unthinkable to destroy it."

"I object," Edmond Harsh cried out as he rose from his seat.

Mr. Hale's eyes turned upward for a brief moment as Harsh strode to the vacant microphone. "We don't need a stay of demolition, and we don't need a buyer who wants to keep that house around. What we need in this town is progressive thinking and a way to keep revenue flowing into our coffers."

The room grew quiet. In the back row, Alexandra managed to find the front of the room again, and fixed her eyes on the podiums. Dwight and Irene sat at attention, wide-eyed with grim lips.

Mr. Harsh continued. "Folks, if we saved every home for every sentimental history buff who walked the streets, we'd never survive. We'd stay rooted back in the 1800's, stuck back in horse and buggy days with no change or progress. Nobody would care about visiting this place. We need people here who can spend money, pay taxes. We have to move forward. Keeping that mansion doesn't do anything for the community." He turned a disapproving eye in Kit's direction. "Miss Millinger, I hate to be the party for bad news, but unfortunately, the historical society offers nothing to this community, really." A series of murmurs spread around the room as if someone has tossed a gas-soaked rag on a round trail of gasoline. From Kit's view, Alexandra's eyes widened, lips tightening in irritation. Mr. Crispin shook his head, eyes turned toward his lap, while Irene sat on the edge of her seat, fists clenched, sliding her gaze from Dwight to Harsh.

Harsh's words struck a sour chord with Kit. Inside, indignation swelled as she quickly processed the insensitivity. Squaring up her shoulders, she spoke into the microphone, braving an occasional glance in her opponent's direction.

"I beg to differ, Mr. Harsh. First of all, your words are truly offensive. Dismissing the work of the Society is an outrage not only to me, but for many of you who hear these ill words, especially to my comrades who are also here." She summoned up every nerve in her body and began her speech. "First of all, we do a great deal of good for the community. We teach the value of preserving history, and how we can learn from it. Much of the history of this town lives on in the stories we tell during tours. Families share those stories with others, encouraging new people to come visit so they can hear for themselves. We teach families how to care for their treasured items handed down for generations.

During Halloween, we tell ghost stories on the steps and offer candy to the kids. The whole square participates based on what we do. At Christmas, we have our lighting of the tree and give out gifts to more unfortunate children. In the spring, we have orchestras playing beautiful music on the lawn. In our gardens, we have authors from all over who come and read from their books."

All eyes were on Kit. She continued. "We continually find ways to create community events so the people have activities they can enjoy and look forward to. How on Earth is that not a value? When people come to our events, they spend money when they're on the square. Restaurants get business and the antique shops sell more items. I could go on."

"My plan would bring more people with more money. Restaurants would be packed until the wee hours of the morning. Shops would continually have fresh turns of merchandise on their shelves. How is that bad? And just who else is crazy enough to disagree with me?" Harsh's voice rang out over the microphone. His cheeks had turned a rich pink.

"At least one hundred fifty people and counting, Mr. Harsh. There are people in the community who haven't had a chance to sign our petition, but rest assured, we will collect those signatures and more." Kit waved her papers at him, gloating to herself as she witnessed his eyes nearly bulging out of his head.

"Um, Miss Millinger, do you mind if I have those?" Mr. Hale offered a polite smile as she handed over the sheets, each one bearing rows of precious signatures, the voice of the people. "Good move on your part. There's power in numbers. And when you have the others, Miss Millinger, please send them to me."

"Alexandra, do you actually agree with this insanity?" Harsh glared in Alexandra's direction. "I thought we had a deal."

"Miss Stothwell, would you mind coming to the front, please?" Mr. Hale motioned her forward. Sighing with resignation, Alexandra pulled herself out of the seat and made her way next to Kit.

"Look, I know this comes as a surprise, from both sides." Alexandra spoke easily into the microphone. "Ed, I had every intention of selling the land to you, and maybe now, looking back on everything, maybe I shouldn't have acted so fast."

Harsh shook his head, faking a light chuckle. "Act fast? I'd say I've never seen anyone move as slow as you did. I literally had to chase you down...." He stopped, eyes scanning the room as if he'd been caught at something tasteless. He stretched his neck from side to side, trying to maintain what was left of his composure.

"I'll expand on your comment, Ed. For the record, this man kept at me like a hunter during deer season, and I'll leave it at that."

Mr. Hale's gaze bounced between Alexandra and Harsh. "I see. Miss Stothwell, do you feel like you've made a decision under duress? Is there a signed contract?"

Alexandra hung her head. "There is."

Harsh nodded.

"But Mr. Hale, and to the good people in this room – to the people of Windham Springs – I've reached a point in my life where I'm ready to move on. I agree wholeheartedly with the good work the Historical Society does. My mother believed in them and supported them long before I did. I think they offer a great service to this town. I hope everyone knows, including Mr. Harsh, that selling the land isn't a problem for me, nor waiting for another buyer who intends to preserve my home. After all, it was mine all my life, and a part of me would always be sad to see it destroyed and the memories along with it."

Behind the passion of Alexandra's words, Kit detected a certain weariness in her cousin's voice. For the first time, she wished she'd taken another job somewhere else, with people who were total strangers. Her father had always warned her about doing business with family. Now she knew why.

Kit broke in with her final words while Alexandra shrank back from the microphone. "And for this gracious consideration, we at the Society thank Miss Stothwell wholeheartedly. For those of you who respectfully disagree with Mr. Harsh and don't wish to experience the negative living conditions that come with overcrowding, please feel free to add your name to my petition or tell the Committee how you really feel about preserving Windham Spring's history. Thank you, Mr. Hale, and all of you for hearing our request."

Mr. Hale stepped up to the microphone. "Thank you, Miss Millinger and Mr. Harsh. The Committee will consider both sides. When we reach our decision, all three parties will be notified." Kit stepped away from the podium, blowing out a silent breath. Out of the corner of her eye she spied Dwight staring at her, a glow of admiration on his face. The memory of high school graduation struck her to the core, assaulting the present moment. Somehow the presence of Dwight wasn't enough. She wished Steven sat in his place, smiling, loving, encouraging. High school graduation had been a special moment on her timeline, one she would have loved to have enjoyed with Austin. This forging forward, standing up for something she believed in, scored another big moment on the timeline, a courageous first step during her first job after graduate school. Why she wanted to share this moment with a total stranger perplexed her. It was as if she were missing a certain acknowledgment now, just as she had then. The sad part was, Steven's signature never made it onto her petition.

"Whew, I'm glad that's over." Alexandra patted Kit on the back. "I hope a decision is made soon. No need to have this turn ugly and drag on out."

"Kit, you were amazing." Dwight came up, hugging her close.

"You wowed the crowd, girl. Couldn't have said it better myself." Irene beamed. "Alex, thanks so much for going along with this. I know this is such a bump in the road for your plans."

"Don't even worry about it, Irene. You folks deserve a shot at the house, especially my cuz here." Alexandra dropped a quick maternal kiss on Kit's cheek.

"It means a lot, Alex, but at this point, the rest of this is up to the Committee." Kit returned her cousin's hug.

All four gazed at the sight of a man brushing past, face drawn up in solid irritation, eyes smoldering. "I wouldn't look so smug. This battle's not over." Harsh's voice tumbled out in iron, gritty tones. One last look, and he disappeared though the crowd and slipped out the door.

***

The kitchen smelled of Italian spices. On a sleek, tile counter, Dwight worked a corkscrew into a bottle of Cabernet while Kit tapped a wooden spoon clean against a steel pot full of chicken simmering in a seasoned mixture of tomato sauce and cream. Another pot held pasta cooking in boiling water. One last douse of cooking oil, and she turned off the stove eye.

"Here's a colander." Dwight slipped up behind Kit, nuzzling against her neck. He smelled of spiced vanilla and opoponax, probably one of his exotic French colognes he enjoyed wearing. The scent of him charged her with a brief streak of lust. Tonight, they celebrated her proposal to the Committee. Any more caresses or adoring looks, and she'd be all over him. The troublesome issue tonight: thoughts of Steven paraded across her mind, insistent. Just the memory of him set her on fire.

"Why don't you get the dishes ready, and I'll mix everything together and bring it in to the dining room." Kit turned and smiled.

"As you wish." Dwight backed away, busying himself pulling out dishes and silverware. "You're a good cook, Kit. I should be doing this for you after your performance this afternoon."

"I was nervous. Did you see how Harsh looked?"

"Hopefully we'll get an answer soon, and this whole thing can be laid to rest. Then we'll need to come up with a plan on how to raise money."

Kit followed Dwight into the dining room, placing the food on the table between them. She liked his Frank Lloyd Wright house, with the generous number of large paned windows and airy rooms. The living room held luxurious, rich leather seating, including a sofa wide enough for both of them to cuddle together. She had briefly seen the upstairs, which held more eye-catching designer pieces. What did Steven's bedroom look like?

"You do a mean Italian meal, Kit. Is that a favorite of yours?"

She thought a minute. "Yeah, I guess it is. I tend to gravitate to anything Italian." True enough. She liked the history, the culture, the architecture, and especially the food. What foods did Steven liked to eat? His name sounded Italian. Did he like Italian food too? Did he even know how to cook? What would it be like to kiss him after he'd taken a sip of wine, and to taste the tartness on her own tongue as she stroked over his?

"Hey, are you listening to anything I'm saying?" Dwight glanced over at her with impatience. "You are miles away. Are you thinking about beating out Harsh?"

"Um, yes. That's it. I'm thinking about that." Kit reached for her wine and took a hefty draw from the glass. Dwight wrinkled his brow, studying her with too much intensity for comfort. She scolded herself. Daydreaming about Steven needed to happen when Dwight wasn't around.

No such luck. No matter how hard she fought, her thoughts turned back to their last meeting. Fortunately, Steven had suggested getting together this weekend, and that was tomorrow. Good, problem solved! But she knew Dwight would ask about doing something for the weekend too. Problem not solved.

After the meal, she and Dwight sat on the sofa. A soft jazzy tune filled the air. Nothing like the best in a Bose audio system to pump out a great sound.

"You must be tired. I see it in your eyes, and you didn't talk much at dinner." Dwight ran his fingers through her hair. "The steam in you dwindled down." He grinned.

"I'm sorry. It's like my body charges with a ton of energy before I have to do something really big, and when it's all over, I just feel exhausted." She looked at him and smiled.

"So, what do you want to do this weekend?"

Kit's heart skipped a beat. Ugh, the dreaded question, but what could she expect? Dwight had entered her life before Steven. Why this sudden obsession when she already had a nice relationship going? "I don't know." Could she finish the tour with Steven and make it back in time for a night out with Dwight? She stifled a small laugh. Juggling two men wasn't easy. How did other people pull this stunt off? "You know, Dwight, I think I may need this weekend off to get some things done. If I finish early, can I call you?"

"Like what things?" He frowned and set his wine glass down on the coffee table. "You know, I've never seen you this distracted. Are you okay?"

"I'm fine," she said. "Let me see what I can do. If not this weekend, how about something during the week to break things up a little?"

"Fine." Dwight leaned back against the sofa, pulling Kit close. He moved in for a passionate kiss, the artful dancing of his tongue over hers sending her into another dimension. When they finished, she rested her head on his shoulder. And no sooner than she'd recovered, the thoughts came again. She considered in more detail how she wanted to entertain Steven. How much of the town did she want to show him? Just the historical area only? Or maybe she might expand the date to show him the non-historical side, where he could do more extensive shopping when the need arose.

The more she thought about the situation, the more the idea of keeping it simple seemed better. The historical district didn't include only the square, but streets lined with gorgeous old homes sitting on more expansive lawns than one usually found in the newer neighborhoods. She often liked to take walks in the residential areas herself, finding them peaceful and containing an air of romance. Some of the homes had their own history, even a ghost or two. Mr. D'Astolo might enjoy hearing some fun ghost stories.

"Hey, Dwight? I think it's time for me to head on home." Kit rubbed her hand over the top of his thigh. For a moment, she closed her eyes and imagined Steven holding her in his arms, kissing away every fear, every doubt, and insecurity that threatened to sneak up from behind and try to drag her down. In his embrace, she imagined the world more perfect, safe. She got up from the sofa, Dwight following.

"Before I go, let me help you clean everything up." Kit moved to the dining room, clearing the table as Dwight loaded the dishwasher. The remainder of the evening passed with light conversation.

Driving down the road, Kit stared off into the darkness, taking the turns cautiously as she headed back to her apartment. While driving, she entertained herself with thoughts of Steven's body pressed tightly to hers, the steady beating of his heart drumming against her ear. The same drumming had filled her ear when she rested against Dwight earlier this evening. His kiss still lingered on her lips, burning as hot as the necklace had burned her that eerie night.

Fumbling inside her purse, she pulled out some lip gloss and ran the tip over her mouth, hoping to cover the pangs of guilt more than anything. Turning her thoughts back to Steven, she remembered the look in his eyes each time they'd conversed. He'd shown interest, his eyes had filled with a certain brilliance and animation all men expressed when a girl interested them. Whether she wanted to, she couldn't shake the feeling that the meeting with Steven held something more. His touch reminded her of someone trying to connect, holding on to the present lest it leave completely and vanish forever. As if the lingering contact might spark a remembrance of something, a moment lost in time.

At least she'd move forward tomorrow, showing him the historical district. What a way to kick off the weekend. She picked up her cell phone and selected Irene's phone number from her contacts list. Irene was safe, a listening ear, and a sounding board. Kit needed that right now more than ever.

* * *

Kit jerked awake, glancing at the clock on the nightstand. She sprang out of bed and threw on a robe. Morning had already slipped by. Remembering the evening plans with Steven sent flutters of excitement rippling all through her. She still hadn't finalized the details of this tour, or even determined what he may want to see.

Since he was an artist, would he want to see homes with a certain architectural style? Or would he want to hear the history and some of the legendary stories?

She made some coffee and ate a quick bite. When she finished, she'd decided the only way to give him the tour he wanted was to ask him. Kit showered and dressed. By twelve twenty-five, she headed out the door and down the steps to the outside world. Her heart pounded faster with each step. The sight of his shop filled her with an onslaught of nerves, and she slowed down a little to catch her breath. She had already rehearsed some of the routes they could take, and the homes she'd tell him about. What if she drew a blank and forgot the stories to go along with the homes? Nothing like telling someone 'Oh, here's a pretty house, and it's really old too.' Would he find her ghost tales silly, or would he enjoy them? Would she mix up the design styles of the houses and come across as foolish? Enough, no more second-guessing herself! The hands on her watch pointed to twelve thirty on the nose.

Standing in front of the shop, she took a deep breath, opened the door, and stepped into an empty room. Perhaps he was in the back washing out brushes. Nerves getting the best of her the last time they met, she'd scarcely noticed how nicely he'd fixed up the place. The walls glowed with the new paint, and rows of track lighting illuminated the canvases. Men liked it when women complimented them on their work. Had his feelings been hurt because she failed to acknowledge his transforming the shop into a showplace? Soft music played in the background. She walked over to one of the paintings, which depicted a nude female with honey-golden hair, soulful eyes, and pouty lips, reclining back on a brocade divan. For a moment, the figure startled her. If she stared long enough, she almost thought the lady resembled her. Kit shook her head, blinked a few times, and stared at the picture again, thinking this must be a simple coincidence. She whirled around at the light touch on her shoulder.

"Hi again!" Steven stood behind her with a big, sunny smile on his face.

When she opened her mouth to speak, no words came out. Her face heated up with embarrassment.

"Sorry about that. I didn't mean to startle you." His hand moved to the small of her back.

"I didn't hear you come in." Kit bent her knees a little and inhaled deeply several times, trying with desperation to calm down. His handsome features nearly bowled her over. This time he wore jeans and a plaid shirt with the first two buttons undone. His face glowed as he smiled, and the touch of his hand set her on fire. Yes, *Divine Angel* suited him to a tee.

"I was in the back." He pulled her closer. "Nice seeing you again." His face clouded briefly. "You haven't come to cancel on me have you?"

"Oh, I could never do that." She blushed. "I haven't been around because I figured you needed a little time alone to get everything ready." Her eyes scanned the room. "It all looks so nice in here now. The paintings are really interesting."

"I see you've been getting acquainted with this piece." He angled his head toward the nude.

Kit stepped back, giving him a little smile. "I like it. It's quite nice." Another attack of nerves made her tongue-tied, and words slipped her mind. She swallowed and started again. "Did you use a live model for this particular piece?"

This time, his cheeks turned a bright pink. "Yes." He turned and stared directly into Kit's eyes. "Come to think of it, the more I see this painting, the more I'm convinced she shares some of your features. Beautiful hair, angelic eyes, and amazing body, not to mention a cute button nose and sweet smile."

Kit's cheeks grew warm, and she grinned. Inside her stomach the fluttery feeling came again. "Thank you. She's a great model. I don't think I could ever do that."

He shook his head. "No, not true at all." His eyes brightened up, enhancing the blueness. "I think a lot of people would make great models for art, though they may not think so themselves."

They stood together, studying the painting for a few moments, with Steven interjecting how he'd made decisions in posing, as well as in color choices. He took his eyes off the artwork, turning back to face her.

She stared at his handsome face, drinking in with her eyes every line and curve. "I came back here today so you could tell me what you wanted in a tour, such as more architecture or more history and stories about the people who lived in the homes."

"How about I let you do this your way? You tell me what *you* think are the most exciting stories, and show me the best of the homes. After that, maybe we could grab a bite at the coffee shop. My treat to you for being such a wonderful, personable guide."

"You don't have to do that." She reached out to touch him. An intense warmth filled her hand, and moved its way up her arm. There it was again, the same type of energy she'd experienced from him the first time, with the same influx of emotions.

"I insist." He brushed a small wisp of hair away from her shoulder. "I can't wait until tonight. A change of pace will do me some good."

"Same here." Her stomach quieted a little, but the sensation of his touch still burned. "I'll come back at five, then."

"Perfect." He followed her to the door.

With a wave, she left and walked back home. Entering her apartment, she breathed a sigh of relief. In a few hours, she'd be enjoying Steven's company. Still puzzling her was the way she trembled inside when standing near him. Swirling in a sea of raw emotions confused her. Where did all this come from, and why? After making a hot mug of tea, she settled on the sofa, staring out the window. The October air already held a chill, and the leaves blazed in wonderful colors of reds and yellows. This was her favorite time of year, crisp, clear, fresh, bewitching. And what a way to enjoy this favorite time, in the company of an equally bewitching gentleman, who held her under a magical spell. The way his eyes bore straight through her at times filled her with vulnerability. Part of her found it exciting; part of her wanted to hide. Thinking back, Austin had often gazed at her with dreamy eyes, when they sat across the table from each other in a restaurant, or during study hall when both of them needed a quick break from math equations. Dwight of late had given her the same stare, intense, penetrating, knowing.

Resting back on a couple of throw pillows, she drifted into the deepest corners of her mind, thinking about the more important relationships in her life. She started at the beginning, remembering how she and Austin had enjoyed Saturday nights watching TV, seated on the floor as she cradled his head in her lap. Holding him the first time had sent her into gales of excitement, the way Steven thrilled her now. Moments with Dwight had moved down the same path.

Reflecting back on it with a mature mind, teen love wasn't refined but it certainly was real at the time, with all the anticipation, expectations, and heartache that come along for the ride. As teens, one didn't think about love's elusive qualities, how easily it slipped through the fingers. No one thought about the future in great detail, and how situations would play out.

A whole world, a whole lifetime waited, and one decision changed life's course. As an adult, she viewed love differently. Maturity had a way of sharpening the lens through which one viewed their life, and each romantic encounter held possibilities of permanence if finding a mate meant anything. Decisions stemmed from astute observation and honing in on what one decided they wanted from life.

She sipped some tea, the heat warming her throat. One thing she had learned for certain – a broken heart still hurt regardless of age. If she didn't proceed with caution, the nasty broken heart business stood a real chance of rearing its ugly head. But cracked emotions often became water under the bridge, and most of the time the ugliness couldn't be changed. If so, things were never quite the same as before, the rawness of transgressions cutting a gash too deep to ever go totally away.

She glanced at the clock on the mantel. Only a few hours remained before she'd enjoy the privilege of basking in Steven's presence and his undivided attention, even sharing a meal with him in her favorite place! The sight of the fireplace led to daydreams of sitting in front of hot flames, with him cuddled up in her arms. Maybe one day soon, if everything worked out, she'd find herself holding *his* head in her lap. Through all the warmth in the apartment, she experienced a sudden chill, shivering as an icy sensation seeped toward her spine. Time for a hot bath! She tipped her cup, catching the last drops of tea onto her tongue before pulling herself up from the sofa. Off to the bathroom to spend the remainder of time soaking in a nice, hot tub and getting dressed for the evening.

CHAPTER 7

"Are you ready to go?" Kit stepped through the door of *Celestial Temptation Gallery*, refreshed from her long soak, dressed for a chilly evening walk.

"I am. Been thinking about it all day long, actually." Steven smiled as he switched off all but a couple of lights. The glow from the street lights shone through the windows. Kit craned her neck in the direction of the doorway leading to the back of the shop. The hallway remained illumined by a small lamp he'd left on. She tried to guess what his living space looked like, how he'd arranged all his furnishings to create a home in the back of a shop. Nothing in the least like Dwight's place, she was sure.

"Maybe I'll show you my place sometime." He landed his hand on the small of her back and guided her to the door.

"I'm sorry. I wasn't trying to be nosy or anything." Kit blushed at being caught in the act of snooping.

Steven ushered her outside the shop and locked the door. "That's okay. Believe it or not, I've fixed up quite a cozy spot back there. Like I've said before, I have just the basics, nothing fancy." He faced Kit. "I bet your place is nice."

"It's simple. Like you said, just the basics, but I like it a lot." She smiled up at him. How handsome he looked tonight, wearing a sweatshirt bearing the Dallas Cowboys logo. On his lean hips, form-fitting jeans covered a pair of muscular legs. Her heart caught in her throat and she looked away for a moment, collecting her thoughts. Thank goodness, he didn't read minds, which might have gotten her in big trouble right now.

"Where do we start?" Steven turned his head from one side to the other. "Did you have a favorite spot or special place you like more than others?" His eyes focused back on hers. "Any historical old homes with a good story behind them?"

"You mean, like a ghost story?" Kit wiped a wisp of hair out of her eyes.

Grinning, he shrugged. "Sure, why not? A ghost story's good."

"I guess you've been around the square by now, haven't you?"

"Yeah, I've made a quick run. I've even seen where you live – over Mr. Crispin's law office, right?"

"Okay then, why don't we just start with the neighborhood behind the square? There's some gorgeous old homes, and even some with a good spooky story or two. This should take about an hour and a half."

"Great, let's go, then. Lead the way."

Kit stood for a moment, thinking which direction to take. "Let's go this way." She turned left from the shop, leading the way to the first street. "We'll start here. I love this neighborhood, and I've got a couple of special homes in mind."

The pair turned left, walking into a residential area where stately oak trees lined the street and magnificent old homes had rested for years, still holding up strong under all kinds of weather. House lights beamed from the front porches, giving the street a friendlier appeal. Some homeowners sitting closer to the street had left their windows open. As they passed the houses, Kit and Steven caught glimpses of a cozy dens filled with people reading or watching television. Some dining rooms showcased antique china cabinets filled with porcelain.

Other rooms suggested a guest room, with a view of four-poster beds and matching dressers and chests of drawers. Neat rows of street lamps lit their way. The sky had turned to the soft gray of evening, still infused with enough light to see before giving way to the charcoal black of night. Stars had already come out, twinkling above. A light breeze kicked up clumps of fallen leaves, creating a miniature cyclone around their feet as they walked. Kit took a deep breath, inhaling the woody, nutty scent, the heady perfume of a perfect autumn night.

"Wow, you're right, it's beautiful back here." Steven sniffed in the air. "I like the smell. Seems like some folks are burning fires already." He turned to Kit. "Do you have a fireplace in your apartment?"

"I do, and this afternoon I was just thinking about using it too. I don't guess you have one hidden away in your shop, do you? I've never noticed a chimney."

"No, no fireplace for me. Just regular heating and air, or I could plug in a tiny heater, but that's not the same, is it?" A warm smile covered his face.

"You can't beat real flames." She laughed. "I remember one time my father started a fire in our fireplace, and, for some reason, he forgot which way to move the lever to open the flue. Next thing we knew, the whole house filled with smoke. We opened all the doors and windows, and nearly froze trying to air the place out."

Steven threw back his head and laughed. "Did you ever get rid of the smell? That can be pretty strong, you know, and last for days."

"Dad finally had to go to a hardware store and pick up a can of deodorizer. We had the soot marks on the front part of the mantel until mom washed them off with some Pine-Sol."

They continued walking down the street until they arrived in front of a large old home sitting farther back on the lawn, a little more isolated than the other homes. The house displayed the best in Italianate architecture, and was one of the oldest homes in Windham Springs.

Steven stopped close to Kit, brushing lightly against her. The heat from his body reduced the chill of the night air, and she found herself moving in close to get warmer. In an instant, he slipped an arm around her waist.

For a second, her grounding in reality briefly disappeared, leaving her with a sense of having disconnected from herself, only to return to the present space-time once again. Nothing had prepared her for his full touch. If putting an arm around her caused this much of a physical and mental disturbance, she'd surely die if he held her in his arms.

She gulped in a dose of cold air. "Sorry. The wind makes the air colder than I'd expected. Should have known better and brought a jacket."

He smiled. "That's okay. So tell me about this house."

"Well, let's see." Kit glanced up at the large home, scrambling to gather her wits after the mental kerfuffle. Quickly she recalled the story and all the details.

"This house is the Stowenworth Mansion, one of the first homes in Windham Springs. The first owner, Ezra Stowenworth, cheated on his wife Clara with one of the servant girls, Aggie. Apparently one afternoon, she happened to catch Ezra and Aggie kissing behind the smokehouse. Filled with anger, Clara had it out for Aggie. She spent days plotting out her revenge, outlining just the right day, right time, and all the particulars to get rid of her servant. A few days later, Clara took her revenge, poisoning Aggie with some tainted soup when they were cooking in the kitchen together one day."

"The mistress of the house actually cooked meals too?" Steven raised his eyebrows. "I wouldn't have thought she'd do that. Wouldn't it be beneath her station?"

"I think there were many ladies of the house who took their management duties seriously, and made sure the help did things the way they wanted them done." She smiled at Steven. "Many people suspect, like I do, that Clara slipped back into the kitchen while Aggie was out doing something else for a moment, and poisoned the soup. A good cook should always taste what they prepare, so there you go. Aggie did her job, and boom, she died!"

"Probably shouldn't have been cheating with her mistress's husband." He held his gaze on Kit. "Cheating doesn't usually pay off."

Kit squirmed, clearing her throat. "Unfortunately, I think there was a lot of that sort of thing going on back then. More available females gave the masters too many choices. But yes, cheating doesn't pay off."

Steven turned toward the house. "So, what happened to Clara? Did anyone ever find out what she did?"

"She told the police and everyone else that she came into the kitchen and found Aggie slumped over on the table, ill, at which point she sent her to her quarters to rest. Later that night, the servant girl died. Everyone thought she'd come down with something, or at least ate some spoiled food. No one suspected the wife of committing actual murder. And of course, they couldn't do forensic testing like we do now. She apparently did a great job of acting all casual, like she didn't know about her wayward husband. The stunning revelation came when her last will and testament was read after her death. She actually confessed to the crime!"

Steven nodded in sympathy, slipping his arm away from Kit. "Ah, as they say, confession's good for the soul. There's a release in it somehow. So where does the ghost come in? You still haven't told me that part."

Kit continued, "If you ever go inside for one of the regular tours, you might see Aggie's ghost walking the halls of the house. Sometimes strange noises can be heard from the kitchen during late evening tours, like lids clanging against pots. Others have seen apparitions in the hallways or in rooms later in the afternoon."

They started down the sidewalk again. His hand found hers, the warmth unleashing a new kind of magic as it calmed her nerves. With each step, her comfort level increased. She always enjoyed walks like this, taking her mind off troubles by surrounding herself with old homes and historic neighborhoods. The sight of it all soothed her soul. The homes exuded beauty in the daytime, flaunting all their rich color and architectural decor in the light of day.

But at night, they assumed a different air. Wrapping themselves in the wings of darkness, they stood watchful, pensive and brooding, and in some instances, almost sinister. Houses sitting farther from the curb, shadowed by faithful trees, held secrets. Kit knew it. They held every impression of joy, sorrow, act of violence, or revenge from the day the last nail found its resting place.

"Let's go this way." She stopped and pulled Steven along until they reached the other side of the street. They landed on another sidewalk, following it down another street, deeper into the neighborhood. "There's another home I want to show you."

In silence, they made their way to the end of the street. This house boasted the opulent Rococo Revival style and, like its friend on the other street, sat back on a wide, neatly groomed lawn.

Steven stood with open mouth, staring at the house in front of them. "Gosh, these homes just get better and better." He faced Kit straight on, beaming. "What's the story for this one?"

She closed her eyes, briefly savoring his hot breath against her ear. The whisper of his voice lulled her to the precipice of another world. Using every ounce of will, she forced her eyes open and began the story.

"This house also has an interesting bit of history." Words slipped from her lips, thick and halting, like someone had shoved a large wad of cotton inside her mouth. With iron determination, she continued speaking. "This home is the Aldingham Mansion, built by Maddox Aldingham when he came here in the mid-eighteen hundreds. His wife Corrine lived here with him. They had two daughters, Sarah and Lula, and two sons, Josiah and Rutherford. About two years after the house was built, Corrine gave birth to their third daughter, Irvinia. One day, when Irvinia was only five years old, she was playing outside with her ball."

Steven shook his head. "Oh, I think I see where this story's going, but go on."

"Yes, as you would guess, the ball rolled into the middle of the street, into the path of a rolling buggy. Irvinia, not paying attention, ran to get it, and the buggy rolled right over her. Killed her instantly. It simply couldn't stop in time."

"I guess the laws of physics just weren't in her favor, were they?"

"No, they weren't. And on some nights, in the wee hours, some people have heard a horse and buggy running through the streets, though the road is completely empty of any traffic. Others have said they've seen a face of a woman in the upstairs window that was Irvinia's bedroom. Many think it's Corrine searching for her daughter."

"Does anyone ever run across a child's ball by any chance?"

Kit giggled. "You know, I've never heard anyone mention finding a ball, but that would be really creepy."

For the next forty minutes, under the light of a glowing full moon, Kit showed Steven three more houses on the official Windham Springs Historical Tour, sharing all the best lore the town had to offer. When they finished, he said, "Kit, I've enjoyed this lively walk, but I'm starving. How 'bout we head on back to that coffee shop, and I'll buy us a bite to eat?"

"I'm game. Let's go."

* * *

A Cup Above the Roast hummed with its usual crowd of patrons. Thankful for the warmth, Kit found a table tucked away in the far back corner of the shop. She enjoyed another turkey brie panini sandwich with her usual *Red Velvet Fantasy* cake, while Steven bit into a roast beef and Swiss combination on rye bread. He'd bypassed dessert but, like his companion, sipped on the new coffee flavor, *Divine Angel*.

"You love coming here?" He stretched out his legs, brushing against the lower part of Kit's, never once moving his away.

"It's my favorite place in the whole wide world." She laughed. "I know that sounds silly, but it really doesn't take too much to please me. I'm rather simple, if you want to know the truth."

"Really?" He lifted his cup to his lips.

"Oh, yeah. What about you? What are your tastes, what do you like?"

He shrugged. "I'm pretty much like you. I'm not all about fancy trappings. Of course, you can guess I love art, holding a brush in my hands, laying down layers of paint on a piece of canvas. But I also like the feel of a pencil or pen in my hand while I sketch something that's caught my eye."

"I'm not that creative myself, though I wish I were." Kit swallowed a bite of sandwich. "I notice from your sweatshirt you seem to like sports."

"I love sports. In high school, I played football. I totally got a charge out of being on the field. The adrenaline rush I got on game nights made me feel ultra-alive. I can't describe it."

Kit sat, taking in every word. "You played football, and you like art?"

Steven stared back, his lips turned up into a sly grin. "Sounds like a weird combo, a jock and an artist? Someone who's supposed to be rough and tough, but yet has a gentle, pensive side?" He bit into his sandwich again.

"Oh, I don't think it's such an unusual combo. I actually knew someone like that long ago." She took a sip of *Divine Angel*, reminding herself that many people she knew possessed all kinds of talents. Take Dwight, for example. Just by looking at him, one didn't expect his skills in music. In an instant, a pang of guilt shot through her. No, she would not be meeting with Dwight tonight. A whirl of emotions injected visions of him alone at home, maybe sipping some wine and either reading or listening to music. Maybe he had fixed himself a sandwich for dinner. The most heart-wrenching part, the grim look she imagined on his face if he knew where she was right now. She couldn't think of it anymore and cast her gaze to the ceiling a second to regroup.

Steven said nothing, but kept his eyes on her.

She dipped the fork in her cake and tasted a bite before speaking again. "Did you enjoy our walk tonight?"

"I loved it. Thanks for showing me around the neighborhood. I may go back out one day and sketch those old homes we visited. The architecture is stunning."

Resting an elbow on the table, she studied him for a few moments. "Do you believe in ghosts?"

He shot her a startled look. "Why do you ask?"

"Well, you mentioned going out, and then you asked about homes with a good ghost story. I just thought maybe you liked that sort of stuff. Irene, a lady I work with, gets off on all that. I tease her all the time about it."

After a swallow of coffee, he answered. "I think there are things that go on beyond our immediate awareness of them, if that's what you're asking."

"Hmm, I guess so." She smiled at him. "I was just wondering, that's all."

"No, it's okay, Kit. You can ask me anything, anytime you want." Steven reached out and gave her hand a gentle squeeze. "I like it when you talk to me."

She leaned toward him. "Which story did you like the best?"

He narrowed his eyes in thought. "I think stories of infidelity hit me the hardest, so the first story, definitely."

"Infidelity? As opposed to death and loss?" She pushed another bite of cake into her mouth.

Steven kept his eyes steady. "Infidelity can lead to cruelty, especially from the one who feels wronged or slighted." He finished off the last bite of his sandwich and leaned forward, placing a hand over hers. "You know what, though? I'm glad we're here together, right here, right now."

"Me too!" Kit smiled.

For another forty-five minutes, they sat chatting and drinking another round of coffee. Steven glanced at his watch.

"It's getting late. C'mon. I'll walk you home." He scooted his chair back and stood up, picking up his empty dishes and cup. Kit did likewise, and within moments, they'd exited the coffee shop and made their way back to her apartment. When they reached the outside front door to the building, she turned to say goodbye.

"Thanks for dinner and going walking with me. I really enjoyed getting out tonight."

"You were a great tour guide, and I liked the stories, though they were tragic." He leaned against the doorframe, his body hemming her in against the door. "But I guess that's what makes them intriguing in their own twisted way."

An unexplained shyness crept over her again. He was so close to her, warm breath caressing her ear. She managed a grin. "Yes, tragedy has its own appeal."

Steven's breathing picked up a faster pace, and his eyes glistened with urgency. "Kit, do you mind me being forward and doing one last thing before I go?"

A rush of excitement quickened her pulse. He didn't need to ask permission or speak. All he needed to do was act. She didn't flinch when he turned up her face to his with a gentle lift of his finger, and settled his lips onto hers with the most intense kiss. Her mouth opened, receiving his insistent tongue, soft and moist, gracing her with tender flicks and caresses. Time stood still while she briefly drowned in his embrace. The inside of her body mimicked a blazing fire. What she wouldn't give to let this moment with him last forever. When the reality of it hit her senses, she tensed a little and pulled away, overwhelmed and unable to handle more.

"Did I do something wrong?" He hugged her. "Maybe I jumped too soon. I'm so sorry."

"No, it's okay. You're fine. I promise." Kit delivered him a nervous grin, stroking his cheek. "You're, um, awfully good at kissing. The best I've had in a long time."

"Yeah?" He let out a soft chuckle. "I find that hard to believe."

She grimaced. "I wish I was lying, but then I'd be lying."

He laughed again. "You're cute, you know that?" The smile left his face, and he peered down at her again. "Can I have one more kiss before I go back to my place?" Not waiting for an answer, he kissed her again, with more passion than before, leaving her breathless. "There, now I think that ought to do it." With a stroke of his finger, he brushed away a wisp of hair from her forehead. "Go ahead and unlock the door so I can see that you got inside safe and sound."

She inserted the key and opened the door. "Okay, I'm in now. My apartment is just at the top of those stairs. I'll lock this one."

"Very good." He stepped back. "Can we get together again?"

Kit shot him a wide grin. "I'd love to. We'll hook up and work out the details."

"Can't wait." Steven waved before heading off into the night. When he'd become no more than a ghostly etch in the darkness, she turned around and went inside.

Across the street, the clock from the church chimed the nighttime hour. Time for bed, or time for a new beginning? For the moment, both sounded right. And who really was the best kisser now? Dwight or Steven?

***

"Oh my god, he did?" Irene's voice squealed with excitement.

Kit held the phone away from her eardrum, lessening the vocal assault.

"Yes! I thought I'd died and gone to heaven. Nobody's ever kissed me the way he did." She thought for a moment. "I take that back. That's not entirely true, but his ranks high up there." Steven's kiss carried her away to another dimension in a way Dwight's didn't. Frowning, she compared the two in more detail, trying to determine what she liked best about each one.

"Are you listening, Kit?"

"Yes, I'm listening. Yes, we ate at the coffee shop."

"Hey, I thought that was supposed to be our place, just for us gals." Irene laughed. "What did you two eat?"

"He ate roast beef, and I ordered what Dwight got for me last week."

"Poor Dwight." Irene clicked her tongue in mock disapproval. "You know he'll be beside himself when he finds out you went out with someone else. What are you going to do?"

Kit let out a soft growl of frustration. "Damn, he's bound to find out sooner or later. I can't hide this from him forever. Dwight's great, but there's something about Steven that I simply cannot pass up. Can't put my finger on it, but with him I feel a sense of connection. Don't know where it comes from. But I can't string Dwight along, either, if Steven and I continue seeing each other."

"Don't worry about it. That's just the way things go sometimes, you know?" Irene paused to yell at her cat, and continued talking to Kit. "Listen, I got an idea about your dream."

"My dream?" She adjusted a pillow and wriggled on the sofa to get more comfortable.

"Yes, you're still having it, aren't you?"

She thought a few seconds. "Come to think of it, it's died down a little in the past few days. Can't imagine why, exactly. I've had so much on my mind. But what's your idea?"

"I don't have time to go into detail right now. How about I come over to your place one night this week. Maybe we can order out, or something. The pub does delivery, if it's in the immediate area."

"I like that. All this time, and I never knew they did that."

Irene chuckled. "It's one of their best kept secrets. I've asked them to bring food over to the mansion when we've had late-night meetings, but that was quite a while ago."

"When do you want to come over?" Kit thought hard, mentally reviewing her calendar.

"Wednesday works for me if it does for you."

"Sounds good. Nothing planned that night."

"All right, girl, I'll let you go. See you tomorrow." Irene hung up the phone.

Kit basked in the afternoon sun blazing through the windows, and thought how nice it would be if Steven were snuggled up beside her. Should she call Dwight? It's not like she and Steven had become an item overnight. For the first time in her dealings with men, she felt a rush of confusion. If a relationship blossomed between her and Steven, she'd have no choice but to let Dwight down easy.

She compared the two, like how each one made her feel when he touched her. They created different reactions. Steven's hands sent her into orbit, plain and simple, while Dwight's hands grounded her. Both men offered security, unique, yet powerful. Dwight always managed to surprise her with little things, romantic gestures, tokens of affection. Steven embodied a touch of familiarity, while infusing her with a fresh, unique sense of adventure.

Steven's kiss compelled her to surrender everything to him, body and spirit. After he left, she'd imagined his hands exploring every inch of her, infusing a light kiss in the most sensitive areas. She'd stalled those types of thoughts with Dwight until recently, slowly indulging her libidinous side. Dwight didn't have a skittish bone in his body, and would do anything for her. With him, she had finally let her guard down a little. The meal she ate at the coffee shop reminded her of him. She'd almost considered herself a traitor, sharing *his* meal selection with another man.

Grimacing, she turned her thoughts back to the mansion. Planning an event was so much easier than figuring out men.

CHAPTER 8

Dwight sat in front of Kit's desk, beaming as she waved an envelope in her hand. "We have a letter from the Commission. Got it just now."

"Have you read it?" Dwight sat straight up, eying her intently.

"I wanted us to read it together. They sure came up with an answer fast. Only two weeks ago, I stood in front of everyone, scared to death." She let out a slow trickle of breath. "And now I'm scared at what the answer will be." Her eyes fixed on Dwight's.

"Go ahead and open it. We can speculate all day long, but the answer is in your hands." He cocked his head in the direction of the envelope dangling from her fingers.

Kit sliced open the top of the envelope with a letter opener from her desk. Her eyes skipped over the words, her pulse racing faster.

"Well?" Dwight didn't wait for an answer, but strode to Kit behind the desk and gazed over her shoulder.

"We got it!" Both spoke in unison, high-fiving as they nodded with excitement.

"Uh-oh, look here." Dwight pointed to the last paragraph, repeating the line stating the conditions. He glanced at Kit. "We have forty-five days to come up with a down payment before the window of opportunity closes, and Harsh steps back into the picture."

Frowning, she read the line again, before letting out a groan. "Most people have longer than that, usually ninety days, at least. Sometimes six months."

"Bet old Harsh gave 'em hell and the Commission compromised by cutting the time in half." Dwight shook his head and returned to his seat.

Drumming her fingers on top of the desk, eyes narrowed in thought, Kit's mind raced. "That's only a month and a half, Dwight. That hardly gives us enough time to plan anything."

"And we're coming up on the holidays, too, which becomes a tricky time for everyone."

She retrieved the pad of paper on her desk, nodding at intervals as he spoke, scribbling a list of ways to raise money for the down payment. Kit tapped a pen against the desktop. "I say we do this the weekend before Thanksgiving. Maybe we can scrounge up some generous people who will fit us into their holiday budget." She sat back in her chair. "Ugh, I hate the timing of all this."

"Don't disagree, there, *cherie*, but that's the hand we've been dealt. Nothing wrong with coming a little under the deadline, but we've got to move fast, no matter what."

The whole prospect seemed dismal at this point. The community in Windham Springs liked any reason for a party, coming in droves for an event. Even smaller outlying towns joined in. Kit propped her head in her hand and looked at Dwight. "What are your thoughts about how we can raise money? And we need to do this as cheaply as possible without looking too cheap."

"I'm sure there are groups or organizations who wouldn't mind pitching in at a low cost for a good cause." He wrapped his hands behind his head and stretched out a little. "What do you have written on that pad of yours? Looked like some ideas were percolating hot and heavy, the way you were going at it." He grinned.

Returning the grin, Kit said, "So which of these ideas did you like the best? A silent auction, artisan sale, or gala?"

He tapped a forefinger against his lower lip and stared off across the room. "Tell you what we could do. Why don't we combine a gala and silent auction? We could hire a band to perform, and there could be an open bar, dining, dancing, and of course, the silent auction."

"I love that idea, Dwight. But again, how do we do this so we're not spending an arm and a leg? We're trying to earn money, you know."

"I know that." He stuck his tongue out, sending Kit into a fit of giggles. "There's a culinary school in Charlotte. I say we hit up some of the students who need a project marked off their list."

"You could be a one-man show and sing for us. Just bring that trusty guitar of yours, and we've got this gig in the bag." Kit made a funny face at Dwight. "You'd do it for free, wouldn't you?"

Dwight laughed. "You crack me up. Back to school, again. I know music students who need recital projects."

Kit raised an eyebrow at him. "What's with you and school, already? But I have to admit, you make good points." She turned her attention back to the pad. "We need to take donations as well as charge for the event. No matter how much we advertise and invite the public, there won't be enough in ticket sales alone to meet a down payment need. There also may not be enough from the silent auction, either."

"Any way we could start advertising this week? And we need to advertise this, not only in Windham Springs, but in adjoining counties. Philanthropists abound in other areas, and there are people who love nothing better than an excuse to get out and support a good cause."

She winked. "I'm sure good booze and dancing don't hurt, either." With a teasing grin on her face, she asked, "I'm sure you know some good bartenders?"

"Mmm, now you have me stumped on that, but surely the culinary folks know people. You gotta appreciate connections." His smile lightened, turning his face into one with a soberer look. "Do you have your formal gown ready, Kit? I'm prepared to dance the night away with you."

With a laugh, she waved him off. "Oh, you know what, I'll have to buy something for this event. I'm flat out of fancy ball gowns at the moment."

"Maybe Irene will have a dress you can borrow. I know Jim whisks her away on glitzy trips every now and then. She may have needed a glitzy dress for one of those occasions."

"We are about the same size. But you're right, I could at least check with her first." She rested back in her chair. "Good, I think we're on the right path. So we'll do this event on the Saturday before Thanksgiving week." Clicking on her calendar icon, she input the date with a few more clicks. "There, it's official."

"That will have to work. On Monday, we'll go to the bank."

"We?" Kit stared at him. "You're the finance guy. Wouldn't you handle that?"

"And this, in some small way, is your house, isn't it?" Dwight shot her a questioning look.

"Huh." She jerked her head up straighter, pondering his words. "Yeah," she said softly, "I guess it is." He spoke the truth, if only in a small way. This purchase was a business deal for the Society. But her connection solidified the desire burning inside of her to see this house stand for eternity, if possible.

"How does it feel to finally have the home of your childhood?"

"I don't know. I don't think it's all settled in yet." Kit gazed back at him, taking in his thoughtful expression. She loved seeing that look on his face, muscles relaxed, eyes sparkling with easy warmth. "Tell you what, I'll get some flyers printed up tonight after work, and you, me, and Irene can start putting these up tomorrow. That'll work until we can get some larger posters made. I'll get to work on an announcement for our website."

"When I get to my office, I'll drum up advertising for the radio. And I can get Irene to have the printer get some posters made along with special invitations for VIPs."

Struck with an idea, Kit clapped a hand over her mouth, eyes wide. "Dwight." She peered at him with shining eyes. "Why don't we make this gala a masquerade ball, in the style of the old Venetian carnivals? We can come up with a standard time after the first one, but an event like this would probably intrigue everybody. We all like dressing up. And I know we have artisans here who would be itching to create masks and costumes for sale."

He stared at her a few seconds, digesting this suggestion. His face lit up. "You're a genius, you know that? I love the idea, and it'd be unique too. Nobody does this type of fanfare much anymore."

Excited, she reached for a pen, writing furiously on her pad. "And we'll need big tents with heaters. We have plenty of room on the property to hold this event."

He nodded slowly. "You want to be in charge of finding a company who can set up all the equipment?"

"I can do that. No problem. We need to start collecting items for the silent auction. Want to start that this weekend?"

"I'm in. We'll ask Irene. She'll do whatever we need her to do." Dwight smiled.

"Good." Kit sat rocking back and forth in her chair. "Love it when a plan comes together, and it looks like the three of us will be pretty busy until the day this is over. But I'm hoping this will be a huge success, and we get the money we need."

"I think we'll make a great team." Dwight's words tumbled out in a soft whisper.

"Yeah." Kit's eyes met his. Somehow, she suspected that 'team' didn't include Irene. "Let's get to work, then. I'll get online and start hunting for tents, and tomorrow, we start posting fliers. Tonight, I may even hit up some of the residents I know personally, and see if they have something they'd like to put up for auction."

Dwight walked to the door. Before leaving, he turned around and winked, "I like where all this is going. We're starting a new tradition."

"You bet." She waved as he left her office. Inside, Kit's nerves fired off a warning cry. All the 'we' business tugged at her heartstrings. She dropped her head on the top of the desk and let out a soft cry of anguish.

"Oh, my. Having a bad day, are we?" Irene popped her head inside the doorway before strolling on inside. "You sure couldn't tell anything was wrong by looking at Dwight, all smiles, strutting down the hall like he owns the place. At one point, I swear I almost saw him float." She dropped down in the chair in front of Kit's desk. "I saw he was in here for a while. What did you two talk about?"

Kit lifted her head and smiled at her friend. "We just won a shot at purchasing this house."

Irene lifted her eyebrows. "That's wonderful! You didn't look happy for someone who got what she wanted." She clapped her hands. "Is that what you two were talking about?"

"Yes, but don't get all excited yet." Kit spent several minutes bringing her friend up-to-date on what had transpired.

"Sounds like you came up with some great ideas, and I really like the idea of Carnival. Jim and I have been to a couple of those. They're magnificent, with all the costumes and masks." She closed her eyes, face drawn up in satisfaction. "And to think we'll have something like it closer to home."

"You don't mind doing posters and invitations, do you?"

"Not at all, and I'll start working on the guest list and finding a speedy printing company. Damn! Harsh knows how to put the screws to someone, doesn't he? I'm with you and Dwight on the time issue. Anything else?"

Kit narrowed her eyes, pretending to think. "Yes, forgot to add, since *we* are a team, because that's what Dwight said – *we* – I want us to spend this weekend taking up auction donation commitments."

"*We*, huh?" Irene chuckled. "I'm sure he was referring to you and him. Forget *moi* over here."

"You're silly! But I think we split up like we did the last time. That worked really well."

"Sounds like a plan." Irene smiled. "I'm in one hundred percent. I'm so excited we're getting this place. And really, you've been the one to get all this together."

"Thanks, but I can't go it alone."

Irene's face clouded. "How do you think old Harsh will take this when he gets wind that his ship won't be sailing over Stothwell waters?"

Kit grimaced. "Eww, I try not to think about it too much. I mean, he was hot at the Commission meeting. Did you see those eyes?"

"I wonder if his bark is worse than his bite. He may be good with using his resources and putting pressure on people, but surely, he's no crazier than that. Connections mean a lot, and he probably has them."

"True. We'll just hope he puts on his big boy briefs and deals with it."

Irene shot her a doubtful look and pulled herself out of the chair. "Okay, I'm off to create posters, invitations, and a VIP guest list. I'll get with Dwight to see what else I can do to help him –maybe make some phone calls."

"Take care." Kit waved as her friend passed into the hallway.

For the next couple of hours, she hunched over her desk, making a list of all the merchants she'd visit the next day, including the residents she planned on seeing after work. The last hour of work, she spent time surfing the Internet for tent companies.

"Excuse me, Miss, I've got a package for you."

Kit froze a moment at the interruption, and glanced up to see a deliveryman standing in front of her. He stood a good six feet tall, with thick dirty-blond hair, and wore brown slacks and a matching shirt. His brawny arms stretched over the desk, thrusting a box in her direction.

"Didn't mean to scare you there. You looked like you were awfully busy. You working on a big project or something?" He craned his neck a little, eyes darting about the room and viewing all the papers scattered on her desk.

She smiled. "Oh, that's okay. I didn't hear you come in. I wasn't expecting a package, though."

The man glanced down at the box and read the label. "Well, it says right here that this is supposed to go to you. The address, I believe, is correct. This is the Windham Springs Historical Society, and you are Kit Millinger, aren't you?"

"Yes." She just blinked at him.

"Then I'm leaving this with you." He placed the box on the desk with a thump, disregarding her paperwork.

How rude! She frowned. "Thank you. Don't I need to sign something?"

For a moment he stood still, leering at her. "Um, no, that won't be necessary. I'll let the sender know you got it." Without another word, he turned out of the office.

She cleared her throat. "Hey, you!"

The man kept on walking, apparently determined to leave the office in a hurry. Damn him! Kit bolted out of her seat and raced toward the entrance hall. Too late, the door had just closed. In a blind fury, she ran toward one of long windows next to the door and peered out from behind the lace curtain. Parked on the street, she saw a plain white car. The man had already gotten inside, started the engine, and was pulling out onto the street. Within seconds, he drove off, tires screeching.

Still cursing, she returned to her office and glared at the box. The label had both her name and the Society's on it, but no return label. She picked up the parcel and peeled away the tape. Who sent this? Was Dwight up to something new, resorting to having gifts delivered? If so, he had lousy taste in couriers, which would be the first time he had bad taste in anything. Once all the tape rested in a heap on top of her desk, she laid the box down, opened up the side flaps, and plunged her hand inside.

To her surprise, she pulled out a large skull, which she nearly dropped. It was similar to those used in anatomy classes. Upon further inspection, the box had been lined in plastic, and the skull resting on dirt. Kit inspected the piece with great care. In her estimation, everything appeared authentic, from the soft yellow- brown surface to the glossy, grayish sheen of the teeth. Even the sutures on top appeared sharp, with the tiny curvatures of the bones fitting neatly into each other like a puzzle. She swallowed hard, lifting her head away. No doubt about it, this skull was the real deal. A wave of uneasiness swept over her.

Something white peeking through the dirt caught her eye, and she pulled out a small envelope. Great, now she'd learn the identity of this twisted sender who must have liked the idea of grossing her out completely. Kit grabbed a couple of napkins from the drawer of the desk and, picking up the skull, dropped it back in the box. She tore open the envelope, which held a piece of paper with a typed message: *"This will be you."* Stunned and speechless, she stood still, trying to make sense of this package. The sender wanted to give her a message, all right. If anything, this person had succeeded in getting her full attention.

Grabbing up the box, she charged out of her office and ran down the hall to Irene. Not bothering to knock, she stormed in. "Irene, you won't believe what I just got!" Kit held out the box with both hands.

"What's wrong?" Irene tossed her pen on a notebook and came out from behind the desk. "And where did you get this?"

"It's not what you think." Kit's eyes widened in fear, and her hands trembled.

"Kit, sit down here for a second, and calm down." Irene's usual playfulness vanished, and her take-charge mode kicked in. "Here, give this to me." She took the box and put it on her desk.

"What's all the commotion?" Dwight stopped in the doorway. Without invitation, he strode into the office and placed an arm on Kit's shoulder. He knelt down by the chair and cupped her face in his hands. "What's wrong? Why are you so upset?"

"She just got something through the mail, and we're trying to figure out what's going on." Irene started to open the box.

"I didn't get it through the mail. Some weirdo delivery dude came into my office and gave it to me."

Irene drove her hand into the box. She gasped. "Oh, look at this!" She pulled out the skull, cringing at the site of it as the hollowed eye sockets came into view.

When Dwight looked back up at Irene, he jumped up and ran to her side. "What on earth? And what's this?" He pulled out the envelope.

"Yeah, get a load of what that says." By this time, Kit had joined her friends at the desk.

"This will be you." Dwight handed the note to Irene. "Great, the note isn't signed or hand-written. We can't even do a handwriting analysis on it." He hugged Kit close. "Don't worry, we'll get to the bottom of this."

Irene ran her hands through the box. "Wow, this person is a little morbid, packing that thing with dirt." She shook her head, letting the soil run through her fingers. "I'm beginning to get a sense of who could be behind this."

Dwight groaned. "Surely not. This is so unprofessional, not to mention immature."

"You don't mean Edmond Harsh would send something like this, do you?" Kit stared at her friends. "If so, you're right; that is ridiculous."

"Or it could just be a silly, practical joke, but I couldn't even begin to think who'd be up to something like this."

"Could it be the new artist who's come to town or someone he knows? You never can tell about these artsy people. They sometimes have a twisted sense of humor." Dwight slipped the envelope back in the box.

"Oh, good grief, Dwight." Irene's eyes moved with a frustrated expression. "Why on earth would someone new in town do something like this to someone they've been out...?" She caught herself in time. "I mean, I highly doubt the new guy would do something like this. He wouldn't know much of what's going on locally, and definitely has no interest in this property."

He frowned back. "I'm just saying you never know about people, that's all. They'll surprise you every time."

Kit patted Dwight on the back. "You're right, Dwight, people can surprise you, but I'm beginning to agree with Irene. Harsh is starting to get his digs in early by trying to scare me or us off from buying this place."

Dwight glanced at Kit. "What are you going to do with it?"

"Ugh, I have no clue. I don't want it in my office, nor do I want to carry it all the way back to my apartment, either. That's just ..." Kit shuddered.

"Tell you what. I'll take it and put it down in the basement. We'll have it if we need it for evidence, if it comes to something that drastic, and it's still out of everybody's way." Dwight stuffed the paper back in the envelope and tossed it into the box.

Irene nodded. "Good idea. I don't think I'd like that thing around me either, and can you imagine tossing it into a dumpster and someone finding it?"

"I'm off to the basement, ladies. We'll just keep our eyes and ears open for anything that looks suspicious."

Irene grinned as Dwight left. "The knight in shining armor to the rescue. Taking that nasty thing away. What about Steven, now that he's graced your lips with such a sensuous kiss?" She patted her friend's arm and went back to sit behind her desk.

"I'll have to decide soon, see how it goes. One thing I'll say, I adore his kisses and his touch." She whispered. "The thing is, they're both so different."

"They're two different men. You'll have to make a choice at some point."

Kit looked toward the door. "I hear you loud and clear."

"How about we have some dinner together tonight?" Irene smiled. "After this little ordeal, I think you need some company. You up for it?"

Kit blinked a few times, thinking. Did she want company, or did she want some time to herself? No, she wanted Irene's company to help process all the things that had happened. "I think you're right. I am a little shaken up, and somehow, I don't care about spending tonight alone. And I'm not that far along with Steven that I would feel comfortable asking him to keep me company."

"Tell you what, I'll get an order placed at the pub and give them a delivery time, and we'll go from there." Irene shrugged.

"Great, just come on by the apartment whenever you want. I may leave a bit earlier so I can get everything tidied up a bit. For the moment I just can't concentrate, so I'll be pretty worthless the rest of the day." Kit left Irene's office and walked back to her own. For two hours, she focused on a project involving the creation of a podcast on how to preserve antique textiles and linens. Selecting suitable photographs for inclusion as examples did little to take her mind off things. Script writing for the audio portion became more difficult because her mind refused to cooperate. After one more hour of pushing through the material and agonizing over how to organize it all, she gathered up her purse and left the mansion. At least she had Irene's company to look forward to.

CHAPTER 9

Outside on the streets, cars sped by and Kit searched for a plain white vehicle driven by a male who looked like the delivery person who'd stood in her office. No luck. No luck with cars parked on the streets, either. Kit thought about the hateful box tucked away in the darkness of the basement. Too bad she hadn't thought of refusing the package and having the delivery guy return it to the sender. Hindsight was always better than foresight, and thinking on the fly had never been her strong suit, anyway. From across the street, she viewed the inside of *Celestial Temptation Gallery*, the 'Open' sign blazing in the window. For an instant, she considered running across the street to see Steven and cry on his shoulder. Though she had found Dwight's arm around her soothing enough, Steven's arm around her would make her forget Edmond Harsh altogether. Another burning kiss from his lips would make her believe the world was truly an angelic place, a reflection of Heaven where nothing bad ever happened.

No, she needed to hurry home and get ready for an evening with Irene. She'd visit Steven later. Memories of the deliveryman still left her with an uneasy sensation. The sender knew her and where she worked; he apparently knew how to get someone to do his dirty work too. But why just her and not the others? She hadn't attended that meeting alone. Should she give Alexandra a call and tell her what happened? She hadn't spoken to her cousin since the meeting. Most likely keeping a low profile. Kit couldn't blame her much.

The ugly truth was, old Harsh would go after anyone standing in his way. Unfortunately, as conservation manager, she held the honor of instigator, the bold one who'd stepped up to that podium, taking a stand for what she believed in. As a result, she'd have to deal with it for the sake of the Society. She could only hope the others would be left alone.

* * *

The buzz from a communication panel in the apartment blared out Irene's arrival. Kit pushed a button, which opened the main door below. Within seconds, Irene knocked on the door.

"Hello!" She beamed, sailing into the apartment, food in tow. Underneath one arm she held a box.

"Here, let me help you with all this." Kit relieved her friend from the sack of food and carried it to the kitchen. "Oh, what have we here?" She dipped her nose into the bag and inhaled. "Gosh, that smells so good. I'm starved. I didn't even eat lunch today."

Irene tapped her friend on the shoulder. "Hey, I had to convince Dwight to go on home after work."

"Convince him? Why?"

"He was dead set on coming over here and staying with you for a while to make sure you were safe. I finally had to let the cat out of the bag and tell him we had plans here tonight."

"Speaking of letting cats out of bags, you almost spilled the beans on me and Steven going out."

"I know, I'm sorry about that." Irene gave Kit an apologetic smile. "But I saved face and caught myself in time. Because he was so interested in what was going on, I don't think he suspected a thing. Do I at least get brownie points for that?"

"I forgive you." Kit eyed the box Irene had placed on the rocking chair. "So, what's in the box?"

Irene grinned. "I brought something that can help us with the dream you've been having. I know you said something about not having it as much anymore, but I still think it'll rear its head. These things don't just up and go away without a reason."

Kit thought a moment. "Does ignoring it help? I swear I think not paying attention has its merits, but you won't believe me." Since the time she took Steven on the tour, the dreams had come to a brief halt. Had his presence served as a substitute incarnate, dredging up sparks of the old pain and pleasures she'd experienced with Austin? The paradox left her both confused and intrigued, and right now, no amount of reasoning from Irene would allow her to resolve it with any great satisfaction.

"Still, we need to get to the bottom of that dream. Like I said before, I think your old flame wants to talk to you."

"Let's eat, and then we can play with whatever you brought."

After the meal and some small talk, Kit stepped outside onto her balcony. From a storage room, she brought out a log and returned to the living room.

"Why don't we do this in front of the fireplace? It's cool enough outside, and somehow a fire seems like the perfect way to create a good environment for conjuring up spirits."

"Great idea. Do you need any help?"

"Nah, I got it." Kit trotted over to the fireplace. Within a few minutes, a small fire burned. Irene had situated everything to her satisfaction.

"Geez, I feel silly. I've never done this sort of thing before." Kit seated herself in a cross-legged position facing Irene.

"You've never used a spirit board? Didn't you play with something like this as a kid?"

Shuddering, Kit shook her head. "Uh-uh, no way. I hear all this is evil, so I've done my best stay away from it. She smiled at her friend.

Irene, said in a matter-of-fact tone, "The spirit board is really no different than tarot cards or pendulums. Again, they're just tools for showing what's really going on in any given situation."

"Do they work? I mean, how can cards or a board tell you anything? Isn't it just like life? Luck of the draw?"

"Nothing's pure chance. Everything stems from a purpose, free choice, intent."

"Okay. Then I'm exercising my free choice to use this board because I intend to put a stop to these dreams, or anything else that bugs me. And right now, the dreams are honestly taking a back seat to that crazy skull that got dumped on my desk by some lunatic out there who wants to toy with me. Let's get on with this."

"I'm just as nervous as you are, Kit. We care about you. What happens to you affects all of us."

"Well, what do we do now?"

"Let's just focus on the dream first. I have a hunch there's more going on with that. I just can't shake the feeling."

Turning her face down toward the board, Kit viewed the glossy surface. In the firelight, it harbored an almost sinister glow. Irene already had her fingers on top of the planchette. "Put your fingertips on this, Kit, just like me."

Kit stifled a grin and did as Irene instructed.

"Okay, I want us to clear our minds, and open ourselves up to the free flow of energy." Irene closed her eyes, took in a deep breath and, after holding it a few seconds, exhaled slowly. Her head dropped back a little, giving the appearance of one in a trance. The only sounds in the room came from the fireplace, with tiny sizzles from the log and the clock on the mantel, clicking out rhythmic tick-tocks. In an instant, whether it was a true change of energy or out of respect for her friend, Kit felt her mood shift from lighthearted to somber. Eyes closed, she settled down long enough to focus on the moment and sink deeper into concentration.

Each breath became deeper, slower, more controlled and deliberate. The ambient air grew more charged, with an unseen hand taking hold and pulling her into another dimension, a spiritual pull she'd never experienced before. It set her nerves on edge. Her pulse quickened, and inside her head, a host of images flashed before her, turning her into a spectator in a cosmic theater featuring a strange silent movie.

Irene broke the silence, whispering to Kit. "What's your friend's name?"

"Austin," Kit whispered back. Shuddering, she closed her eyes and tried to concentrate, wishing more than anything to shut out everything around her. The old adage '*there's power in the spoken word*' never rang truer for her than now. Saying Austin's name aloud infused the present moment with a strong shot of reality. Somewhere in her gut, she knew the outcome of this night could set the stage for change, reframing how she would view herself and what had really happened between her and Austin from this point forward.

"Very good." Irene closed her eyes again and took several deeper breaths before she spoke. "First, we need to determine if Austin is mere symbolism, or if he's really trying to talk to you." In an intense, monotone voice, she asked the following question, "Dear Austin, friend of Kit, we come in peace and goodwill. We seek to help you and mean no harm. Please tell us, do you represent something symbolic in Kit's life?"

Silence filled the room, and as the ladies sat in concentration over the board, the planchette moved in short jerks, settling into a smooth sail across the surface.

Opening one eye, Kit's heart fluttered. When she saw where it had landed, a chill shot up her spine. "No" filled the little round window.

"Austin, do you have a message for Kit, something you wish to share with her?"

Kit couldn't bear to look. Every nerve in her body tingled, and her ears picked up the slightest sound. The planchette glided to the opposite side of the board. When she opened her eyes, she saw Irene viewing the answer in the window: "Yes."

Infused with a new ambience, the room had transformed into an unnerving place, surreal, holding dark secrets to the unknown. Worse, this board held the key to her past. Though the fire had reached a vibrant peak, with large, dancing flames transmitting a soft heat, a quick, light chill passed through, leaving as quickly as it had come. Kit shivered, and viewed her friend on the other side of the board. Irene appeared oblivious to the immediate surroundings, throwing herself into the work of contacting someone who, in Kit's mind, would most likely be better off left alone and allowed to rest in peace forever.

Swallowing hard, Kit took a deep breath, trying desperately to calm her nerves. She didn't know which was worse, getting a package with a nasty warning, or dabbling in the spirit realm where the playing field didn't resemble the earth plane or anything on it.

Irene spoke again. "Austin, can you tell us what you want from Kit?"

Both women held their fingers on the planchette, which darted down toward the letters, and began spelling out an answer. Filled with a mix of awe and horror, Kit opened her eyes just enough to peek at the planchette as it glided over letters, spelling out a message: F-O-R-G-I-V-E.

A wave of emotional heat erupted, welling up in her chest, threatening to suffocate the vitality right out of her. Kit mumbled the word, the one singular, awful word eluding her the most during all these years. The fact that this divination tool, out of the blue it seemed, had managed to conjure up such a message chilled her blood. On the walls, shadows from the flames in the fireplace danced, their black lines gyrating to the unheard beat of music from some dystopian realm. For a moment, she wanted to scream at Irene to stop this séance, this nasty business of contacting the dead.

She'd heard about these spirit boards and how they could sometimes drum up trouble. Maybe Austin just needed to be left alone after all. But why had he come to her in dreams, during sleep, where the power of speech and the ability to run often escaped her? And why had the dream subsided? Inside, her stomach lurched with a queasy sensation. Irene took a deep breath. Kit closed her eyes, reluctant to see any more. The planchette moved toward the next letter of the message.

A loud knock at the door startled them both, with Irene letting out a short screech. The planchette came to a halt. Open-mouthed, she stared at Kit. "Oh, the spirits come a knockin'!"

"Irene!" Kit pursed her lips and shook her head. "Stop that!"

Irene wore a look of panic on her face. "What do we do?"

"Did you remember to lock the door downstairs when you came in? Nobody can just come up here, unless the door's unlocked."

Her friend's eyes widened. "I know I locked that door behind me. I wouldn't forget something like that."

The knock sounded again, a little louder.

Irene motioned toward the door. "Go ahead, I'm here. I can help if something happens."

Kit got up, glancing one last time at Irene. "Are you sure?" she whispered.

Irene flicked her hand toward the door, mouthing silently for Kit to go on.

Creeping slowly, Kit reached the door at last, and jerked it wide open.

"Hi, are you in the mood for some company tonight?"

She unclenched her other fist. Her breathing returned to normal. "Steven!"

He stood in the doorway, looking handsome, wearing jeans, a printed sports shirt, and a jacket to ward off the night chill. A bottle of wine peeked out from underneath his arm. At Kit's insistence, he entered the apartment, fixing his eyes on the board as he walked toward the fireplace. Irene remained rooted to the floor, lips open in surprise.

"I'm Steven, nice to meet you." He smiled at Irene, but glanced back to the board. "Am I interrupting anything?"

"No, of course not. I was just leaving." Irene pulled herself up from the floor, board in hand, and rushed to the chair, tossing everything back into the box. "Kit, I'm going on home. I need to feed my cat."

Kit returned the hug as Irene opened the apartment door. "Thanks so much. I enjoyed having dinner with you and ..."

"Don't mention it. Had a great time. I'll see you tomorrow. Steven, nice to meet you."

The door closed, followed by Irene's footsteps echoing down the stairs.

"I'm so sorry for just barging in like this, but I didn't have your number to call you." Steven stood by the sofa, uncertain what to do next.

She walked toward him, relieving him from the bottle of wine and his jacket. "No worries. Irene was right, we were done." She took Steven's jacket and placed in on top of her bed. Without any formalities, Kit quickly popped the cork from the wine bottle and poured up two glasses while Steven made himself comfortable on the sofa.

She returned, placing the glasses on the coffee table. "It's great to see you. And just for your information, you never need an excuse to come over."

He opened his arm, indicating for her to sit down next to him, which she did with a grateful heart. Just what her body and spirit craved, shelter and warmth in his embrace. Her head nestled into his neck and she inhaled, breathing in his clean, natural scent.

He delivered a light kiss on the top of her head and hugged her tighter. "I've been missing you since we went out. I just had to come over."

Both of them sat in silence for several minutes watching the fire, like they sat this way all the time. Kit basked in pure bliss, taking in the moment for what it offered, Steven and his presence. His breathing sounded in her ears like a soft musical whisper, or an answer to a prayer. It didn't matter. Snuggling next to him was enough.

"I'm sorry if I interrupted you and your friend. She didn't have to go. There's plenty of wine for all of us." He smiled and took a quick sip from his glass.

"You didn't interrupt anything. We came here right after work, so we were finished with everything."

"I couldn't help but notice a spirit board on the floor. Do you mind my asking why you were using it? I find the use of them rather interesting myself."

Kit's internal alarm bells went off. She had no intention of sharing the whys and wherefores regarding this subject, not even to someone she thought she liked a lot. Her voice remained steady and casual-sounding. "Oh, Irene loves to dabble in the spirit realm. She wanted to show me how it worked, so we were just playing around, that's all."

He tipped his glass to his lips, eyes never leaving her face. "Did you – did she get the answer she was looking for?"

The heat rushed to her face. "Yes, as a matter of fact she did."

Steven squinted at his glass of wine, gave a light shrug, and nodded. "Good, good." A few seconds passed before he spoke again. "So tell me, have you been doing okay? Anything new going on in your life since we last got together?" He leaned over to give her a light kiss on the lips.

The scent of wine from his breath as he leaned in close aroused her for a second, and she fought hard to refrain from throwing caution to the wind and smothering him with hard, passionate kisses. Kit took a deep breath and thought for a moment. Vamping him right then and there remained completely out of the question, but did she dare burden him with her problems, her deepest concern for the moment?

Steven placed his wine glass on the coffee table and turned to face her. "Something's bothering you. I can see it on your face, and you seem a little tense, whether you know it or not."

"I-I don't know what to say." She stared at her glass, running a finger around the rim as she thought. "But you're right, something happened to me at work today."

"Tell me about it, then." He took her hand in his and rested it on his thigh. The warmth from his palm touching her skin gave her the reassurance she needed.

For the next several minutes she told him all the latest happenings involving the Historical Society, ending with how she became the unlucky recipient of a macabre package. When she finished the story, Steven sat in silence, thinking.

He took a deep breath and shared his thoughts on the matter. "Sounds like the one who sent you this skull amounts to nothing more than a big coward, in my opinion. And to have someone else do the dirty work so he won't get caught is even lower, especially because it puts someone else in danger of being the fall guy." He pressed his palm against her hand. "No, I don't like the sound of this, either."

Kit sighed. "I just don't know what to do, that's all. I try to ignore everything, but somehow I can't help but think it's just the beginning."

Steven smiled and pulled her close. "All I can suggest is that some things can't be ignored, but let's hope you don't get any more packages. Keep your chin up. I'm here for you." He leaned over and graced her with a longer tender kiss. "I care about what happens to you, Kit. You don't have to keep all this to yourself. I'm here, right now." His kisses fell on her lips, urgent, greedy, almost smothering her. Inside her mouth, his tongue courted hers in tantalizing *adagio* movements. She almost begged out loud for more. Before she could think, he pushed her back on the sofa, hands brushing over sensitive parts of her body, turning up the arousal more than a notch. She let out a light whimper, and he held her tighter, kissed her harder.

Little by little, she worked her hands under his shirt, meeting with heat from his skin and a light film of sweat. With fluttery movements, she crisscrossed over his flesh, smiling with inner satisfaction as he shivered on top of her. He paused his kisses and smiled down at her.

"You're wonderful!"

The words, a light whisper, sent her heart soaring. Captured under his spell, the current world fell away, and she enjoyed letting doubt, indecision, and deep-seated restlessness go along with it. Every night since they'd met she'd lived moments like this in her head, hoping when she opened her eyes she'd find him there next to her. Tonight, this moment, she didn't have to wish. He'd come of his own free will, seeking her, wanting her.

They spent the remainder of the evening gazing at the fire, holding each other, indulging over and over in a cascade of hot, passionate kisses. In his arms, she discovered a connection, a magnetic pull bridging a lost part of herself to him, and back to the part of herself that lived now. Only one thing overshadowed Steven's presence. The message from the spirit board. The bigger question, why did a pang of sadness loom in her heart when she and Steven kissed?

CHAPTER 10

"That whole spirit board deal was totally unnerving." Sitting in Irene's kitchen, Kit glanced up at her friend, enjoying the surroundings of pale sage-colored walls and white ruffled curtains around the window above the sink. Minx the cat purred at her feet, finally settling down for a quick nap. Irene's place provided a fresh change from everything antique and name-brand in the arena of historical architecture and designs. "Does the little wooden thingy always move around so much? I could barely keep up with it."

An iron chandelier, with five old Mason jars acting as light shades, illuminated the shabby chic table where the two women sat. Kit sipped her jasmine tea in a dainty porcelain teacup, waiting for her friend's answer.

Irene chuckled. "It does when there are ready answers. Did the word 'forgive' mean anything to you?" She tilted her head to one side, studying her friend.

Kit shrugged, stomach tightening. "I dunno. We'll never know what the entire message was now."

"I think that word alone was pretty powerful. What needs to be forgiven, Kit? Austin sure wasted no time in spelling it out for you, if you'll forgive the pun."

"Double entendre." Kit tried to grin, but shook her head. "I'm sure there were things we did way back when. Honestly, I can't remember." Lie.

"He hasn't forgotten. What are you going to do?" Irene poured another cup of tea from a matching teapot.

"Not sure." Kit's mouth curved into a wan smile. "I'll have to give it all some more thought."

"Okay, fine. I'll change the subject. But if you want that message to be worthwhile, pay attention and do something with it." Irene winked. "Did you and Steven have a nice time? That was a surprise. Were you expecting him at all?"

"Total surprise. We never made an official date when he walked me home." Kit sipped from her cup, swirling the tea around in her mouth, marveling at the strong floral taste, like she'd swallowed a field of wildflowers. "I'm drawn to him, like I've known him from somewhere before. *Deja vu*, I guess."

"There are some people we feel an attraction to like that. Nothing strange there. So you want to see him again. Did you make a date this time?"

"Nothing official. I'm going to his place to see if he'll donate a painting for the auction. I'd love to see what kind of money one of his would bring."

"Speaking of the auction, do you want to give Dwight a call and tell him that we're meeting up this Saturday to get donations?"

Kit's pulse quickened. Of course, she'd like to call Dwight. His nighttime calls had diminished somewhat, and part of her missed that, even with thoughts of Steven. "Yeah, I'll call right now so I won't get busy and forget."

Irene shot her an oh-get-real look and fidgeted with the candle sitting in the center of the table while her friend punched the numbers on her cell phone.

"Hey, Dwight, it's Kit. I'm good ... You? Listen, I'm at Irene's, and we wanted to remind you that we're getting together on Saturday." Kit grinned. "Just letting you know in case you forgot. Yeah, I know. Time's ticking away, but we'll get this done." Kit's cheeks flushed, and she lowered her voice mumbling the words, "Yeah, I miss you too. I know, I know. We've just all been so busy lately." A few more words of conversation, and Kit pushed the button on her phone, ending the call.

"What?" Kit frowned at Irene. "I do miss him." Flames of guilt burned hard and fierce. He'd tried so hard to act like nothing had come between them, with her talking to him and trying to keep the conversation on work and little else. "Tell me where you are in the planning, Irene. I'm still looking for tent companies."

"I've written up some of the guest list, and I'm working on the posters. I think Dwight already has some radio ads ready to go, and he gave me some numbers for bands. He said he'd find a caterer. I think we're moving along."

"Great." Kit smiled at her friend. "This is a last-minute idea, but I may see if some artists about town want to create carnival masks. We can have a day of selling these the weekend after this upcoming one. People will want masks and costumes."

Smiling, Irene said, "I love the creativity of it all. I think this whole thing will be fun. And are you going to invite Steven to the event as your date?" Irene grinned and gave Kit's foot a light kick.

"That's pretty much what I've been thinking." Kit stared at the half-empty teacup. "You bringing Jim?"

"Not sure. Only because he might be going out of town on business, but the other reason may be so Dwight doesn't have to come stag." Irene said the words so seriously, gazing down at her cup as if she were the one tangled between two loves.

"You're so evil." Kit stuck out her tongue. "You just said that to drive the sword through my heart, didn't you?"

"Somehow I think someone's going to end up sad, and if you don't watch it, that someone could be you."

Kit hung her head, face forlorn. "You said it. I dread breaking the news to him. Even so, Steven's a merchant, so he needs to be included on the VIP list and get a personal invitation."

Irene patted her friend's hand. "Don't you worry; I'll make sure darling Steven is on the guest list."

* * *

The weekend arrived, another bright Saturday rolling by without ceremony. As the Society members walked their assigned streets, each collected names of families willing to donate to the auction. At the end, Irene suggested going to dinner, but Kit kindly bowed out, claiming housework and laundry had gone long enough without attention. The look of disappointment in Dwight's face bothered her, but keeping up pretenses had become wearing. Waving her friends off as they headed back to the mansion where they'd parked their cars, Kit turned in the direction of her apartment.

Her thoughts wandered back to the skull, shuddering at the fact that it had found residence inside the mansion's basement. Dwight would need to dispose of it at some point. He'd seemed so knowledgeable about colleges and their programs; maybe he knew of a good biology department in search of a new skull. The wind had picked up. As she wrapped her jacket tighter around her, she gazed up at the sky.

The stars twinkled bright, silvery flashes of light against obsidian black. The longer she studied the darkness, the more the night transformed into something ominous. The moon glowed in the distance, casting mournful shadows. Another shot of cold air whipped around her, this time penetrating through to the inside. Her whole body instantly chilled. She didn't know why, but her gut clenched. Her senses heightened; she grew nervous.

Without another thought, Kit ran the rest of the way to her place, heading to the back of the building where she parked her car. Instinct pulled hard, creating a compelling need to check and make sure everything was okay before turning in for the night. The sense of dread creeping inside her body suggested things were not all right. She'd spent a pleasant, productive evening with friends. Why this ill feeling gnawing away at her? A streetlight mounted on a post gave off the only light in the back lot. Glancing around, she didn't see anyone, but that didn't dispel the onslaught of nerves.

Slowly her car, her beloved Beetle, came into view. As she approached the front of the car, horror filled her to the marrow. The windshield had been shattered. Shards lay in a heap around her car, sparkling like the most hateful diamonds on earth. Stunned, she didn't move, staring at the vehicle in disbelief. When had this happened, and why? Vandalism occurred at times, even on a town square in a smaller town like Windham Springs. This didn't feel like vandalism, though. The insult to her car smacked of revenge. It felt personal, like someone keeping tabs on a sinister score card.

Tears filled her eyes as she gazed at her car. The expense of fixing a damaged vehicle didn't fit her budget. She circled the VW, looking for other damage, but found none. Kit whipped out her cell phone for a picture. The light from the lamp and the flash on her camera would be good enough for a close-up. She snapped a shot of her license tag, too, for good measure. Thankful for no other destruction, she ran back to the entrance of her building, racing up the stairs and into her apartment. Nothing to do but wait until tomorrow, when she could call a tow service.

Then she realized she could call the police. Her fingers raced over the numbers on her phone. "Hello? Yes, I would like to report a vandalized vehicle ..."

There, she'd done that much. On her sofa she sat, trembling, phone in her hand. Should she call Dwight? He'd turn around and be there in a flash. Irene?

"Steven?" Her voice faltered as a young man's voice answered on the other end of the line. "Do you think you could come over? Something's happened, and I'm scared."

* * *

Monday, back in her office, Kit spent the greater part of her morning in a gloomy state of mind, finishing up one project before moving on to another; this included storyboarding a video tutorial on how to preserve family heirloom documents and records. With her mind reeling, she sat back in her chair and stretched a little to relieve the stiffness in her body. Her head ached. No matter how hard she tried to concentrate on work, she barely got through her task list.

Reaching inside a desk drawer she pulled out a bottle, dumping two aspirin in her hand. She swallowed them down with some remaining coffee, cringing at the bitter taste mixing with lukewarm liquid in her cup.

"Why didn't you call me when you saw your car, Kit?" Dwight stepped into her office, unannounced, and sat down. The muscles in his face tight, he stared hard at her.

"Sorry. I told Irene about it only this morning."

"Why?" Dwight frowned. "I would have stayed with you or brought you to my place."

Kit's face colored. "That's okay. I'm a big girl, but thank you." The truth, Steven had spent not only Saturday night with her, but Sunday, too, leaving just before she'd awakened for work this cloudy morning. Should she tell Dwight, own up, confess? Should she also confess she'd sneaked down to the basement earlier and nearly tore the place apart until she found the hideous skull, taking a picture of it as well?

"Let me know if you need a ride to the garage when your car is ready." His face had softened a little.

"I may do that, or ask Irene." Kit rested her head back against the chair. "I personally think someone was behind all that. It wasn't a random act. I can't prove it, but I sense it."

Dwight shook his head, brows furrowed. "I'll admit it seems too coincidental that it should happen to you, and especially right now, with everything that's going on. Or maybe it's just vandalism. Have you called your cousin about any of this?"

Gazing ahead past Dwight, Kit considered his question. "No, as a matter of fact I haven't. It's crossed my mind, but I've really wanted to avoid putting her in any compromising situations. If anyone needs to lay low, she does."

"That may be true, but I just wonder if she doesn't need to know."

"I'll think about it. If anything else comes up, I'll definitely give her a call. I don't want to worry her, either."

"Promise me you'll call anytime you're nervous or you think something's going on. Especially call me when something like this happens."

His face stiffened with admonishment, like a father scolding a naughty child. Kit wondered for a second what Dwight would be like as a father, holding a baby on his lap, or showing his little daughter the flowers in the garden or a butterfly. Would he teach his son how to play the guitar or take him out for a burger, a boy's night out kind of treat? He'd definitely make a good husband and father. Her instincts told her so. Part of her felt a momentary sadness that she may never be the other half of the equation.

"I have a bit of good news. I've got us tents and all the trappings to make this carnival everything we want it to be. Made a final call first thing this morning so I could get it off my plate." She grinned at Dwight.

He smiled back. "That's a good thing. We're lucky we can have this right here on the square. I think it'll be more fun and easier to manage this way."

"Did you start the radio ads yet?"

"Yep. Personally, I like the idea of making this an annual tradition, a way to raise money to make payments throughout the year."

Kit nodded in agreement. "I think so too." While he continued sharing his thoughts on the carnival, the Society, the world, she studied him in detail, paying close attention to the curves of his nose, lips, chin, the style and color of his hair, and then his whole body. As she viewed his strong jaw line, complete with lean, athletic build, her mind lapsed into a brief mental walk on the lusty side of her nature. For a moment, she envisioned his hands instead of Steven's, trailing soft and gentle over her bare shoulders, stroking her abdomen, grazing over the inner part of her thigh and coursing down ..."

"Did you and Irene have a nice evening together the other night?" Dwight's steady gaze burned hard and fierce.

Her cheeks flamed scarlet while she forced her brain to re-orient itself. "Yeah, we did. Had a quiet evening with some sandwiches and ale from the pub."

He said nothing, never veering his eyes from her.

"What? Why are you staring at me that way?" Perhaps the lusty gleam in his eye mirrored her own thoughts? Deep in the quiet depths of his mind, did he often undress her, anticipating the sensation of her skin under his fingertips as they showered her with the deftest, sensual touches?

"Oh, nothing." A somber expression covered his face, and his eyes remained glued in her direction. He tilted his head from side to side, engrossed in thought. "I was worried about you. If Irene hadn't told me she was spending some time with you, I'd planned to show up myself."

"She told me you were concerned. Sorry for all the worry." Kit let out a light laugh.

Dwight didn't smile back. "Kit, are we ever going to have some time just for us again? I feel like life has been so topsy-turvy these past few weeks. Ever since Alexandra announced wanting to sell the mansion, nothing has been quite the same."

Kit fixed her gaze on him, blinking and nodding lightly. "It seems once – what's his name, that artist guy? Once he came to town, you haven't been the same. You avoid me. We don't get together like we used to. Only when there's work involved. Don't think you can fool me, Kit. I know when I'm being snubbed, even though you act nice, like nothing's happened."

Shifting uncomfortably in her chair, she cleared her throat and tugged lightly at her collar. She twisted a little in her chair, adjusting her blouse. The room had become warm all of a sudden. "Listen, Dwight, it's true. Steven and I have seen each other a little. I really can't say what will happen. Pretty much, we're just friends." She nearly choked on the words.

They'd moved fast, Steven and her, based on her conservative opinion regarding intimacy and relationships. The chemistry between them flowed without effort, as if they'd been together for a long time. Neither had to think, but just do, moving along with each other in a tide of unexplained urgency, engaging with such intensity as if an invisible time clock ticked away, and the sharp dinging of the bell would end the dream. No matter how hard she tried to convince herself that Steven was a stranger, he didn't fit the category where her heart was concerned, and this left her stymied. Why so cautious with Dwight and not so with Steven? Now she was glad she'd taken things so slowly with her co-worker. The decision lessened the blow.

Dwight broke the silence. "I found a way to get rid of that damned skull. Irene has a friend who wants it."

Kit shuddered. "Be my guest. I sure as hell don't want it, and the quicker you can get it to Irene's weird friend, the better."

"Now that we've received donation promises from the community, when do you plan on getting donated items from the merchants? We still have that to do. Do you want me and Irene to help?"

"No." Kit's eyes turned up to his. "I can handle the merchants on the square and the ones on the side streets. That'll be easy and shouldn't take long. I'll take a day during work to do that. You and Irene could check out the other merchants in Windham Springs."

"Good, will do," said Dwight. "Irene's still waiting on posters, but they should be here today or tomorrow." His voice held steady, but this time it held a tone of coldness, his struggle to keep the conversation civil at best. Kit decided she wanted this conversation to end. Enough for one day.

"I think we're nearly done with this. We'll have an artisan sale, like Irene and I talked about, and I think that will wrap things up." She shook her head, grabbing up her pen and shuffling some papers on her desk. "I'll be so glad when all this rushing is over. It's so tiresome."

Dwight got up from his chair. "Me, too, but all this will be worth it in the long run."

When he left the office, Kit viewed her calendar. She'd work tomorrow on the merchants, and Steven was number one on her list. But no matter how much she tried focusing on her work for the remainder of the day, the issue with Dwight still bothered her. How long would it take to get over him?

* * *

"Well, now, I'm glad you asked. I'd love to donate something to a good cause." Steven had come out from behind the counter, smiling when Kit came through the door. He stood in front of her, happy like he'd just won a million dollars. He also planted a succulent kiss on her lips and hugged her in his arms before walking to one side of the room. "So, which painting would you like?"

"Oh, dear, Steven, I wouldn't even know where to begin. I know I definitely want one that you did. I mean, do you carry works by other artists in here?"

"Nope, just me." He turned back around and placed an arm around her shoulder while they studied the paintings in more detail.

"How about that naked lady?" Kit giggled.

He scrunched up his nose. "No, I don't think so. As much as I like it, I don't think nudity would be suitable for an auction."

"Why not? We have people around here who appreciate the human body for what it is."

He grinned. "Eh, bodies, they come, they go. What can I say?"

Kit let out a huff. "Well, you're mighty cavalier about your own work."

"I'm just kidding. I like bodies. Honestly, I'd have more fun painting this one standing next to me." He lowered his face and kissed her again. "Would you ever let me paint you like that?"

She opened her mouth in surprise and shrank back in horror. "No, I'd never let you do that! Not in a million years!"

"Never? Up in your apartment? Alone? Just the two of us?" He laughed. "C'mon, surely you're not that shy."

"Surely I am, thank you very much." After slipping an arm around him, she motioned back toward the wall. "Okay, naked lady's out. What else ya got?"

"Why don't I let you have *The World*?"

"What? Which one?" She blinked, thinking a moment before clapping a hand to her forehead. "Oh, yes, that one, the one with the hands holding the Earth."

"Yeah, that one!" He mocked her in a teasing tone of voice, and took few steps toward the painting. "Do you want me to give this to you now?"

"Mmm, you know what, I hadn't thought about that part. I don't guess I'll be collecting things literally, will I?"

"Not unless you have some mighty big arms." He pulled her close, lifting her face up to his. "Why don't you pick a day, and all of us can deliver our goods to you at the mansion? That way you'll have everything when you set up for the carnival."

"Do you like the idea of the traditional Venetian carnival?"

"Are you kidding? I love the idea. I think you'll have one hell of a smashing event."

"You'll come, won't you?" Her eyes searched his.

He hesitated. "I guess so. Don't you have to be invited or something? This sounds like a fancy, uppity gig to me, kind of like those charity balls you see featured on the society pages of a high-end magazine."

Kit ran a hand up and down his back. "How about you and I attend this together? And that way you can see how well your painting sells."

"Or won't. People may not like it, may not get it." His fingers slipped into her hair, taking up small locks, and letting them fall gently back into place.

She snuggled closer to him. "You might get lots of money for it."

"*You'll* get lots of money for it. Aren't you raising money for the house?"

"True. So yes, I hope we get lots of money for it." She rested her head in the nape of his neck. For a moment, she wished they were back at her apartment. Maybe she needed to reconsider the offer of being painted in the buff. Too bad she wasn't adept with a brush so she could paint him.

"Have you been to any of the other merchants, yet?" He cradled her head in his hands. "If you want, I could come with you and help out. All I have to do is put a note on the door that I'll be gone for an hour. Then I'll have to come back."

"Are you getting some good business since you've opened?" Kit's eyes scanned one side of the room, then the other. All the walls were covered now, showing canvases with all kinds of themes. Some showed animals, people, while others touted more abstract or philosophical subjects.

"Um, yes." He looked around the shop too. "I do get email requests for pics. I do private showings, or I'll take several pieces to a client's home if they can't come here."

She stood and listened while gazing at the painting of *The World*. As odd as this one seemed, he'd done a masterful job of setting up the image, applying the colors, and adding touches to make the work significant in the way he intended. Yes, it would be a wonderful addition for the auction.

"Would you like me to donate a second painting for the auction? Perhaps something a little more traditional?"

"I couldn't ask you to do that. Offering one is more than generous. These paintings took a lot of time and hard work, I imagine."

"I don't normally give away my work, but for you and your noble cause, I'll make an exception." He inched his face close to hers.

She closed her eyes and rested her head against him, the warmth from his cheek warming hers. His words flirted with a 'come hither' tone, soft and mesmerizing, leaving her almost spellbound. Why couldn't they just hang out here in his shop for a while longer? Better yet, why couldn't they forgo collecting other peoples' belongings and just head on back to her apartment and take care of business, complete with wine and a good fire?

He loosened his grip around her and pulled back. "I guess if you've got work to do, you'd better get on it. You sure you don't want me to come with you?" His smile, the one rivaling the sun, spilled across his lips.

"I bet you've met most everybody here on the square by now, haven't you?"

"I bet I haven't. I keep mostly to myself, working, working, working." He winked.

"Then, let's get you out some so you don't become stale and moldy."

He gave the tip of her nose a soft kiss. "I don't worry about it that much. Stale and moldy is usually par for the course for me."

Kit shook her head and chuckled. "C'mon, let's go."

"Let me put a note on the door." He ran behind the counter and scribbled a quick note. "There, that oughta do it." Leading her by the hand, Steven headed for the door, where he taped the paper in place. "After you." Kit stepped outside first.

A twist of the key in the lock, and the two of them walked over to the next shop. Each merchant around the square promised items for the auction. Kit remembered she still had a few families she had missed in the neighborhood, so a brisk walk and knocks on doors garnered more success. Families offered all sorts of fine collectibles they didn't want any longer, or simply wanted out of their attics. Secretly, she wondered how far above their means some of these families lived. How much longer would the money hold out for many of them? At the moment, she didn't care much. As long as she got her treasured auction items and kept the Historical Society in its present location, nothing else mattered. Nothing else except Steven.

CHAPTER 11

Kit shut the apartment door, Steven having already passed inside. He made his way over to the sofa and settled down. The weekend had come again. After *Celestial Temptation* closed, they watched the golden hues of the afternoon slip quietly to the pastel purple of evening, with the charcoal night taking its rightful place before another day slipped into motion. A quick dinner at *JJ's Grille* left them satisfied and content. While placing Steven's jacket in her bedroom, she took advantage of the opportunity to change and freshen up.

Tucked away inside a dresser drawer reserved for lingerie, she spied a little strappy baby blue tank top and matching boy short bottoms she'd purchased a couple of weeks ago. She slipped from the clutches of her street clothes and into the baby soft fabric, admiring how it felt against her skin. Standing in front of the mirror, Kit gave herself the once-over, making sure everything looked in place. Something was missing, and she stood a few extra seconds determining what it was.

The heart necklace hadn't been touched since she'd replaced it back in the box, but tonight, thoughts of that particular piece of jewelry gripped her hard. The more she studied her reflection, the more the image of the heart nestling in the hollow of her throat seemed as natural as anything else she might wear tonight. Wearing it made all the sense in the world right now. She cautiously opened the drawer holding the jewelry box and removed the necklace. The gold metal rested cold and easy in her hand as she held the piece with some trepidation, almost expecting it to combust. Should she wear it or not? Would Steven like it? The jewelry won. With quick, nimble fingers, she fastened the piece around her neck.

She looked forward to the evening. Steven's presence acted as rain to a parched garden. Every moment with him awakened something new in her body, mind, and in many ways, her spirit. Nestled in his arms, she discovered a certain peace. Each passing minute, pressed against him, drew her deeper into another realm. Smiling at herself, she turned away from the mirror and walked back to the living room.

"Cute outfit. Shows off all the important things I like most about you." Steven grinned, staring at her as she approached and sat down beside him. "I like your necklace too." His eyes fixated on the piece as he fingered the heart. The touch of his fingers against her throat sent a jolt of heat radiating through her, and for a moment, fear set in. What if the heart burned again? How would she explain this to him? The notion of such a possibility set her on edge. She flinched slightly.

Steven broke his gaze, landing a quick, juicy kiss on her neck. "I had a great time tonight. *JJ's* has some great food."

"The square has some of the best dining and shopping. I honestly think it's the most highly kept secret in Windham Springs."

His eyes glinted in the dim light. "Do you want me to start a fire? It's kind of chilly in here." He picked at one of the straps on Kit's top, sliding it back over her shoulder.

"Sounds good. You know where everything is. Since we didn't have dessert, I'll get us a little something sweet to nibble on."

Within minutes, the couple found themselves in front of a friendly fire, with glasses of wine, a fondue pot of chocolate, and a companion bowl of fruit within easy reach.

She watched as Steven picked up a skewer and speared a plump pineapple chunk. After dipping the fruit into the pot, he popped the bite into his mouth. He closed his eyes and smiled. "Mmm, this is so good. What a great idea."

"I thought we might enjoy this, something we haven't done yet." Before she could snare a piece out of the bowl, he'd re-loaded the skewer and aimed for the pot. This time, he propelled a drenched bite of apple toward her mouth. "You're right, this is good." Smiling and licking her lips, she returned the favor a couple of times, feeding him some melon and then a strawberry. After several more bites, they sank down on the floor, sipped wine, and watched the flames for a while.

Steven, relaxed from the wine and food, stretched out and rested his head in Kit's lap. He reached up, gently moving a finger across her lips. "I love coming over here. I love being with you."

Her cheeks warmed at his touch. She gazed down and, as she had often done with Austin, ran her fingers through his hair. In one startling instant, her mind shot back in time with such force and clarity, she saw Austin's face between her hands instead of Steven's. Instead of the piercing look from a man with maturity and inner wisdom, it was Austin's eyes she beheld, filled with waning innocence and the lusty anticipation of youth.

"Hey." Steven snapped his fingers. "Come back."

"Sorry." She blinked a few times. While clearing her mind, she traced along his jaw line, finally dropping her face over his to give him a light kiss on the lips. "My mind just wandered a bit, that's all."

He pulled himself free and sat up. "What do you think about when your mind wanders? Where were you just now?"

Kit sat in silence. Did she really want to answer that question? "Oh, I don't know. Nowhere, really."

"Fine, don't tell me, then." He pushed her down on the floor, pinning her hands over her head, grinning as he kissed her earlobe.

She giggled, hoping to make light of the situation, but mostly to hide her welling discomfort. "What about you, Steven? Where does your mind wander off to at times? I'm sure you have moments like that too."

"You're right. I do. Lately, I'm finding myself thinking a lot about the past. I'm at a point in my journey where I'm taking an accounting of myself, where I've been, and where I need to go." His face nearly touched hers.

Kit gazed up into his eyes. So soulful they were, almost wistful. "Steven, do you ever have moments in your life when the past starts creeping up on you again, suddenly, out of the blue?"

His eyes remained expressionless, but she knew he listened with the acuity of a hunting hound. He always did, taking in his surroundings, paying close attention.

"I must be going through one of those phases where I'm thinking back to days when I was younger, when life was just starting out, and everything seemed fresh and exciting."

"Does your life not feel fresh and exciting anymore?" He released her hands, smoothing his palm over the left side of her waist and over her abdomen. The soft, rhythmic movements of his hands settled her back into a new comfort level, and words fell a little freer than before.

"You'd think with a great job and living here and having the friends I do, everything would be perfect and settled, but something's ..." She stared off into space for a moment.

His hands slipped inside the cotton bottoms and around her buttocks. As his fingers rubbed against her cool skin, nice and easy, the hot sensation of his touch warmed her all over.

"What's missing, then? Or what is it you're looking for?" His face relaxed into a thoughtful expression.

"I don't know." She glanced back at him. He wore a serene look, and his eyes showed understanding.

"Why are you thinking about old times? Is it about a specific time or someone in particular?" His hands rubbed a little faster, sometimes grazing his nails gently over her flesh. She closed her eyes, melting at his touch, but part of her wanted to run away.

His question startled her, scared her. She didn't want to go there, not now, not with him. "I think it's what you said, being at the crossroads in your life." She smiled at him. "I like that answer, and I think it sums everything up pretty well." Good, she'd held her ground. "But you know what they say about the past. It's over and done. You can't change it."

"Do you really believe everything is so final like that?" His words came out soft, reflective.

She didn't answer.

"Enough talk. Sometimes it's better to enjoy the present." His lips came down on hers with a series of earnest kisses, beginning soft and tender, and building to a crescendo so strong she feared she'd drown.

The air became charged with a new excitement. Sliding his hands underneath, he removed her top. When he hooked his fingers over the waistband of her shorts, she lifted her hips. He stripped off the bottoms, leaving her bare before him. She reached with eager anticipation for the zipper of his jeans as he whisked off his shirt. He finished the job of ridding himself of his remaining clothes.

They both lay naked. In the stillness of the room, their breaths came in rapid succession. Without wasting another second, he propped himself up and used his fingers to take note of each curve and crevice her body possessed. He let her do the same to him, resting easily on his back, letting her fingers explore every inch of him, especially the wondrous parts that made him male. The touch of her fingers on his sensitive flesh encouraged the lust burning in his eyes, and the lingering glow of pleasure on his face pushed her to please him more.

"You're so beautiful." His words fell out in a whisper, and his eyes gleamed as they drank in every bit of her. "I wish I could stay here with you forever, the two of us, just like this."

Her head landed softly against his chest. "Me too."

The fire had reached full swing, with lapping flames, giving off a small crack of relief every now and then. Feeling the full effects of the wine, Kit loosened up more. Better yet, her mind had slowed down to a pace where it absorbed every sound and touch in this moment. Steven pulled her on top of him, both engaging in full-body contact.

The sound of his heart beat loud and clear into her ear. She thought of nothing else but the two of them together, basking by the fire. Within moments she became limp, letting herself fall heavier into him. Her pelvic area, in full contact with his, felt warm and soothed, instead of pounding with the raw arousal she normally experienced. A tingling sensation filled her abdomen and heart, working its way up to her throat. At one point, she swore she sensed it in her head. How strange, yet wonderful. She'd never felt such peace and contentment before, and she barely breathed for fear this experience would simply vanish, and she'd find herself alone as if waking from a dream. Several minutes passed as they lay together like this, each one absorbing the essence of the other.

Just as she lulled herself into what might have been some elementary form of a transcendent state, an image of Dwight came barging in, disrupting her whole mindset. For a micron of a second, the unhappiness on his face when they'd broached the subject of their own relationship blared in her mind. The vision ended as fast as it had come, but left her swimming in a sea of dismay. She squeezed her eyes tighter and took a few deep breaths, trying desperately to refocus.

After several minutes, she gave up, unable to continue enjoying herself. Try as she might to focus on Steven's heartbeat or something else, her mind kept wandering back to Dwight and what it would be like to feel his naked body next to hers, how his hands would grace her skin as her fingers fluttered over him. She squeezed her eyes shut, hoping to shut her mind down. Self-consciousness had set up house in her mind, with guilt playing the part of an uninvited guest. In one last-ditch effort to break the horrible spell of Dwight's image, she lifted her head and stared down at Steven.

"What's wrong?" He opened his eyes.

"Nothing." She smiled down at him.

In the firelight she detected the way he studied her, trying to determine if he believed her or not. Did he sense doubt? Instead, he gave her an easy, reassuring grin. "Being together like this is total perfection, isn't it?"

She nodded. "Couldn't agree more."

Their eyes locked. The longer they held each other, the more the carnal ache grew stronger, and each one begged the other with silent words. They wanted each other. His smile softened, and the light in his eyes showed tenderness and caring. He turned his attention to pleasuring her, rubbing and massaging over sensitive areas, ending with a gentle squeeze every now and then where it mattered most, setting her body on fire. Like a flower opening up its petals in the golden morning sun, she responded to his touch, her body igniting in a fury of blissful heat. A hard ache swelling deep inside threatened to send her into a temporary state of madness, and she silently prayed for him to still the pleasure pain, lest she cry out in desperation. He slid his fingers into the warmest, most sacred part of her. The rhythmic movements against her flesh acted like a tonic, soothing her into a deeper state of tranquility.

She concentrated on nothing but his touch, the way he teased the hidden parts of herself, the way he derived joy from seeing her happy and content. In a grand finale of finesse and great care, his fingers nudged and danced over the most sensitive part of her feminine region, and he smiled as she lost herself in a moment of passion.

When the climax stopped, he leaned over and kissed her, kissed the heart pendant. But it was his turn now. The yearning in his eyes spoke the same language as hers. He reclined back. The fluttering touches of her fingers in all the right places brought a smile to his lips. Beneath his skin, muscles quivered as she caressed and teased the velvety soft flesh, the masculine part every man treasures the most.

Viewing his closed eyes and tightening jaw line, she sank deep into the heart of anticipation, joining him on the journey to his release, the free-fall, where time remained suspended, and the body rejoiced, vibrant and vital. Every touch from her, pushing him closer to the edge, gave her a sense of gentle power. He sucked in his breath: Then came the fall. As he drowned in his own ecstasy, she marveled at the sight of him, strong, yet vulnerable.

They cuddled in each other's arms. The flames in the fireplace reached a dull glow, and a light chill had settled over the room. At last Kit stood up and reached out to Steven. "Let's go to bed. It's late."

* * *

Carnival night was a little over three weeks away, and Kit had managed to set up an artisan sale. She'd also managed to obtain more signatures she needed for the Commission, taking three days from work to visit nearby towns. Her on-line petition had helped gather seventy-five names she needed. She needed thirty-five more to reach her goal.

Time ticked on, and she scrambled to rise to the occasion, using every resource at her disposal. Dwight had driven her to the garage to pick up her car. With her beloved vehicle restored, she'd driven to neighboring towns in search of interested participants. She'd spent time on the phone, calling crafting organizations and artisan shops in hopes the word would get out.

In the end, hard work paid off. The Stothwell Mansion found itself surrounded by artisans and costumers set up in booths on the front lawn. Hit with a little warmer weather and bright sunshine, people came out to the square to shop. Outside on the lawn, a huge sign read 'Save Our Historical Society.' Some of the other society members paraded down the sidewalks of the square, holding smaller signs with similar wording, taking time to answer questions from passersby. The lawn held booths filled with stunning, colorful masks, each one constructed with ornate scrollwork, gilt surfaces, and elaborate decorations. Some masks were quite simple, while others reflected the image of a bird or jester.

Other booths contained glitzy beaded jewelry, various accessories, and costumes, creating a fine selection of lavish capes, flowing robes, tunics, and frilly jabots. Some of the more ambitious seamstresses had constructed intricate, flamboyant gowns and suits for would-be party-goers with deeper financial pockets.

Kit and Irene, in the meantime, busied themselves inside the mansion, lining up auction items brought in by community members.

"Wow, there's some nice things in here." Irene picked up a handsome Rosenthal nude figurine, admiring the beautiful simplicity of the woman, sitting on her haunches and staring heavenward. "Who would ever want to part with this piece?" She ran her finger over the smooth porcelain surface.

Kit stood over a set of fine Havilland china, cooing over the delicate floral motif. "And I love this."

Both ladies surveyed the room they'd selected for housing the items until carnival night. Each donation had been labeled with the name of the person or merchant who'd owned it. They had determined to spend some time after the auction writing thank-you notes to each contributor, including the dollar amounts from the final bid on the donated item. This way, each person knew how much they'd helped the Historical Society.

"Excuse me, do I leave this here?" A man entered the room, holding a painting.

"Steven!" Kit skirted through several items to reach him, and greeted him with a quick kiss on the lips. "You brought it."

"I promised you I would." He smiled as she took the painting.

Irene stood in a designated corner of the room and quickly filled out a slip of paper with the name of the shop and his name as the artist. She walked over and grabbed the painting from Kit and placed it against the wall in a vacant spot. "Oh goodness, Steven, is this one of yours?"

He smiled over at Irene. "Yeah, I did that one. It's a little strange, but I thought someone might like it."

"This is great! I love it. What's it supposed to represent?" Irene gave Kit a quick wink and turned back to study the painting in more detail.

Steven walked over and stood next to her. "It's supposed to represent *The World*, one of the major arcana cards in a tarot deck."

"Do you use or understand tarot cards? Are you into spirituality?" She perused him up and down as he spoke.

"You might say I'm into spirituality – in more ways than one – and I'll leave it at that." He turned and smiled at her.

Irene narrowed her eyes, nodding. "Well, it's a lovely piece of work, and I'm sure it will fetch a mighty fine price."

"I hope so. It'll be nice to help raise money for a good cause." He focused his attention on Kit, who'd sidled up and placed her arm around him. "Looks like you got a great turnout. I saw all kinds of people milling around out there."

"Are they buying anything? I really want the vendors to do well so this day will be worth their while."

Steven nodded. "There were several people carrying bags, so I guess so."

"We don't have *our* costumes yet." Slipping an arm through his, she rested her head against his shoulder.

"What say we head outside and get ours?" He turned and gave her a quick kiss on the lips. Irene suddenly cleared her throat.

"Hi there, Dwight." She whirled back around, facing Kit with an 'Oh-my-god-look-who's-here' grin. "Did you finally pick out a neat mask? Looks like there's some mighty nice ones from what I've seen."

Dwight stood in the doorway, face red, glaring at Kit and Steven. As she read the dismay on Dwight's face, she wished the floor would just magically swallow her up. He held a beautiful mask in his hands, a painted orange one, depicting a human Jack-O-Lantern face. Around the eyes, a circle of painted black webbing gave the face a diabolical look, and the orange sparkles on top added a party-like flair. He said nothing, but walked over to Irene, who'd distanced herself from the couple, and struck up a conversation.

Kit pulled Steven to the door. "Come on, let's get out of here and see what's outside."

She silently cursed herself for being so careless. So much for the 'we're just friends' routine she'd given him earlier. One thing remained at the top of her to-do list, and that was getting away from Dwight.

Outside the mansion, a shot of fresh air cleared her head. She and Steven spent a good deal of time wandering around the different booths, chatting with the artists, and getting familiar with the merchandise. Finally, Steven pulled Kit in front of one booth to look at a spectacular mask, painted silver on one side and covered with scroll-like cutouts. The other side, a beautiful color of indigo, held no decorations. Grommets accented the eyes, making them stand out. Overall, the mask held a cosmic look, something Kit couldn't quite grasp.

"You like this one?" She touched her fingertip lightly over the surface.

"I think I do." Steven picked up the mask, examining the decorations. "If I wear a billowy head-covering and a silken robe of some kind, I think I can pull off a pretty cool look."

"I think so too. But before you get this one, don't you think you should look around a little more, see if there's something else you might like better? After all, if we make this an annual celebration, then you'll want a mask you really like since you'll be wearing it each time."

At once, her thoughts turned toward the future as she envisioned with anticipation moments like this one. There would be plenty of parties and bright spots in their lives, each one shining like a brilliant star as she and Steven intertwined their threads of individual existence into one strong, cohesive fabric of enduring love.

The unexpected flash of sorrow in his eyes and silence as a response sent a chill down her spine, leaving a dull sadness hitting hard at her heart. Why had he not agreed with her? Where had his enthusiasm gone? Surely he wasn't so easily spooked by references to the future. A cool breeze blew, rustling the ribbons on the mask. Steven glanced back down to his hands. In an instant, he brightened up, wearing his usual warm smile.

"I think I really like this one. I've panned the place, and nothing jumped out at me like this one did."

"Okay." Haunted by Steven's hesitation and forced smile in reference to future events, she tried to perk up and not view his behavior with such an analytical mind. She smiled back. "Then I'd go ahead and get it before someone else snatches it up." She pushed him closer to the young lady behind the table, who manned the cash box. "I think he wants to buy this one."

"Great choice." The lady got up from her chair and reached across the table for Steven's money, which he'd withdrawn from his wallet. "I remember making this mask, and how I just fell in love with it when I finished." She glanced at him. "Do you have an idea of what you're going to wear with it?"

"I think I have some ideas rolling around in my head."

"Great. I'm sure whatever you do, you'll look like a million bucks. Thanks so much for buying it." The lady gave him change, wrapped up the mask, and handed it to him.

The couple spent the next hour roaming over the lawn several more times, Kit being undecided on what to buy. All the masks held their own charm and unique display of artistic creativity, making the choices more difficult. Steven pulled her over to one booth, and pulled off a mask from a display stand.

"How about this one? I think a cat would be great for you, Kit, like a kitty cat." He handed her the mask.

"How cute! Or pretty, I should say." She inspected the mask, depicting the face of a cat. A crackled antiqued cream finish covered the surface, and black lacy cutouts adorned the ears, one side of the cheek, and underneath the nose. Crystal flat backs, artfully placed, sparkled in the light.

"Let me see. Put it up to your face." He tipped his head from side to side. "I think this one suits you. You can be my kitty cat."

Kit giggled. "Meow! Do I look funny, or what?" She pulled her hand down. "So you really like it?"

"I love it. Like you told me, better get it before somebody else snatches it up."

"I guess you're right. We've gone all over this place, and this one's as cute as anything else I've seen."

The artist, a heavy-set, older woman working the booth, sauntered up. "You like my cat mask?" She smiled, showing off a full row of big, white teeth. "This one is my favorite. You don't see many like it."

"You know what, I think you're the only one who has a cat mask." Steven took the piece and handed it to the lady. "This is Kit, the conservation manager for the Historical Society. I'm trying to tell her she needs this one because it reflects her name."

The lady opened her mouth in surprise. "Well, you don't say! Nice to meet you." She held out a plump hand, which Kit accepted and gently shook. "Tell you what I'll do. I'm going to do a manager's deal for you and give you fifteen percent off. How about that?"

"Oh, I wouldn't dream of you doing that. You worked so hard on this." Kit reached over the table and patted the lady's hand.

"Honey, I'd love nothing better than to give you a deal. With all the hard work you do, trying to save beautiful homes and such." She gave her hand a light flutter up and down. "You deserve this piece if anyone does."

Kit returned a smile filled with gratitude. "Well, thank you. I'm just hoping all of you are selling well so you can make some money too."

"Doll, we're all happy to be here. This gave us a chance to put our minds to work and do something different." The woman turned and looked around. "I think people are having a good time, and the sales have been pretty good." She took Kit's money and wrapped up the mask.

"Thank you so much." Kit accepted her new piece, and she and Steven turned around to leave.

"What about costumes? Don't we need something to wear?" He stood and surveyed the lawn.

"I guess you're right. We do need something. I don't
have extra clothing or costumes hanging around in my closet
or filling up my drawers at home." Kit latched on to his hand
and headed toward one of the booths, where several pieces of
clothing hung from hangers attached to grid wall. "I've been
eying these for a while." She fingered a black robe, rubbing
over the silky finish. "I don't have the extra cash to buy one
of those heavy-duty Elizabethan gowns that I'd really like,
but something simple would work just as well."

Steven flipped over a price tag attached to an ornate suit
with a ruffled top. "Yeah, I hear you on that one. I think
something simple would work for me too." He moved over to
the back of the booth, and removed a colorful top and
breeches from a rack of clothing.

The owner came over to assist. "I have stockings to
match that outfit, if you're interested in it." The older
gentleman smiled and pointed over to a table filled with an
assortment of scarves, gloves, and stockings. "Do you have
your mask with you? Maybe I can help you pick out
something."

Kit, satisfied someone was helping Steven, concentrated
on making a final selection. She pored over the clothing,
rifling through all the robes and capes, one by one. For
several minutes, time lost its essence. The interest of culling
through the costumes pulled her into the moment, and she'd
become oblivious to everyone and everything. The sound of
someone moving close by attracted her attention, and she
turned around to look up.

Her heart nearly stopped. Only a few feet away, a man entertained himself pulling out certain articles of clothing and holding them up against his body, only to return them back to the rack. Though his back faced her, the height and blond hair reminded her of the delivery person who'd brought the hateful package. If only she could be sure. Kit moved over, hiding behind a mannequin sporting full costume regalia. She lingered and watched, praying he'd turn around enough so she could see his face.

She got her wish. He'd grown bored with the clothes and began roving over the accessories on the table. No mistake about it, the deliveryman, now dressed in old jeans and a sweatshirt, stood only a few feet away! Filled with a surge of panic, she slipped out from behind the mannequin, turning her face away, and scrambled from the booth. In a fit of desperation, she ran for the nearest crowd. Another booth several yards away afforded her the opportunity to blend into the middle of a small group who'd gathered at a table loaded with beaded jewelry. Taking a deep breath, she turned around. At least she didn't see him anywhere else. Most likely he was still shopping in the same booth.

Why was this man here, and how long had they been in the same area? Did he see her first and come in just to spy some more? Surely his inquisitive nature hadn't translated into stalking someone. Kit tried to reason with herself. Maybe running into him was mere coincidence. After all, the sale and carnival were public events, barring no one. The touch on her shoulder startled her, and she whirled around.

"There you are. Why did you leave so fast?" Steven wrapped an arm around her. "One minute I was talking with the owner, and the next thing I know, you're sneaking off."

She pressed her lips close to his ear. "You're not going to believe this, but I just saw the same guy who brought me my package."

Steven stared at her, face void of emotion.

"The same dude who came to my office with that horrible package was standing nearly right next to me."

"He's here? Are you sure?" His face reflected disbelief.

"I'm one hundred percent sure. He turned around just enough for me to catch sight of his face." Kit hugged Steven close. "I know for a fact it was him. I'd know him anywhere."

"So, what do you want to do?"

She scowled. "Not sure at the moment. I'm trying to rack my brain and hope that it's nothing more than him wanting to check out the events."

Steven gazed out across the lawn. "I've learned over time that nothing is coincidence. You may be right, he wants to check things out and see what's going on."

"Well, I wish he'd just stay away from me. I personally don't think he was in that booth to buy some fancy costume for an event he's most likely not attending." Kit shielded her eyes from the bright afternoon sun and scanned the crowds.

"Maybe so, but who knows what this guy's up to, or who's getting him to do what? He may be a fall guy or being used as a puppet."

Kit tapped Steven's arm. "Oh, boy, there he is. Look."

Several yards away, near another booth closer to the mansion, stood the figure of a man.

To the casual eye, he didn't appear to have a care in the world, watching people as they filed by. In Kit's opinion, however, he checked out the others with the sole purpose of finding her. She bounced lightly on her feet, impatient to leave again. "Don't let him see us!"

"What on earth are you doing?" Steven craned his neck around as she scurried behind him.

"I don't want him to know I'm here."

"Hey, I've got an idea. We have some masks we can wear so nobody will know who we are. Why don't we just put them on and practice for the carnival?" His lips twitched into a wicked grin. "I'll wear mine if you'll wear yours."

She swatted him on the arm. "Stop that. No teasing."

With a laugh, he pulled her along, away from the crowd.

"Stop! What are you doing?" Kit staggered a little before tightening her grip on his arm, and dug her heels into the ground.

"Come on, we're going to get costumes. Let's go back where we were before." With a light tug, he wrenched her loose.

"We can't go back there. He'll find us."

Steven gathered her in his arms and stood her in front of him. From the look in his eyes, she knew he meant business. "Kit, he's gone. I don't think he'll be back at that other booth again. Let's go."

Swallowing hard, she blinked a few times and took a deep breath. "Okay, if you're sure."

"Of course, I'm sure. That man has no reason to go back to that booth. If his only objective was to scope out the place, I doubt he's here to buy. He came, he saw, he's done."

"Let's do it fast, then. I don't want to hang around here much longer."

His face softened. "We'll make this quick." With an arm looped through hers, he led them back to the previous vendor.

"Well, well, I wondered if you'd be back. You two ran out in a hurry." The gentleman got up from a chair and walked over to them.

With a glance at Kit, Steven managed a quick, save-face reply. "Sorry about that. My girlfriend here apparently saw an old friend of hers, and had to chase her down to say hi."

The gentleman shrugged. "Not to worry. I understand."

"We saw some things we wanted to buy." She walked over to the rack of clothing and pulled down a simple black robe with a ruffled collar. "I liked this when I saw it last."

"Nice choice. It's simple, so you can add more accessories to it if you like." The man reached out for the robe and began to write up a ticket. "Is there anything else you'd like to go with it, or are you wanting to keep it simple?"

She shook her head. "No, thank you. Just the robe."

Steven came up beside her, holding a white robe with pleated, puffed sleeves. "And I think I'll take this one."

The owner looked up at him in surprise. "Oh, you've decided against some of the tops and bottoms we looked at earlier?"

"I think it's better to keep it simple so we can dress everything up more later on."

"Don't blame you, sir. A lot of people like all that accessorizing." He took Steven's robe and placed it on the table alongside Kit's. "Will this be together or separate?"

"Put everything on one ticket. I'll pay for it."

"You can't be serious!" She grabbed his hand. "Steven, that's too much. I can pay for my own."

"Ignore her. I'm buying." He motioned for the gentleman to place everything in one bag and removed his wallet from the back of his jeans.

"So, are the two of you dressing up as a duo of some kind?"

Kit answered. "No, I don't think so, but we have two of the neatest masks around."

The man kept scribbling the item descriptions and prices on the tickets as he chatted. "There are some incredible masks out here today. I'm the guy with the sewing machine and fabric rather than the sculptor with paper, paint, and cardboard. I guess it takes all kinds." He smiled and gave Steven the ticket.

When Steven paid for everything, he turned to Kit and kissed her on the lips. "I think we have everything now. Let's grab a bite for lunch. I'm starved."

"Agreed! And then it's back to work I go." She clasped a hand around his, following as he led the way to *JJ's*. If only she could rid herself of thoughts about the deliveryman. Most of all she wanted to vanquish the uneasiness about Steven welling up in her mind.

CHAPTER 12

"Have you seen Dwight at all since the artisan sale?" Irene sat in Kit's office, enjoying a cup of hot tea.

Kit made a few flourishes with a pen on a couple of sheets of paper, and threw them into a folder.

"Come to think of it, he's been rather scarce."

"I wonder why?" said Irene, glancing sideways at Kit.

"Well, I don't know. What would be your take on it, Irene?" She threw down her pen and stuck out her tongue.

Irene shook her head a little before taking another sip of tea. "You know he saw everything, the way you and Steven were huddled up, the kiss he gave you."

"It wasn't like we were rolling on the floor, lip-locked and naked." Kit blew out her breath in a huff. "But you're right. I'm busted, though I've tried to be gentle about everything."

"He'll get over it. That's the way it goes, sometimes. You and Dwight were really settling into what looked like a nice relationship. Steven seems nice, but part of me hates to see Dwight go."

Kit wrinkled up her nose. "Steven has taken us all by surprise, it seems. As for Dwight, I miss him. He's a sweetheart."

"I can imagine. All that attention, little back massages, sandwiches, coffee, little frou-frou gifts." Her friend winked and went back to swirling the contents in her cup. "Don't deny it. It's true."

"True, Steven does none of that. And yes, the treats are nice, but I miss Dwight coming in here, hanging out, and us doing things together like we were starting to do."

"It'll all work out. At least everything is set for the carnival. Dwight and I finally got our part nailed down, and I took a day to hang up posters everywhere."

"And the invitations?" Kit quirked an eyebrow at her friend.

"Never to worry. All that has been sent out."

"Good, that's what I like hearing." Kit thought a moment and suddenly clapped a hand over her mouth. "What about decorations? I hadn't really given that a whole lot of thought."

Irene waved her off. "Let's keep it simple. Everyone else will be dressed up. That'll be enough decoration right there. And if I know Dwight, he'll have all those caterers jumping to get the food prepared and presented in the classy way he likes things done."

"He is a classy one, I'll grant you that." Kit stared back at Irene. "That's another trait I like about him. He's a guy who has standards."

Irene polished off her tea. "Couldn't agree more."

"Maybe I ought to take him some coffee as a peace offering. I could let him know that I still would like to at least be friends."

"You could, or you could just not do anything." Irene wagged her foot back and forth in front of her, tapping her fingers against an empty cup. "As much as we both like Dwight, that doesn't mean you've done anything wrong. You have a new boyfriend who seems to adore you, and there's nothing wrong with that. You deserve to be with someone you like."

"Thanks, Irene. I appreciate that comment." Kit bowed her head in gratitude, quickly turning her attention to several sheets of paper on her desk. "Oh, there is something I forgot to tell you. I saw the deliveryman hanging around at the artisan sale. He actually stood a few feet away from me in one of the booths I was in."

Irene's mouth dropped open. "You're kidding!"

"Nope, I'm not kidding. He was within spitting distance, just about."

"What was he doing at the sale? Surely, he wouldn't be thinking about coming to the carnival. I wouldn't think he'd want to pay the price of the tickets, and he sure isn't on the formal guest list. I know everyone on it."

"I think he was spying on me, that's what."

"So, what did you do?"

"I got the hell out of dodge. But Steven made me go back to the booth once the man left. Said he'd most likely not be back."

"Kit, I'd be careful if I were you. Let's just hope this guy gives up or whomever is egging him on will grow bored."

"Yeah, I'm hoping beyond hope." Kit propped her head in her hand, resting easily on the desk. "Do you think Harsh could be behind any of this? Maybe hiring toadies for his dirty work?"

Stifling a yawn, Irene stretched and pulled herself out of the chair. "Who knows? Your car could have been anybody. The skull? That incident is fishy. Anyway, I have some work to finish up. Call me if you ever get scared. I may not be able to come over, but I can at least talk on the phone and help make you feel better."

"You're a true pal, Irene. Thanks, but let's hope I don't have to take you up on that offer."

Irene smiled and headed out of the office.

* * *

Engrossed in her work, Kit glanced up at a shuffling sound in front of her desk. Her eyes landed on a pair of men's slacks, which she followed all the way up until she saw the owner's face. Dwight held out a cup of steaming coffee from *A Cup Above the Roast*. In his other hand, he held a few sheets of paper. The only thing missing was the smile he usually wore when he saw her.

"How sweet of you. You didn't have to do that, but thanks." She put down her pen and took the coffee, sniffing the steam. "Mmm, I always love coffee from there."

Without elaborating further, Dwight seated himself and organized the papers with careful deliberation. "Would you like to help me with this menu? I've got the caterer lined up, so all we need to do is tell them the food we want." He glanced at Kit. "Let me know if you're not interested."

"Of course I'm interested. I needed a break, anyway." She waved her hand toward the vacant chair. "You just sit right down, make yourself all comfy, and we'll go over that menu as much as you'd like." Kit cringed. What was up with the squeaky voice? Definitely overdoing it, trying to sound natural, as if nothing had come between them. He must have noticed it, too, because he flashed her a stony stare as he sat down on the seat. She sank back in her chair, listening.

"I have food lists for the event, one for hors d'oeuvres during cocktails, the main meal, and then dessert."

"Oh, goody, desserts are my favorite." Kit lightly clapped her hands.

"Yes, we couldn't forget dessert." Dwight still hadn't mustered up even a small hint of a grin on his solemn face.

She found the sight of him rather hot, so hoity-toity and business-like that she almost considered coming out from behind her desk and running her hands all over him. Their last time together at his house still lingered in her memory, the way they'd sat close together, filled with the happiness of new lovers. She swallowed hard, stifling her animal urge, hoping he'd lighten up soon. "So what choices do we have, and who's catering this?"

Dwight removed the pen resting behind his ear and gave the lists a studious once-over. "We have lots of choices, and the catering company I'm going with is *The Elegant Epicure.*"

"Fantastic! And they weren't already taken? That's a surprise."

"Yeah, I got lucky. Someone had canceled on our same date, so I grabbed it."

Kit sipped some of her coffee and smiled. He'd brought her *Divine Angel* again. "Let's hear it, then, what are the choices?"

Dwight read through all the lists, while they bantered back and forth about why one choice made more sense and worked better for the event while another didn't. After about an hour and a half of decisions followed by reconsiderations and back again, they finally reached an amiable agreement for all the courses.

"Whew, I'm glad we finally decided. That was hard." She swiped a loose lock of hair straggling over her eye and leaned back in her chair, taking a deep breath.

"You and me both. You'd be a hard one to plan a wedding menu with."

Her eyes popped open, and she took a big gulp. His words threw her into a brief moment of confusion. Did he just say the 'W' word, and in reference to her?

"A wedding?" Her voice barely came out as a whisper.

For the first time, he smiled a little. "Yeah, a wedding. Those are hard to plan too."

With a few deep breaths and few seconds to compose herself, her senses returned. "Lucky you, we're not doing that today."

The intrusive thoughts came again, tumbling through her head, one after the other. In another amorous side trip, she found herself imagining Dwight's hands doing to her what Steven's had done the other night. She envisioned what a honeymoon night with Dwight might be like, tucked away in a cozy mountain cabin, or in their room on a magnificent cruise liner on their way to some exotic island. She pictured the two of them by the fire, feeding each other fruit, and whispering sweet words of endearment into each other's ears. How wonderful it would be in that beautiful designer home of his.

When the mental movie came to the scene where her reclining figure lay open, aching with anticipation, as his long fingers slid into dark, moist places, she dug her fingernails into her palm to stop the psychic projector. Did he have the capacity to please her as much as Steven, in similar ways? Did she have the capacity to stop these thoughts from springing up whenever he came around? Lately, she found herself comparing him to Steven, using an unmerciful pro-con technique where a careful count of numbers led to a final answer.

One thing she knew for sure, Steven's arrival to Windham Springs and their subsequent involvement with each other had opened up a part of herself she'd closed off for quite a while. Their intimacy pushed her to think more about what she wanted out of life, what she wanted out of a prospective mate.

So far, she believed Steven held the winning hand. He knew how to approach her, knew all the right things to say and do. If the soul had windows, he saw straight through, and still seemed to love her. It was like he knew her on some inner level, as if they'd known each other for years. All this struck her as rather odd given how well she and Dwight had always connected. How did Steven have the ability to merely sail into town with nothing more than a smile?

"Kit, are you paying attention?"

She jumped at the sound of Dwight's voice. He'd gone off on another tangent, and she had heard only snatches of words. "Oh, I'm sorry, I guess I was still thinking about the menus."

"Then you're thinking about those menus awfully hard, from the look of concentration on your face. I thought we'd wrapped them up already."

The heat of embarrassment colored her cheeks. "Sorry, I think I'm just tired today. All this planning and worrying is wearing me out."

"No need to stress out. You're doing an excellent job. I'd give myself a pat on the back if I were you." The old dreamy gleam in his eyes had returned.

"You and Irene need to give yourselves a pat on the back. It's hard work trying to find bands and the people to make food for an event like this."

"We've loved every minute of helping you, and now the Society gets to have a permanent home."

"I saw a little bit of the mask you bought. Looked pretty interesting. What was it?"

His eyes clouded over, and his lips flat-lined. She'd have paid all the money in the world to retract such a thoughtless question, given what he'd seen between her and Steven.

He shrugged. "Just an orange mask representing a pumpkin face. Nothing special."

"From what I saw, it looked really neat, Dwight. I bet you'll have a great costume."

"Maybe. I'm sure there'll be lots of fun costumes." He rifled through the menus, pretending to study over them again.

Pandora's Box had been opened, and Kit decided to go with the flow. "Will you still have a dance saved for me?" She grinned, flipping her hair back with a quick flick of her head.

"You'll most likely be too busy to worry about a dance with me. I think you'll have others wanting your attention." The shuffling of the menus became more emphatic.

Kit lightly drummed her fingers on a stack of papers. Trying to regain lost ground with him may prove a losing battle, but she didn't want hurt feelings or animosity on his part to ruin a good working relationship, at least. "No matter how many people are there that night, I want a dance or two with you, Dwight. Can you at least promise me I can have a couple?"

He put the menus down, glanced up, and studied her for a few seconds. "Yeah, sure. I can do that." With a light grunt, he stood up and made his way toward the door.

"Hey, thanks again for the coffee." She winked. "You always know what I like."

His smile, though genuine, contained a hint of doubt. "I try. I really do try."

The sound of his shoes sounding out a dull thud against the wooden hallway floor mimicked the dull ache thudding in her heart. Though she adored Steven, hurting Dwight's feelings was not something she'd ever intended to do. Irene spoke the truth about him getting over it at some point. And yes, right now in her life, she had a boyfriend who seemed to love her, flaws and all.

* * *

The clock on the wall showed five o'clock, signaling the end of another working day. Kit straightened up her desk before grabbing her purse and jacket for the trek back home. Outside, an overcast sky infused the cold with a strong bite as the light wind nipped at her cheeks. In the air, a hint of snow threatened to invade Windham Springs a little earlier than normal. Lights from the coffee shop tempted her to come inside and sip something warm, but spending time alone there tonight held a sense of emptiness and isolation. Irene had already slipped out of the office, and the thoughts of asking Dwight didn't appeal to her, even as friends. He hadn't tried to ask her out anymore, especially since he'd seen her and Steven together. Still, she didn't quite want to head on back home so fast, either.

Across the street inside *Celestial Temptation Gallery*, the large room showed no signs of Steven anywhere. The track lights still illumined the paintings. Perhaps a last-minute customer would slip inside to steal a peek before closing time. How odd she never saw customers milling around in his shop, and none came in during times she'd been there. Irene, on occasion, referenced Steven in conversations, but otherwise acted as if he didn't exist.

Never had Irene suggested she and Steven go out with her and Jim as other couples might do. Somehow, she sensed she'd have better luck in this department if she and Dwight were dating. Of course, Dwight preferred to ignore anyone who stood between him and her getting together. Neither of them seemed all that interested in checking out his paintings in more detail, which struck Kit as unusual. Dwight's home held several unique pieces of art work. Irene expressed great interest in the piece he'd donated to the auction, but never alluded to bidding on it. Perhaps he truly sold more to private customers, as he'd suggested earlier.

She glanced back at the coffee shop, debating what to do next, almost opting to purchase a cup of coffee and a pastry to enjoy later. Her cell phone rang. Kit pulled open the side pocket of her purse and glanced at the display. The number showed up as Alexandra's. Her pulse quickened.

"Hey, Alex. What's up?"

"Hey, Kit. How are you? Haven't talked to you in a bit."

"I'm okay. Anything going on?" From the sound of Alexandra's voice, she hadn't called for idle chit chat.

"Have you had any weird things happen to you lately? Are you okay?"

Kit jerked her head up in alarm. "Why do you ask?"

"After the Commission meeting, Ed Harsh called me a couple of times, really insisting that I talk to you, get you and everybody at the house to let him go ahead with his plans. I simply told him that I was not getting involved in this, and that things needed to pan out with no interference from me."

"Yeah? And what did he say?" Kit turned back around, facing the mansion, glimpsing its facade, barely discernible in the darkness.

"Nothing much after that. Just hung up on me, but get this. When I stepped off my porch earlier today, the stairs broke, like someone had pulled the nails out or removed the supports. Didn't notice anything odd when I came out of the house."

"Did you break an ankle or leg? Do I need to come over?" Kit contorted her face in disbelief.

"No, don't come over. Luckily I just twisted my ankle. It's sore, but not broken. I'll be fine. I'm just a bit spooked by the fall."

Deciding she needed to come clean, she shared with her cousin the incident with the skull and her car.

"Oh my gosh, Kit." Alexandra's tone played out in wailing tones. "Do you want to come stay with me?"

"No, that's okay. Dwight's already offered. From the sound of things, you're not necessarily that safe, either. Let's just ignore this if we can, and get to the business of getting through this party."

"I got my invitation."

"Good. Irene sent you one. You are coming, aren't you? When I get to work tomorrow, I'll email you a list of artisans who sell masks and costumes. Support a local. That's what I always say."

"You bet, honey. I'd love to do that. In the meantime, we'll just keep these shenanigans between us. Don't want to scare anyone, or act like we're afraid. But call me if anything else happens." The voice on the other end of the line had calmed considerably. After another few minutes of idle chatter, Kit ended the call.

Gazing across the street again, she mulled over her next plan of action. Coffee with Steven had seemed like a fun idea. Catching him at his shop on-the-fly would have been nice, but after the conversation with Alexandra, Kit wanted to head on home, unwind, and settle her nerves. She'd focus on the upcoming carnival and how to spruce up the costume for her cat mask. A feeling of pride rushed over her, even in the dismal gloom. The Society had taken the first steps toward purchasing the Stothwell Mansion, acting as pioneers in the effort to secure a permanent home for pursuing their work efforts. The community could also look forward to a glitzy annual event each year, another highlight of things to do in Windham Springs while preserving its history.

With quick steps, eyes focused straight ahead, she moved over the sidewalk toward her apartment. In the distance, the figure of a man caught her attention, and she came to a screeching halt. Something about him looked familiar, too familiar for comfort. His tall, thick frame filled the small space under the awning over the entrance to the building, and he stood close to the front door, holding a brown box under his arm. Turning his head from side to side, he surveyed everything around him before reaching for the doorknob. To her horror, she recognized the man as the one who'd delivered the first package, and the one who had stood nearby in the same booth where she bought her costume. Kit's anger flared. When he saw the intercom panel, he reached out and pressed the button, the one people used to notify her or Mr. Crispin of their arrival. To her dismay, no one answered the door.

Kit's heart sank. Mr. Crispin must have cut out early tonight. If he was in his office, he always accepted packages when she couldn't. Later that night or the next day, he'd deliver them to her. The man looked around once more before leaving the package by the door. Overtaken by a surge of indignation, she ran toward him, clipping along at a more rapid pace, hoping he wouldn't see her right away. She clutched the cell phone in her hand, pausing when she was a few yards away. Her fingers trembled as she touched the app opening up the camera function on her phone. The street lights illuminated the side walk, and the lamplight attached to the building added more light. If she could get his attention and move in closer at the last minute, she could possibly get a shot of his face.

"Hey, you!" She shouted at him, attracting his attention. She'd already focused the camera on his face, and moved her fingers across the phone screen for a close-up. The man jerked his head in her direction, staring, his mouth open in surprise. Ready. Aim. Snap. The flash went off as the camera made the familiar hiss-click sound when capturing an image. "Wait – I want to talk to you!" Her words tumbled out, raspy with a mix of fear and excitement.

The man didn't wait around any longer. He turned on his heel and fled down the street away from Kit, darting around a building and into a small alleyway.

Her voice rang out with a loud screech, her breath rattling in her throat. "Come back here!" She'd rounded the corner, only to hear a door slam. Though it was useless at this distance, she aimed her camera in the direction of a white car and pressed the button, watching helplessly as the vehicle sped off down the alley, made a left, and disappeared into the darkness.

"Damn!" Stamping her foot on the sidewalk in frustration, she clutched her purse and phone tighter. On the phone screen, she pressed the button to bring up her camera roll. The picture of the man's face showed fuzzy features due to poor lighting and distance, but overall better than nothing. The car shot turned out to be useless, but she decided against deleting it because one still made out the image of a car. She headed back to her apartment, viewing the ominous package hidden in the shadows where the man had placed it far back in the corner. Luckily the building had the awning to protect most packages from the elements and to offer a little discretion from prying eyes. Unless someone came to see Kit or Mr. Crispin, most people walked by the door and continued on to the main part of the square to do some shopping. This time Kit would have loved nothing better than to have this box stolen right out from under her. But no such luck. She paused a minute, in a quandary whether to pick up the box or leave it and let Mr. Crispin deal with it. At least she'd have some moral support opening it up in front of him. Then again, morbid curiosity had already inched its way inside her, and there was no turning back now.

Kit picked up the box, reading her name and address neatly typed on the label. Then reality hit her. The deliveryman must have been watching her for a while; how else would he have known where she lived? A brief breeze blew through the air, chilling her to the core. With shaking fingers, she inserted the key into the lock. Usually she looked forward to Mr. Crispin leaving so she'd have the entire building to herself, able to enjoy complete privacy. But now she wished more than ever he'd somehow show up, return to take care of one last bit of business he'd forgotten.

Inside the apartment, she caught her breath, winded from the trek up the stairs. A flick of a switch, and the heat warmed the room. Kit placed the package on the kitchen counter where she simply stared at it for several minutes. This particular box created a higher discomfort level. Because of who delivered it, the box couldn't have held anything good. A quick bite of dinner, and then she'd figure out how to deal with this delivery. In a flurry of excitement – not the good kind – she made a small salad and a sandwich, and carried everything over to the sofa in the living area.

A bottle of wine in the refrigerator held enough for a last generous serving. Her nerves needed a drink strong enough to dull the anxiety gnawing at her belly, but not too much to dull her senses completely. Whatever was going on, she needed full awareness for fighting back, or preparation for the ugliness being dished out. In between bites, she surveyed her apartment, taking in every detail. Up until now, this place called home, this town, had been a refuge, a place for happiness and safety. But now it seemed like the Big Man upstairs wanted to entertain himself by upsetting her apple cart and turning her world upside down. A feeling of doubt seeped in, overshadowing her former confidence. Would obtaining the mansion, the place of her childhood memories, be worth it? Surely the carnival would set the pace for stopping this harassment. The carnival signified intent, commitment. The Society had taken on a tremendous responsibility, one not ending any time soon.

Struck with an idea, Kit scrambled off the sofa and walked to the bedroom where she stored her laptop. While eating, she surfed the Internet for anything on Edmond Harsh. After scrolling down, she spotted his website link and clicked the mouse button.

There he was, a full photo of him, with the same thin, dark hair, eyes giving off that glaring hawk-like glint, and thin lips curled into a light, empty grin. Once thing rang true: nobody could prove Harsh was involved with her receiving packages from a strange deliveryman who seemed hell-bent on avoiding any confrontation with her. But the motive and strange coincidences added up way too much for liking.

She took a long draw from her glass, the alcohol revving up the effects of a light buzz. Harsh's picture glared back at her from her laptop with a haughtiness that mocked everything she sought to achieve regarding the Mansion. The information on the website touted his success as a contractor. He'd apparently made laudable contributions to areas where blight and decay had seeped in. Fine residents and business owners had dribbled out in search of better real estate, leaving behind sagging buildings and landscapes choked with weeds, unruly bushes, and gangly trees. Because of his work, these restored areas now flourished with a vibrant new life, attracting prosperous inhabitants and new merchants with a wonderful assortment of goods and services.

Kit clicked off the browser and closed the laptop, swirling the last taste of wine in her mouth before swallowing. Like it or not, she had to admit old Ed Harsh had his merits. As a conservation manager, anyone who tried to restore, preserve, or revitalize neighborhoods, towns, and cities usually ranked high in her esteem, but Harsh left a bad taste in her mouth, and the way he'd looked at her and Alexandra during the Commission meeting still sent chills down her spine. Why bother the historical district of Windham Springs? Everyone liked the area, and she'd never heard of complaints about it lacking in any way. The square definitely didn't need any revitalizing. Harsh needed to back off and leave her and the staff at the Historical Society alone.

With a new resolve, she made the decision right then and there to continue fighting this battle, this cowardly, unseen intruder to the end. She glanced over her shoulder, back at the kitchen.

The box jeered at her from the counter. After placing the dishes in the sink, she crouched on the floor, pulling out a utility knife from a toolbox under the sink. Taking in a deep breath, she walked over to the box and made a slit in the tape on the top side before prying the flaps apart. When the contents came into view, she let out a loud scream. The knife slipped from her hand, clattering against the floor. Inside, on a pile of small rocks, lay a rattlesnake. It didn't move or try to slither out of the box, but lay there, neatly coiled. The rattle on its tail had been prominently positioned, and the severed head lay next to the top of its body, close to the cut.

She stepped back, blinked a few times, and peeked inside again to make sure this all wasn't a dream. No, her eyes hadn't deceived her. Everything about the lifeless reptile spelled reality, from its stale, cloudy eyes to the forked tongue lolling out of its mouth. This horrific sight turned the skull incident into a silly high school prank. Harsh, or someone out there, meant business.

Kit backed away from the box, tears burning in her eyes, and stole out of the kitchen. For a split second the room spun and she reached out, steadying herself with unsure arms against the wall. Time slowed as she stumbled to her room. One thing for sure, she needed to get out, and fast. Inside her purse, the keys to her apartment lay buried among tissues, cosmetics, and a host of other items. With shaking hands, she dumped the contents in a heap on the bed and fumbled for the keys. In troubled times, she needed sanctuary. Such a place existed in none other than Our Lady of Eternal Blessings, that solid building watching over the square as a sentinel might guard her most precious treasures. So much had happened in such little time.

She needed something else: her crystal rosary. This special rosary had been given to her as a little girl by an old woman who'd never had children of her own. Somehow the lady must have thought Kit would get some use out of it at some point during her life. Though she'd had some disheartening times, none compared to this one.

Inside the nightstand, in a small, black velvet drawstring pouch, the rosary lay tucked away for safe keeping. Kit rummaged around before grasping the strings of the bag and yanking it free, sending the contents in the drawer flying all directions. A dreadful combination of fear and disgust roiled inside her gut, creating a queasiness inside her stomach; but no time remained for hugging the toilet.

Desperation grew more intense as she bounded down the stairs, making it to the bottom in record time. The clock from Our Lady of Eternal Blessings chimed the nighttime hour, and she scurried across the street toward the main entrance of the church like her life depended on it.

The doors always remained open until nine every night, and people often came to engage in prayer or light a candle. Tonight, Kit felt in dire need of both. As usual, the church lights had been dimmed. Relief washed over her as she stepped inside, losing herself in the vastness of the interior. She walked with care, trying to keep her steps measured and quiet against the stone tiles. The rack of candles up front looked dark, as if everyone had abandoned prayer for the day. A day without worry or some kind of excitement seemed like a long-ago luxury, and if her little votive burned alone without kindred spirits tonight, so be it. If evil hid this day, it would surely rear its ugly head tomorrow.

The figure of one lone male sitting several pews down attracted her attention. He seemed engrossed in prayer or some form of meditation because he didn't lift his head at the sound of her footsteps. Upon closer inspection, she discovered the identity of the gentleman.

"Steven!" She stated his name in a soft tone and hurried over by his side.

"Kit!" His face lit up into a smile. He extended a hand and pulled her down close to him. "What are you doing here?"

"That's my question for you."

His lips curved up into a teasing grin. "Maybe you don't come here that much. Since I've been in town, I come here every Sunday, and other times when I need to."

She sat staring at him for a moment. His words triggered a memory, one that lay buried deep in the past – forgotten memories of her and Austin attending the same church from childhood until the day they graduated from high school and went their separate ways. When they were little, they didn't speak to one another while they attended classes on the catechism of the Catholic church, better known in other denominations as Sunday School. The boys cared only for the company of their peers, as did the little girls.

But Kit remembered Austin as he had sat with his friends, cutting up with the others, leaning over and whispering something to one of his friends. When the friend carried on in response to his suggestion, he'd throw his head back, squeeze his eyes shut, and let out a cute, high-pitched, whispery giggle. Austin always threw himself wholeheartedly into his laughter, letting it out with all the sincerity his little soul could muster. That's the way it was with him. He threw himself into life and pursued activities and passions with gusto. Those traits had endeared him to Kit from the beginning – until the end. Sometimes she saw the same type of laughter from Steven, but more toned down, tamed by maturity and the moderation of emotions that came as part of being an adult. If Austin had lived, would he have laughed the same way as a grown man?

"Kit, are you listening?" Steven lips grazed her ear.

Somehow or another, she'd tuned out the rest of his comments, and struggled to save face. This mind-wandering definitely had set in as a bad habit, with Dwight, with Steven. "Oh, yes, you wanted know why I came in tonight." She tried to look as if her brain hadn't zoned out on him completely.

"Yes." A serious expression covered his face, and his arm found its way around her shoulders. "Like I said earlier, I haven't seen you here. Something must be up for you to come tonight." He whispered in her ear. "Is something wrong? Did something scare you again?" His spare hand reached over and tapped the rosary bag sitting in her lap.

Kit stared at his fingers resting on the bag, words coming to a standstill. Reliving the earlier events of the day stirred up fear again. How on earth would she explain to him, with any credibility, that a dead snake lay resting in peace in her kitchen? She paused a moment, unsure how to begin telling him what happened after work.

Her eyes found his, and, in a quivering voice, she related every detail leading to her entering the church on this particular night. "I'm fighting the devil, and I need guidance. I'm hoping something will step in and make it all go away, a miracle or something." She looked up at him, tears stinging in her eyes. "Steven, the Historical Society deserves that property. We've kept it in good shape for years, and we try to preserve nice buildings and keep the arts and history alive. We do good things for the community."

"And here's me playing devil's advocate. You could also say Harsh has improved living conditions before, and he wants to generate revenue for cities that need it."

Kit grew testy with this reasoning. "We also generate revenue for businesses around here because of the events we hold, the people we invite. We stimulate the mind, intensify culture, give people something to look forward to in their day-to-day routines. We provide enjoyment and opportunities for others to sprout their wings and pursue their dreams. Isn't that what self-development and evolution is about? It's more than money or the physical, structural side of all this. It's spiritual, too, and you can't price that."

Steven raised his eyebrows. "Well put."

"All Harsh wants is revenue generated for him. He couldn't care less about anybody but himself. And Windham Springs isn't in a deplorable state. He can go get property somewhere else and just leave us alone. We don't want him or anything he has to offer. He's pure evil."

He smiled lightly and shook his head. "Is he pure evil? Probably not. No one is all good or all bad. Even good people have flaws. When it comes to spirit, the universe is impartial, and doesn't look at good and evil the way our human minds do. Both of you think you have a good reason and good right to have what you want. The question is, do you have a stronger will than he does, and do you have a way to set that intent so you don't lose sight of it?"

She sat glaring at him, stunned at his words. "I'll never lose sight of this as long as I live and breathe. I've put the Society at a huge, financial risk trying to push the purchase of this mansion, and I believe in our work. My intent will never waver, and at this point, I should be cracking a little. I'm not." Frowning, she added, "I thought you were on my side."

He smiled. "Trust me, I am on your side, more than you give me credit for. But I've learned to realize my power potential, and I've also learned how to roll with the punches, even if I don't like it. When we don't get our way, there's usually a good reason for it that we may not understand at the time."

She insisted. "We have first right to buy this property. Period. Mr. Crispin and the Planning Commission say we do. Alexandra Stothwell says we do." The ignition of anger, the indignant tone of her voice, all these feelings fueled her with new determination. The snake incident still repulsed her, but now, instead of cold fear, all she felt was frustration toward potential obstacles. The Historical Society would get that land, come hell or high water.

With a face void of emotion, Steven sat gazing at Kit. His hand on her shoulder radiated an uncommon heat, one that blazed to the core.

"I think I'll light a candle now." Her eyes countered his, and she spoke with a hint of defiance.

He said nothing, but uncurled his arm and let her slide out of the pew.

Her sneakers squeaked against the tile floor as she walked toward the rack of candles. She would set her intent now, with Steven serving as a witness. The words he spoke, hateful against her ears, rang with a hint of truth. The picture of Harsh flashed through her mind, forcing her to remember the article, bullet-pointing all the good he'd done in the world. Picking up a match from the holder, she closed her eyes, said a quick prayer, and lit a wick. The votive holder glowed red, a confirmation of her sincerest request. There, it was done, complete, finished, and, with this gesture, hopefully all the other bad stuff was finished too.

In silence, she made her way back to Steven, who'd stepped out of the pew and stood in the aisle. He wrapped an arm around her and pulled her close. "Let's go back to your place, and I'll help you take care of a few things."

Two lone souls, who had arrived separately to seek their own sanctuary in a church, left together for a small apartment, where they sought solace in each other's arms before a roaring fireplace.

CHAPTER 13

"Where is this snake you told me about?" Steven turned his head from one side to the other, surveying the apartment until he spied the box on the kitchen counter. He made his way over and opened the flaps with great care.

"It's pretty gross, so don't freak out when you see it." Kit shut the front door and tossed the rosary pouch on her bed before joining him. "I've seen it already, and I don't care to see it again." She contorted her face in an exaggerated grimace and shuddered with disgust.

He let out a whistle. "Wow, this is the most bizarre thing I've ever seen."

"What are you doing, now? Ugh, Steven, are you going to touch that thing?" She heard him rustling around in the box.

"Chill! You said you'd seen everything, but you didn't tell me about a note."

"A note?" Curiosity getting the better of her, she sidled up next to him.

"Yeah, it says right here, *You could be next.*"

Kit felt the blood drain from her face. All the candle-lighting stuff went by the wayside again. "Is that a death threat?"

"It could easily be taken as one, or whomever sent this wants to scare you, at least. If we could prove Harsh is behind this, he'd be in a lot of trouble." Steven returned the envelope to the box.

"The problem is, I can't even manage to get a license plate number. That asshole delivery guy is way too fast. The first time, he sped out from the mansion and I barely saw what he was driving. At the sale, I didn't see him get into or out of a car. Tonight, it was a little too dark, and he drove off like a bat out of hell before I could get a clear picture of anything." She stopped pacing for a moment and returned to Steven. "I know it was the same guy tonight because of his height, and I can remember what he looks like. I took a picture too."

"Do you want to leave this box out on your balcony until you decide what you want to do? Or we could take a picture in case you need it later."

She paced some more, trying to decide what to do. Thoughts of harboring a dead snake, even outside the apartment, creeped her out. "Would you take a picture of it with my phone first, and then put the box on the balcony? I definitely don't want it in here."

Steven picked up Kit's phone and snapped a couple of clear pictures of the dead animal before closing down the flaps and carrying the box outside. He came back, rubbing his hands together. "It's a little nippy out there tonight. I think your little friend will keep pretty well until morning."

"I can't wait to get rid of my 'little friend.' I don't know how I'll be able to sleep tonight, knowing that thing's out there." Her face contorted into an expression of disgust.

With a smile, he took her in his arms and they kissed. "Would you like for me to stay a little while with you? It's not too late, I don't think." He gave a quick turn of his wrist, checking the time.

"I'd love nothing better. Great idea. Glad I thought of it." She let out a light chuckle, while he entertained himself with kissing the side of her neck.

"Do you want me to get a log for the fireplace?" His eyes wandered over to the fireplace and back to her.

"Yeah, why don't you do that, and I'll get us some wine and a blanket for the floor."

Within minutes, they settled together in front of the fire. Kit took the time to slip into something comfy, not to mention something Steven could easily remove. The snake ordeal had set off a bad case of the jitters, and she wanted more than anything right now to cuddle up in his arms where he'd keep her safe. After swallowing some wine, the numbing effects kicked in, taking the edge off her fears.

She stroked Steven's arm. "Have you come up with anything else to wear with your mask? I'm thinking of making a snood for my hair covering, maybe some black silk gloves and black shoes, and calling it a day on that one, especially if I don't find something else I like better."

He took a sip of wine before answering. "I'll probably get some white veil or a poufy material of some kind, and create a simple headdress to resemble clouds. I'd love to do something like angel wings, but everything may get more complicated if I do that."

"I think wings would be nice. You don't see many male angels, except in the Bible, of course." Her lips turned up into a smile. "You'd be a wonderful angel."

His eyes sparkled in the dim light. "You think so? Do you like angels?" He changed from his supine position and propped himself up on his side. His finger teased over sensitive areas of her body. Her nipples hardened to the point where they pressed their firmness against her thin top.

He was doing it to her all over again, starting up the internal fire with no mercy. With a gulp, she tried thinking of an answer to the question. "I love angels. I think they're beautiful." Stifling a light giggle, she turned her head, gazing up at him. "I have a confession. The coffee shop has a new flavor called *Divine Angel*, and I think of you when I drink some."

He threw back his head and sounded off a soft, airy, high-pitched laugh, one that nearly stilled her heart. "Oh, great! I remind you of coffee? Is that it? That's not too flattering, or romantic."

For the first time, she focused on his laugh and tightly closed eyes. The sound and vision flared up memories of Austin all over again. The only difference, this one bore a mature, masculine quality, which had ripened and rendered it with both a haunting familiarity and a uniqueness of its own.

Steven sat up. "You're doing it again."

Kit shook her head, refocusing on the here and now. "I'm sorry, what did you say?"

"You see? It's like I mentioned last time. You seem to drift off to another world. What's there?" His face wore a new earnestness, and his eyes sought hers. His hands no longer touched her, and a quick chill slammed through her body. While the fire blazed out its brilliant climax before them, a brooding sadness wound around her heart.

With a trembling voice, she finally decided to break the ice on this troubling issue, at least a little. He may not learn all the truth tonight, but this internal emotional block needed some relief from the pressure that had been building up all this time. Besides, trying to ignore everything had become a drain on her energy level. "Sometimes you remind me of someone in my past."

Steven sat motionless, the occasional blinking of his eyes the only affirmation of understanding.

"Lately, especially before you came, I'd been having dreams about him." A small pop from the fireplace startled her, and she glanced in its direction.

"So what happened? What's so disturbing about those dreams?" His hands searched for hers.

"They're pretty vague. It's not like I hear anything or we do anything in particular. It's just seeing him. And he just stands there looking at me, but we don't speak."

"You talked about the past coming back to you. Did you *not* do some things that maybe you regret now? Did you *say* things you regret now?" He seemed to emphasize the questions, intent on learning the answer.

The blood rushed to her face, and Kit turned to stare at the floor. "It's been so long ago." She paused a moment. "In the end, we just went our separate ways."

"You just went your separate ways? That's it? Tell me what happened." The tone in Steven's voice told her he didn't believe her for one minute.

"You know what, I'm just not ready to dig that deep right now. That'll be some work on my brain." She grinned. "Let's just say the dreams stirred things up at this point. My life was pretty easy overall. Can't complain too much."

He continued staring, rubbing his thumbs over the tops of her hands, no judgment showing in his mood or demeanor. But she'd resolved not to say anything more, preferring to keep her private shame buried for a while longer. Sharing this much brought a tiny bit of relief, just a little and no more. Maybe one day he'd learn the rest of the story, but not now, not tonight.

He didn't ask anything else, accepting her answers for now. However, the look on his face and the thoughtfulness reflected in his eyes hinted of inner suspicion. It created an uneasy sensation.

"Come here." He pulled her into his arms, and stretched out with her resting on top of him. "Let's see if I can lighten you up a little." The words came out in a whisper, tickling her ear. She giggled, nuzzling against his neck while his fingers flitted over her back. In seconds, his fingers slipped inside the cotton bottoms and trailed over the satiny flesh of her buttocks. The touch of his hands worked magic in untangling the tension she felt moments ago. The hot, fervent kisses from his lips plunged her deeper into the pit of forgetfulness as the past slipped away to take a brief rest on a gray mental shelf in her mind.

His tongue, loaded with fiery determination, explored her mouth as if searching for answers to the questions he'd asked earlier. A few easy maneuvers and their clothing lay in an untidy heap on the floor. Kit didn't need instructions this time, but settled on top of him, returning his kisses with equal vigor. She loved the way he tasted, the way his body fit hers. The interplay of energy between them became hotter, filled with an 'other-world' quality not described in easy words.

She wrapped her thighs around his, pressed against him harder, and buried her face in his neck. His hands encased her head, holding on with a gentle firmness. Closing her eyes blocked out the immediate surroundings, and she concentrated on nothing but the here and now. In Steven's arms, she could hide and leave everything behind for a little while. Perhaps he'd take her to another world where no harm would come her way, no hateful deliverymen giving ill gifts, and no greedy soul wanting to take away something she loved. Desperate to find this world and lose herself in it, she permitted herself to sink into a concentrated peace. Her breathing soon matched his. It seemed as if their heartbeats tapped in unison. Deeper and deeper she fell into darkness, almost feeling weightless, suspended in space. For once, she liked this detachment from the world, yet still tethered to it.

From the sound of Steven's breathing, he had already achieved his divine connection, wherever, whatever that was for him. His earlier words, almost a telepathic replay in her head, reminded her to let the moment last. For once, she put away earthly concerns, worldly goals, and reached out to a source far greater than anything else. In an instant, time stood still.

As she and Steven reclined together, basking in front of the fire, something strange happened. His body tensed for a second, and he inhaled a quick, short breath. At the exact same time, a fullness gathered at the base of her spine, pulsing with an energy so strong, her whole body vibrated. Without warning, this force unleashed its full power, surging through her with lightning speed, exiting through the top of her head. In her mind's eye, she saw it blaze a neat linear path of flaming, spinning orbs as it flashed upwards. Red, orange, yellow, green, blue, purple, and violet, they'd each ignited, setting her soul on fire; the tips of her limbs tingled. Her whole body reacted as if it had experienced a total orgasm. The sensation of being wholly consumed left her almost breathless.

Steven ran his fingers up and down her spine, pressing gently at intervals. Had he felt the same thing? As he touched her, the tingling dissipated. When he determined this was enough, he rolled over, flipping her with ease so she rested on her back. Taking her hands in his, he rubbed over her fingers, and then her palms until the tingling feeling stopped.

"What just happened?" Kit stared up at him, glassy-eyed with wonder.

He gave her a broad, knowing grin, leaning down to kiss her lips. His eyes held an almost unearthly glow, displaying his own pleasure. Though his body hadn't shown the usual male signs of arousal and impending release, the energy and demeanor he exuded now proved otherwise.

His lips moved down her neck, over each one of her breasts, and continued kissing down until they reached the sensitive spot between her thighs. Kit arched her back and dug her head harder against the floor as the tender work of lips and tongue ignited the passion inside her, which blazed like the end of a fireworks finale. The pounding ache threatening madness subsided slowly. Muscles constricted and released; nerves sang in vibratory unison. She closed her eyes again and drowned in sweet darkness, reveling in a sensation she at least understood. Her hands reached down in an effort to capture his flesh, but he caught her wrists and held them in a secure grip.

"I'm fine. Trust me!" He grinned.

When he finished, they cuddled together for a long while. The fire had nearly burned out, with only one lapping flame remaining. After a valiant battle to stay alive, it finally resigned itself to a red glow. Sleep slipped its fingers over her eyelids, closing them for rest and sweet dreams.

Sometime during the night Kit awoke briefly and found herself in bed. Groggy with fatigue, she somehow sensed Steven had returned home, and fell back asleep without rolling over to see for sure. He'd allayed her fears, protected her, left her body swooning. She'd face the morning with a clearer head and brighter heart.

CHAPTER 14

Inside *JJ's Grille*, the usual crowd gathered around tables, enjoying drinks and food. At times, a loud sizzling sound came from the kitchen, and the smell of fresh food permeated the air. In one corner of the room, four players stood back from a dart board, cheering or booing the others as darts landed. At the bar, a line of men sat yelling or cheering at the large screen television sets, armchair quarterbacking as a football game stirred up ire or envy. Several people sat at the long table in the middle, laptops plugged in while they nursed beers and mixed drinks and nibbled on succulent appetizers.

Steven ordered for them both while she searched out a table where they could enjoy some privacy. She seated herself, viewing the scenery outside the window. The moon and streetlights glowed like magic brewing inside crystal balls. The nightlife had fallen into full swing, and the air held a contagious charge. A bump of a tray on the table ended her mind-wandering; Steven had arrived with the food.

"Coffee and a *Reuben* sandwich for you, and let's not forget dessert." He grinned as he placed the items in front of her. "You love your sweets, don't you?"

Kit laughed and pulled a set of silverware and a napkin off the tray. "I always make looking at the dessert menu a priority. The entree is just an afterthought."

"For dessert, I'll just have you, sunny side up!" He moved his plate closer, eager to dive into the roast beef and Swiss on rye. A bottle of beer rested close by.

Blushing, she let out a light chuckle. "I doubt I taste better than chocolate." She grinned.

"Trust me, you're tastier than any confection." Steven winked.

Kit had already bitten into her sandwich, taking a small sip of coffee to wash it down. "Thank you for treating me to dinner. This is becoming our place."

Steven's expression changed to the one she saw the day of the artisan sale at the mansion. Her heart did that funny flip-flop again. Inside, her stomach tightened. Why did he do this?

He nodded a couple of times, intent on his food. "This is a fun place." He glanced around, taking a drink of beer. "I can see why you enjoy it here. Definitely a good place to hide out, more so than church, it seems."

Filled with more concern, she turned her eyes up to his. "Does that bother you, about me not being an avid mass-goer, I mean? Many Catholics are devout about that."

His pursed his lips, signaling a noncommittal attitude about the issue. "Not really. I personally think you can commune with the divine anywhere, anytime you want to. There's no sacramental day, time, or place."

"Commune with the divine?" She kept a steadfast gaze on his face, taking a quick sip from her coffee cup.

"Yeah, commune with the divine." He glanced at the bar as a few of the men let out a whoop.

The somber tone in his voice caught her attention. A vacant expression covered his face, giving the impression he'd relapsed to that quiet place of communion they'd just discussed. She wanted to ask him about the future, and why he looked at her the way he did at times. But an answer would upset her if it didn't contain what she wanted to hear. Better to put certain conversations on hold a little longer. After all, no rush.

Kit cleared her throat, sitting up straighter on her seat. "Was that what you were doing the night we met at church? Communing?"

He swallowed a bite of sandwich before speaking. "You could say it was something like that." Thoughtful silence followed.

Given his mood, Kit knew their conversation tonight would be of the serious sort. Their times together weren't always giggles and grins, but when his mood leaned in this direction of philosophical reflection, she usually braced herself for some bit of wisdom or spiritual observation. Thinking back over their relationship, she discovered his words often hit her, swift and true. Sometimes his casual way of teaching held an allure, refreshingly practical, when she gave it all more thought. Other times, he challenged her. Hating when this happened, she mostly had to admit he made valid points. When they found themselves entangled in intimate moments, his approach often left her in a state of wonder.

She persisted. "So what do you do during your communion? What do you say, how do you do it?"

Halting the bottle mid-lift to his lips, he stared at her a few moments before placing it back down on the table. "Kit, have you paid any attention to some of the things we talk about, or to some of the things I hope you've experienced when we're physically together?"

The question startled her. "Was I supposed to, necessarily? I mean, you say some things that make me think at times." Her eyes focused on the sandwich in front of her, and suddenly she felt like a little girl being scolded.

He smiled, placing his hand on top of hers. "It seems to me like we have some different opinions on things, or at least a different approach to the way we tackle things in life. Let's just say for a long time, I've been in a special position where working on myself has been the main focus. I've learned how choices can make or break me, how to use my will to get what I want, that sort of thing."

"Seems like I'm mustering up some will to keep fighting off crazy deliverymen, or at least trying to ignore him and stick to my main task."

"And that would be trying to purchase the mansion you love so much." Steven took a brief drink. "Learning to call on divine power when the chips are down is one thing, but the important thing is to simply be quiet and listen, which is what I try to make time for every day. It helps me put everything into perspective."

Kit stared into his eyes, viewing the earnestness there. She'd heard this before, and as always, it had gone in one ear and out the other. Only Irene most likely had a clue about what Steven had just said. Then it occurred to her, the difference in the last time she and Steven had held each other in front of the fireplace. The sensations she experienced were like nothing she'd ever felt before. For the first time, she tried recollecting some semblance of what he had told her earlier. And she just decided to let go, let it all go for a while without a care in the world.

"So what about last time, when we were together? Something odd happened to me then. What do I make of that?"

He squinted at her in confusion. "The last time? Oh, yes!" The corners of his lips turned up into a bright smile. "Yes, that was a divine experience, a complete connection. Neat, wasn't it?"

"You knew, didn't you?" She read the expression on his face. He did know; he hadn't forgotten, either. Did he have the same sensation; did they share it together at the same time?

"I did, and I didn't want to spoil the moment with explanations. I knew we'd be talking about it sooner or later, so I just decided to leave it alone for the time being."

As much as she hated to say so, the entire sensation put others to shame by comparison. But why did she still want to have the usual, the predictable when she could have more?

As if reading her mind, Steven spoke up. "I had the same experience you did. If you're anything like me, you'll soon find yourself just as satisfied with what we experienced the other night."

"I see." She still didn't quite understand, but refused to ask any more questions.

"I also enjoy making you happy. You make me happy." The light in his eyes dimmed a bit, and a hint of sadness edged its way in. "But lately, I'm wanting to make things last, because nothing lasts forever. Once it's over, it's over." The words were spoken more to himself than to her.

Kit waved him off. "I see what you mean."

Steven stared off, face emotionless.

Now she wanted to change the subject. He affirmed something new, and it was time to move on. "Tell me something. We've never talked much about what it was like for you growing up. I've mentioned high school to you. Did you enjoy yourself then, have any other special hobbies other than art and football?" She leaned over the table a little more, speaking in clear tones. "Like you've asked me, did you have any regrets, or things you wish you had done differently?" A light grin flickered on her face, and somehow asking the questions back to him filled her with triumph in some small way. At least the pressure decreased for her.

He sank back in his chair. "Where to start?" On the table, his fingers drummed out a light, nervous *tap-tap-tap*. "First of all, my household wasn't the kindest place to be, living with a dad who cared more about my being a man rather than helping me find my kind, sensitive side. He loved the fact I played football: '*It'll make a man out of ya!*' he'd always bellow at me, right as I'd head out the door to a game. That's when he was the proudest of me. The rest didn't matter quite as much."

Steven's eyes turned up to Kit's, and an old sadness made itself at home on his usually cheerful face. "As for the art, he thought that was for sissies, and the last thing he wanted was a sissy for a son. But lucky me, as long as I stayed in sports, he tolerated the paintbrushes and pencils."

Fearful one slight move would break the spell between them, Kit listened hard, not even so much as giving a smidgen of attention to the food in front of her. The story sounded too familiar, one heard long ago from a young lover who'd cried on her shoulder every now and then, when his heart somehow couldn't hold whatever sadness had intruded upon it that day.

"I loved sports more than anything, but in art, I could lose myself, paint or draw whatever world or fantasy I wanted. If I didn't like something, I'd toss it and start over. As far as friends, I had lots of friends. But looking back on it now, I ran with a dangerous crowd sometimes, ones I should have left by the wayside. Instead, trying to prove I was manly, I'd run around with them anyway. We'd drink, drive too fast. It's no wonder ..." He stopped, stared at his beer, and took another sip.

"No wonder what?" Kit shifted in her seat.

"Nothing. I guess I should have spent my time studying or doing something else. Maybe getting better at my artwork, working my creativity harder. Instead, I was more interested in drinking, trying to be popular, and scoring ..." For some reason, Steven's food attracted his attention, and he devoured his sandwich like a starved urchin who hadn't eaten in days.

Kit let out a light breath of relief. This seemed as good a time as any to follow his lead and finish up her own sandwich. If the truth be known, Steven's suggestive narrative on 'scoring' hit a nerve. What was it about guys and scoring?

All these years she'd managed to stuff the memories of 'scoring' with Austin in dark closets of her mind, never wanting to think about them again. After all, being the first love also meant being the one with first rights to her virginity. Youth and lust, at certain times, made ill bedfellows, and memory stepped in, imposing cruel reminders that it was she who had been only too willing to give it all to him when the time presented itself.

If memory wanted to make one last jab, it also reminded her that she had been the one who invited Austin over, planning in advance for something 'special' to happen. She had wanted him as much as he had wanted her. Scoring wasn't a preferred word she wanted to use for describing their first time. It sounded so stilted and shallow. Is that how he'd viewed it, viewed her? Scoring? She shook her head, trying to shake off the unsavory thoughts.

The story was a typical one, parents gone for the weekend, with daughter staying behind, claiming she needed to work on a project for school. Not one to doubt their daughter, her parents headed off without a second thought. Finding themselves alone that Saturday night, she and Austin took advantage of the situation and headed down to a spare room in the basement of her house. Neither had been a stranger to alcohol at such a young age and, filled with just enough of a buzz to make inhibitions turn a blind eye, they'd finally done it.

If she allowed her mind to relapse back in time and concentrated hard enough, she remembered the lust in his eyes as clearly as if it had happened yesterday. In the dim lamplight they'd undressed, both somewhat shy. She remembered feeling strange and self-conscious being naked in front of a guy, even if it was Austin. They'd each taken turns, touching and exploring those tender parts which had previously been filled with the dull ache of virginal youth.

Every touch from his enthusiastic hands, those of one not quite a man, but not a boy, either, had called forth a beautiful storm of strange sensations she'd never felt before. When his fingers found the special bundle of nerves tucked away, hidden in the dark recess of an area she'd been taught to hide, the resulting internal hot explosion carried her away to another world, leaving her breathless.

Once they'd both reached a certain comfort level, they threw caution to the wind, and finally united. Austin's gentle side came through in full force that night as he tried to be as easy as possible. The alcohol had numbed the pain a little, but most of all it allowed her to put religious dogma aside and accept his entry without passing judgment on herself, him, or the act of giving in to lusty needs.

Did she and Steven dare finish the current thread of conversation, or should the subject be changed to something entirely different, avoiding deeply personal subjects altogether? As for Kit, sweeping unpleasantness under the rug had always worked for her. Why change now? But the mood had already caught her up by the heels. Leaving the subject matter unfinished would only leave her dangling.

"So what about regrets, Steven? Were you a kind, sweet person in high school, so you really never had to regret anything you ever did?" Kit stabbed a fork into her cake, savoring the strong chocolate flavor as it hit her taste buds.

Steven glanced up after helping himself to a tiny bite of her dessert. A wry smile spread across his lips. "You think I was kind and sweet then?"

"Well, you're a nice guy now. I just thought it was probably in your nature."

"My nature's been fine-tuned and elevated with time, and I mean lots of time and special attention." His words bit and snapped, almost chastising her.

Kit took in a deep breath. "Okay, so you weren't nice, then. Why not? What did you do?" She swallowed another bite of cake.

His cheeks colored for a second, and he seemed entangled in a personal war over whether or not to share the thoughts on his mind. Instead he peeked at his watch, stalling a little. "Oh, I tried to be nice with everyone, in general, but I think my own attitude and arrogance got the better of me at times. I did some things I'm not proud of now, but, at the time, I didn't think about consequences too much." The steely gleam in his eyes caught her off guard. A light tingle ran up her spine. "I'd give just about anything to make up for some of that now."

Uneasy, Kit turned her eyes in the direction of her cake, not sure if she wanted to hear any more about what he was like in the past, or how he wanted to make amends. She knew what she'd been like, and a brief comparison of their histories hinted at an uncanny similarity. What would she give to atone for some of her past transgressions?

"Hey, enough about me. What about you?" He reached over and took one of her hands in his.

With a little shrug, she noted with a casual air, "I was pretty lucky, I guess. Had great parents, everything I wanted. Most would say I was a little princess. But overall, my life was pretty tame and uneventful."

He'd kept his eyes fixed on hers, nodding while she spoke. With a quick maneuver of a fork, he helped himself to another bite of cake. "I see. Good, good for you."

She hoped he'd buy her answer, which was mostly true, and let the rest go. Confession still didn't hold enough purge-appeal to make the tongue loosen and wag out nasty secrets, and noting the earlier hesitation in his voice, he echoed the sentiment. Why shed light any sooner than necessary on a personality bearing a facet composed of virtual acid, a veritable bitter side, which allowed verbal bile to spew forth when wronged? Like an old pulp fiction monster creeping out of a dark space, the word from the spirit board, F-O-R-G-I-V-E, rose up in her mind. Could she do that, forgive Austin, forgive herself? No, not now, still not ready.

Steven spoke first after their brief silence. "So, going back to where we started, you can be anywhere and plug into the raw power and intellect of a world we don't readily see with our eyes."

She nodded. "Yes, I see your point. And I think since we've met, I've been trying to do this thing you're talking about, even when we're not together."

"Please, keep at it." His hand squeezed hers so hard she nearly winced in pain. "If I know you like I think I do, you'll learn to love yourself again."

Kit sat in disbelief, the words hammering in the nails of hard truth into her soul.

"Something tells me you've lost your way, Kit, and you need to get back on track. You don't seem to like yourself very much these days. I can sense it."

Getting up enough courage, mostly in an effort to sweep personal discomfort under the rug again, she blurted out, "You seem to sense a lot about me, considering the short time we've known each other." A light smile graced her words, and she prayed for sincerity to come through.

"The short time we've known each other?" He glanced around the coffee shop, casting a courteous smile on a customer passing by. "Okay, if you say so, but just remember what I've told you. You're holding something back. I can feel it."

A little exasperated, Kit forced herself to keep her temper intact. "You know what, Steven, there are some things right now I just don't feel comfortable talking about. Maybe one day, but not right now."

With a light nod, he backed down and didn't press the subject any more. The remainder of time passed with small talk, nothing too deep and thought-provoking. By the time the evening ended, the mood had swung back under the 'pleasant' radar. Taking another look at his watch, Steven motioned for them to get up and leave. Since this evening wasn't a weekend night, each one felt compelled to head on home. Steven walked Kit home and saw her safely inside before walking back to his shop.

Inside her apartment, the clock on the mantle chimed nine o'clock. Too early for slipping into nighties and dropping off to sleep, especially with a sugar buzz from the dessert humming through her nervous system. She walked to the refrigerator for some milk. Settling back on the sofa, her mind wandered as she stared at the ceiling. The night of the carnival was nearing fast, and everything seemed in order. For her cat costume, she only needed some gloves and a headdress of some kind. An old black shirt and slacks hung in her closet. She'd wear those under the robe she purchased. On the square, Flora's antiques featured a booth where a dealer specialized in vintage accessories and odd slips of fabric. Maybe she'd take Steven and they could go shop there one day.

From the bookcase across the room, the yearbooks winked at her, taunting. Tonight's conversation with Steven had inflamed the old memories again. She and Austin had cared about each other, as much as teens could, floundering in the remnant trappings of youth while stepping gingerly into the adult realm, holding hands and hoping neither would stumble and fall too hard along the way.

Austin had his merits, strength of character, talent. He had loved her, so she thought. Looking back, she'd seen him blossoming into manhood just as she had into womanhood, both unaware, yet very much aware on an inner level neither quite understood.

Closing her eyes, she rested her head on a small pillow, thinking about youthful times, some of the happy moments she and Austin had shared, just the two of them, sometimes with a group of close friends. The more she concentrated, the more vividly the images slipped through her mind. Inside the apartment, the energy had changed, as if someone had set an electric current loose through the air. Her body tingled. In the space between her eyes, a vibration hummed, strong, insistent.

The sound of a book falling from the bookcase broke the silence, shattering her concentration. Damn! Not again. She bolted upright. On the floor lay one of the high school annuals. A chill shot through the air. She got up, shivering, and walked over, only to discover it was the senior annual that had fallen. As always, this one. Kit stared at the cover a few seconds, too spooked to pick it up. Filled with dread, yet compelled to find an answer, she overcame her nerves and picked up the annual.

Seated on the sofa, she thumbed through the pages until the section of senior class pictures came into view. Skimming over the other photos, her eyes finally landed on Austin's. Her brain homed in on the features captured on the page. His light grin appeared innocent enough, with a soulful gaze spilling out from his eyes. But Kit knew better than fall prey to his beguiling charms again, even if they now stemmed only from ink and paper. For a moment, she'd almost be willing to let the past go and move on. But there were too many unanswered questions, and the more she called up the memories, the more the old pain throbbed in her heart as if it all had happened yesterday.

She snapped the book shut, and returned the annual back to its space on the shelf. Enough of this crazy book and facing old ghosts. Someday, when the time was right, she'd make a pledge to put closure to it all. Maybe then she'd be ready to forgive, ready to like herself a little more, just as Steven suggested.

In the meantime, she had him all to herself. He'd be there with her to guide, teach, and love her, seeing her through any storm. Her eyes burned with fatigue. The clock struck ten. On that note, she trudged to the bedroom. Before her head hit the pillow, her eyes had closed with sleep.

CHAPTER 15

Everyone was talking about the big event. People called to ask questions, volunteer their help. Time passed. The carnival had morphed from a mere concept to a rapidly approaching reality. Artists called, thanking Kit for helping them show off their creative side. Even Alexandra told her people had called, telling her how nice it was that the Society had the option of buying the house, and that she'd be missed as she retired to a quieter life.

All the guests on the VIP list had returned their RSVPs, complete with checks for their tickets. The posters achieved their goal of bringing in merchants and residents from the historical district. Not ones to shy away from fun, even the bigwigs from neighboring towns had gotten in on the event, offering generous donations for the mansion's cause. Between her online petition and reaching out to other homeowners in neighborhoods away from the square, Kit received the remainder of her signatures. In the end, she even received ten additional ones.

She sat in Dwight's office, watching him pull checks from envelopes. On the guest list, he checked off names. If the person wasn't on the list, he wrote down the name so they could write a proper thank you note later. The smile on his face raged for several minutes as he placed the checks in one neat little pile.

He glanced up and beamed. "I like the looks of this already, Kit. We're getting some cash here for a down payment. If it keeps moving in this direction, we may be able to meet the minimum."

"May? Let's hope it all comes in. We have to get this house." She turned toward the remaining stack of unopened envelopes. There were at least fifty more to go. "Tell you what, I'll go ahead and open these for you so you can start adding things up. If you want, I'll track the names too, and just hand you the checks."

Dwight looked like someone had handed him a personal check for a million dollars. For the first time, Kit saw his face flush. "You want to take time out of your busy schedule to help me do this?"

"Oh, I need a break. I just so happen to have a small lull, which is unusual for me. I know Irene just got hit with a bunch of projects to do, so she won't be much help."

"I love Irene to death, but as for me, I think you'd make a much more efficient envelope-opener check-puller kind of gal." He winked and mouthed her a kiss from across his desk.

"I heard that. Thanks a lot, Dwight." Irene stepped into the office, flashing Kit an 'oh-my-gosh-he's-at-it-again' stare. She tossed some more envelopes on the desk. "Here you go. Somehow some of these got stuck in my mail by mistake."

"Thanks, Irene, appreciate it." He turned his face up long enough to smile at her. "We're starting to see some progress."

"Fantastic. Catch you guys later. I've got some more work to do."

Alone again, Kit and Dwight fell into a natural rhythm in their work as Kit slit open envelopes and placed checks in a special pile on the desk. Dwight stopped, taking off his glasses and rubbing his fingers over his eyes. When he replaced his lenses, he sat back in his chair, legs outstretched, gazing at Kit.

"What?" She jerked her head up when she caught him looking at her. "Is there something wrong? You look like you want to say something."

He rubbed a finger lightly over his lower lip a couple of seconds. Wrapping his hands behind his head, he leaned back further in his chair. "Kit, why didn't you tell me about the recent package you got?"

Her eyes popped open, followed by her mouth. "Huh?" She blinked a few times to clear her head. "Was I supposed to?"

"Irene told me about your newly acquired reptilian friend, Mr. Snaky-poo. Are you two enjoying each other's company?" His jaw tightened, cheeks flushing a light pink.

Kit mimicked someone regurgitating and shuddered. "I got Ste … Mr. Crispin picked it up and threw it out. Won't have to worry about that thing again."

"Why didn't you tell me about all this? You think I wouldn't want to know something like that, especially since you, Irene, and I have been going through all this together?"

The hurt in his eyes tugged at Kit's heart, leaving her lost for words. "Dwight, I'm sorry. It's not like I was trying to hide anything. I really just wanted to put the whole thing out of my mind." She waved him off. "Anyway, I'm sure you've got better things to do than sit around and listen to me caterwaul about shit all day long." Her voice dropped to a lower tone. "Really, you'd grow tired of it fast, let me tell you."

He sat still, his eyes fixed on hers, as if his brain struggled to comprehend her explanation. After brief contemplation, he ran his fingers through his hair and sat up straight at his desk again. His words came out, measured and filled with warmth, sending a surge of goosebumps breaking out over her arms. "Kit, I always care about what happens to you. I'm always here if you ever need a shoulder to cry on, or if you're scared and need someone there for support. You can call me or come to me anytime, night or day. Please don't ever forget where we were."

The words and the way in which they were spoken reminded her of Steven, so much so that she almost believed for a fraction of a second she heard him instead of Dwight.

She breathed in a big dose of air. This time, a quiet calm settled itself all over her, rather than the usual tug-of-war reactions when he made comments like this. "You know what, I appreciate that. I really do." Overcome with an influx of urgency, words of gratitude tumbled out of her mouth. "Dwight, I just want you to know that no matter what happens, I appreciate the things you do for me and all the nice things you say. I'm lucky to have someone who's so concerned and caring. You don't find that a lot in people these days. And one thing I'll guarantee you, you'll always be top-notch in my book."

If someone had stepped into his office, smacked him in the face, and walked out, he wouldn't have appeared any more stunned. Without a word, he got up from his chair, walked over to where Kit sat, and knelt down beside her. He cupped her head in his hands and gazed up into her eyes. "Just know that I'm not saying these things to hear myself talk. I mean every word. I do things for you because I enjoy you, everything about you, even if what I do anymore is limited to when we are in this house." His hands tightened a bit more. "You're a fine lady and a good person, Kit. I just hope you know that about yourself."

Kit blushed, not intending for Dwight to speak his mind the way he did. Perhaps, like her, he'd kept his thoughts locked away, with the voice playing the role of an astute gatekeeper. But what had she done to make him think her a fine lady? She went at her work with vigor, with passion, putting her whole heart and soul into every project finding its way on her desk. When it came to mingling with others, she'd always made an effort to be courteous, sympathetic, and kind. What would he think of her darker side, the insensitive side where she sometimes turned a blind eye, and, most importantly, a deaf ear?

Dwight returned to his desk, gazing at the mountain of envelopes. "It looks like we got through most of these. Believe it or not, we're at about twenty thousand dollars and still counting. I know more people will be signing up and sending in their money." Sitting back in his chair, he gave the ledger in front of him a few taps with his pencil and smiled back at Kit.

"Do you think we can raise another twenty thousand dollars in the time we have left? That's still such a large amount for so little time."

"It's cutting it close, isn't it?" He glanced at the unopened envelopes on the desk.

"Do you still want me to stay and help you open the rest of those? Maybe we'll get our windfall in one of them. There's about fifteen left."

"You know what, I think we're fine. You've been a big enough help this afternoon. I think I can get through the rest of these and at least let you get back to your office so you can get some of your own work done."

She got up from the chair. "Okay, I'll head off back to my own domain and work on a few things. Don't forget this project is not just one person's, so I don't mind scheduling it in with my other stuff."

The rays of afternoon sunlight fell on his hair, reflecting back a golden glow. The strong contours of his face caught her attention more than ever as she stood gazing at him. For a moment, her feet didn't want to move, nor her eyes. If she could have gotten away with it, she'd have stayed a while longer just to look at him some more. The warm smile on his lips lit up his handsome features, setting off a strong urge to suddenly run over and kiss him. Her mind raced. What if she quickly moved in for a light touch on the lips, kind of like the way they used to do, just a tiny kiss, not a deep, significant one?

Kit cleared her throat and uprooted her feet, moving toward the door, trying to keep her thoughts from running amok. Across the desk, Dwight had been scrutinizing every move, or lack thereof.

"You okay?" His voice sounded out, strong and rich, every bit as handsome in its quality as his physical features.

"Yes, I'm fine. I was just trying to think if there were any last-minute things we might be forgetting before I head on back to my place." Oh, what a lie! She needed to leave, and fast. Left with nothing else to say or do, she turned and nearly ran for the door. Back in the safety of her office, she settled down behind her desk and began organizing the papers scattered on top.

There it was, sitting on a small notepad, a small light blue box tied up with a red silk bow. Who on earth gave her a gift? The bigger question, why? It wasn't her birthday or any special holiday. She tugged one corner of the bow and pulled the top off.

Chocolates, a set of eight, rested neatly in cut-out paper cups. Their beauty took her breath away. Each one competed for her attention, glistening with swirls of vibrant colors, red, orange, turquoise, and green. They were the loveliest set of confections she'd ever seen. Only in magazines featuring world-renowned chocolatiers did she see this type of art brandished on a piece of candy. Steven definitely would give her a gift such as this, one bearing the hallmark of a true artist. Unable to resist, she plucked out one of the chocolates and popped it into her mouth. The hint of pepper and another unidentified flavor coated her tongue, and after a few swirls, she swallowed. Interesting taste, not quite like anything she'd eaten before, but still good. She picked up the phone and dialed the number to his shop.

"Celestial Temptation Gallery, can I help you?"

"Steven, you doll, you!"

"Hey, Kit, what's going on? Taking a break from work?"

"Yes." Her voice took on a coy, flirty tone, and she smiled, fluttering her lashes as though he stood in front of her. "I have something."

He chuckled. "Oh? And what's that?"

"You don't have to pretend like you don't know, because I already know."

Silence.

"Steven?"

"Yes, I'm still here."

"What's wrong?" Now the conversation became a little frustrating. "You know what I'm talking about, the box of chocolates you dropped off here. I must have been in Dwight's office helping him with opening invitations and collecting money. I'm sorry I wasn't around when you came by. I would have loved to have seen you."

Silence.

Oh, goodness, had her mentioning Dwight made him angry for some reason? She and Steven never talked about him, but that didn't mean he couldn't become jealous if he thought another man was giving her gifts. "Steven?" Now her voice contained a tinge of uneasiness. "You did give me a box of chocolates, didn't you? Huh? Sweetie?"

He sighed. "Kit, I swear by all that's holy that I never gave you a box of chocolates today." He cleared his throat. "Do you think someone else did, perhaps a friend, someone you know?"

Kit leaned back in her chair and rubbed her eyes. If Steven hadn't given them to her, there was only one person left she could think of, and he sat down the hallway and around the corner, busy crunching numbers. He hadn't let on that he'd given her a gift. "Gosh, Steven, I'm so sorry. I don't know what to say. This is a little awkward for me right now. I feel a little silly, honestly."

"Don't feel silly. It's all good. Maybe Irene wanted to give you something. After all, why not? You two are good friends. I could totally see that."

"All I can say is these chocolates don't look like your typical candy."

"Really? What do you mean?"

"They're just fancy, and I mean, fancy-schmancy. I tasted one. Pretty good. But the colors are incredible, all swirly. Somehow, I don't think these are your run-of-the-mill commercial grade sweets." She ate another one, this piece tasting of cloves and something spicy – and then that other unique flavor she couldn't quite put her finger on.

"Wow, Kit, they sound awfully nice. Someone thinks you're special. But you know what, they couldn't think any more of you than I do. You know that, don't you?" He sounded off kissy sounds into the receiver.

She chuckled. "You think that much of me? Are you sure?"

"You are the best! And I'm sorry I didn't think of giving you a box of new-fangled, swirly treats. We're still on for this weekend, aren't we, or do I need to be worried about someone else?"

"Of course. And no, you don't need to worry about another man." After the giggles subsided, she spoke. "You're so funny! And I can't wait. Let me get off here and find out who I need to thank."

"Okay. See you tomorrow."

Kit said good-bye and hung up the phone. She ate another chocolate filled with some kind of liqueur and cream. Interesting taste, she thought. By the end of the day, only two pieces remained. She stared at the box, embarrassed. Working on projects made one lose count where chocolates were concerned. How should she thank Dwight? Call him? March right down to his office and give him a hug? She got up from her chair and headed down the hallway. She'd figure something out, play it by ear.

"Knock, knock." Her fingers struck a few soft taps against the doorframe. Dwight glanced up, and his lips turned into a wide smile when he saw her. "Come on in here. What's up?"

A few strides across the room, and the next thing Kit knew, her arms encircled his neck. With her lips almost on his ear, she whispered, "Thanks for the chocolates."

Dwight pulled away from her as if she had a disease, rumpled brow showing clear dismay. "Chocolates?"

She stepped back, clapping her hand over her mouth. "You didn't give them to me, either?"

He sank back in his chair, frowning. "I'm afraid art boy would come and bust my chops if I did something like that, so no, nothing from me."

"Hey guys, just saying tootles for the weekend. Hope everyone has a nice one." Irene stepped into the office.

Dwight wore one of those over-exaggerated smiles, and spoke with a voice tinged with sarcasm. "Well, Kit is celebrating hers early, aren't you? She just got chocolates."

Irene's lips twisted in an expression of surprise. "Oh? How nice."

"No, not nice, because I have no idea who sent them." Kit scowled at both of them.

The room became quiet, and all three friends passed glances like a well thought-out football play. Dwight broke the silence with rat-a-tap-taps on his desk.

"Have you eaten any?" Irene turned to look at Kit.

"Let's just say I've taken the liberty of indulging myself and leave it at that."

"Was it a big box?"

"It had eight pieces." Kit shifted from one foot to the other.

"And how many are left?" Dwight's face remained expressionless.

"Does that matter?"

Irene shrugged. "Maybe, maybe not. We don't know yet." She snapped her fingers. "Why don't we ask one of the administrative assistants if they put the chocolates on your desk? Maybe they can tell us who delivered them."

"Great idea, Irene, but they've gone home now. They leave earlier than we do, remember?" Dwight's lips turned down in disappointment.

"That's true. Damn! I forgot about that, and it's Friday." Irene, glancing at the clock, repositioned the purse over her shoulder and walked over to hug Kit. "Just call me if something weird happens or you need anybody. I'll come right over. In the meantime, I gotta run. Big weekend planned with Jim." With a wave, she left the office.

Dwight said nothing for a moment, but stared down at his papers.

Kit moved toward the door. "I guess there's nothing else for me to do but go on home. I'm sorry I interrupted the rest of your afternoon, Dwight."

"Hey, no, you're okay. I just don't know what to say right now, that's all. But I'm like Irene. If you need anybody, you can call me too." He finally managed a forced grin.

"Thanks. I think I'm going to go home and relax, watch some TV or something. I'll see you next week."

Within minutes, she'd returned to her office, gathered up her things, including the box of candy, and hurried out of the mansion. Dear god, why hadn't she checked with everyone first before wolfing down all those chocolates? A feeling of doom set in, clutching her in its grip, and fear added its two cents worth by chiming in. Thoughts of going home to an empty apartment scared her right now. What if she got sick and died? What would they think if she didn't show up to work on Monday? What would Steven think if he tried to come over, but couldn't get in touch with her?

Ruminating over sickness and death made her nerves more frantic. All of a sudden, a wave of nausea hit her stomach, and her thoughts spun out of control. *"Oh dear lord! Here it is right now! The grim reaper's come to take me away."* Stopping in her tracks, she took a deep breath, glanced over at *Celestial Temptation Gallery*, and scurried across the street.

CHAPTER 16

"Are you okay?" Steven scrambled out from behind the counter and ran across the floor, intercepting Kit in his arms. "You don't look so good. Come here, sit down." He led her to the chair he'd occupied and helped her down.

She took a series of deep breaths, fanning her hand in front of her face trying to cool off. "Oh, wow, it's cold outside, but I'm so hot. Jesus help me ..." A light belch slipped out of her mouth. "Sorry about that." She fanned herself again.

"What on earth is wrong with you?" Steven knelt down beside her and peered up into her face.

Tears, which had been lurking behind her eyes ever since she left Dwight's office, tumbled out in droves, and she whimpered. "Steven, I don't want to die. I'm too young to go now."

At those words, Steven's look of concern went blank. The warmth in his eyes grew cold, as if some unseen force had reached down and pulled a hidden plug.

"What? Why are you looking at me that way?" She lifted her hand, muffling a light hiccup. "Sorry, I must look horrible. I feel so awful." After fanning her face some more, she spoke again. "I didn't mean to barge in on you like this, but I'm scared to go home."

"What's going on? I've never seen you like this." Care and empathy kicked in, because he rubbed his hand over her shoulders and the back of her neck.

"Remember the chocolates?"

"Yes." He began to frown a little. "One of your friends gave them to you, right?"

She shook her head. "No. I asked my co-workers, and none of them gave me candy."

Steven said nothing, but ran his fingers through his hair, trying to think. "I don't know what to say, but this is a little weird. Did you bring the box with you?"

"Yeah, I have it right here."

He picked up the box. "Looks nice, pretty ribbon. Was it sealed?"

"No!" Kit sniffled. "I guess that should have been my first clue. But it looked so pretty, harmless, really. And sometimes Dwi ... No, it wasn't sealed."

"There's only two left in here. How many were there?"

"Oh, don't you start! I've already gotten the third degree from my friends."

"How many, Kit? How many of these things did you eat?"

"Six, and yes, I know I'm a glutton when it comes to sweets. You know that." Her head hung in shame.

Chuckling, he replaced the top on the box and set it down. "Are you sure you don't just have a good old-fashioned bellyache?"

"I've eaten my share of chocolates, and had my share of being ill afterwards, but never to the point of wanting to hurl and then go somewhere and croak."

"Tell you what. Let me close up here, and I'll take you home." He ran to the back of his shop for a moment, returning again to switch off the lights in the front room, and flip the 'Open' sign in the window.

As he moved, Kit couldn't help but notice that the same paintings hung on the walls. Why hadn't he sold anything? How could he keep this place open without sales?

"There, I'm done." He smiled at Kit.

"Steven, I feel so bad about this. I can go on home and wait until you close. It won't be that long."

"No, I'm done for the day. Let's go."

They walked out of the shop. He locked the door, and they headed toward Kit's apartment. The trip up the stairs seemed longer this evening, each step up rattling her brain and nerves. Leaning against him, she felt the power exuding from his body. His presence acted as a safe harbor, which she acknowledged with a thankful heart. Kit unlocked the door and they entered the hallway.

"Go sit down, and I'll get you some water. Maybe that'll help."

Kit staggered to the sofa, dropped down, and took some deep breaths, wincing at the cramps throwing sucker punches in her stomach. She doubled over to calm everything down.

"Here, drink a little." Steven handed her a glass of ice water. "There's some soda in the refrigerator; do you think that might be better?"

"I don't think so. If I have something bubbly, I think I'll explode." She sipped the water, holding on to his hand while he watched and waited beside her. At least home wasn't so scary now, and if she did croak, at least he could see to a proper funeral and burial.

"Is it letting up any? Do we need to take you to the emergency room?" He placed a cool hand on the side of her cheek. "You feel a little warm."

"Your hand feels so good. Keep it there." She pushed her face harder against his palm. "Thank you so much for coming home with me. Will you stay with me tonight? At least until I fall asleep?"

"Yeah, sure." He hugged her close.

His warm breath against her face acted like a form of life support for her wounded spirit, and his gentle massaging of her shoulders took the edge off the war raging in her belly. Why did all this have to happen to her? Most of all, why did she act like such a glutton and eat all those chocolates? It served her right. After all, church teachings spoke out against gluttony, pointing out this as one of the deadly sins. She held her head in her hands and took a deep breath. If she had to die, passing away in Steven's arms wouldn't be such a bad thing.

Unfortunately, his tender loving care failed to quell the rumblings of the intestinal battle brewing inside. Kit closed her eyes, took some deep breaths, and tried desperately to imagine something pleasant. But the sweating had kicked in, and she wanted to faint.

"Steven, I don't think ..." She bolted upright and made a dash for the bedroom. Standing over the toilet, she opened her mouth. Every impurity she'd ever consumed, breathed, or even believed came out in a torrential gush. Her bowels threw in the white flag of surrender, and Kit morphed into a filthy, foul-smelling creature who wanted more than anything to get away and hide.

"What's going on? Kit?" Steven stood in the doorway and sniffed the air. "Are you okay?"

"Don't come in here!" Kit yelled out as she turned her head in his direction.

But he ignored her, stepping in to open the linen closet where he pulled out some towels and wash cloths.

"Get out!" She shrieked louder, hoping he'd leave her alone. "Please get out! I'll be okay."

Steven stood rooted to the floor. "Are you sure?"

Kit coughed and gagged a little before calming down enough to talk in a more civilized manner. "I'm sure. Just go back and let me clean up. I'll be done in a minute."

"Can I at least get you a trash bag? Where do you keep them?"

"Under the sink. You'll find a box of them." Thankful to have him gone, Kit shifted to keep her balance, holding on to the back of the toilet for support.

Never in her worst nightmare would she have dreamt of finding herself in a situation like this one. Lovers weren't supposed to see each other like this, weak and covered in their own filth. What would he think of her now? After this horrendous scenario, he'd never see her the same way again. Her attempts at maintaining a facade of perfection had just been busted by none other than Mother Nature herself, and of course, the deadly sin, Gluttony, who'd made his point with a swift punch in the gut.

Within seconds, Steven returned with a bag. "Do you need help getting out of these clothes?"

"No, I can do it myself. You can go back out there. Don't come any closer." She'd finally forced herself to turn around and face him. "I feel so embarrassed, you seeing me like this."

"Kit, I don't mind." He'd opened the bag to catch her slacks, panties, and top. Next came bra and socks.

"Do you want me to start the shower for you?"

She shook her head. "No, I'll get it. You can put the bag on top of the washing machine. I'll decide later if I want to wash them or simply toss them out."

He grinned at her. "Or we could start a nice, toasty fire and burn them."

Kit laughed, and pushed him gently out the door. As she stood in the shower, Kit prayed this hot baptism of water would cleanse her from all the unpleasantness going on. Come Monday, she'd think of what to do next.

* * *

Sunday afternoon found Kit crawling into bed, with Steven snuggling in from behind. What had been planned as a weekend for fun and love-making had ended up with Kit spending much of the time trying to recoup. Steven played the attentive nurse, attending to every need, and spending nights with her to make sure she was safe. Dwight and Irene called Saturday to check in on her. She'd especially enjoyed chatting with Dwight, the conversations and easy talk bringing back memories. Today some semblance of normalcy had crept back into her body.

"Talk about killing your libido!" Kit smiled into Steven's face and landed a kiss on his lips.

"You've been pretty sick. I'm just glad you're feeling better." He wiggled closer, and as she stretched out, his hand cupped one of her breasts. While his thumb and forefinger busied themselves, she closed her eyes, savoring the lusty storm brewing inside her chest. Within moments, the storm erupted, creeping down into her abdomen and exploding throughout the rest of her body, landing where it counted most.

"You feel so good!"

"So do you!" He grinned. Her hands wandered down, each finger prancing over his velvety flesh in a flirty dance, pressing in, retracing, fluttering over all the right places with her own artful touch.

Their lips met and Kit drowned in his kiss, tasting and sucking his tongue, greedy for more. She wrapped her arms around him and held on with a firm grip, fearful he might vanish in an instant. Deeper and deeper she sank, closing her eyes, wrapping herself in darkness. Every thought inside her mind stilled and retreated into dark recesses. The world faded away, and nothing mattered but the present, she and Steven in each other's arms. The kissing slowly came to a halt. Kit gave herself over to the moment, merging her energy with his.

In the flash of an instant, the core of her body felt like a switch had been thrown, revving up every nerve with a life of its own. The rush came, the unleashing of the serpent, that bundle of raw energy coiled at the base of the spine, springing forth like a snake striking at its target. If colors could be felt, Kit sensed herself bathed in all the glorious shades she'd seen before.

She dipped her head down, licking his earlobe, before giving it a tiny kiss.

With a lazy grin, he pulled her tighter in his arms. "I think we came together on this one."

With a tiny giggle, she answered with a kiss on his lips. "You think?"

"In a special sort of way. Our special way." His eyes took on a dreamy glaze, as his fingers ruffled through the strands of her hair.

Kit winked, and moved her head toward the area below his belt line.

In an agile move, he intervened, flipping her to a supine position just as her lips landed on the flesh between his thighs. "A little eager, aren't you? Don't you know they say good things come to those who wait? Huh?" He delivered a few playful tickles to the sides of her ribs, going at it with greater gusto the more she squealed with laughter.

For the next hour, they engaged in a tantalizing round of play, filled with excitement and fascination, as if experiencing each other for the first time. All sense of time disappeared, leaving the couple in a world they'd created. Touches and kisses of endearment branded loving imprints on the heart, leaving shallow speeches of tender adoration locked in silence. Steven entertained himself with roving fingers and tongue, bringing her to the heights of raging ecstasy. Kit, in turn, delighted in rousing him to the fullest level a man can reach. With deft movements, she coaxed him into a hard release. They ended in a sweaty, breathless heap, entangled in each other's arms.

"Looks like you're bouncing back to the old you." Steven gave her a soft kiss on the tip of her nose.

"I think I'm mostly there, but I must admit, I'm a little exhausted right now." She ran a finger up and down his chest, lost in thought. "Tomorrow, I may call old Harsh. It may be a long shot, and I know I'll be pretty much accusing him, but I've got to confront him some way. It's high time he knows I'm on to him. Maybe I'll at least scare him."

He cradled her tighter. "What'll you say to him? Have you thought about that?"

"I'm not sure. I'll probably make it up on the fly. Sounds a little nutty, but sometimes it works better for me that way." Her eyes searched his. "I'm nervous, though. What if things get worse? The night of the carnival is creeping up fast."

Steven loosened his grip and stretched out, staring at the ceiling. "My real concern is that he may never give up, even after the carnival. Remember, your Society will be working on raising money for the property until it's paid for. That will take years."

"I can't be tormented for years, Steven, I just can't. There's got to be an Achilles' heel for him somewhere. I just have to figure out where it is. And I still can't prove anything. There's a motive, but no direct proof."

He nodded, glancing in the direction of his jacket.

"What? You're not thinking of going home right now, are you?" She propped herself up, stretched out a hand, and turned his face back to hers. "Don't go. Not right now."

"I'm not leaving, but I need to get something." He crawled off the bed toward his jacket. From one of the side pockets, he pulled out a tiny vial.

"What's that?" She craned her neck for a better look.

"I'll tell you in a second." He slipped back into bed and held the vial out in front of her. "I created this for you."

"What is it?"

"It's an anointing oil. We're Catholic, so you've heard of anointing."

"Yeah, but isn't that reserved for priests? You can't just do that yourself, can you?"

The vial glistened in the lamplight, showing off an amber liquid.

"I beg to differ. Yes, we think priests are the only ones who can anoint, but I've learned that anyone can do this. Healers have been doing it for thousands of years. The oils are healing, and they allow one to set an intent."

Kit's eyes grew wide, and she gently took the vial from his hand and brought it to her nose. "Can I smell it?"

"Go ahead, open it up. Just be careful and don't spill anything."

An earthy smell mixed with other spicy scents permeated her nostrils. "Interesting." She glanced over at Steven. "I like the scent."

"This particular blend is for protection and for counteracting fear." He took the bottle from her hand. "We know how well your candle-lighting went. Now it's my turn."

She wrinkled her nose at him, before grinning back. "I tried, anyway. But you're right, I think I was too scared to even think that night."

"Your desire to take action is the first step to your own healing. The follow-through will be the next step. Believe it or not, we have more choice and influence in our lives than we're taught, Kit. Trust me on this one."

"So what do you do with this oil? Rub some on my forehead, splash some around the room, like you're chasing way vampires or evil spirits? This is something Irene would do, though I've never heard her talking about anything like this before."

"You can anoint in different ways, no set rules. There's only a little bit in this bottle. I had enough made to use in one session. I'm going to rub it on different parts of your body, and while I do, I'm going to say some prayers. I want you to relax, be receptive, and see yourself as strong and powerful."

Unlike the spirit board experience, Kit liked the idea of anointing much better. On a deeper level, this engagement with Steven seemed much more personal and intimate than playing 'Twenty Questions' with a board. He'd gone out of his way to create an oil just for her, demonstrating kindness and devotion to the highest degree. Why not try his magic oil? Her feeble attempts at candle-lighting had failed miserably.

She dropped back down on the bed and closed her eyes. "Okay, I'm ready. You can start anytime you want."

Steven pulled back all the covers. The cool room air hit her flesh, and for the first time, she became acutely aware of her nakedness. She swallowed hard, struggling to keep her arms at her side. This physical exposure went way beyond making a simple cross on the forehead of an ill person. Her thoughts turned to Adam when he became aware of his unclothed flesh. Many a sermon she'd heard ranted on and on about standing bare before the Lord, and as she mulled over the concept, it all became clear. We had to come before the Almighty, naked, and bringing with us all fears, shame, and doubts, knowing we were still loved and cared for just the same.

It took total trust to do this willingly and pull it off without a hitch, but she was slowly beginning to understand how shame, fear, and doubt painted one into a corner, holding the body and soul captive and left to die. Kit close her eyes and settled into that blank state she'd been practicing since Steven's first introduction to the concept. She had to admit, practice made perfect, and she'd been working diligently to perfect this skill each day.

Steven settled into a comfortable position and opened the vial. Tipping the bottle, he caught a little of the liquid on his fingers and, with tender strokes, applied the oil on her forehead, behind her ears, and down the sides of her neck. Kit opened her mouth to say how much she liked this anointing process already, but caught herself in time. On a gut level, intuition guided her back to the old adage that silence was golden. Besides, she knew no one most likely spoke when being anointed. She closed her mouth and let out a soft sigh instead.

Tempted to steal a peek at Steven to see what else he was doing, maybe catch him mouthing some weird incantation, she opened up her eyes just enough to view him through squinted lids. She snapped them closed again. It didn't feel right spying on him. But why not? This anointing was for her, wasn't it? Why shouldn't she be able to peep or say something, like how much she liked his hands rubbing over the top of her sternum?

"Kit, you're not paying attention and doing what I told you to do."

Her heart nearly leaped out of her chest as his lips brushed against her ear. Caught red-handed! Could he read her mind, or did her face show lack of piety? Maybe she'd started to grin or even giggle. She didn't recall any giggle creeping its way out. What would happen if he touched a ticklish part?

"Ki-i-t, concentrate!" He whispered a little louder and firmer this time.

Heavens, she had no other choice but to do what he told her! Next time, he'd be mad. With a deep gulp of air, she tried clearing her mind, and, after a few seconds, it calmed down and went blank. Concentrating on nothing but his touch and the fragrance of the oil, she tried visioning herself as strong and powerful. Inside her mind, snapshots of scenes, playing like video clips, raced by in succession. Some visions showed her holding a sword, ready to slay an enemy. Other images depicted her surrounded by white light. An instant flash of Austin's face, filled with a radiant smile, startled her as it morphed into an image of Steven, bathed in a blaze of glorious white light. What did all of this mean? Everything struck her as prophetic, suggesting safety and success.

Is this what meditation or setting an intent was like? Is this why Steven liked what he called "just being?" Maybe he would understand why the inside of her head mirrored a theater screen.

He landed a light kiss on her earlobe. "You're doing great."

The even pressure of his fingers massaging over her wrists and abdomen had done wonders in calming her, and in the end, he'd taken the remainder of the oil and rubbed it into her feet. When the last of the oil had been applied, Steven sat, allowing her to awaken on her own time. Little by little, Kit roused from her reflective state. Her eyes fluttered opened, and she blinked a few times.

He leaned over, gracing her lips with a light kiss. "There, we're done." Taking her hands in his, he spoke in a soft voice: "May all you say and do serve the highest and greatest good. May the spirits on high grant you the most benevolent outcome. May Grace bestow upon you a gentle kiss as the lamp of Love lights your way in darkness. As you follow the path of Truth, may the hand of Strength cast away Fear and Doubt. When Evil seeks to block the way, may Courage and Wisdom be your steadfast companions."

She sat up and stared at him. "How beautiful! Is that what you said while you were using the oil?"

"Yes. It's my blessing for you, Kit."

His eyes reflected an indisputable authority. This act of intercession left her dumbstruck. No one had ever gone to such great lengths to make her affairs and well-being a personal concern.

"I've never been blessed before." The warmth from his hands heated every part of her, creating the effects of a security blanket, one she wanted to hide under for a long time.

"I know without a doubt you'll get all of it. You have to believe it yourself." His eyes searched hers. "You do believe, don't you?"

Kit thought back to the visions she'd experienced a few minutes earlier. The pictures rolling around in her head, though cryptic, filled her with a certain peace. Yes, a good part of her did believe. "Yes, I think so. Let's just say I do now more than ever before."

"Good. And don't forget any of this." Steven got up to replace the empty vial back in his jacket.

"Hey, by the way, what if I need more of that oil?"

Steven gave her a startled look. "I made this myself, so this is it." He smiled. "Besides, you may not need any more. I have a feeling you'll be okay."

"You know that for sure? How?" She slid out of bed and tiptoed over, wrapping her arms around his waist. His back felt solid and warm against her cheek as she held him close.

"I just know, Kit." He cleared his throat. "Everything comes in cycles. You're going through a rough spot, but it will all turn around."

"Really?" Her eyes narrowed into slits, and she licked the bottom of her lip. Suddenly her body became tired. All the physical and mental activity had fatigued her, creating a sluggish feeling. Shrugging the whole conversation off, she turned around and crept back into bed. "Good to know."

"Besides, if you want a regular anointing oil, you can purchase it in any New Age shop or a religious supply house."

She'd slipped beneath the covers, snuggling down for a nap. With a yawn, she closed her eyes. "Another good thing to know. Maybe Irene and I can make a blend of our own. Maybe a BFF blend."

He chuckled, slipping in beside her, lips brushing against her ear. "Kit, you'll be fine, really."

"Mmm, if you say so." In an instant, she'd dropped off to sleep, with Steven cradling her in his arms, joining her in that special place where dreamers go.

CHAPTER 17

All morning long Kit sat in her office, occupied with compiling a list of churches in Windham Springs, along with the names of the deceased buried in their respective churchyards. It was her plan to place the complete list on the Society's website for genealogical use. Taking a break, she rested her head in her hands and stared at the phone. There was definitely someone who seemed intent on spooking her, rattling their chains with horrid packages and destruction. She'd been watching her back and calling her cousin to make sure she was okay too.

One question kept rolling through her mind, especially since the horrible chocolate incident. Should she contact Edmond Harsh and let him have it with both barrels, giving him her nasty two cents worth? Or should she continue ignoring everything and just be extra careful from here on out? Steven had made a point. Old Harsh or his cronies could spend his time dogging her at every corner if she or someone didn't put a stop to it. She drummed her fingers on the desk. Do it, or forget about it? What would she say if Harsh answered?

Screw it! She'd always winged it before; she'd do it again now. With her stomach flipping and turning like an acrobat inside her, she tapped out his name in the search box of the Internet browser. "Edmond Harsh Contractors" came up at the top of the page listing. His company phone number, in bold, came up under the address. Her fingers punched out the numbers, quivering over each one. A sour taste filled her mouth as the phone rang on the other end. No one had answered, yet. There was still time to hang up the phone and go about her business, forgetting this craziness altogether.

"Ed Harsh speaking." The man on the other end paused for a response.

Kit's heart pounded so hard she heard the blood rush in her ears. For such a hateful person, his voice sounded smooth, almost pleasant.

"Hello? This is Ed Harsh speaking. Can I help you?"

Hearing him speak brought back memories of the Commission meeting, the anger in his eyes, the rage in his tone of voice. Without a word, Kit hung up the receiver. She thought back over all that had happened to her since that time, and what had happened to Alexandra. All of it appeared coincidental, a little too much for her taste. She had no hard proof, and as she played out the what-ifs of hiring a lawyer or private investigator to follow him, the whole deal wore her out. Several options came up for paying off the mansion, but she had no one to help her pay legal fees.

She thought about Mr. Crispin, and how he'd told her about lawyers and the practice of law in general. Many times he'd only use bluffing tactics, which sometimes sent his opponents scrambling. Would that work on a greedy, wealthy person like Harsh? Snapping her finger, Kit jumped out of her seat. Those pictures on her phone need not go to waste. She took them for a reason. Her plan was worth a shot. If Mr. Crispin could bluff, so could she. If it didn't work, she'd truly have to go to plan B if the nonsense didn't stop. She grabbed up her purse and phone and bolted toward the door.

"Whoa, there!" She and Irene nearly collided. "You're running out of here like a bat out of hell. Where are you going in such a hurry?" Irene backed up, steadying herself.

"Sorry, but I have some business I have to deal with." Kit hoisted her purse strap over her shoulder, phone and car keys gripped tightly in the other hand.

Irene looked at her in earnest. "You need someone for moral support? I'm your gal."

"Mmm, I think I better handle this one on my own. No need for too many cooks in the kitchen, if you know what I mean." Kit grinned at her friend, patting her on the arm.

"What are you going to do?"

"I'm going to put someone in their place, or at least try to scare the shit out of them, if I'm that lucky."

"Like who?" Irene raised an eyebrow, face contorted in surprise.

"Look, I gotta run. I'll fill you in later." Kit moved past Irene, walking boldly to the door.

"Don't do anything foolish. And we're as close as a phone."

Irene's words trailed off as Kit shut the door of the Stothwell Mansion behind her.

The afternoon blazed bright and sunny, vibrant colors of autumn enhanced by a brilliant sun, the way afternoons often looked this time of year. The crisp air swiped at her face, rustling her hair as she walked to her apartment. If she didn't have so much on her mind, she would have enjoyed taking an extended lunch. She ran the remainder of the last few yards to the front door of the building and bounded up the stairs to her apartment.

In her room, she sat at a small desk. After raising the lid on her laptop, she clicked on her email app. On her phone, she accessed her camera and emailed herself all the pictures she'd taken since the arrival of that hateful skull, grinning at her, eye sockets showing off horrific gaping holes. After switching out the regular paper in her printer with photo paper, she printed each picture. She opened the top desk drawer and retrieved the box of chocolates with the remaining two pieces. She'd kept this gift as more tangible evidence. Might as well take it too. Go for broke.

She thought a minute before leaving her room. Should she at least tell someone her plan in case something happened? Mr. Crispin was working downstairs. Kit took up everything she needed and made her way to her landlord's office.

"Knock, knock." She tapped on the doorframe.

The gentleman glanced up and smiled. "Taking a quick lunch break at home?"

"Hardly, but there are some things I want to tell you, if you have a few minutes."

Crispin sat back in his leather chair. "Go ahead. I'm all ears."

For the next several minutes, Kit brought him up to speed on what had occurred.

He wrinkled his brow, frowning with concern. "And why didn't you tell me all this much earlier?"

"Don't know. I was hoping maybe these shenanigans would stop. But if you don't see me tonight, send out the search party." She grinned, somewhat cringing as she spoke.

"Just don't do anything too rash. If he is indeed behind all this, maybe he'll get the point and back down." He shook his head. "Boy, he's got balls if he is the mastermind. If he's not, then maybe he'll warn whomever is, if he knows them."

"Can't hurt to try, so wish me luck." Kit headed for the door.

"You have my best, and if you need me, let me know." Crispin gave her a thumbs up.

Kit's mind raced as she drove to Harsh's office, leaving the quaint world of the square behind. How would she approach him? What would she say? How would he react? This tactic was her immediate ace in the hole, the best she could do to hopefully stop strange and destructive things from happening. She had to sound convincing, while maintaining some sense of professionalism. There was always a risk of him lashing back out at her.

As she drove, the buildings displayed modern architecture, and the activity flowed at a more hectic pace. People walked the sidewalks, some carrying bags, others enjoying a more leisurely stroll. Making a right turn onto Compton Avenue, she guided the Beetle down two more blocks before spying Harsh's office, a modest brick building in an upscale business park. Her pulse quickened and her stomach tightened, matching in scale to the tingling of her nerves. She parked the car, taking up her photos and box of candy before opening the door. Hopefully he'd still be in his office.

The receptionist greeted her with a pleasant smile. "Good afternoon, is Mr. Harsh expecting you?" She glanced up from her computer as her chubby fingers paused over the keyboard.

Returning the smile, Kit roused up every ounce of courage. "No, but I really need to talk to him. I'm Kit Millinger, from the Historical Society." Never had Kit seen a person's expression sober up so quickly.

"I'll definitely tell him you're here. I'm sure he'll be glad to make some time for you. One moment please." The lady slipped out from behind the desk and headed toward a closed door.

Kit surveyed her surroundings. Nice office space, carpet of navy blue, and light salmon-colored walls displaying neatly framed before-and-after photos of buildings. Across from the lady's desk, a waiting area had been made, complete with a simple sofa and two armchairs and a coffee table. On an end table a lamp glowed, softening the ambience. The silence in the room nearly smothered her. In the far corner, she spied a large table and chairs, most likely for meetings. However the scene would play out between her and Harsh, she'd have to remember to keep her voice down. *Don't get riled, stay in control.*

The lady returned, pleasant smile in tow. "Mr. Harsh will see you now."

"Thank you." Kit nodded, moving toward Harsh's office. *Here we go!*

Behind an enormous executive's desk sat a thin man surrounded by layers of what appeared to be blueprints. His computer screen gleamed open to a real estate site focusing on foreclosures. Just as she figured. He could have his pick of land without bothering hers. Forcing her eyes away from the screen, she choked down the bitter annoyance bubbling inside her already.

"To what do I owe this surprise visit, Miss Millinger?" His voice came across pleasant enough, but not without a steely edge in the tone. He waved her to the vacant chair in front of his desk, a forced light smile on his face. Kit noted the cold flash in his eyes. She braced herself for the worst, just in case. But she'd decided to not get caught up in the emotions. Just get down to business.

"Good afternoon, Mr. Harsh," Kit also put on her best fake smile face. "I'll stand, if you don't mind." She planted herself against the front of his desk, ignoring the offer of the chair. "Before I get started, would you like a chocolate? Surely a man of your caliber appreciates fine confections." Kit opened the box and pushed it close to his face.

Harsh's eyes widened, face flushing. "Excuse me?"

"Go ahead. Eat one. They're really very good." Kit pushed the box closer.

The man pushed the box away. "No, thank you." The coolness in his voice dropped several degrees.

"Why? Isn't this from your favorite chocolatier? Really, you should have one." She stifled a grin, eyes never leaving his face. The boldness bug bit her hard, leaving her with a new sense of smugness. Maybe Mr. Crispin was right about this notion of bluffing.

"Miss Millinger. I'm a very busy man. So what is it, please? Have you had a change of heart about the mansion?"

Kit replaced the top on the box. "I know why you don't want a piece of this chocolate, Mr. Harsh. Do you?"

"Damn the chocolates, Miss Millinger. Get on with the reason you're here."

Kit thrilled at the sight of him clenching his teeth, fingers white, drawing up in irritation. Yes, she'd definitely get on with the reason she came.

"Because they're poisoned, Mr. Harsh. Deliberately tampered with or allowed to spoil. Either way, you got your wish."

"What the hell are you talking about?" Harsh's face contorted with surprise before irritation set in. "You little ..."

Holding out her hand to silence him, Kit clicked her tongue in mock chastisement. "Oh, let me finish, and I'll be out of here as quickly as I came." She placed each photograph on his desk, peeling them from the stack in her hand like a dealer hands out cards in a poker game, satisfied as his facial expression turned blank. But his eyes still held that same, irritating glint.

"Look familiar?" Kit tapped each photograph a few times for emphasis. "Did you have fun dreaming up all this?" She leaned in close to his face. "Did you have fun beating up my car, smashing it to smithereens? And my cousin could have broken her leg when she fell from her porch."

Harsh fell back in his seat, shaking his head. "I have no idea what you're talking about."

"Bullshit!" Kit took several deep breaths. "You know exactly what I'm talking about. Don't look so innocent, like you don't know the things that are going on. How could you not know? Other than you, who else gives a damn about that house?"

"Apparently you do, because you're hell-bent on keeping it, putting up with whatever it is that's going on in these photos." He pointed at the pictures, a smirk flitting across his lips.

Kit stood up, aiming her finger straight at him. "Let me tell you something. If anything else happens to me or my cousin – I don't care how big or small the incident is – I'll hire a lawyer. I'm looking up private investigators as we speak. I'm going next to see the news channel. They'll love a good story on how a man like you kills poor defenseless animals, snakes included. Fighting off animal rights activists won't be fun."

The man behind the desk stared out at her with expressionless eyes – cold, dead, dark, like someone had knocked him senseless. Kit took a quick breath, digesting everything she'd said.

"You're crazy. I could get you for slander, coming in here and accusing me like you are. Or for trespassing." Harsh started to get up.

"Save it." Kit didn't budge. "Don't you dare threaten me. You and your crony will stop because I'm done with this. It will be years paying off this mansion, and I'm not spending the entire time looking over my shoulder, dealing with damaged property, or fearing for my life." She gathered up the photos and the chocolate box. "Now I'm done." Whirling around, she left the office, not minding the door shutting a little on the loud side. Nodding coldly to a stunned administrative assistant, who watched with wide eyes and open mouth, Kit reached the office door, throwing it open and sailing out into the afternoon sun.

* * *

Back inside her office, Kit reviewed the scene at Harsh's office over and over again in her head. She'd entered the mansion with such speed and purpose, rushing back to her office, no one dared asked her what was wrong. Luckily, Irene and Dwight were tucked away elsewhere, and for that she was glad. After her verbal spar with old Harsh, she wanted to be alone, unwind, process everything that had just happened. How much would a private investigator really cost? Especially in comparison with a lawyer? She hoped she'd showed him enough to send him running in the opposite direction.

The phone rang. She yelped, startled, fearful of picking up the receiver as if it were possessed. With a huff, she answered. If she could toss out accusations once, she surely could defend herself if old Harsh had called back to give her a piece of his mind.

"Hey, baby, are you feeling better today?"

She let out a breath of relief. The suave voice on the other end of the line never sounded as sweet as it did that moment. "Steven, thank goodness it's you!"

"Oka-a-a-y, thank you? You sound worried. What's going on?"

"Sorry. It's just that you'll never guess where I've been this afternoon. It wasn't pleasant, but I told him where to get off."

"Yeah? Where? And who got told off?"

"Edmond Harsh's office. I told him to lay the hell off, or else."

"What? You went over to his place?"

Kit chuckled. "I'll tell you all about it later, but I'm hoping I bluffed him enough to stop, or at least he'll tell his henchman to stop. Either one is fine with me."

"Hmm, interesting. So you waltzed right in there and just let fur fly, huh?"

"Yeah, and it flew too. I took all my evidence. And I was so insulted. He didn't even take one of the chocolates I offered him." Kit grinned as she drew some doodle figures on a scratch pad, one being the caricature of a man's face with horns on top of the head.

Steven laughed. "Did you really do that?"

"I did." Kit chuckled.

"Do you feel better now?"

"A little."

"So do you regret doing it?"

"I won't lie, Steven. It's unnerved me a little, but overall, I'm glad he's at least in the know."

"Good. You took a stand, and that's at least something. You can't do anything about the way he chooses to handle this. Maybe things will stop and you can rest easy."

She leaned back in her chair, gazing at the ceiling. "I hope so. God, I'm so tired of all this. It needs to stop once and for all."

"I have a feeling it'll get better. Somebody hell-bent on being shady gets found out one way or another. They don't last long."

"Hey, by the way, thank you for the weekend. I think your oil kicked in."

Steven laughed. "Sounds like it did. I'm glad you're feeling better. But I'm glad you stood up to him. I don't normally agree with going around accusing people of things, but I have a suspicion he needed to be told."

"Steven, on another note, do you think we might be able to steal away and look for some other pieces for our costumes? Can you take some time so we can visit an antique shop for a little while? Some of the dealers in these places have great items."

"Sure, I can get away. Did you want to do it this weekend? Because next weekend it's show time."

"True. And like we said, we're not looking to buy the most extravagant things."

"I hear you. We'll see what's out there. Well, gotta run. We'll hook up later."

Kit hung up the phone. Whew, close call! At least she'd received some validation for her actions.

Steven didn't always agree with her, but when he did, or at least showed some semblance of agreement, situations always seemed less dramatic and chaotic in her mind. Picking up a pencil, she engrossed herself in editing the church listing some more before committing the information to an electronic document.

"Dwight, what are you staring at?" Kit looked up at the sound of rustling and grinned as he perched easily on top of her desk. The intent gaze showed he'd come with some purpose, and the smile shrank from her lips. "I can tell by the look on your face something's up. Are you okay, or do you know a secret I don't?"

"Yeah, Kit, I do have something I want to share with you. It's been on my mind, and I'm not sure how to go about this, even now." He ran his fingers through his hair, eyes narrowed with thought. "Here, let me shut the door, if you don't mind. Like I've said before, I adore Irene, but I really need this to stay between you and me." He got up from the desk and shut the door. When he returned, he walked around and knelt beside Kit's chair.

Her stomach lurched. Somehow, she'd already suspected that this conversation would most likely not be a normal one. On the other hand, facing fears and uncomfortable subjects had, as of late, appeared to pop up as missions, tests for some kind of crazy character-building. Time to hunker down for another one.

She watched as he stared at the ground a few moments, his face showing a certain inner turmoil. The next several seconds held a charge of excitement, one riddled with anticipation and dread.

"On Sunday, later in the afternoon, I was at home and decided to take a nap. Not sure why I was tired, but for some reason, I needed a quick round of shut-eye."

Kit nodded and leaned forward a little in her chair. "Yeah, and?"

"I fell asleep, pretty quickly, mind you. And, as you might guess, I'm not one to put much stock into dreams, but this one has followed me around since the moment I woke up."

"Okay. So what was it?"

"When I fell asleep, I dreamed about ..." He paused, studying the floor again.

She cocked her head a bit, but the pick-up pace of her heartbeat caused some alarm. "What did you dream about, Dwight? And somehow, I doubt the carpet has anything useful to offer. Look at me." His cheeks flushed, and the sight of his eyes, with tears threatening to sneak out, hit a soft spot in her heart. "Tell me, what did you dream about? It's okay to tell."

He swallowed hard, and his voice nearly cracked in his throat. "I dreamed about us. I dreamed we were in bed – and we were making love." His face colored even more.

"Go on, Dwight, I won't be shocked or mad. Just tell me." The chair creaked as she leaned forward. Part of her dreaded what she was about to hear, but a bigger part of her wanted to hear. All the details, all the emotions, she needed to hear it.

"We were making love." He closed his eyes and smiled, and every pent up thought or desire he held came tumbling out.

"In the dim lamplight of the room, we were in bed, naked, and making love. I felt your skin under my fingertips, soft like the finest silk. Your lips, when I kissed them, touched mine with all the velvety softness of rose petals. And your tongue, I wanted to hold it in my mouth so I could caress and taste it forever. My fingers touched every part of your body. I went slow so I could memorize every curve, every line. For some odd reason, I knew just what made you happy. An unseen force seemed to guide everything. When I dipped my finger inside you, your excitement matched mine. And when I rubbed over that sweet spot of yours, I watched you drown in the sensations every woman craves. I knew you were ready for me, and I slipped inside you. At that moment, I honestly didn't think my heart could handle such happiness, that I wasn't worthy."

He paused a moment, then looked directly at her. "But you know what, Kit? The love in your eyes – it was there; I saw it – saw it all. You wanted me like I wanted you."

Kit's eyes widened with every word, and now her mouth dropped open.

Dwight continued his poetic monologue. "And your hands brushed over my skin, and I declared I was in the presence of an angel. You knew how to bring out all the sensations a man likes to feel, and in all the right places. When your body accepted mine, I rejoiced in the surrender."

The attempt to stop him at this point stuck in her throat, but it didn't matter, because he'd lifted up a hand, requesting silence.

"But that's not it, Kit. No, not in the least is that all of the dream. What happened next was the strangest, but most amazing thing. You and I both felt it. Somehow, in this dream, I knew we had. You see, at one point during all the climaxing, there was a moment where we held each other. All at once, without warning, my body became consumed by this all-encompassing energy, one so strong I still felt the tingling in my hands when I woke up. The sensation was like nothing I'd ever experienced before. I swear I saw every color in the rainbow in that one instant. I don't know which I liked better, the delicious explosion of power rushing over me, or the pleasure of climax as we knew it."

Stunned by his revelation, Kit had moved so far over the edge of her seat, she nearly slipped to the floor. She gasped. The fact that the dream had occurred at the same time and on the same day she and Steven had been together filled her with such horror that a wave of nausea rumbled in her gut. Dwight caught her in his arms, and lifted her up so both of them stood, face-to-face.

He held her close and stared into her eyes. "Is this what would have happened had we continued our relationship with no interruptions? Why would I dream something so vivid like that, Kit?"

All she managed to do was gaze up at him and shake her head. His words had already created a frenzy inside her head. The warmth of his body nearly ignited hers, and the strength of his arms as they encircled her rivaled Steven's.

"I'll tell you why." He held her tighter and tipped his head to her ear. "It's because thoughts of you like this consume me, day and night. And now, after this dream, I can't keep this to myself anymore. You know I've cared about you from the moment we met. I'd always hoped maybe there'd be a chance you'd feel the same way about me. And we nearly had it. Since that man across the street swaggered into town, I'm not sure there is any hope for me, for us, anymore. But just know how strong my love is for you, Kit. I'll just throw pride away and say it. You can trample on my heart all you want, but nothing will change the way I feel about you."

In an instant, he moved in for a kiss, passionate and deep, slipping in his tongue to search for hers. Once he captured his prize, he lived out his dream in real time, tasting and sucking with a tender greed as if this moment offered one last morsel for his starving soul. If he hadn't been holding her, she'd have fainted. For the moment Kit put thoughts of Steven aside. Irene's warning of having to make a choice at some point played like a broken record over and over in her head. Yes, Kit needed to know her true feelings between the two, thereby justifying everything happening right now.

Without overthinking or rationalizing, Kit took advantage of the situation and opened her mouth wider, letting his breath filter in all the way to the depths of her lungs. His kiss, strong and persistent, created a frustrating ache in all the right places. If she knew without a doubt Dwight had locked the office door, she would jerk his fly open and then they both could make his dream come true. She held her breath. His hand worked its way under her blouse and gently brushed across her left breast.

Thoughts of ripping his pants open may have gone by the wayside, but her desire segued into the smooth sliding of her hand inside his pants and down to that special masculine area she had no business exploring. His taut flesh greeted her fingers with a sound welcome, and his hips jerked a little in response to her touch before he relented and pressed himself against her hand. His fingers moved in frantic motions over her bra, doing little to combat the weakness in her knees.

As quickly as the careless interlude had started, however, it came to a dead halt. A pang of guilt struck out and hit like a lightning bolt. She pulled her hand free and stared up at him, paralyzed with a mix of twisted relief and self-loathing.

"I'm sorry, Dwight. I didn't mean to ..."

Squaring up his shoulders, he gave her a light smile. "I'm not a bit sorry, Kit. We can finish this off right here and now, if you want. I locked the door. I won't say anything if you won't. Nobody will ever have to know but us."

"No, that's okay. Let's not do something we'll both regret. And besides I am seeing – "

"I really don't give a damn who you're seeing." He gazed down at her. Hostility and sadness brewed in his eyes. "I have no regrets over what just happened, or what could have happened if we'd kept going." He placed his hands around her shoulders. "I'll confess right now that I hate him. I hate that he came into town, that he's wormed his way into your life. Honestly, I wish he'd just go away and ..."

"No, Dwight, please don't say any more." Her words came out soft and pleading. She lifted a couple of fingers to his lips. "Sh-h-h, it's okay. I'm not mad at you, but please don't say anything else." Her arms wrapped around him, hands rubbing over his back, trying to soothe a man in anguish.

He lifted her face to his for one last quick kiss and stepped around the desk, striding to the door. "Very well, then. This is just our secret, Kit, no one else's." The sadness and frustration still lingered on his face as he turned away and closed the door behind him.

The second the door clicked shut, she collapsed back down in her chair and threw her head back. Her mind reeled in confusion. How could she have let this incident go as far as it did? The instant their lips touched, she could have pulled away or stopped his advances. And then Dwight's comments, wishing Steven would go away and ... Kit shuddered, trying to shut out the hateful words. They hit too close to home, too close to the heart. Straggling through all the whys led to one ugly remaining truth: she wanted his touch almost as much as he wanted hers.

But the 'almost' is what made the difference. As long as Steven cared about her, she wanted him, plain and simple. The clock on the wall showed a few more hours of work before quitting time. Turning back to her project on the church lists, she spent the remainder of the day between productive work and wrestling with lingering lust and simmering guilt.

CHAPTER 18

"I know you're not telling me the truth about what happened last week. I can just feel it."

Inside *A Cup Above The Roast*, Irene sat across from Kit as they chatted over a couple of lattes. Darkness had already settled over the sky for the evening, and the lights on the square created a unique, cozy feel to the night.

"So talk to me, Kit, what happened after you left work last Friday? I could tell then you weren't looking all that good."

Kit took a quick sip of her latte. "The truth is, I ran over to Steven's. I didn't want to be home alone." She leaned over toward her friend. "I got sick as sick could be, a total wreck."

"Did he go home with you?"

"Yes, thank goodness. I thought I'd seen the last of this world. I'm thinking the chocolates had either spoiled, or someone tampered with them."

Irene shook her head. "Oh dear, and then your visit with Harsh. That took guts, but it sounds like you made your case."

"Pretty much. I'm just hoping he'll go away now."

"What did you and Dwight talk about when I left? I noticed he was still hanging around."

Irene's eyes pinned Kit down, penetrating into her darkest thoughts.

Kit squirmed a little in her chair. "Nothing much. We just chatted a bit about the money coming in from donors. We're slowly getting the amount for a down payment."

"You're such a poor liar." Irene shook her head, tapping her fingers against her cup.

The psychic alarm bell sounded off in Kit's gut, and her internal muscles clenched. "Excuse me? And why would you call me a liar, Irene?"

The corner of Irene's lips twitched into a sarcastic grin. "Because ever since we left work, you've had this 'caught with your hand in the cookie jar' look on your face. Besides, I can feel the charge from your body so strong right now."

Annoyed, Kit set her latte on the table. "Are you so psychic that you can pick up on all this shit as well as you claim you can?"

"Oh my, testy, testy! That's telling me something right there." Irene rested an elbow on the table and showed Kit a sadistic smile. "So what really happened behind closed doors? Did old Dwight finally move in for the kill? Did you two go at it with reckless abandon, and do the nasty on the floor? Make up for lost time, so to speak?"

If Kit's nerves had been rendered as a stage set, one would have witnessed a scene of red lights flashing, with electric live wires sparking and slithering about in a chaotic mess as they snapped and sizzled, unable to handle the voltage igniting through them.

Instead, she laughed and waved off her friend with the most casual air she could muster. "Heavens, no. Why would we do such a thing, and at work too?"

Irene's eyes scrutinized Kit with such intensity, she'd have put the finest hawk to shame. Instead, she merely picked up her cup and continued nursing the latte. "Hey, you know what? I had a strange phone call from an old friend the other day, and I thought maybe you could help me answer this question. She's seeing a new guy, but there's this other guy who wants her too."

"Mmm, okay." Kit eyed Irene with dismay. Somehow she guessed this was no ordinary question, but didn't let on.

"Anyway, one day the other guy and my friend happened to find themselves in a sort of compromised situation. Long story short, out of the blue, one thing led to another, and they found themselves on the brink of giving in to their own lust. At what point would you say my friend cheated on her boyfriend?"

For the first time, Kit wished she were sitting in the coffee shop sipping a latte by herself. Sometimes being alone allowed one to think more. Most of all, being alone allowed one to hide awhile longer and not be outed by friends. She tapped her fingers on the large cup before taking another sip. "I guess I'd say if they stopped before going all the way or didn't get too far into copping a great feel, then they pushed the envelope, but didn't necessarily cheat."

Irene nodded slowly and pressed her lips together in thought. "Yeah, that's kind of what I'm thinking, too, but boy, all that starts to cross a gray line, doesn't it?"

Kit choked down some of her latte, studying the tabletop in more detail than usual. "It does, yes. But again, if they stopped, then I'd chalk it up to a really close call, and they need to be more careful next time."

"Like I've said before, choices, choices. One has to make them, like it or not."

"I hear you, Irene." Kit glanced up at her friend. "No doubt you told your friend that, too, right?"

"I think I've said things like that more than once to people. Maybe it's me being egotistical, but I wish they would listen to me sometimes."

Nodding, Kit stared out the window while Irene sat back to let their conversation digest. Kit wanted nothing more than to slip out into the night and dissolve in the air. Knowing her friend as well as she did, being sneaky or unkind was never Irene's intention. For all her outspoken tendencies, this lady always kept loyalty and trust in the forefront. Lately, however, her inner knowing had left Kit more on edge, and the gentle confrontations kept her on her toes. But there was a question that burned in Kit's mind, and maybe Irene could help again. Since the shop didn't have many patrons tonight, this time seemed as good as any for answers to questions.

Kit blurted out, "I've been wondering about this, and since we're on the subject of boyfriends and amorous co-workers, maybe your sixth sense can help me with this question."

"Go on, I'm all ears." Irene perked up.

"Sometimes I wonder if Steven really loves me or not. I want to know where he stands concerning us."

"Fair enough, and I have just the thing that can help answer some of these questions." Irene slipped her purse from the back of her chair and spent a few moments rustling through the contents until she pulled out a black velvet drawstring bag. "I always carry this with me. It's not bulky like tarot cards, and it's definitely smaller than a spirit board." She opened the bag and pulled out a pendulum. The clear quartz point dangled from the end of a silver chain.

Kit smiled. "You come prepared, don't you?"

"Always!" Irene grinned back. "But before we begin, I need to calibrate this thing just to make sure it's working okay." She dangled the point, holding the piece a few inches off the table.

"You mean a pendulum can actually malfunction?" Kit wrinkled her brows and shook her head. "I wouldn't have imagined something like that breaking down."

Irene gave her the look of a teacher lecturing before a group of students. "If the energy isn't right, they can refuse to move, and you won't get any answers during the current session. You'll have to wait for another time and try again."

"I see. I don't want to wait until another time, so here's to hoping we're in luck."

"I'm going to ask it a simple yes or no question. When it moves clockwise, that means yes, and when it moves counterclockwise, that means no." Irene straightened up and focused her eyes on the pendulum. "Is Kit here with me tonight?" She repeated the question in a soft voice. Within seconds, the pendulum moved. As Irene repeated the question, the point swung in a clockwise direction. "Stop – neutral – neutral – new question. Is snow green?" The pendulum shuddered to a stop, and as Irene repeated the question, the pendulum swung in a counterclockwise direction.

Stunned, Kit remained silent, not daring to break the mood with silly remarks.

Irene smiled up a Kit. "Terrific. Looks like we're in business tonight. So what's the question?"

Pushing her latte aside, Kit straightened up in her chair and leaned toward Irene. "I want to know whether Steven truly loves me."

"Very well, we'll ask." She dangled the pendulum in front of her once again, holding the chain at the end. "Does Steven love Kit?" Within seconds, the quartz point swung a little, gathering momentum the more Irene asked the same question. The pendulum moved in a clear clockwise direction, thus answering the question in the affirmative.

Wide-eyed, Kit glanced from the pendulum to her friend. "Wow, that was something. And you think it's accurate?"

"I'm the one holding this, and don't forget I have a subconscious mind too. But you're also providing energy, as you tap into the deeper, unseen wisdom you have." Irene gazed directly at Kit. "You have your answer to this question. Do you have another one?"

"Yes, I do have one more. Is there a future between Steven and myself?"

Irene steadied the pendulum and asked the question. "Will Steven and Kit be together in the future?"

The coffee shop grew quieter than usual, with the clatter of dishes and coffee grinding coming to a halt. Remaining customers had dwindled down to around two, and they'd been sitting for a while with their eyes transfixed to computer screens. Kit and Irene remained on task, immersed in their own world, the one of seekers. After a few times of asking the same question, the pendulum shimmied. These movements turned into tiny convulsions on the end of the chain. Both ladies stared in amazed silence. In an unexpected turn of events, the quartz drop split in two parts, followed in rapid succession by the chain breaking. The pendulum fell in a heap of disconnected, useless parts on the table between the two ladies.

"Holy shit! What just happened?" Kit shrank back in her chair.

Irene sat blinking at the destroyed pendulum, shaking her head. "Oh, dear. I'm not sure what just happened. I've never had that sort of thing go down like this before." She turned her eyes up to her friend. "That pendulum was not about to give us any answers, and, quite frankly, I'm not sure why. Apparently the spirit world wants to keep that answer under wraps for right now." She shifted in her seat. "This whole thing has me baffled, and a little nervous. Let's talk about something else, like the carnival."

Disturbed by the events she'd just experienced with Irene, even discussion of the carnival didn't dispel the ominous feeling enveloping her. Kit and Irene spent the remainder of their time in forced conversation and artificial discussion as each tried to dismiss the eerie events that had just transpired. At last, the friends said their good-byes, and Kit walked by *Celestial Temptation Gallery*, more desperate now than ever to see Steven.

The 'Open' sign was turned off. Peering through the windows, she saw him perched on a small stepladder, busying himself with re-arranging paintings. She stood back in the shadows to avoid detection. The desire to spend some time with him burned strong in her heart. However, the sight of him stirred up an equally strong level of discomfort, as if a big scarlet letter glowed from her chest. Would she ever be able to face Steven again after what had happened with Dwight? Would he even want a future with her if he ever learned what they had done?

The chimes from Our Lady of Eternal Blessings rang out seven o'clock. A few hours still lingered before bedtime, and staring at the church filled her with a sudden urge to pray. Kit headed off to her apartment. Once inside, she bounded into her room and snatched up her crystal rosary from the nightstand. This big sin she'd committed, putting a blight on their relationship, needed immediate redressing if she wanted to face Steven without guilt and shame. Within seconds, she returned to the sidewalk, moving with swift steps back toward the church.

For the transgression against Dwight, herself, and especially Steven, she intended to pray hard for forgiveness. Most devout Catholics went to confession, but confessing to a priest didn't figure into her personal equation. Only the spirits above needed to know, and Kit liked them only because they didn't ask sly questions or expect answers. They also didn't meddle or pry.

The night breeze held a stinging chill, and the brief walk to the church seemed to last an eternity. Upon reaching the doors, she slipped inside, hoping for solitude. Up front beside the altar, some of the votive candles flickered. Tonight the church held a rather ominous vibe, magnified no doubt by her own personal demons. Eyes from the figures in the stained-glass windows appeared to glare at her as she made her way down the main aisle, chastising her for falling prey to a moment of weakness. Each timid step echoed against the tiles, and the trek to the rack of candles never seemed longer than it did tonight, an eternal stretch down an endless road. With trembling hands, she reached into the holder, grasped a match, and grazed it against the striker, lighting the tip.

If she could get through this, everything would be better – almost. An unlit candle sparked into a tiny blaze of glory, and the extinguished match lay smoldering in a small brass container of sand. Kit crept back over to the first row of pews. After sinking down onto the kneeler, she pulled out the crystal rosary. Catch-me-if-you-can rainbow flashes zipped and dodged about in a game of chase as the church lights struck each facet on the beads. Normally she loved gazing at this piece, admiring its beauty, but not tonight. Confused, she didn't know whether to pray the traditional rosary or merely hold it while saying her own prayer.

Lifting a hand to make the sign of the cross with one hand, she grasped the crucifix at the bottom of the rosary with the other. With a deep breath, she began the Apostle's Creed: "*I believe in God, the Father Almighty, Creator of heaven and earth ...*" Oh dear! How did the rest of the creed go? She closed her eyes and started over again, faltering at the same place. Giving up in despair, she sat still a moment. Maybe if she came to church more often, she'd at least know the prayers. Steven most likely knew them, as well as other good churchgoers. After chiding herself for several minutes, she tried again to come up with something, even if reciting the Apostle's Creed had been an utter failure.

Words swirled in her head, each competing for a voice. With a little concentration, verbal chaos soon fell into a semblance of order, and one by one, each word slipped out in a desperate plea for mercy and forgiveness.

Dear Lord, Jesus, all the apostles and saints, I'm not worthy, but humbly seek your benevolence and grace. I ask that you cleanse me of all my transgressions. Show me the path to righteousness and humility, so I may walk in the light of divine beauty and perfection forever. Amen.

As she uttered the last word, one of the church doors opened, letting in a gust of wind. Startled, Kit turned around, but the entryway remained dim and empty. A chill sailed through the air. She shivered and turned back to the votives, their flames waving around in frenetic gyrations. Kit glanced up, catching a view of the lights overhead swaying back and forth, their movement so subtle she looked twice to make sure she hadn't imagined it. At once they flickered, threatening to go out altogether. Frightened, Kit cowered down with bowed head and eyes squeezed shut, wishing more than ever for Steven's presence. She lifted her head and strained her ears, listening. Did she hear footsteps behind her? Had someone slipped in unseen? She jerked her head up and turned around again to make sure.

In the vestibule her eyes caught the shadowy figure of a young male. Kit, filled with uneasiness, strained harder to see him better in the dim light. He walked toward her a few steps and stopped. Her eyes widened in horror as the lights of the sanctuary revealed the identity of the youth. It was Austin standing there, staring at her with luminous, imploring eyes. All at once a chill consumed her body, and she grabbed the back of the pew, steadying herself from the dizziness setting in. Her vision grew dark. With every ounce of will inside her, she fought the urge to faint. Austin's face, untouched by time, wore an expression of sadness, reminding her of the last time they'd spoken to each other.

He seemed so real, but yet he couldn't be real. Shaking, Kit fought the tears brimming in her eyes. Part of her wanted to run to him and share all the things locked in her heart for all these years. She tried standing, but her body, numb and heavy, refused. The sight of him incited a fear so strong, she couldn't look anymore. Gathering up some nerve, she called out in a squeaky voice, "Austin?"

He remained motionless and silent.

Brilliant flashes from the crystal rosary beads distracted her for a second, and she glanced down, praying this was nothing more than her eyes playing tricks or hallucinations stemming from stress.

When she looked up again, he was gone. The church doors were closed, and the temperature had returned to normal. Everything, the candles and lights, had settled down to their usual glow. Kit shivered, taking several deep breaths to clear her head. She knew it. Of course, Austin's appearance had only been a figment of her imagination, extreme fright toying with her sanity. But the vision left her shaken and jittery.

Enough with prayers! First a pendulum breaks apart for no apparent reason, and now a deceased lover shows up. The whole evening had turned into one horrid nightmare. Would Austin ever leave her alone? The desire to leave the church hit her hard. Maybe Heaven didn't like her feeble attempt at penance after all. Kit crammed the rosary back in its pouch, pushed up the kneeler, and scrambled out of the pew. When she exited the church, she breathed a sigh of relief. The cold night air held a refreshing quality, restoring a befuddled mind back to normal and, most important of all, back to reality.

At least she'd made an effort to make things right. And it's not like she and Dwight had gone all the way. Though taking him up on his offer to finish things up had been tempting, she'd refused. Next time, if one came around again, she'd be more careful. With a few more deep breaths, Kit walked toward Steven's shop.

Though he'd already closed for the evening, a compelling need to see him propelled her forward. He didn't have to know anything; she wouldn't let on. And she'd never tell him about seeing the ghost of her old boyfriend.

Before tapping on the shop door, she peered a moment through the window. This time, he sat behind the counter in front of a large canvas, adding color with bold strokes of a brush. When he heard her knock, Steven glanced across the room and moved quickly to the door.

"Hey, what are you doing out?" His eyes turned down to her hand, and he smiled. "I see you've got your rosary. Were you in church?"

Kit's lips curled up in a nervous smile. "Oh, I was going to go, but decided what I really wanted was to see you instead." Her body pressed close against his, and her eyes held a lusty, hungry look.

The smile left his face as quickly as it had come. Kit's pulse quickened. In her opinion, he almost seemed displeased. Restoring himself to his previous humor, he merely stated, "Hmm, putting me before church? You sure that's a good idea?" With a light shake of his head, he clicked his tongue, in mock disapproval.

"You're heavenly enough for me. That should count for something."

His gaze hovered over her for several seconds, his facial expression kind, but intent. Kit held her breath. Did he believe her, or did he smell sin when it wafted under his nose? She buried her face in the curve of his neck and gave him a soft kiss, wishing more to hide her face. He took her in his arms and gave her lips a greedy kiss. Kit opened her mouth and let his tongue chase hers, before indulging herself in tasting his, the way she and Dwight had done earlier. Guilt tried to push its way into her conscience again, but this time she managed to fight off the feeling with a vengeance. Though she could have enjoyed Dwight without a doubt, Steven ruled. A strong comfort level lingered between them, one stemming from the depths of the heart and soul. In all her adult relationships, none compared to the one with Steven.

"Are you busy tonight?" Her fingers rubbed over his chest, and started the trek over his abdomen and down to the top of his jeans.

He smiled. "Never too busy for you."

"Let's go back to my place."

Steven grinned, and put his paints and brushes away.

The two of them made their way to Kit's apartment where they spent the rest of the night in rounds of frenzied love-making. Every move, every earnest touch resulted in climaxes so strong, Kit wondered if she and Steven still existed in this world. Sweaty and drained of energy, the couple cuddled up together and fell asleep. Sometime in the early hours of morning, he awakened quietly and returned home.

CHAPTER 19

Saturday rolled around, brimming with sunshine and a nippy breeze. Hand-in-hand, Kit and Steven ambled down the sidewalk to *Flora's Antique Mart*, tucked away in the corner section of the square. Only one week before the carnival, and the couple scrambled to pick up last-minute pieces for their costumes. The 'Open' signs flashed in all the shop windows, and traffic picked up at an animated pace. Browsers strolled along without a care, glancing here and there through the display windows. Two brass bells jingled out their arrival as they opened the door to the antique store. From behind the counter, the perky *vendeuse du jour* smiled at them and said a warm hello. Kit returned the smile, wasting no time in leading Steven down to the far aisle on the right-hand side of the shop.

Excited, she pulled him along. "There's a dealer here who sells all kinds of fun merchandise. Maybe we can find something in this booth."

Steven's eyes darted all around. He paused at one booth, fingering through a tiny prayer book before an impatient Kit tugged him away.

"Here it is." With a triumphant smile, she pulled him into a booth filled with textiles, vintage clothing, and a host of boudoir items. A scattered collection of glassware and other oddities had been placed haphazardly on an eclectic assortment of furniture. "Neat, huh?"

"I think so." He loosened himself from her grasp and side-stepped over to the left side of the booth where a rocking chair rested in the corner. On the seat perched a generous portion of white tulle.

"You could do something with that!" Kit sidled up to him, wrapping her arm around his waist while running her finger over the material's surface.

"Exactly what I was thinking. I could make an elaborate headdress. I'll find some wire I can use as a form, and drape this over it. It'll look really cool by the time I finish with it." He smiled at Kit as she quickly moved to another part of the booth, standing in front of a vintage dresser, lording over a large wooden jewelry box.

"Come here a minute." With a wave of her hand, she motioned him over while plucking an item from the box. "What do you think about this for an accent piece? Maybe something you can wear over a pair of gloves?"

He picked up a ring, examining the large faceted glass centerpiece. "Hmm, I don't think I can get this over my finger, but seeing it's only two dollars, it's clearly a costume piece." After studying the ring some more, he slid the shank around the top part of his finger. "You know, I could lop off the top part and glue it to the finger of a glove. That would work."

"Great idea. I love the way you get so creative." Kit nuzzled her cheek against his before giving him a light kiss. "Oh look, here are some white gloves in this drawer." She pulled out the gloves and turned them back and forth, inspecting the size.

"Those definitely won't fit." Steven shook his head.

"Well, they stretch a little. At least try them on." She shoved one of them in his direction.

With a few gradual tugs and working of the fingers, he managed to slide it over his hand. "Tight. I hope they don't rip."

"They look like a larger size, though. You might try wearing them so they'll stretch a little." Kit grabbed the mate and passed it on to him.

Steven checked over the items in his hands. "Okay, I think I have what I need. Head covering, ring, and gloves, I think that's it for me. What about you?"

"Look, what's this?" She stooped down to one of the large drawers at the bottom of the dresser. Peeking out from a back corner, a black feather hat lay tucked away. She promptly rescued the hat from its hiding place and ran her fingers over the soft feathers covering the brim.

"Nice." Steven nodded in approval. "This has a lot of fluff to it. It'll go great with your mask."

Kit's eyes lit up with excitement. "I think so too. And it's the right color. How lucky is that?"

"Did you want to look around some more, in case we find something else?" He stepped out and glanced down the aisle. "Let's go down some more."

As they made their way down the aisle, a man with short blond hair, neatly parted on one side, stepped around the corner ahead and walked toward them. With an easy manner, he viewed booths on one side, then the other. The red designer sweater, khaki slacks and loafers fit his toned, lean body to perfection. However, when Kit caught sight of his dark-rimmed glasses, she came to an abrupt halt. Dwight. He took his time strolling down the aisle, picking up items at intervals for further inspection. Stifling the urge to scream, Kit grabbed Steven and pulled him in the opposite direction.

"Hey, slow down! What's wrong?" He slowed his pace. A quizzical look played across his face.

She pulled harder at his arm. "C'mon, let's go check out. I think we're done."

Steven stayed put and pulled her back. "Not so fast. We were still looking around."

By this time, the footsteps suddenly stopped. Kit didn't dare look behind her. Urgency soared to unadulterated panic.

With one last tug, she managed to wrench Steven forward, and neither stopped until they'd reached the counter. "Can you ring us up fast? We're in a hurry." Breathless, Kit turned around, catching sight of Dwight coming out of the aisle. He stood with his face turned in their direction, and from what she could discern, his stare showed a man riddled with hostility and dismay.

She jerked her head around and kept her eyes on the counter, where the clerk had placed their items in a small plastic sack. What was Dwight doing here? He hadn't mentioned coming to the square this weekend. And why today, of all days? He never waited until the last minute for anything. If they didn't get out of here fast, her heart stood the chance of exploding and killing her dead on the spot. As a matter of fact, the idea rather appealed to her right now. At least dead people didn't have to explain themselves. As Steven took out his wallet, he cast her a glance of confusion. "What's your problem?"

"Nothing. I just wanted to finish up." With a trembling hand, she rubbed up and down his back, trying hard to appear casual, praying harder he believed her.

"You folks have a great day, and thanks for shopping with us." The clerk smiled and handed Steven his credit card. Kit picked up the bags and sailed out the door.

Steven caught up with her and grabbed her hand. "Stop, would you?" His face showed signs of annoyance. Kit wished more than ever she had reacted differently. So what if Dwight had caught up to them? He would have either acknowledged her or kept on walking. None of it would have mattered at this point.

"I'm sorry. It's just that I was done and ready to leave. I'm not one to spend money on things like this, and I get panicky when I do."

"You've been acting weird since last night, all lovey-dovey and clingy and stuff. You're not usually that overboard. Something's up. So out with it." His eyes flashed with irritation, which stirred up an old feeling of uneasiness. Austin had often given her similar looks when he was frustrated at something she said or did.

"Sweetheart, can we just forget about this and get some lunch? We can go back to my place. I'll make something special just for you, anything, whatever you want."

Steven ignored her suggestion and tipped his head toward the door of the antique shop. "Hey, isn't that your friend from work? I remember him." With a smile, he threw up his hand and waved. Leaning close to her ear, he murmured, "Say hi to your friend, Kit. He's coming this way."

The blood rushed from her face. She couldn't look. If looking like the most foolish person on earth hadn't bothered her, she would have sprinted down the sidewalk to her apartment where she'd lock herself away forever. Why had she insisted on antique shopping in the first place? Guys hated doing this. Steven could have found pieces for his costume without her help.

Dwight's shuffling footsteps stopped when he landed next to her. From the strained look on his face, he appeared to have wanted a fast getaway as much as she did. With Steven attracting his attention, he'd been hooked, netted, and hauled out of the water. True to his nature, Dwight usually put manners ahead of personal prejudices.

"How's it going?" Steven held out his hand, which Dwight accepted, with the most artificial smile in the world plastered on his face. Steven continued talking. "Are you getting ready for next weekend?"

"I guess. Not having much luck today. Looks like you two have fared pretty well."

Steven glanced down at the bags. "We did all right."

Dwight, drumming up every ounce of resolve, finally looked over at Kit, giving her a soft pat on the shoulder. "And how are you?"

To her horror, his touch lit up her internal fire, nearly sending her reeling. "Fine." She swallowed hard, a stiff smile on her face. Shifting from one foot to the other, she discovered a strong urge to use the restroom. She'd always heard extreme fear caused some people to lose control of their bladder. Fear itself may not have been the culprit, but extreme guilt and anxiety made for a good runner up. Maybe she could find an excuse to mosey over to the coffee shop and use their facilities.

Steven stood back a little, watching. The smile had deflated to a faint grin. An amusing glint danced in his eyes, and Kit's nerves reared up in high gear again. He spoke to Dwight. "We were thinking of grabbing some lunch; did you want to come?"

Both Kit and Dwight stared back at him, jaws slack, eyes wide open.

Dwight removed his glasses, rubbed an eye, and shook his head. "No thanks. I ate before I came." He gave Kit and Steven one last once-over and turned to leave. "Gotta go. I have some other errands to run. Have a good weekend."

"He seems like a nice guy." Steven stared off after Dwight. "Would have been nice to talk to him the day everyone was dropping things off for the silent auction."

"Mmm." Kit blinked a few times, taking deep breaths to subdue a racing heart.

The couple walked to Kit's apartment. Steven turned and asked, "So do you two ever do lunch together or get involved with other projects at work? You talk about your other friend a lot, but never about him."

She stared ahead, struggling to stay calm. "We don't see each other much. Dwight's the finance guru. We're all usually busy." Out of the corner of her eye, she caught sight of Steven's eyes bearing down on her and, with a heavy heart, detected an expression of doubt.

Neither said another word until they reached the apartment. Steven headed straight for the sofa and stretched out. Kit took their bags and placed them in the bedroom.

"So, what's the something special you had in mind? I'm starved." He turned his face up, gracing her with a smile as she headed toward the kitchen.

"I went to the grocery store earlier this week. Let me check out what I have. I'll surprise you." Whew! Hopefully he'd let her off the hook about her strange behavior and toss more talk about Dwight by the wayside. This generosity alone warranted an extra special meal, complete with wine and an after-dessert treat. For the next hour, Kit clattered around in the kitchen, pan-frying steaks, baking potatoes, seasoning bread, and tossing together a crunchy, colorful salad. For dessert, she whipped up a confection she liked to call *Chocolate Majestic Delight*.

While Kit stood at the counter, finishing up last-minute work, Steven crept up from behind. She let out a scream, followed by laughter. He wrapped his arms around her and, starting with an earlobe, nibbled his way down to her neck, where he offered a flurry of tiny kisses.

"Smells great. I didn't expect all this." He maneuvered himself around in front of her and delivered a fervent kiss on the lips.

"I promised you something special, so here it is." She rested against him, while a flash of heat seared through her body. His hands slithered under her top, and with deft strokes, he toyed with the peaks of her breasts. For a moment, nothing mattered but the present and letting him have his way with her. When he satisfied himself above her waistline, he concentrated on the area below. Slipping his fingers into her jeans, he moved over all the right spots, setting off one of the strongest orgasms she'd experienced. He held her tight in his arms.

"You like that?" His words, tickling against her ear, teased her as much as his hands. The grazing of his tongue against her neck aroused her to such a degree she nearly came again.

"Steven!" Kit murmured his name as she hooked her fingers around the top of his jeans, pulling him closer. Nestling her face in the curve of his neck, she breathed in his scent, masculine and clean. She wedged her hands inside his jeans, moving down to complete what she'd dared not do with Dwight.

Nice and slow, her fingers took their time working over him, tracing over delicate curves and sliding a finger through his moisture. Within moments, he shuddered against her, muttering into her ear a stream of unintelligible words sounding like whispers trapped in a waterfall. His breath fell hot and fast against her neck. For a second, she lost all sense of time. Worries lifted away; no intrusive thoughts clouded the space between them. If only this state of bliss could last.

The rude ding from the timer broke the spell. Steven pulled away. Kit checked on the oven. She tidied up, while lifting lids and prodding at the food. Everything had cooked fully, or needed a last-minute dash of salt or lemon juice.

"Good, everything looks ready to me. I'll get the dishes and silverware, if you'll open some wine."

He grinned and chucked her playfully under the chin. "I'm on it."

To top off the ambience, he built a fire in the fireplace. They seated themselves at the table and ate.

"Mmm, this is so good!" He closed his eyes, savoring a bite of steak.

Kit sipped a bit of wine. "Not bad for such a quick fix. Luckily I had a great seasoning rub I picked up from a spice shop in town."

"You're a great cook. Everything's always top notch." He displayed one of his charming smiles before digging his fork into the salad.

"I don't mind cooking. It helps me decompress when I'm stressed out."

"Painting and sketching help me when I'm stressed out. Cooking, not so much."

An hour later, they had finished their meal, cleaned up the kitchen, and settled down together on the sofa.

Steven pulled her on top of himself where she snuggled close, moving in for a warm, deep kiss. For several minutes, their tongues courted each other before she caught his in her mouth and suckled gently. The taste of Cabernet lingered in his mouth. As always, the remnants of wine from his lips aroused her. With frisky hands, she wandered down over the outside of his right thigh before crossing to the inside. He stiffened under her grasp. With closed eyes, she clenched her buttocks in response to his hands finding their way under her bra to fondle the tips of her breasts. His fingers squeezed harder this time, creating a strong ache bearing the paradox of pleasure and pain.

Is this the way Dwight would have touched her, creating a buildup to the ultimate climax? Her mind shot back to the image of them alone together in her office, and how those beautiful, strong fingers had made her burn hot the way Steven's did now. Her eyes snapped open, and she peered down at him. A searing heat flared throughout her body, and his toying with her nipples ceased.

"Sorry, too hard?" His face filled with alarm.

She shook her head. "No, not at all." Confused, her mind whirled. Shit! How on earth could she have thought about Dwight at a time like this? After all, she'd made a special trip to church to pray this whole ordeal away, and then prepared a romantic meal for a man she adored more than anyone.

Now, lying in his arms, thoughts of someone else had paraded over her mental stage. Gathering some composure, she sank her head down on Steven's chest, desperately thinking of what to say next. The beating of his heart sounded like a defiant protest of betrayal. His hands stroked over her head and through her hair. They remained this way for several minutes before he steered her face over his.

Staring deep into her eyes a few seconds, he dropped the bomb: "I can't help but think your friend likes you."

Stunned, Kit said nothing.

"Not meaning to break the mood here, but I keep seeing him in my mind."

Her heart pounded hard. "Um, you mean Dwight?"

Steven nodded, his face solemn.

A black cloud of doom settled over Kit, filling her with despair. Would this ever end? She licked her lips. "What made you think about him?"

"I can still see the way he looked at you while we were standing together, the way he touched you when he said hello."

Kit swallowed hard. "He didn't look any different to me. Just plain old Dwight."

"The energy between the two of you was strong. I almost could see it: a vibrant red cloud, with fringes of pink around the edges."

She glared down at him in disbelief. "No way! You did not! Besides, he's simply a friendly person. Doesn't mean a thing."

"I know things, Kit. I can sense them." He reached up, pushing a strand of her hair back.

"Now you sound like Irene. Do you know how much I have to hear that crap all the time?" The annoyance in her voice came through loud and clear. In fact, she was pissed. What could have been a great mood with some terrific petting going on had now ended up in idle chatter about someone else.

To her surprise, Steven pulled her face down over his, smothering her lips with another round of kissing. When he finished, he gazed up. "I'm sorry. I didn't mean any of this in a bad way. It was just an observation on my part, that's all. I didn't mean to be stern with you this afternoon, either."

"It was my fault for rushing around like an idiot, so don't beat yourself up." She gave him an earnest look. "Steven, despite what you might be thinking, you mean the world to me. I care about you so much. You've got to believe me. Promise me all this will never change, ever."

In silence, he studied her face for a long time. His finger strayed back and forth over her cheek and down over her lips. He pulled her down close for a soft kiss before holding her tight against him.

CHAPTER 20

Kit and Irene stood on the back lawn, watching the workmen as they strained, hoisting a gigantic white tent erect, fastening it securely in place. Tomorrow night cleverly masked party-goers in brilliant costumes would be gathered under that same tent, eating, drinking, and donating money. But the most thrilling of all was the pride of the Historical Society being able to call the Stothwell Mansion their own home. Every staff member had tabled their current projects and helped set up for this event. Items for the auction had been carefully lined up inside the entrance hall so they could be placed inside the tent the next day.

"Tomorrow the caterers and band will set up before the party starts. We'll be displaying the auction items too." Irene glanced at Kit, gracing her friend with a big smile. "We finally did it, didn't we, girl?"

"Yes. Now we can see the fruits of our labor. Kind of exciting, isn't it?"

Irene turned her attention back to the workers. "It is, and a little scary too. This is a big responsibility."

"Nothing we can't handle, and I have all kinds of ideas for raising money." She slipped a hand in a pocket of her jacket. The chill had worsened.

"Where's Dwight? I thought he'd surely be out here supervising and making sure everything was being set up without a hitch." Irene kept an intent gaze on the workers. "Of course, there's tomorrow, with the food, band, and items for the auction. Surely he wouldn't leave all that for us to manage."

In the brisk air, Kit felt warm all of a sudden. Any mention of Dwight these days unnerved her, and during work hours, she'd been trying so hard to avoid him altogether. "He'll show up. Maybe he's in his counting house counting all his money."

Irene let out a loud laugh. "Like a king! Too bad it's not his. Of course, from what I hear, his own coffers are none too shabby. Comes from a well-off family, you know."

"I'd heard the rumors, but somehow it doesn't surprise me. He seems to have impeccable taste in everything."

"Have you noticed how strange he's been acting lately? He's keeping out of sight and more to himself. Doesn't seem like the usual debonair Dwight we know and love so well." Irene faced Kit, sweeping back her dark hair, which had become briefly disheveled by the wind.

"I haven't been paying much attention, I guess."

Irene frowned a little. "Well, I have, and it makes me a little sad. I kind of miss him, especially watching him flirt with you. You two made such a cute couple."

Kit shot a glance over at her friend. "Does it entertain you that much?"

"I just think you two would be nice for each other, that's all. You'd do very well with him."

"Don't you think Steven and I are nice for each other?" Irene's comment acted like a sharp sting in her heart.

"Sure. But somehow, I have a hard time getting a grasp on him. Can't quite put my finger on it, but he seems to have an illusory quality. You know what I mean? Like he's invisible, almost." Irene gazed hard at Kit.

With a little shrug, Kit shook her head. "He's not illusory in the least. I feel things with him I've never felt with anyone else before. He's different." She frowned at Irene. "And how can you say he's invisible? That's just not nice."

"Sorry, Kit. I didn't mean that in a rude way. It's just that Steven's hard to pin down in my mind, that's all."

Irene's words had hit a chord, leaving her in deeper confusion. Never admitting it to herself until now, she had to agree that Steven, at times, came across as someone from another world. Instead, she'd often detected an inner wisdom, one she admired and respected. He carried himself with authority and confidence, but crowned, at the same time, with humility. The distant gleam in his eyes when he was in the height of ecstasy, the occasional chill coursing down her spine when he touched her, the total rush consuming her body when they made love, all these experiences didn't strike her as merely ordinary. On the contrary, these visceral sensations of late had forced her to perk up and pay attention.

"Hey, Irene, I have a question for you." Kit had been debating with herself whether she wanted to hear an answer to this one, or just let it go. She decided to have a go at it and hear her friend out.

"Shoot. What is it?"

"What does seeing a cloud of red fringed with pink mean?"

Her friend wrinkled her brow and turned her attention away from the tent. "You mean something like an aura?"

"Hell, I don't know what an aura is. Maybe?"

Irene straightened up, moving closer to Kit. "People who are spiritually developed often see auras, or cloud-like colors hovering around a person. Think Kirlian photography. The camera captures the subject's energy field at a given moment, and when you look at the photograph, you see areas of different colors, or you may see the person shrouded mostly by a single color with small shaded areas in different parts. It all has meaning."

"You mean someone can be like a camera, but see things with their own eyes?" Kit's eyes widened.

"Yes, exactly. Why do you ask?" Irene's face lit up with a big smile. "Are you seeing them?"

"Are you kidding me? No, of course not. Remember, I didn't even know what they were. But I guess that doesn't mean I couldn't see them." Kit grinned. "Sorry to burst your bubble, but I'm not seeing colors around anyone."

"Who is, then?"

"Okay, I'll just come clean. Steven and I ran into Dwight over the weekend, at Flora's Antique Mart."

"Surely you're joking, aren't you? What was he doing there?" Irene's face clouded with dismay.

"Beats the hell out of me. At any rate, I tried to get Steven and myself out of there pronto. I thought I just about had it in the bag until we got outside. No, as luck would have it, when Dwight stepped out the door, Steven waved him over to us."

Irene closed her eyes and lowered her face. "Lord have mercy. What happened?"

"What else could he do? Dwight came over, we chatted a few seconds, and Steven and I headed on back to my place. Simple as that." Kit lowered her voice. "But here's the weird part. After we ate, he suddenly piped up and said he thought Dwight liked me. He said he saw a cloud of red fringed with pink."

"Around whom?" Irene blinked with astonishment.

"I don't know. He didn't say. But he mentioned seeing the energy between us, and that it was strong."

Irene's face colored. "Kit, a red aura means vitality, and the pink means love and romance. Pink is also the color for soulmates."

"Love, romance – soulmates?" A cold chill took a dive straight into Kit's spine, radiating with fury up and down her body. She frowned at her friend. "Do you see auras?"

"I don't, but I get strange vibes about things, like a strong intuition or something. And I'm telling you, Kit, there's something about Steven I'm just not getting a handle on. I've tried, but I just can't."

The ladies remained silent for a long time, watching the men put the finishing touches on the main tent. The workers now turned their attention to setting up the tents for the portable toilets, one for men, the other for women. Satisfied everything was shaping up for the big event, Kit and Irene headed back inside the mansion.

* * *

Dwight and Kit nearly collided as she turned out of her office, rushing to hand in a project before it became overdue.

"Oh, sorry, Dwight. Didn't see you coming."

He hung his head low, mumbled a return apology, and tried to dodge her.

Irene's words came back to haunt her. Kit hated to admit that she'd been concentrating so hard on trying to avoid him herself, his absence had almost been welcome. But this avoidant behavior by both of them had to stop. As long as they worked together, they needed to have a comfortable working relationship.

Kit grabbed his arm and pulled him back inside her office. "Hey, what's up with you? Irene said you've been acting weird lately. And were you so rushed you couldn't even say hi to me? That's not like you, Dwight."

His cheeks turned a bright pink as he tried to free his arm. "Nothing, I'm fine." He tugged again, but somehow remained unsuccessful in extricating himself. "Kit, I'm in a hurry, so if you'll kindly let go of my arm, I have some things I have to check on."

Whether it was nerves or a quick surge of humor, she couldn't resist teasing him. "If you're worried about the tent set-up, Irene and I have your back. We supervised everything to a tee, and threatened everyone that you'd have their necks in a noose if they fouled anything up."

He scowled at her, giving his arm one last yank. "Very funny. Now I've gotta get moving." As he turned to leave, Kit grabbed his arm again. The irritation in his eyes, though disconcerting, failed to scare her into total submission. She pulled him in further and shut the door.

Dwight glared at her. If he'd yelled at her and stormed out of the office, she wouldn't have been surprised or blamed him. However, he spoke in a quiet, but strained voice. "If you're shutting that door to tease me, or do god knows what, I'll not have it." He moved toward the door, nearly landing his hand on the knob when Kit intervened.

"I'm begging you please, hear me out, Dwight." Startled at the sting of tears in her eyes, she took a gulp of fresh air and started speaking again. "First of all, I want to say again how sorry I am for what happened in here last time. None of that was your fault, and I'd never blame you or be angry. And I feel bad Steven put you in an awkward position this past weekend. I felt as horrible about it as you did."

His jaw tightened. "I'm sure lover boy had himself a good laugh over the whole thing. I should have snubbed you both and gone on my merry way."

"Dwight, I understand your feelings. I've had them myself before, but honestly, Steven thinks you're very nice." Kit reached for Dwight's hand. "He even said he wished you two had been able to talk more the day we were collecting things for the silent auction. He'd never say or do anything to humiliate or belittle anyone."

"How convenient." Dwight's lips twisted into a wry smile.

Good! She at least had his attention without him trying to bolt and run. Giving his hand a light squeeze, she stared up into his eyes. "I want to say that no matter what, nothing will change our friendship. You mean a lot to me, and I don't ever want that to change."

He straightened up without pulling his hand away. The anger had dissipated, and in its place, a cool air of composure had settled over him. His voice rang out with conviction, so solid it nearly took her breath away.

"Pardon me for being a cold-hearted bastard, but I don't think friendship alone will satisfy me, Kit. I want more, and now I'm damned if I can't have it. I can usually buy my way into or out of things with the snap of a finger, but I can't buy you or your love. I'll say it again. I'll rot in Hell before I settle for friendship. That much you can bank on!"

Stunned beyond words, Kit watched in silence as he opened the door and closed it behind him. She glanced at the clock. There was still enough time to get her project turned in, but right now, she needed a good cry. Fighting desperately to hold back the tears spilling from her eyes, she stumbled to her chair, collapsed down in the seat, and grabbed a tissue from her desk. Heaving with emotion, Kit sat for the next twenty minutes sobbing hot tears of pain and sadness.

Though her love for Steven burned strong, the affection she still held for Dwight would not let go. And she didn't know what to do about it. A part of her felt the same way as he did for her. Cooking dinner in his kitchen, fragrant flowers, lunch from the coffee shop – all these endearments had tugged at her heartstrings. Most of all, the physical nature of him equally appealed to her. But Dwight had cut her off. Steven had already shared his observations, and she certainly didn't want to hear any more of them. Talking to Irene didn't sound like a better idea, either. She'd definitely weighed in on the subject.

When every tear she could muster up had been cried into her soaked tissue, she got up from the chair to turn in her project. Before facing the other co-workers, she took a moment and pulled out a compact and lipstick, touching up her tear-stained face. There was nothing else she could do about Dwight; he'd made that perfectly clear. From this point forward, she'd simply work around him when they were at the mansion. She'd still be polite, but any future events for raising money could be done with Irene or other staff members. There, problem solved. She stood up, grabbed her assignment, and strode out of the office.

For the moment, she tried to think about nothing but the carnival. She and Steven would enjoy themselves tomorrow night in flashy costumes along with the others, eating, dancing, and merry-making. Afterward, they'd go back to her place and frolic in pure, naked bliss before a blazing fire. At least Steven wasn't going anywhere fast. After all, he'd sealed his promise with a kiss.

CHAPTER 21

Carnival night arrived in all its anticipated, splendid glory. Steven pulled off his costume's look with skill, looking like a being from another dimension, with the white shift robe and head covering he'd crafted from material purchased at Flora's. Kit had coordinated her antique feather hat with the black shirt, slacks, and robe, transforming herself into the most charming cat. Glistening around her neck was the tiny gold heart necklace. Steven had insisted she wear it. Though she'd tried to discourage him, she broke down and gave in.

Each donned their masks, admiring one another before they headed out of Kit's apartment. Distant sounds of a lively band drifted in their direction. Kit squeezed Steven's hand. In the air, the stinging chill carried with it a breath of exhilaration and anticipation. Participants on both sides of the square filed in droves toward Stothwell Mansion. Rough silhouettes suggested all styles of flamboyant attire, and Kit pulled Steven along at a faster pace, straining her eyes for a better view.

Steven pulled her back, laughing. "The party's not going anywhere. Slow down a minute."

"Sorry. Can't help myself. I'll be able to see better when we get inside the tent. How do you think we look compared to everyone else?"

"I think our costumes are just as good." He gripped her hand tighter. "Besides, being together for a night of fun means the most to me."

She turned her face in Steven's direction. "You're right. That's the most important thing, isn't?"

After blending into the crowd, they wound through the lawn to the back side of the mansion, and found themselves at the entrance of the tent. A costumed figure wearing an elegant Victorian gown and a mask bearing feathers and jewels greeted them at the door.

"Tickets please." A dainty gloved hand extended out in front of Kit, whose heart stopped in her chest. Oh, no, she'd forgotten to bring the tickets or any ID. The masked face moved closer to her, intent on staring her down. "Who's under there?"

"Irene?" Kit recognized her friend's voice, at which point she spoke louder. "It's me."

"Kit! And I presume you are Steven?" Irene held her hand out in his direction.

"Hi there." Steven shook her hand. "Looks like you've got a great band tonight."

"Aren't they the best?" Irene turned around and motioned toward a group of smartly dressed gentlemen in flashy jackets and slacks playing instruments. A lead singer accompanied them, belting out some snappy lyrics to a lively tune. Several couples danced together, while other people dined on food from the buffet.

Irene pulled Steven over next to her. "People are already bidding on your piece. It's generating quite a bit of money."

Steven nodded his head in approval and patted Irene on the back. "That's great."

While Irene and Steven engaged in small talk, Kit scanned the crowd. Where was Alexandra? She'd promised to come. Both had been so busy, neither had chatted about costumes. Besides, Alexandra loved keeping secrets. Flowing gowns of all colors, embroidered suits, billowy pants with matching shirts hailed in all styles and colors.

Fancy head coverings came in all shapes and textures, and the masks ranged from traditional to comical to outright scary. One person wore a jeweled skull mask and shimmering black robes, and held a scythe. Kit marveled at the creativity and use of accessories. Supporters of the Stothwell Mansion had gone to great lengths to make this night a reality, and pulled out all the stops for this party. This lavish display of thought, care, and support from the community overwhelmed her heart with gratitude.

Near the buffet, she caught sight of Harold Crispin wearing his brilliant-striped jester outfit, topped with cap 'n bells. He'd removed his mask to eat. Next to him stood Dwight, decked out in his brilliant jack o' lantern mask and a nineteenth century-style orange suit with dashing cloak to match. A black jabot adorned the front of his shirt, and he sported a black top hat. In one hand, he held a matching black lacquered walking stick. Kit gazed at him for several moments, imagining herself pressed up against him, wrapped inside his cloak, while her hands roamed....

Steven tapped her on the arm and grabbed her hand. "Hey, let's get something to eat. I'm starving."

The buffet teemed with steaming delectable food. Her thoughts shot back to the day she and Dwight had planned out the menu, the moment he'd mentioned the word 'wedding.' *Kit Vandergard.* She said the name a few times under her breath, letting the words roll off her tongue. Embarrassed, she stopped herself. *What about Kit D'Astolo?* Or *Mrs. Steven D'Astolo.* That had a better ring to it. The whole concept hit her as warm and fuzzy. Steven interrupted her thoughts by handing her a plate and some silverware.

"How do we eat with these masks on?" he asked.

"Once we load up and sit down, we'll just take them off for a bit. I've seen many people having to do that. Maybe we should have picked out simpler masks."

"Never! I love what we got. We'll figure it out." He moved down the line, selecting tidbits here and there.

Kit did the same. When they reached the end of the line, they headed toward the tables. There were two empty chairs beside Mr. Crispin, who'd finally seated himself. Kit turned her head for a brief view of the tent entrance and saw Dwight and Irene talking. At one moment, he appeared to be looking in her direction. With a flash of discomfort, she turned her attention back to Mr. Crispin.

"Of course, you can join me! Sit right down." Mr. Crispin motioned toward the chairs. "You look really cute tonight, Kit. Love the mask."

"Mr. Crispin, I'd like for you to meet Steven. You've heard me talk a lot about him." Steven had seated himself and removed his mask.

"Nice to meet you." The gentleman intercepted Steven's outstretched hand. "Kit speaks highly of your artistic talent. Is that your painting I see up there, getting all the bids?"

Steven threw back his head and laughed. "Yes. Who knew people would like it so much? I painted it on a flash of inspiration one day."

"I was telling Kit I needed something cheery for my office. I need to stop by your place sometime."

"Come in any time. I'll help you pick out something."

Kit swallowed a bite of her entree. "Looks like this is turning into a great party. You think they'll show this much enthusiasm each year?"

The attorney smiled. "I don't see why not. People look forward to shindigs like this. Gives 'em a chance to do something different."

The three spent a while talking and eating while several more couples headed to the floor, persuaded by the new jazzy tune searing through the air. Many lined up around the auction tables, frantically placing bids on their favorite items. Several studied the goods, glanced at their checkbooks and back again, in a quandary over how much to plunk down on something they most likely didn't need. Five people stood in line to bid on *The World*.

Irene sauntered up to Steven with an outstretched hand. "Would you like to dance, sir?"

He glanced up and smiled. "I'd love to." Excusing himself and quickly replacing his mask, he followed Irene to the dance floor.

"How about you and me, Kit? Since everyone is having such a riot out there, why don't we join them?"

"That would be great, Mr. Crispin."

Both replaced their masks and wormed their way into the crowd. The older gentleman impressed Kit with his dancing skills. Irene and Steven seemed to have stolen the spotlight with a snazzy impromptu free-style routine, garnering them a fan base of admirers. The current tune soon wound to a close, and everyone clapped with satisfaction. As the lights dimmed, the lead singer encouraged everyone to keep bidding to benefit the mansion, and announced the next song as a slow dance for guys and their favorite gals. Couples snuggled into each other's arms, as much as their costumes would allow, and the band struck up a sultry melody.

"May I cut in?" The voice sounded off from behind a jack o' lantern-masked face.

"Sure, Dwight. I'd keep this lovely lady all to myself, but that would be too rude of me, wouldn't it?" Mr. Crispin chuckled and stepped back as Dwight took Kit in his arms. "I'm going to get something to drink. All this dancing has left me parched." The lawyer wound his way out of the crowd and back to the drinks table.

Kit breathed as easily as she could between new anxiety flaring up and Dwight's masked face. Inside her chest, a beating heart nearly exploded. She'd all but put the notion out of her head concerning Dwight wanting a dance with her.

"At the beginning of this project, we promised each other a dance and, as you know, I'm a man of my word." Dwight wrapped his arms around her and held her close.

"You don't have to do this if you don't want to. I won't hold you to it." Despite the comment, Kit rested her head on his shoulder.

"I'm sorry for being so ugly with you the other day. I went home and thought about it some more. You didn't deserve that." His hand rubbed over her back, creating inside her a tormenting, lusty ache. Where had Irene and Steven gone? Her eyes skimmed the crowd, but caught no sight of them. Still no sight of Alexandra, who was no doubt making her way around the crowd.

"I hope you haven't been beating yourself up over it." She tilted her head up.

"I've discovered this, Kit; I don't like being at odds with you. It puts a damper on my day when I wake up in the morning, and plagues me in my dreams when I go to bed at night."

She giggled. "You're so dramatic. Do I really have that kind of effect on you?"

Dwight answered by tightening his grip around her and leading her through a few smooth steps, keeping time with the music. Kit swore if they hadn't been wearing masks, he would have planted another kiss on her and, like the last time, she'd have enjoyed it just as much. For a few moments they didn't speak, but merely swayed back and forth.

Without warning, Irene materialized behind Dwight and clapped her hands around his shoulders. He loosened his grip on Kit and whirled around. "Oh, it's you."

"Yes, my dear, it's me. Time for our dance. I know you didn't promise me one, but I don't care."

He paused and turned to Kit.

Kit waved them on. "Go ahead. I think I need something to drink. You guys have fun." Before leaving, she patted him on the shoulder. "Dwight, it was a pleasure." She turned around and strolled toward some empty tables. Midway through the crowd, someone grabbed her arm.

"Steven, there you are!"

His arm encircled her waist, and the dance with Dwight took a brief backseat in her thoughts. The warmth of Steven's touch reminded her how much she enjoyed him, wanted him.

"Kit, my painting is now over two thousand dollars! Can you believe that? And people are still in line to bid on it."

"Wow, that's really cool. You did an awesome job on that piece. Anybody would want it."

He led her back to the dance floor, arms holding on around her waist with a secure grip. The band kept everyone comfy cozy with another slow piece, and now it was their turn to enjoy a moment of intimacy. Together they moved, Kit following his lead as he guided her through a few turns and steps, moving forward, backward, sideways, and ending with a quick turn and a small dip when the song ended.

"You're good. Where did you learn to do all that?" She threaded her arms around his neck, her face inches from his.

"I've had a few lessons. Glad I did too. Did you see me and Irene out there? We had it going on, didn't we?" He threw back his head and laughed. "I really like her. No wonder you enjoy being with her so much. I would too."

For a moment, a surge of jealousy shot through her like a bullet out of a gun. They did seem mighty happy out there, cutting a rug before an adoring crowd. Irene and Jim weren't married. If Steven wanted her, he could use the art of gentle persuasion and charm to win her over. They had several commonalities already. It wouldn't take much. Kit fought her thoughts from spinning out of control, and finally brought them to a screeching halt.

So this is how Dwight must view her relationship with Steven, a threat to some fantasy he wanted desperately as a reality. And when the fantasy threatened to slip away, it cut to the core, leaving an empty, black hole inside.

The truth, she reminded herself, summoning up her rational mind, was that Irene loved Jim. Something needed to give where Dwight figured in, but she'd have to give that some more thought. At least he'd come to some resolution himself. Maybe they could just be friends and be done with it.

The music ended, and Steven pulled Kit toward the buffet. "I'm thirsty," he said.

When they reached the beverage table, each one ladled out a healthy serving of punch before seating themselves in a couple of empty seats. The band had lightened the mood again with a catchy piece, but many of the couples had resigned from the dance floor, seeking chairs where they rested their feet and chatted amongst themselves.

"I'm glad you came with me tonight." Kit rested her head on Steven's shoulder.

"I wouldn't have missed this for anything. You'll have fun with this each year."

She lifted up her head, staring at him in confusion. "What do you mean *I'll* have fun with this each year? You'll be here, too, so we'll both have fun."

Steven stared back, silent, and took a sip of his drink before returning his sight on the crowd.

The comment troubled her, setting off an internal alarm. He'd given her these looks before. Anytime they'd talked about the future, he gave cryptic answers, or didn't answer at all, changing the subject instead. Great, what if he turned out to be a commitment-phobe, one who'd be happy dating for a lifetime but refuses a more permanent relationship? Would she be happy with that kind of situation? Another thought struck her: What if he'd grown tired of her and wanted to move on to someone new, like Irene, but didn't quite know how to say so?

The inside of the tent had heated up with all the lights, bodies, and hot food. A fit of claustrophobia caught her in its grasp, and suddenly, she needed to take a break and go outside for a breath of fresh, cold air.

She leaned close to his ear. "I'll be right back. I need to check on something."

He nodded. "Do you want me to come with you?"

"No, this won't take long." She got up and maneuvered her way through chairs and people until she reached the opening of the tent. Outside a cool breeze blew and, taking in a deep breath, she filled her lungs with a good dose of cold air. Her head cleared the moment she exhaled. Moving further away from the hub of activity improved her disposition.

When her head cleared more, she chided herself for having gotten so wound up. This was a party, after all. Of course, Steven would dance with other people. Their relationship needed time, like anything else, to blossom and grow. Right now, her life contained him, a great job, wonderful apartment, and loyal friends. Nothing else mattered, and the future would take care of itself.

Kit walked toward the gardens. The moon waxed full and tonight it beamed from the sky in full glory, lighting up the lawn in a sharp, white glow. The tent loomed in the distance like a large ghost. Several yards away, in the shadow of the trees, she glimpsed what looked like two people in deep conversation. She walked until she landed beside a tall garden statue of a young woman holding out her apron. The Society used it for a bird feeder, and on warm afternoons Kit had rested here to eat lunch. She stared up at the starry sky, taking slow, even breaths.

A soft rustling sound disturbed her quiet moment, and she jerked her face in the direction of a figure standing in front of her. It was the person she'd seen earlier, wearing the jeweled skull mask and the grim reaper outfit.

At this moment, a small breeze swept through, ruffling the hood. The moonbeams struck the surface of the jewels on the mask, giving the form an eerie presentation. Her memories shot back to the horrid skull she'd received that fateful afternoon, the incident that had started the cascade of warnings and disasters.

Alarmed, Kit spoke first. "Yes, can I help you?"

"Hey, honey." Alexandra's voice slipped out from behind the mask.

"Alex!" Kit breathed a sigh of relief. "You're the one wearing that creepy costume? I've seen it off and on all night long."

Alexandra chuckled and removed the mask. "Bet you never would have guessed I'd wear something like this, would you?"

Kit laughed. "I expected a costume more like Irene's, but I have to admit, I kind of like the lady of death theme you got going on there."

Her cousin shrugged. "Sometimes you need to do something different, make a change. Since I'm all about that right now, I couldn't resist. I wanted something to reflect death, change, like the Death card in the tarot deck."

"You're into all that, Alex? You've never told me that." Kit removed her mask and gazed at her cousin in wonder.

"No, I'm not. Irene suggested it when we chatted a couple of weeks ago. Besides, I thought it might ward off anything evil. Know what I mean?"

Shivering, Kit nodded. "I'm surprised he's not done something to sabotage this party, but I guess my scare tactics worked."

"He?" Alexandra wrinkled her brow.

"Old Harsh. I didn't tell you I went to his place and told him off." Kit grinned.

"You too?"

"Huh?" It was Kit's turn for surprises.

Alexandra pursed her lips, shaking her head. "The porch incident was one thing, but other strange things happened too. I'd see this one car driving slowly by the house at different hours of the day. One morning I came out and nearly stepped on a dead rabbit on my doorstep. The phone would ring, and when I answered, the person would hang up. My mail was destroyed and placed back in the mailbox more than once. Just crazy things. I decided enough was enough. I figured it had to be him or someone working for him."

"When did you go see Harsh?"

"I went last Tuesday afternoon." Alexandra's face lit up with a smug smile. "I marched right into his office and threatened him with a lawsuit and everything else I could think of. He knows I've got the funds to do just about anything I need to do."

"I guess hearing it twice was too much. At this point, he probably thinks we're in cahoots."

The older lady passed the scythe from one hand to the other, staring thoughtfully in the distance. "I think all this has stopped. And I'm so glad, Kit, that you and the Society will have this house. I'll always believe this was a good decision, and I don't want anyone messing that up for you." She leaned forward, hugging Kit in a warm embrace.

"You two ladies enjoying the night air?" Dwight sauntered up behind Kit, placing his hand lightly on her shoulder.

"Just catching up, Dwight." Alexandra smiled at him. "You're the most handsome jack o'lantern I've ever seen."

"And you, Miss, are a most convincing specter of death. I quake in your presence." Dwight removed his hat, presenting Alexandra a low, courteous bow.

"I adore you, Dwight," Alexandra said, laughing. "You're so funny." Her face returned to a sober expression. "And you're quite a man of men." She passed her gaze back and forth between Dwight and Kit. "I'll mosey on back to the tent. Maybe I can sneak in a dance at the last minute."

Dwight and Kit watched until Alexandra faded from sight.

He whispered in Kit's ear. "All this has turned out pretty well. A huge success."

"And for that I'm glad." Kit sank back into his arms, enjoying the heat of him as he wrapped her in his cloak.

"So what were you two talking about?" His warm breath brushed against her ear, and Kit closed her eyes.

"Just how two conniving ladies told Harsh to lay off."

"Whatever you told him, it must have worked." Dwight pulled away, turning her around. "Just what did you tell him?"

"I'll fill you in later. Maybe a lunch break at the coffee shop is in order."

He grinned, giving her forehead a light kiss. "Let's go back inside. I'm thirsty."

As they walked back toward the tent, Kit spied a lone person standing several feet away beside a grove of azalea bushes. She paused, scrutinizing the features, which struck her with a certain familiarity. The figure pulled off his mask and headed in her direction.

"Steven! How long have you been standing there?" Kit glanced back and forth between him and Dwight.

"Long enough for a breath of fresh air." He acknowledged Dwight with a quick smile and nod of his head. Dwight gently pushed Kit into Steven's open arm.

As Kit wrapped her arm around his waist, Dwight slipped away without a word. In the distance, she viewed his silhouette at the entrance of the tent. The sensation of his warm kiss lingered on her forehead.

Inside the tent, the merry-making still churned in full force. The lead singer announced the closing time for bidding. Last-minute bidders scurried to the auction tables for a shot at winning their coveted item.

Kit pulled Steven along to the table where *The World* sat patiently, waiting for its new owner. She glanced at the bid sheet and saw the bid up to two thousand eight hundred dollars, and several more people in line to bid on the painting.

"That will be a hefty donation from the person who purchases it." Kit gave Steven a congratulatory kiss on the lips. "I'm so proud of you."

"Thanks. Glad to help." He stared at the painting, and in his eyes, Kit detected a hint of sadness.

She rubbed her hand up and down his back. "Hate to see it go?"

"Yeah, I do."

"Would you like to nibble on some more food and take in a few more dances before the night's over?"

He perked up. "I'd love nothing better. Let's have at it."

Together, they strolled over to the buffet, picked out some favorite choice tidbits, and spent the remainder of the night enjoying each other's company. When the lead singer announced 'last call,' people began leaving, picking up a last-minute drink and paying for their winning bids. Dwight and Irene stood with other co-workers behind the auction tables, collecting money.

"Hey, I'm ready to go if you are." Steven tapped Kit on the shoulder and stood up.

Wrapped arm in arm, they said their goodbyes and exited the tent into the cold night air. Along the square, a few cars remained, waiting for their owners who seemed bent on stretching out this festive occasion as long as possible. The lamplights glowed along the street, giving the dark shops a ghostly air. The chimes from Our Lady of Eternal Blessings announced the time, midnight.

Kit and Steven reached the outside of her apartment. On the way back, neither said much. He seemed lost to his own thoughts, and she didn't want to intrude. Perhaps he'd found the night's activities exhausting, or seeing her and Dwight disturbed him.

She unlocked the door and stepped inside. Steven didn't follow. "You coming in?" A pang of uneasiness set in.

"I hate being a party-pooper, but I think I'll head on back to my place. I've got some things I need to do early tomorrow." He glanced around and focused back on her.

"Oh, okay." The knot in her stomach grew bigger, and the night air hit her skin much colder than it had earlier. She didn't remember a moment with him being so awkward. "Steven, are you okay? You've been pretty quiet on the way back here."

"It's nothing. I'm tired more than usual tonight. I don't know why. I think I need to sleep in my own bed."

"Is it that uncomfortable sleeping with me? Are you saying I keep you up?" She shifted from one foot to the other, trying hard to keep the blood moving. If she moved, maybe she'd avoid fainting.

His face showed a light grin. "If you keep me up, it's always for a fun reason."

Desperation set in. "I'll sleep on the sofa and let you have the bed, if that will help."

"No, Kit, you don't have to do that. Go on inside, and I'll head on back."

She didn't move; he stared back.

"Will you stop standing there and go on in?" His voice contained a mix of urgency and exasperation.

Thinking it best not to trifle with him at this hour, she nodded and whispered, "Thanks for going with me tonight." Without giving him time to answer, she stepped inside the building and closed the door. Tears stinging her eyes, she pulled herself up the stairs, dragging one foot behind the other. Time moved in slow motion. He hadn't even kissed her goodnight. Her breath hitched as she stifled the urge to sit down and cry. The walls seemed to close in around her. Had he seen Dwight kiss her? Did Dwight's arms around her upset him?

She stopped midway up, and hurried back down to the bottom again. There still may be time for a peek at him walking back to his shop. Taking great care, she opened the door as softly as she could and poked her head outside. Kit turned her eyes left, searching in the distance. Steven was nowhere in sight. Blinking a few times, she stepped outside, trying to find him. No, the empty streets confirmed her first observation. How had he returned home so fast in such a short time span? He'd left about a minute ago. The urge to run after him hit her hard, but she willed herself back inside and up to her apartment.

When she made it inside and closed the door, she headed straight to her room and fell on the bed, too numb to cry. She lay still, fingering the golden heart. The cold metal sent a sudden chill through her. Jumbled thoughts, none of them making sense, whirled in her mind. After an hour lapsed, she closed her eyes and fell fast asleep.

CHAPTER 22

Kit opened her eyes and sat up, staring around her room in confusion. The sunlight winked through the window curtains, casting whitish orbs of light, skipping and dancing, against the walls. She glanced down and saw her clothing from the previous night. Why had she slept in her clothes? A dark cloud settled over her, and a heaviness of heart gripped her so hard, she struggled to breathe.

A brief review of last night's events reminded her why she found herself in the present position. Right now, she needed a shower and fresh clothing. After that, she'd give more thought on how to handle the situation with Steven. After all, he may have been telling the truth when he said he simply needed a good night's sleep.

She removed the necklace, placing it in the jewelry box. The sight of it conjured up a feeling of woe, the way it had in the past. The clothes came off, landing in a heap on the floor. She turned on the shower and stepped inside the tub. When the hot water splashed over her skin, the floodgates in her eyes opened up. For the next twenty minutes, each tear drowned in the hot water coursing over her. At last, the water turned lukewarm. Having cried herself out, she turned off the faucet and stepped out. Within the hour, she'd dried her hair and dressed.

She stumbled to the living room. Though her stomach rumbled, any appetite she'd possessed had long disappeared. Dropping down on the sofa, she spent the next hour brooding, questioning herself about what had happened. Men did this most of the time, all lovey-dovey for a bit, then without word or warning, poof, they ducked out of sight and disappeared from her life. *Here we go again!*

She let out a loud, exasperated huff. Her married friends had always told her they were glad to be rid of the dating game. If she could find the right mate, she'd hang on to him for dear life. Steven had seemed like the mate she'd always wanted.

Should she call him, see if he'd slept well? Maybe she'd surprise him by taking lunch over to his shop. No, not this time. She vowed no phone calls, no stopping by his place, though that would be the hardest to avoid. This time there would be no adolescent silliness, chasing after someone like she'd done in past relationships. Lesson learned; when a guy bowed out, no matter how he tried to sell it, it was the end, pure and simple. He needed to make the first move, not her. But several minutes of rationalization over the situation did little to improve her mood. The phone rang; she jumped and grabbed the receiver. Her heart pounded so hard she heard her own blood swooshing in her ears.

"Hey, Kit, are you finally up and at 'em?"

Kit's voice fell. "Oh, it's you."

"Well, that's a fine how-do-you-do. What's wrong with you?"

"Sorry, Irene, I've just had something bad happen, that's all."

"Did you get something else through the mail again?"

"No. I wish it were as simple as that. I've learned to deal with that, at least." She stretched out on the sofa. At least talking with Irene loosened her up, got rid of the sensation of her heart being crushed to death.

"So what's happened this time?"

"You ready for this? Steven refused to come inside last night. He went on home instead, claiming he needed some good sleep. I even offered to let him have the bed to himself."

"Eww, that doesn't sound good. With me having Jim, I don't have to deal with that stuff anymore."

Kit rubbed her feet together and shifted to a more comfortable position. "Rub it in, won't you? But what am I supposed to do now?"

Irene sighed. "Geez, I hate it when guys do crap like that. Maybe he was telling you the truth. You could run on over there and see what's up."

"Don't think I haven't considered it. But I think I'll hold off. He backed off first. He can run back to me when he's ready. I'm tired of trying to figure things out with men. I'm getting too old for this silliness, if you want to know the truth." She let out a light chuckle.

"We're not that old. Besides, you could land a guy with the snap of a finger. I know one who'd take you in a flash, but I'm not going there."

"I hear you. I think Dwight and I made peace again. But last night, Steven saw Dwight and me in the garden."

"Hmm, imagine that." Irene's voice fell away from the receiver as she mumbled a few words to Jim. "I'm back. Sorry about that. So do you think Steven's jealous?"

Kit groaned. "I don't know. He just seemed preoccupied at times last night. I saw it in his face, in his eyes, a look I couldn't quite figure out. I've seen it before, though."

"Guys are weird, Kit, I'm telling you. At least with you-know-who, there's no game-playing. Everything's on the up and up. You might want to think about that now."

"Irene, I love Steven. He's the best person I've ever been involved with, and I hate to see all that go down the drain. I just hate it." Her voice cracked. A new round of tears pooled in her eyes.

"C'mon girl, things will brighten up. Don't let that dude get you down. As much as you like him, he's not worth it. I've told you before, there's something about him that's ... I don't know."

"Well, you seemed all nice and jolly dancing with him last night." Kit sensed a snippiness in her voice and backpedaled to smooth it over. "And you two looked fantastic. It's like you flowed together."

Irene laughed. "Overall, I didn't get any specific strange vibes, other than a nice time dancing. But oddly enough, I still couldn't get a good read on him, either. It's like he'd put up an energy shield, some kind of auric protection. I don't know exactly how to describe it any other way. Again, that's the big thing I find troublesome about him."

"I guess only time will tell what happens with this relationship. But I'm just done with foolishness, I'll say that."

"Just be true to yourself, Kit. That's all you can do. And you have us at work to help you through the tough times."

"Thanks, Irene. I appreciate that, I really do."

"Listen girl, gotta run. But hang in there, and I'll see you tomorrow."

When she hung up, the old smothering sensation crept back over her again. This state of mind would never do. Kit pulled herself off the sofa and headed to the bedroom. When the going gets tough, the tough go shopping. At this moment, she wanted more than anything to leave the square behind for a while. She put on some shoes, grabbed up her purse, and headed out of the building into the sunshine.

CHAPTER 23

"Have you still not heard anything from him?" Irene sat perched on top of Kit's desk.

Kit leaned her chair back and shook her head. "Nothing, not a peep."

"Still determined you're not going over there? It's midweek, Kit. I thought he'd have called by now, shown up, done something."

"Nada, no cigar." She straightened up again, tapping a pencil on a stack of papers, trying to alleviate her anxiety, which had never quite settled since the carnival.

Irene grimaced. "You could be the bigger person and just go see him, find out what's going on. You wouldn't look that bad or desperate."

"Thanks, but I'll pass." Kit rested her gaze on the ceiling.

"How do you go past there every day and not swing by? At least peek in the window?"

"So he can catch me doing that very thing? No way! I live on the opposite side, so I just keep my head turned away and try not to give his place a second look."

"You're a better woman than I am. I think I'd have done something by now. At least I'd find out if we were *finito* or not."

"We may be *finito*. I mean finished. He's not the first who's pulled this stunt."

"Tell you what, why don't we do lunch at the coffee shop, and we can both swing by his place before we head on back here. I'll act like I'm wanting to buy a painting for my living room, some cockamamie story like that."

Kit laughed. "You're funny, Irene! I needed a good lift. I'll give it a few more days, and if nothing happens, I'll either go over there and see who's licked the red off his sucker, or move on."

"You serious about that? You're drawing a line in the sand?" Irene's eyes widened, lips twitching into a grin.

"I'm drawing a line in the sand. I'm not playing these silly games anymore."

* * *

Darkness settled in for the evening, and Kit finished cleaning up the kitchen, having made a meal for one as she had done so many times before Steven dumped her. That's how she saw the whole affair. He'd dumped her, fair and square.

She stuck out her tongue in disgust and wandered over to the bookcase for a novel she'd wanted to read for some time. Now was the time. Grabbing the crocheted wrap made by her grandmother, she settled down, covered up, and opened the book.

To her surprise, she spent the next two hours reading, actually enjoying herself. But the happy moments didn't last long, with thoughts of Steven pushing their way into her mind like a hateful, willful intruder. She closed the book and her eyes to think a while. Maybe Irene was right. Why not slip out and go check on *Celestial Temptation Gallery*. It was dark outside. She'd be extra careful, make sure no one caught her prowling. Besides, one more day of work and the weekend was hers to do whatever she wanted, alone.

She ran to her room, slipped on some sweats, a jacket, and shoes, and bounded down the stairs. Judging by the emptiness of the streets, everyone had retired for the evening. The chimes from the church pealed out the nine o'clock hour. Good, at least she wouldn't be out too late. She scurried across the street, making her way down the sidewalk to the gallery. Kit hovered closer to the buildings so she'd be able to see into Steven's shop ahead of time, cutting down the chance of someone catching her outside and nosing around.

In minutes, she spied the gallery. As usual at this hour, only a couple of lights remained on. The rest of the shop sat in darkness. With caution, she turned her eyes toward the inside. She relaxed a little; no one was there. A brisk breeze rustled up the night air, and she wrapped her jacket around tighter, shivering. With a little more resolve, she moved over to see if she could catch the view of a light on in his personal space. The dark hallway suggested he'd either gone out or gone to sleep.

A thought came to mind: Why not go to the back and see if his window provided any clues? Kit grinned to herself. All her self-talk about not being adolescent, not to mention her self-respect, had gone out another window. After glancing around the square, she made her way to the back, avoiding anything that might signal an intruder.

The back proved a desolate place, dark, empty, and neglected. She walked in the direction of a window that would be his. From inside, she detected the faint glow of a lamp, and edged closer for a peek. Another cold blast sliced the air, and for a moment, she wished herself back in the warmth and safety of her apartment. She inched her face closer to the pane, trying to discern anything noteworthy in the dim lighting. The curtain, though thin, still hindered much of her view, but she focused her eyes through the open slit between the two panels.

Losing all sense of time, she stood there, absorbed in studying the surroundings of the room. She didn't see him or anyone else. Did she see any furniture in this room? Suddenly it hit her. During all this time they'd been together, he'd never once invited her over to his place as he promised. Of course, the excuse they'd both given is that she had a comfortable apartment with a fireplace. Reasoning once more with herself, makeshift living quarters at the back of a shop couldn't possibly be all that great. Of course, one of her gay friends back home had a shop, and he made his living area in the back a jaw-dropping showplace.

She stood back and checked the area one more time. The light from the window lured her back, and she peered inside for one last look, hoping for some answers to his private world.

Without warning, an arm wrapped around her waist. A hand clapped over her mouth, stifling her scream. A chill filled her body as the blood moved away from her extremities. Dizzy with fear, she mustered up enough wherewithal to struggle with every muscle. Strong arms held her fast.

"Sh-h-h, it's only me!" A familiar voice whispered in her ear. "Stop, would you?"

Kit stopped and craned her neck. Steven stood behind her. Now she really wished she'd stayed home.

"What on earth are you doing here at this time of night? Have you lost your mind?"

How to answer this question, she didn't harbor a clue. He'd have a hard time believing her, if he believed her at all.

"I was just out walking around, and thought I'd stop by, see if you were okay. I hadn't heard from you."

"You make a habit of walking around here by yourself after dark? Is that wise?"

"I have before, honestly, and I've never had a problem." She glanced up at him, embarrassed. "I don't do it a lot, though."

"Let me walk you back home." He wrapped his arm around her and guided her away from the window.

"Where have you been tonight?"

"If you can go out for a walk late at night, so can I." He pulled her closer, giving her a quick kiss on the cheek.

She pushed herself into him a little, breaking their stride. "That's a lame answer, and you know it."

"Maybe, but it works for me if it works for you." He led her back to the sidewalk and they strode off to her apartment. In the night air, their breathing left lingering clouds of condensation floating like tendrils of smoke as they walked.

"I've been worried about you, Steven. You haven't called or done anything. I couldn't stand it anymore."

"I'm sorry. I've had some personal things come up, that's all."

Out of the corner of her eyes, she noted a solemn expression on his face.

"Are you okay? Is there something I can help you with?"

He didn't answer, but kept walking.

"Steven, you've been acting weird since we left the carnival. Don't hide things from me. I've had to deal with this since high school, men suddenly ducking and running. I can't take it anymore." Her voice choked. Tears stung her eyes.

He stopped and stared at her. "Kit, I'm really sorry about all this. Tell you what, let's get together tomorrow night, and we'll go from there. Deal?"

She nodded, swallowing hard. "Deal."

Cupping her face in his hands, he moved his lips over hers for a warm, soft kiss. They walked back to her apartment in silence.

"How about I stay with you tomorrow night?" He smiled and moved a wisp of hair away from her face.

"Sounds good. You promise?"

"I promise."

When Kit stepped inside the entrance to her apartment, he turned around and headed off into the night. Kit closed the door behind her and didn't bother looking back. Relief flooded her. All she wanted to do was hop in bed and get some sleep.

CHAPTER 24

"Good! Any idea what he's got planned?"

Kit sat inside Irene's office. She'd shared her escapade from the night before. "Not a clue. Nothing fancy, I'll bet. Of course, I don't require that, but sometimes it's nice to do something fancy."

Irene grinned. "It's nice, and I think you need a man who'll do that for you too."

"Don't start!" Kit held up her hand.

"I won't, but I wish you'd listen to me for once."

A ringtone jingled from Irene's cell phone.

"It's Jim. I need to take this call." Irene grabbed her phone.

Saying nothing more, Kit got up from the chair, exchanged waves with her friend, and walked back to her office. When she stepped inside, a large cup of coffee stood at attention on her desk, and beside it a slice of *Red Velvet Fantasy*. The familiar logo from *A Cup Above The Roast* meant only one thing: Dwight had reverted back to his old self.

Smiling, she sat down and took a quick sip. It was her favorite flavor, *Divine Angel*. She sank back in her chair, thinking. Yes, Dwight knew how to treat a woman like a queen. What kind of gifts would he lavish on his best girl, or even more, his wife? Had Steven not entered her life, would she have been that best girl? She took another sip and began working. It didn't matter what Dwight would do. Tonight she'd be spending time with her real divine angel.

* * *

Showered and dressed, ready for the evening, Kit paced up and down in her apartment. She hadn't heard from Steven all day. The clock on the mantel chimed a single tone for the half-hour. It was six thirty-five. What if he had no intention of showing up? Anger swelled up inside her at the thought, and she made a promise to herself. If he pulled a nasty stunt like that, she'd find another guy and never speak to him again. She sat down on the sofa and tried concentrating on the novel she'd started. Several pages into the book, the phone rang.

In a fit of excitement, she almost snatched up the receiver on the first ring before catching herself. Better not look so eager. The phone rang two more times. Should she let it go to her answering machine and call him back a while later? Not wanting to play games, she answered.

"Hello?"

"Hey, Hon, you ready?" Steven's voice purred in her ear.

"I'm ready when you are."

"How about meeting at the coffee shop?"

Kit pursed her lips together. Somewhere in her heart, she'd been hoping he'd spring for something different, a little more upscale. A traditional restaurant chain or chintzy bistro away from the square would have satisfied her craving for something unique tonight. Even *JJ's* would have worked somewhat better.

"Are you there? Did you still want to go?"

"Yes. Sorry, my mind wandered a bit. I'm on my way."

They hung up, and Kit grabbed up her purse. Tonight may not be extraordinary, but she'd be with her man, and at the moment, nothing else mattered.

As she walked out the door and onto the sidewalk, she took in a breath, inhaling the scents of the night, food from the pub and another local eatery, the stench of fuel from a passing car. Somewhere in the distance, she heard a band playing in one of the bars located on another side street. Couples walked hand in hand. A sudden sense of loneliness overpowered her, and no matter how much she tried to shake off the horrible feeling, it stuck to her with its own tenacity. No amount of reasoning and convincing herself otherwise made her spirits lift any quicker. She choked back an onslaught of tears and made her way to the coffee shop, where she found Steven sitting in a far corner by the window. He'd already ordered coffee for them.

Her mood lifted when he smiled. She sat down across from him. He reached for her hand. Kit sipped her coffee, staring at him from across the table.

"You look pretty tonight." He squeezed her hand. "Of course, I think you're beautiful all the time."

She said nothing, but made a kissing motion with her lips. They spent a few moments looking over the menu, and Steven went to the counter where he placed their orders. While they waited, they engaged in safe, idle chitchat. Ten minutes later, the barista called out their number, and Steven retrieved the food. Each one took a bite, eating in silence a few moments.

Kit kept her eye on him, watching every move, every facial expression. He appeared preoccupied, the way he looked when they'd walked home after the carnival, and the other night when they walked back to her apartment after she'd spied on him. Most of the time, she loved his pensive moments, the way his eyes focused on something unseen in front of him, the way his jaw tightened as he sank deeper in thought, or his fingers toyed with a straw in a glass or a paper wrapper.

However, watching him tonight did nothing but crank up the uneasiness rumbling in her gut, the one she'd been carrying around for days and didn't know why. He seemed more tense this time, struggling with himself on whether or not to share what was on his mind. His hands reached out for hers. He looked up at her with an intense gaze that scared her.

She didn't want to ask, but somehow couldn't help herself. "Steven, is there something wrong? You look like you're worried. You've had that look a lot lately."

He swallowed a bite of his sandwich, washing it down with some coffee. "I have a question I've been dying to ask you, Kit, but wasn't sure when would be a good time to do it."

"What's that?" She smiled at him, hoping his question would calm her nerves a little.

He shifted in his seat, getting up the nerve. "I want to ask you once again why you and Irene were playing with a spirit board that night I came up to your apartment? Do you remember that night?"

She thought for a minute and nodded.

"What were you trying to do?"

Startled, she sat there in silence, unclear how to respond. The interlude with the spirit board had taken somewhat of a back seat in her memory, or she'd tried to hide it there as best she could. It was the beginnings of the message that haunted her, just like the earlier dreams of Austin. Finally, she let out a soft chuckle.

"Oh, Steven, you really wouldn't be interested in hearing about that. Irene and I aren't that exciting. And anyway, you'd think I was crazy or something."

"No, as a matter of fact, I wouldn't think you're crazy or something." He sat up straight now, grasping her hand with such earnestness she became more uncomfortable. Her stomach suddenly lurched, filling her with a queasy sensation.

"I want to know why you were playing with a spirit board. What were you trying to get out of it?"

She fidgeted, glancing around the coffee shop. They and a couple of other customers were the only ones present. This struck Kit as rather odd, especially when this shop usually held an ample crowd of adoring customers on a Friday night.

Her eyes turned back to Steven's. "Nothing. Me and Irene were just goofing around, that's all. She had a question, and the board gave her an answer." She pulled her hand out of his and grasped the handle of her cup, taking a quick sip of coffee. The hot liquid burned a path down her throat. How she wished the cup contained heavy shots of the strongest liquor on the market.

When she put down the cup, he regained his stronghold, squeezing both her hands harder. The burning look in his eyes sent goose bumps rising on her arms. "I don't believe you. You're hiding something, and I want to know the truth. I want you to tell me now!"

"Why is it so important, Steven? It's just silly." A nervous laugh slipped out as she tried to pull away from him. He wouldn't let go.

Then she heard it, another song from high school days, playing over the shop speakers, the same song that had kicked off this obsession with old ghosts from the past.

Her stomach clinched, and she swallowed hard. "You know what, I'm feeling a little sick all of a sudden. Must have been something I ate last night. Maybe it's this coffee. Do you think we can just go home?"

For the first time, she didn't want to be around him. Her spying on him the other night had set off an explosion of deep regret. Perhaps things would have been better just left alone.

"No, I think we're fine right here." His voice remained tense while his eyes bore straight through hers. "You said Irene got the answer she was looking for that night, but somehow my instinct says the answer was for you. You were the one searching for an answer."

A burning heat covered Kit's face, kicking up her breathing to a rapid rate. She blinked a few times, keeping her eyes on Steven.

He continued. "Just take a deep breath and calm down for a minute. Tell me what you and Irene were doing that night." He leaned forward a little. "From the day we met in my art gallery, I've sensed something about you – like you're holding back a secret. Even in our closest moments, you can't seem to bring yourself to let go – to totally let go and be free. You've got something on your mind, something that's been eating away at you for a long time – a long time. What was the message you got, Kit?" His voice had softened with his last words.

She looked away for a moment, struggling for the smoothest way to share what had been locked in her heart and mind all these years. Steven's persistence had her cornered, and the look on his face told her he'd stay in the coffee shop all night if the situation so demanded. Her spirits sank. No matter how hard she'd tried to bury the past when Austin died, part of it wouldn't let her go, keeping a grip around her like the ugly, gnarly fingers of an angry banshee. And when she tried to turn away, its angry wails screamed out the announcement of his death over and over. If she didn't get rid of this burden, she'd never move on emotionally. With a gulp, she began her confession.

"Like I told you before, I'd been having some dreams about someone back in high school. Something bad happened between us." Tears welled up in her eyes, her voice shaky. "I ended up saying some really ugly things to that person, and then ..."

"Go on." Steven held his grip on her hands.

"And then he was gone."

"Who was he, and what happened?"

Tears trickled down her face. The words came out, bearing the sadness and pain she'd bottled up and tried to hide away forever. "Back in high school, there was a guy. He was my first love you might say. We seemed to have a good thing going, and all of a sudden ..."

"All of a sudden what?"

Kit cleared her throat, steadying her voice. "You see, like you, he was a football player, one of the cool guys. We were still seeing each other during our last year at school, and I felt so smug and proud, because it made me feel cool, too, just to be seen with him. He was also artistic, just like you." She paused, sniffling and blinking away some tears. "Anyway, one day, out of the blue, he stopped calling me and coming around."

"So what did you do, Kit?"

"Nothing much, really. I tried to talk to him, ask him why he had suddenly pulled away, what was wrong, what did I do ... you know the deal ... the questions girls ask guys when they pull away."

Steven nodded.

"Well, as you can guess, he never gave me a straight answer. Blew me off, if you want to know the truth. Needless to say, I was heartbroken. When I saw him taking another girl out, one who nobody in the whole school liked, that was it for me."

"Okay, when did the bad things come out? You mentioned earlier about saying something awful. What was it?"

Kit hung her head, embarrassed. "After a few weeks of seeing this girl, he came up to me one day after school and wanted to talk." She shook her head, grimacing. "Oh, no, I wasn't going to have any of that shit! No, not me. He'd made the decision to leave and see this girl nobody liked. Everybody thought she was strange. Nobody was very nice to her. And to have him leave me for her? No! I was done!"

"What did you say to him, Kit?" Steven's tone rang out more insistent than ever.

Her lower lip trembled. Tears gathered in her eyes again. "I told him he'd hurt me, that I hated him, and never wanted to see him again. And here's the awful thing: that I wished he would just die and go away. And that's exactly what happened. He got killed in an accident soon after we graduated, and when I heard about it, I tried to put it all out of my mind. I just chalked it all up to coincidence. But now I'm not so sure anymore. He keeps coming back." Her voice had lowered to a whisper.

Steven sank back in his chair and stared at his coffee. A light flush covered his face, and his eyes burned with a bright new energy. He pursed his lips in thought before looking back up at Kit. "Let me tell you what happened to me." His voice softened, as well as his grip on her hands. "One night my football buddies and I were playing a drinking game. We'd been talking about some chick in class and how easy she was. She was a loner, and everyone thought she was a little weird. So they stayed away from her. The deal was the loser of the game had to date this girl for a month. And, of course, try to score with her."

Kit's mouth dropped open. Her eyes widened in horror as she listened to the story. A sinister feeling crept over her, trickling its icy fingers over her shoulders, trailing down her spine, and dripping all the way down to her toes. Her hearing kicked in full force, clinging to each word he spoke.

"Needless to say, I lost the game, fair and square, and I had to pay. I couldn't say no because I wanted to save face with my buddies, but getting up the nerve to go out with this girl was hard. It was even harder because I had a girlfriend I adored. She was the cutest thing I'd ever seen, so full of energy, and simply amazing." His expression softened as he gazed at Kit. "All I can say is youth and screwed up priorities can cause a young man to make foolish choices and do stupid things and, believe me, that was one of them."

She sat there, dizzy with disbelief at what she'd heard. Steven's story slammed against her senses, ringing with a blaring truth that nearly bowled her over. Was this the answer she'd been searching for all these years, the real truth behind how her relationship ended with Austin? If she could talk to him now, would he share a similar story?

"Did the girlfriend ever forgive you?" Kit squared up her shoulders. She grasped his hands, startled at the chill in his fingers.

With an expression of sadness clouding his eyes, he shook his head. "No. I tried to explain it all to her, but she had nothing good to say to me. After that, it was over – for good." After a few seconds of silence, he asked, "So what would you say to him if you had the chance?"

Kit licked her lips, fighting another round of tears. If she couldn't speak these words to Austin, she could at least purge herself by sharing her deepest feelings with someone she adored now. Winding her fingers through his, staring him straight in the eye, she confessed. "I'd tell him I'm sorry, and to please come back." The lump in her throat tightened as she forced out the last words. "I'd also tell him that I forgive him, and most of all that I love him."

Steven's face colored again. In a soft voice, he said, "And I'd do the same for her." He leaned toward Kit. "Just remember, those words we never speak never have to be forgiven. Remember that, would you?"

Kit nodded, silent as she wiped away the tears. A sense of relief flooded over her. After all these years, she'd finally unloaded a heavy burden, a great millstone around her neck, threatening to weigh her down until her dying day. She'd never shared these thoughts with anyone, refusing to acknowledge them herself.

He lifted one of her hands and kissed it. "Thank you for talking to me tonight. I really needed this."

"Me too, Steven."

A veil of shadows had been lifted by this purging of the soul, and Kit saw the effects reflected in the new sparkle in Steven's eyes and the fresh smile on his face. Most of all she sensed a new energy welling up inside, like a page of a book had been turned, allowing her to go on to the next chapter. The couple finished their meal and left the shop. They walked back to Kit's apartment, where they proceeded up the stairs and made their way into her bedroom.

CHAPTER 25

Kit switched on a small lamp sitting on her nightstand while Steven slipped up from behind, wrapping his arms around her waist. For a few minutes, he held her close while she bathed in total happiness. All the sadness from the past few days faded away like a distant bad dream. She'd awakened refreshed and joyful knowing he hadn't left her, but just needed some quiet time for personal reflection.

He whispered in her ear, "Let me love you." The warmth radiating from his body lulled her into the familiar trance-like state she often felt during their quiet times together, when he drew so close she almost seemed to melt right into him. She faced him. Mesmerized by the sapphire blue of his eyes and the glow of his handsome face in the soft lamplight, Kit followed him to the bed. In total submission, she lay quietly, his hands working as they removed her top and bra. He took his time as if wanting to savor every second to the last. His hands slid to her waist, where he unbuckled the leather belt and unzipped her jeans.

Her heart pounded in her chest as he slid them off and tossed them carelessly to the floor. In awe, she watched him remove his own clothing, revealing a strong, lithe body with musculature in all the right places without being too showy or pretentious. The glow of his skin in the lamplight gave him an other-worldly vibe, and his face bore the soft, commanding countenance of the most loving deity.

His eyes landed on her panties. He hooked his fingers at the top of the elastic band and pulled them off. She lay naked before him, trembling. He crawled onto the bed and positioned himself over her. "Kit," he whispered in her ear, "let me in."

And then she closed her eyes and opened herself up, allowing him to enter. As they came together in the most perfect merger, not only did their bodies meet, but so did their spirits. With his deep, burning kisses, each breath she inhaled from him filled her with a vitality she'd never felt before. In an instant, she found herself suspended in a dimension where complete joy reigned, where the present faded, and all earthly sensations slipped way. Cradled in a cocoon of perfect love and total connection, her whole body vibrated with an energy that left the tips of her fingers tingling.

Every earnest thrust from him banished all the old fears, conditions, and shame, allowing her to experience complete union filled with unconditional love. In spiritual communion, she held him close, absorbing every joy and happiness he'd ever experienced, as well as all the deep sorrow and regrets he'd kept locked deep in his heart. In one brilliant flash of awareness, all her deepest emotions burst forth, wrapping at the door of her highest level of consciousness, forcing her to see and feel each and every one of them clearly as they revealed a certain truth.

When he emptied himself, corresponding waves of pleasure washed over her, transmuting all fears, doubts, and hurt into peace. Her arms wrapped around him tighter. She wanted to hold him forever, never let him go, never let him out of her sight. He kept her warm, and his strength kept her safe.

Inside her chest, Kit's heart nearly burst from the thrill of raw, unbridled emotion. Unable to hold back, she opened her eyes, and the words tumbled out as smoothly as if she'd rehearsed them: "I love you."

"And I love you more." His words rang with the sweetest notes, almost heaven-sent. In his eyes, she read passion and joy.

He cradled her in his arms, spooning around her. Both closed their eyes and fell asleep.

* * *

Kit rolled over and stretched out her hand, hoping to find Steven, but landed on nothing but cool sheets where his warm body had been. She rested her head back down on the pillow, straining her ears for any sound of him clinking dishes as he made something to eat, or perhaps the rustling of a magazine or music from the radio. The silence in the apartment pounded against her so strongly, the absolute nothingness of it catapulted her to the brink of a panic attack.

"Steven, where are you?" She turned her eyes to the bathroom, hoping to see a closed door. The door stood wide open. "Steven?" Now she'd fallen over the edge into full-blown panic.

This wasn't the first time he'd left to go back to his shop without waking her, but an inexplicable fear crept into her gut. Instinct hinted something had changed, and she didn't know where to identify the source. Sitting up, her eyes darted around the room and into the living room. She listened hard one last time before throwing off the covers and leaping out of bed. Steven was gone. Nothing had been disturbed. Somewhere in the night or wee hours of the morning, he'd slipped out without a sound.

The heaviness in her stomach grew by leaps and bounds, and her heart pounded hard. Tears stung her eyes, and she struggled for breaths. Kit closed her eyes, talking herself into a calmer state. If she wanted to know what happened to Steven, why not just call him instead of getting worked up over nothing? She walked to the kitchen, picked up the phone, and dialed the shop number. On the other end of the line came ring tone after ring tone, and no hello from anyone. Finally, she hung up. She'd try his cell phone. With shaking fingers, she punched in the numbers, and met with the same experience as the first call, with one strange thing: the call didn't go to voice mail.

Maybe he was busy, had a customer, didn't hear the phone. Maybe the phone provider was having technical difficulties. Kit rolled the possibilities around in her mind, trying to make excuses for why he didn't want to talk with her again. After further questioning, chastising herself for past behaviors, and lots of swearing, she made a decision: shower, dress and go to the shop. They'd see each other, and everything would be fine. All the reasoning she conjured in her head did little to ease the fear and dread threatening to morph her into an insane creature.

Not caring what she looked like, she ran to her room, threw on some clothes, and bounded down the steps to the outside world. The usual hum of the square on a Saturday afternoon fell away unnoticed in this moment where nothing mattered to her but finding Steven. After a few cars cleared the street, she sprinted across and made haste for *Celestial Temptation Gallery*. When she reached the front window, she nearly fainted from shock.

CHAPTER 26

A 'For Lease' sign hung in the window. Kit glanced around. Had she entered another reality? She looked all around. People still walked by, dogs still barked in the distance, and customers still entered and left the coffee shop. The gallery stood empty, everything removed from the room, gone. She still didn't believe it. In a blind rush, she sprinted to the back of the building. One look into the back window would be her last clue.

The curtains had been thrown back. Inside the room, nothing but emptiness, no sign that anyone had been there recently. She stopped and caught her breath. Tears streamed down her cheeks. This simply couldn't be happening. Their evening last night, though off to a rocky start, had ended up better than any moment they'd shared before. Had she missed something, a meta-message somewhere in all these events for the past few months? Had he been trying to tell her something and she simply hadn't listened? Not one to give up, she marched back to the front of the shop, pulled out her cell phone, and dialed Steven's number again. To her horror, she got the following message: *We're sorry. You have dialed a number that has been disconnected. If you feel you have reached this message in error, please hang up and try your call again.*

The 'For Lease' sign showed a contact number at the bottom. Why not call the leasing office? Their staff would surely know what happened to one of their tenants. Taking a deep breath, she dialed the number and, to her relief, a lady answered.

Kit steadied her voice and spoke, "Hello? I'm calling about *Celestial Temptation Gallery*, the storefront located next to the coffee shop on the Windham Springs Square."

"Yes, can I help you?" The lady's pleasant voice sounded reassuring.

"Yesterday, someone occupied that shop, and today it's empty. Can you tell me what happened to the owner?"

"I'm sorry, Miss. I can't say much except that the owner left in a hurry. Said something about having to return home."

"Did he say anything more than that?" Kit's voice became urgent.

"No, that's all the information he would give. I'm sorry I can't tell you more."

Kit choked up again. "That's okay. I really appreciate you talking to me, though."

"Not a problem. Thank you for calling."

The call ended.

In one last confirming attempt, Kit ran behind the building again. With any luck, this was all a bad dream, and maybe the view inside had magically changed.

When she peered through the panes again, though, the view inside hadn't magically changed. The occupant was gone, no question about it. With a heavy heart, she backed away from the window and trudged to the sidewalk, slowly making her way back home.

The whole weekend – no, her whole life – loomed ahead of her, dark and dreary, without Steven. She envisioned the future with disappointment and dread. No one understood her and loved her like he did, at least until now. What drove him to leave without even saying good-bye?

She reached the apartment entrance and took each step upwards with great effort. When she entered the apartment, she laid her phone and keys on the kitchen counter and turned toward the bedroom. The necklace. Thoughts of it consumed her. She shuddered. Did she dare look?

Kit tiptoed into her room, feeling oddly like an intruder in her own home, like she didn't belong here anymore. The sound of her own heartbeat pounded away in her ears, infusing her with a round of lightheadedness. Her fingers trembled so hard she barely secured them around the knob of the dresser drawer. As she pulled, the drawer slid open with a faint squeak. The jewelry box sat undisturbed, or so it seemed, in the back corner like it always did. Then why was she so fearful of opening it? For several seconds she merely stared, hugging herself, undecided what to do. She closed the drawer. No, not now.

Upon returning to the living room, her gaze landed on the coffee table. She jumped with fright, clapping a hand over her mouth, stifling a scream. Right there on top lay her high school yearbook with its pages wide open. As she recalled, nothing had been out of place when she left this morning. The table had nothing on it. Steven didn't have a key to her apartment. No one did. She approached the table with caution.

Surely Harsh, or one of his so-called 'associates,' wasn't up to some sick trick again. Blood pulsing hard in her veins, she picked up the book and sat down on the edge of the sofa. Kit viewed the open pages. Austin's picture had a heart-shaped circle around it, as well as his name circled at the bottom. An arrow from the picture led to the right outside margin, where she saw a tiny sketch of *The World*, a miniature version of the painting. Underneath, she read the words: *Kit, thus we complete our journey. Love, Austin.*

Sitting back in shock, Kit let the book slide to the floor. Without further thought, she ran to her room, tore open the dresser drawer, and flipped open the top of the jewelry box; no necklace. A mixture of emotions overtook her at that moment: fear, anger, relief, sorrow.

There was only one way to finish this. She stole outside to the back of the building, the box clutched tightly in one hand, the yearbooks cradled in her other arm. At the end of the lot sat a dumpster. Kit approached the opening and tossed everything inside, barely cringing when each item thudded to the bottom. She turned away without looking back and headed to her apartment.

Seated on her sofa once again, tears came, one by one, hot and heavy. She cried harder than she'd ever cried in her life. Loud sobs sounded from her throat, and her chest heaved with each breath. Now she understood everything; it all made sense. They'd both been given one last chance to rectify a wrong, make amends, release each other – forgive. She could let go and move on without fear or shame. So could he. But this understanding wouldn't quickly erase the feelings she'd developed, ones for an old ghost who couldn't stay, even if he wanted to. Would she ever get over this? Was making amends worth the aching heart? In the long run, when time healed everything, she might say yes. But now she needed to try and find a way to cope, to go on and move quietly through her life without heavy grief weighing her down. Austin had made choices that most likely had led to his own demise. She'd continue to make her choices, and hopefully she'd choose using solid, inner wisdom.

Kit smiled a little. Wait until Irene heard about this! Maybe her best friend could come up with a way, create some sort of spell or ritual to help mend a broken heart. In an instant, an image of Dwight flashed through her mind, bringing with it a gentle peace that settled over her spirit like a blanket protecting her from the cold. One thing she knew for sure; Dwight, like Irene, had also remained constant in her life since she'd started her position at the Historical Society.

He'd stuck by her through everything, through every hurt, through every uncertainty. Even when the chips seemed stacked against him, through her love for someone else, he still stood his ground and told her he loved her. When she doubted herself, he did not. When she disliked herself, he reminded her of the goodness she possessed.

Wiping her eyes, Kit took a deep breath, letting it out nice and easy. For several minutes, she sat and calmed her mind, thinking of nothing, not the past, not the present, or the future. The tick-tock sounds from the clock kept her grounded, and little by little her whole spirit calmed.

The sharp ringing of the phone sent her sailing off the sofa and over to the kitchen counter, praying hard it was Steven's – Austin's – voice on the other end. Maybe this morning truly had been nothing more than a crazy dream.

"Hello?"

"Hey, Kit, it's Dwight. How are you?"

Kit's eyes widened, and for the first time in several days, her body perked up with some semblance of new life. She took a deep breath and steadied her voice.

"I'm good. Yourself?"

His voice came across the line, smooth and mellow, alluring. "Couldn't be happier. The reason I called is because I'm here on the square. Had an itch to get out and enjoy the sunshine. Would you like to join me for a bite at the coffee shop? It's on me."

She swallowed and licked her lips, fighting the cotton-like dryness in her mouth. Her mind raced, and then she smiled. "I'd love to, Dwight. Give me a few seconds to put myself together." When the call ended, Kit ran to the bathroom and wiped her eyes, fixed her hair, and re-applied some make up. Maybe life would get back to normal again. Moments later, she headed out of the apartment into the glorious light of noon.

... One Year Later ...

Kit lay in bed, staring at her left hand. The morning sun shone through the long windows of the room where Dwight lay sleeping beside her. The rays of light caught the facets of her diamond ring, lighting it up in an explosion of rainbow colors. She moved her hand, admiring the shape of the stone, a marquis – her favorite.

The wedding had been an intimate affair, with Society co-workers and close family in attendance. Both Alexandra and Irene had shed their fair amount of tears, happily acting as maid of honor and bridesmaid. Mr. Crispin and Jim had stood next to Dwight as best man and groomsman. Everyone had watched with adoration as Kit and Dwight gazed into each other's eyes and exchanged vows. Dwight even serenaded her during the wedding ceremony with a special song he'd written.

With a small pang of sadness, Kit moved out of Mr. Crispin's apartment and into the beautiful Frank Lloyd Wright home where she and Dwight enjoyed cooking together and entertaining friends and relatives, especially Alexandra, Mr. Crispin, Irene, and Jim.

She turned her head, gazing at her husband as she thought about the night before when they crawled into bed at last. Just as she'd imagined, he'd made a truly passionate lover, consuming her body, mind, and soul. Every physical merger lifted her higher in spirit, and every day they spent together solidified their reasons for being together.

Dwight stirred. "You up already?" He glanced at the clock on his nightstand. "It's seven-thirty in the morning."

"Just thinking about us. Can you believe last night was our second annual carnival? I think we raised more money this time." She smiled and leaned over, smothering his lips with a kiss.

"It was a huge success. Word's getting out about it. Maybe if we're lucky it'll be one of the most desired events to attend in North Carolina." He grinned back at her. "That would be kind of nice, wouldn't it?"

"You know what would be nice right now?" Kit settled on her back and pulled him in her direction, running her fingers over his flesh. Taking his cue, Dwight settled himself in place, eyes glowing as he prepared himself for her acceptance. She closed her eyes, losing herself as he entered her. With each movement of his hips, time and space vanished, leaving her with a floating feeling, a feeling of nothingness, yet everything.

Through chaos there is order; through pain there is joy; through darkness there is light. Kit found herself in perfect equilibrium with Dwight, where order and joy ruled, and light reigned over darkness.

Acknowledgements:

I'd like to extend warm thanks of appreciation to those who helped me with this book: Dale, for creating an amazing cover. Susan and Pam, who gave me much food for thought. My amazing editor, Jessica West, for her skill in shaping this story into the best that it could be. Most of all, I'd like to thank my dear spouse for his input and being the one who supports me the whole time.

About the Author:

Scarlet Darkwood wields a mighty pen, or at the very least, delivers mighty punches to the computer keys when she's typing furiously on a story. She likes dark and twisted, and the weirder, the better.

Always preferring avant garde themes, her stories take the reader on unusual adventures, exploring the darker parts of the human psyche as she whips out cunning prose wrapped in provocative themes. Sometimes she veers from her beaten path and takes a happy-go-lucky romp in the brighter sides of life, kicking up her style into sharp, snappy dialogue and clever descriptions.

Writing in several genres unleashes her imagination so she never grows bored. From a young age, she's enjoyed writing and keeping diaries, but didn't start creating novels until 2012. She's a Southern girl who lives in Tennessee and enjoys the beauty of the mountains. She lives in Nashville with her spouse and two rambunctious kitties.

For more information about the latest concerning Scarlet and her work, you can do the following:

Visit her BLOG at: www.scarletdarkwood.com

Follow her on Google+ at:
http://google.com/+ScarletDarkwood
Follow her on Twitter at: http://twitter.com/ScarletDarkwood
Follow her on Facebook:
http://www.facebook.com/scarletdarkwoodauthor

Check out Scarlet's other works:
Romance:
Escape From Purgatory

Erotic Romance:
Pleasure House
Dance Of Desire
Taming Bad

Master Of The House
Mistress Of The House

Short Stories:
Hard Way In
Fun With Dick And Peter
Naughty And Nice

If you have any questions, comments, or suggestions, you
can reach Scarlet at **sdarkwood@gmail.com**.
Subscribe to Scarlet's blog at www.scarletdarkwood.com.
Follow her on Facebook:
https://www.facebook.com/scarletdarkwoodauthor
Follow her on Twitter: https://twitter.com/ScarletDarkwood